Jeanette Grey started out with degrees in physics and painting, which she dutifully applied to stunted careers in teaching, technical support and advertising. Almost all of her stories include hints of either science or art. When she isn't writing, Jeanette enjoys making pottery, playing board games, and spending time with her husband and her pet frog. She lives, loves, and writes in upstate New York. Find her online at www.jeanettegrey.com, on Twitter @jeanettelgrey and on Facebook at www.facebook.com/jeanettelgrey.

Be seduced by Jeanette Grey's powerful love stories:

'Jeanette Grey has become a must-read voice in romance. *Seven Nights To Surrender* is lyrical, stunningly sexy, and brings swoons for *days*' Christina Lauren, *New York Times* bestselling author

'With its sexy setting and sensual story, Jeanette Grey's *Seven Nights To Surrender* sparkles' J. Kenner, *New York Times* bestselling author

'A must-read! I couldn't put it down. Jeanette Grey's writing is *so* refreshingly honest. *Seven Nights To Surrender* is intensely emotional and sexy as hell. I need the next book ASAP!' Tara Sue Me, *New York Times* bestselling author

'Sensual, sultry, and exquisite, *Seven Nights To Surrender* will sweep you away and seduce you on every page! Crackling with tension and steamy with sensuality, it's a feast for the senses you don't want to miss' Katy Evans, *New York Times* bestselling author

'Achingly sexy and romantic – I couldn't put it down!' Laura Kaye, *New York Times* bestselling author

'With her unique flair, Jeanette Grey delivers a deliciously sexy and irresistible romance that keeps you turning the pages for more. You'll savor every word so you don't miss a single sizzling moment' K. Bromberg, *New York Times* bestselling author

'I couldn't put it down! I loved every sentence! The writing is outstanding, the setting entrancing, and the characters stole my heart' S. C. Stephens, No. 1 *New York Times* bestselling author

'A sassy and sexy ⬚⬚⬚ full of ⬚⬚⬚⬚⬚⬚⬚⬚⬚. This romance is like a brea⬚⬚⬚⬚⬚⬚⬚⬚⬚⬚⬚⬚⬚⬚⬚⬚⬚⬚⬚⬚⬚⬚⬚⬚⬚⬚⬚ ⬚stselling author

By Jeanette Grey

When The Stars Align
Seven Nights To Surrender
Eight Ways To Ecstasy

SEVEN NIGHTS TO *Surrender*

JEANETTE GREY

headline
ETERNAL

The right of Jeanette Grey to be identified as the Author of
the Work has been asserted by her in accordance with the
Copyright, Designs and Patents Act 1988.

Published by arrangement with Forever,
an imprint of Grand Central Publishing.

First published in Great Britain in 2015
by HEADLINE ETERNAL
An imprint of HEADLINE PUBLISHING GROUP

1

Cataloguing in Publication Data is available from the British Library

ISBN 978 1 4722 2850 5

Offset in 11.5/15.75 pt Garamond LT Std by Jouve (UK)

Printed and bound in Great Britain by CPI Group (UK) Ltd, Croydon, CR0 4YY

Headline's policy is to use papers that are natural, renewable and recyclable
products and made from wood grown in well-managed forests and other
controlled sources. The logging and manufacturing processes are expected
to conform to the environmental regulations of the country of origin.

HEADLINE PUBLISHING GROUP
An Hachette UK Company
Carmelite House
50 Victoria Embankment
London EC4Y 0DZ

www.headlineeternal.com
www.headline.co.uk
www.hachette.co.uk

*To Scott, for all the journeys we've been on so far, and
all the journeys yet to come.*

Acknowledgments

I am so incredibly grateful to the people who've helped make this book a reality. My thanks to:

My editor, Megha Parekh, who saw exactly what the story needed to make it shine.

My agent, Mandy Hubbard, who championed me every step of the way.

My critique partners: Brighton Walsh, for holding my hand, sharing my room, fixing my *furthers/farthers*, and dragging me out of my sad little introvert corner time and time again. And Heather McGovern, for being a voice of sanity when the world was squishy, as well as the best enabler a girl could hope for.

The beautiful blogging ladies of *Bad Girlz Write*, for always raising a glass, and the amazing folks at Capital Region Romance Writers of America, for their constant guidance and support.

And my incredible husband, family, and friends, for accepting me and loving me for precisely the ball of crazy that I am.

chapter ONE

It was ridiculous, how pretty words sounded on Kate's tongue. Right up until the moment she opened her mouth and spoke them aloud.

Worrying the strap of her bag between her forefinger and thumb, she gazed straight ahead at the woman behind the register, repeating the phrase over and over in her head. *Un café au lait, s'il vous plaît.* Coffee with milk, please. No problem. She had this. The person ahead of her in line stepped forward, and Kate nodded to herself, standing up taller. When her turn finally came, she grinned with her most confident smile.

And just about had the wind knocked out of her when someone slammed into her side.

Swearing out loud as she was spun around, she put her arm out to catch herself. A pimply teenager was mumbling what sounded like elaborate apologies, but with her evaporating tenth-grade knowledge of French, he could have been telling *her* off for running into *him*, for all she knew. She was going to choose to believe it was the apologizing thing.

Embarrassed, she waved the kid away, gesturing as best she

could to show that she was fine. As he gave one last attempt at mollifying her, she glanced around. A shockingly attractive guy with dark hair and the kind of jaw that drove women to paint stood behind her, perusing a French-language newspaper with apparent disinterest and a furrow of impatience on his brow. The rest of the people in line wore similar expressions.

She turned from the kid, giving him her best New Yorker cold shoulder. The lady at the register, at least, didn't seem to be in any big rush. Kate managed a quick "Désolé"—*sorry*—as she moved forward to rest her hands on the counter. She could do this. She smiled again, focusing to try to summon the words she'd practiced to her lips. "Un café au lait, s'il vous plaît."

Nope, not nearly as pretty as it had sounded in her head, but as she held her breath, the woman nodded and keyed her order in, calling it out to the girl manning the espresso machine. Then, completely in French, the woman announced Kate's total.

Yes. It was all she could do not to fist-pump the air. She'd been exploring Paris now for two days, and no matter how hard she rehearsed what she was going to say, waiters and waitresses and shopkeepers invariably sniffed her out as an American the instant she opened her mouth. Every one of them had shifted into English to reply.

This woman was probably humoring her, but Kate seized her opportunity, turning the gears in her brain with all her might. She counted in her head the way her high school teacher had taught her to until she'd translated every digit. Three eighty-five. Triumph surged through her as she reached for her purse at her hip.

Only to come up with empty air.

Oh no. With a sense of impending dread, she scrabbled at her shoulder, and her waist, but no. Her bag was gone.

She groaned aloud. How many people had cautioned her about exactly this kind of thing? Paris was full of pickpockets. That was what her mother and Aaron and even the guy at the travel store had told her. An angry laugh bubbled up at the back of her throat, an echo of her father's voice in her mind, yelling at her to be more careful, for God's sake. Pay some damn attention. Crap. It was just— She swore she'd had her purse a second ago. Right before that kid had slammed into her...

Her skin went cold. Of course. The kid who'd slammed into her.

Tears prickled at her eyes. She had no idea how to say all of that in French. Her plans for a quiet afternoon spent sketching in a café evaporated as she patted herself down yet again in the vain hope that somehow, magically, her things would have reappeared.

The thing was, "watch out for pickpockets" wasn't the only advice she'd gotten before she'd left. Everyone she'd told had thought her grand idea of a trip to Paris to find herself and get inspired was insane. It was her first trip abroad, and it was eating up pretty much all of her savings. Worse, she'd insisted on making the journey alone, because how was a girl supposed to reconnect with her own muse unless she spent some good quality time with it? Free from distractions and outside influences. Surrounded by art and history and a beautiful language she barely spoke. It had seemed like a good idea. Like the perfect chance to make some really big decisions.

But maybe they'd all been right.

Not wanting to reveal the security wallet she had strapped around her waist beneath her shirt, she wrote off all her plans for the day. She'd just head back to the hostel. She still had her passport and most of her money. She'd regroup, and she'd be fine.

"Mademoiselle?"

Her vision was blurry as she jerked her gaze up. And up. The gorgeous man—the one with the dark, tousled hair and the glass-cutting jaw from before—was standing right beside her, warm hand gently brushing her elbow. A frisson of electricity hummed through her skin. Had he really been this tall before? Had his shoulders been that broad? It was just a plain black button-down, but her gaze got stuck on the drape of his shirt across his chest, hinting at miles of muscle underneath.

His brow furrowed, two soft lines appearing between brilliant blue eyes.

She shook off her daze and cleared her throat. "Pardon?" she asked, lilting her voice up at the end in her best—still terrible—attempt at a French accent.

He smiled, and her vision almost whited out. In perfect English, with maybe just a hint of New York coloring the edges, he asked, "Are you okay?"

All those times she'd been annoyed when someone spoke English to her. At that moment, she could have kissed him, right on those full, smooth lips. Her face went warmer at the thought. "No. I—" She patted her side again uselessly. "I think that guy ran off with my wallet."

His expression darkened, but he didn't step away or chastise her for being so careless. "I'm sorry."

The woman at the register spoke up, her accent muddy. "You still would like your coffee?"

Kate began to decline, but the man placed a ten-euro note on the counter. In a flurry of French too fast for her to understand, he replied to the woman, who took his money and pressed a half dozen keys. She dropped a couple of coins into his palm, then looked around them toward the next customer in line.

"Um," Kate started.

Shifting his hand from her elbow to the small of her back, the man guided Kate toward the end of the counter and out of the way. It was too intimate a touch. She should have drawn away, but before she could convince herself to, he dropped his arm, turning to face her. Leaving a cold spot where his palm had been.

She worked her jaw a couple of times. "Did you just pay for my coffee?" She might be terrible at French, but she was passable at context clues.

Grinning crookedly, he looked down at her. "You're welcome."

"You really didn't need to."

"Au contraire." His brow arched. "Believe me, when you're having a terrible day, the absolute last thing you should be doing is *not* having coffee."

Well, he did have a point there. "I still have some money. I can pay you back."

"No need."

"No, really." Her earlier reservations gone, she reached for the hem of her shirt to tug it upward, but his hands caught hers before she could get at her money belt.

His eyes were darker now, his fingertips warm. "As much as I hate to stop a beautiful woman from taking off her clothes. It's not necessary."

Was he implying...? No, he couldn't be. She couldn't halt the indignation rising in her throat, though, as she brushed aside his hands and wrestled the hem of her top down. "Stripping is *not* how I was going to pay you."

"Pity. Probably for the best," he added conspiratorially. "The police are much more lenient about that kind of thing here than they are in the States, but still. Risky move."

Two ceramic mugs clinked as they hit the counter, and the barista said something too quickly for Kate to catch.

"Merci," the man said, tucking his paper under his arm and reaching for the cups.

For some reason, Kate had to put in one more little protest before she moved to grab for the one that looked like hers. "You really didn't have to."

"Of course I didn't." Biceps flexing, he pulled both cups in closer to his chest, keeping them out of her reach as she extended her hand. "But it sure did make it easier for me to ask if I could buy you a cup of coffee, didn't it?"

For a second, she boggled.

"Come on, then," he said, heading toward an empty table by the window.

This really, really wasn't what she'd had planned for the day. But as he sat down, his face was cast in profile against the light streaming in from outside. If she hadn't lost her bag, she'd have been tempted to take her sketchbook out right then and there, just to try to map the angles of his cheeks.

As she stood there staring, all her mother's warnings came back to her in a rush. This guy was too smooth. Too practiced and too handsome, and the whole situation had *Bad Idea* written all over it. After the disaster that had been her last attempt at dating, she should know.

But the fact was, she really wanted that cup of coffee. And maybe the chance to make a few more mental studies of his jaw. It wouldn't even be that hard. All she had to do was walk over there and sit down across from him. Except...

Except she didn't *do* this sort of thing.

Which might be exactly why she should.

Fretting, she twisted her fingers in the fabric of her skirt. Then she took a single step forward. She was on vacation, dammit all, and this guy was offering. After everything, she deserved a minute to let go. To maybe actually enjoy herself for once.

Honestly. How much harm could a little conversation with a stranger really do?

Rylan Bellamy had a short, well-tested list of rules for picking up a tourist.

Number one, be trustworthy. Nonthreatening. Tourists were constantly expecting to be taken advantage of.

Number two, be clear about your intentions. No time to mess around when they could fuck off to another country at the drop of the hat.

Number three, make sure they always know they have a choice.

Lifting his cappuccino to his lips, he gazed out the window of the café. It hadn't exactly been the plan to buy the girl in front of him in line a cup of coffee or to pick her up. It *definitely* hadn't been the plan to get so engrossed in the business section of *Le Monde* that he'd managed to completely miss her getting pickpocketed right in front of him. But the whole thing had presented him with quite the set of opportunities.

Trustworthy? Stepping in when she looked about ready to lose it seemed like a good start there. Interceding on her behalf in both English and French were bonuses, too. Paying for her coffee had been a natural after that.

Clear about his intentions? He was still working on that, but he'd been tactile enough. Had gotten into her space and brushed his hands over her skin. Such soft skin, too. Pretty, delicate little hands, stained with ink on the tips.

Just like her pretty, pale face was stained with those big, dark eyes. Those rose-colored lips.

He shifted in his seat, resisting looking over at her for another minute. The third part about making sure this was all her choice was necessary but frustrating. If she didn't come over here of her own free will, she'd never come to his apartment, either, or to his bed. He'd laid down his gauntlet. She could pick it up right now, or she could walk away.

Damn, he hoped she didn't walk away. Giving himself to the count of thirty to keep on playing it cool, he set his cup back down on its saucer. Part of him worried she'd already made a break for it, but no. There was something about her gaze. Hot and penetrating, and he could feel it zoning in on him through the space.

He rather liked that, when he thought about it. Being looked at was nice. As was being appreciated. Sized up. It'd make it all the sweeter once she came to her decision, presuming she chose him.

Bingo.

Things were noisy in the café, but enough of his senses were trained on her that he could make out the sounds of her approach. He paused his counting at thirteen and glanced over at her.

If there'd been any doubts that she was a tourist, they cleared away as he took her in more thoroughly. She wore a pair of purple Converse that all but screamed *American*, and a dark skirt that went to her knees. A plain gray T-shirt and a little canvas jacket. No scarves or belts or any of the other hundred accessories that were so popular among the Parisian ladies this year. Her auburn hair was swept into a twist.

Pretty. American. Repressed. But very, very pretty.

"Your coffee's getting cold," he said as he pushed it across the table toward her and kicked her chair out.

A hundred retorts danced across her lips, but somehow her silence—and her wickedly crooked eyebrow, her considering gaze—said more. She sat down, legs crossed primly, her whole body perched at the very edge of her seat, like she was ready to fly at any moment.

He didn't usually go in for skittish birds. They were too much work, considering how briefly they landed in his nest. He'd already started with this one, though, and there was something about her mouth he liked. Something about her whole aura of innocence and bravery. It was worth the price of a cup of coffee at the very least.

She curled a finger around the handle of her cup and tapped at it with her thumb. Wariness came off her in waves.

"I didn't lace it with anything," he assured her.

"I know. I've been watching you the whole time."

He'd been entirely aware of that, thank you very much. He appreciated the honesty, regardless. "Then what's your hesitation? It's already bought and paid for. If you don't drink it, it's going to go to waste."

She seemed to turn that over in her mind for a moment before reaching for the sugar and adding a more than healthy amount. She gave it a quick stir, then picked it up and took a sip.

"Good?" he asked. He couldn't help the suggestive way his voice dipped. "Sweet enough?"

"Yes." She set the cup down. "Thank you."

"You're welcome."

She closed her mouth and gripped her mug tighter. Reminding himself to be patient, he sat back in his chair and rested his elbow on the arm. He looked her up and down.

Ugh. Forget patience. If he didn't say something soon, they could be sitting here all day. Going with what he knew about her, he gestured in her general vicinity, trying to evoke her total lack of a wallet. "You could report the theft, you know."

Shaking her head, she drummed her finger against the ceramic. "Not worth it. I wasn't a complete idiot. Only had thirty or forty euros in there. And the police won't do much about art supplies and books."

"No, probably not."

The art supplies part fit the profile. Matched the pigment on her hands and the intensity of her eyes.

He let a beat pass, but when she didn't volunteer anything else, he shifted into a more probing stance. Clearly, he'd have to do the conversational heavy lifting here.

Not that he minded. He'd been cooling his heels here in Paris for a year, and he missed speaking English. His French was excellent, but there was something about the language you grew up with. The one you'd left behind. The way it curled around your tongue felt like home.

Home. A sick, bitter pang ran through him at the thought.

He cleared his throat and refocused on his smolder. Eyes on the prize. "So, you're an artist, then?"

"I guess so."

"You guess?"

"I just graduated, actually."

"Congratulations."

She made a little scoffing sound. "Now I just have to figure out what comes next."

Ah. He knew that element of running off to Europe. Intimately. He knew how pointless it all was.

Still. He could spot a cliché when he saw one. "Here to *find yourself*, then?"

"Something like that." A little bit of her reserve chipped away. She darted her gaze up to meet his, and there was something anxious there. Something waiting for approval. "Probably silly, huh?"

"It's a romantic notion." And he'd never been much of a romantic himself. "If it worked, everybody would just run off to Prague and avoid a lifetime of therapy, right? And where would all the headshrinkers be, then?"

She rolled her eyes. "Not everyone can afford a trip to Europe."

Her dismissal wasn't entirely lighthearted. Part of his father's old training kicked in, zeroing in on the tightness around her eyes. This trip was an indulgence for her. Chances were, she'd been saving up for it for years.

Probably best not to mention his own resources, then. Mentally, he shifted their rendezvous from his place to hers. Things would be safer that way.

"True enough," he conceded. "Therapy's not cheap, either, though, and this is a lot more fun."

That finally won him a smile. "I wouldn't know. But I'm guessing so."

"Trust me, it is." He picked up his cappuccino and took another sip. "So, what's the agenda, then? Where have you been so far? What are your must-sees?"

"I only got here a couple days ago. Yesterday, I went out to Monet's gardens."

"Lovely." Lovelier still was the way her whole face softened, just mentioning them.

"I mostly walked around, this morning. Then I was going to sit here and draw for a bit."

Asking if he could see her work some time would be good in terms of making his intentions clear. It was also unbearably trite. He gave a wry smile. "A quintessential Parisian experience."

"And then...I don't know. The Louvre and the Musée d'Orsay, of course." The corner of her mouth twitched downward. "Everything else I had listed in my guidebook."

Ah. "Which I'm imagining just got stolen?"

"Good guess."

Eyeing her up the entire time, he finished the rest of his drink. She still had a little left of hers, but they were closing in on decision time. He didn't have anything else going on today—he never really had anything going on, not since his life had fallen apart. But was he willing to sink an entire afternoon here, offering to show her around?

He tried to be analytical about it. Her body language was still less than open, for all that she'd loosened up a bit. Given her age, probably not a virgin, but he'd bet a lot of money that she wasn't too far off. Not his usual fare. He preferred girls who knew what they were doing—more importantly, ones who knew what *he* was doing. What he was looking for.

This girl...It was going to take some work to get in there.

If it paid off, he had a feeling it'd be worth it, though. When she smiled, her prettiness transcended into beauty.

There was something else there, too. She was romantic and hopeful, and between the story of her lost sketchbook and her delusions about Paris having the power to change her life, she had to be a creative type. Out of nowhere, he wanted to know what kinds of things she made, and what she looked like when she drew.

He kept coming back to her eyes. They hadn't stopped moving the entire time they'd been sitting there, like she was taking absolutely everything in. The sights beyond the window, the faces of the people in the café. Him. It was intriguing. *She* was intriguing, and in a way no other woman had been in so long.

And the idea of going back to the apartment alone made him want to scream.

Decision made, he pushed his chair out and clapped his hands together. "Well, what are we waiting for then?"

"Excuse me?"

"Travel guides are bullshit anyway. Especially when you've got something better." He rose to his feet and extended his hand.

Her expression dripped skepticism. "And what's that?"

He shot her his best, most seductive grin. "Me."

chapter TWO

Kate stayed firmly planted in her seat as he offered to help her up. Trying her best to appear unaffected, she arched one eyebrow. "Does this usually work for you?"

The guy didn't pull his hand back or in any other way appear to alter his strategy, and Kate had to give him points for that. "Yes, actually."

"Interesting."

The sad truth was, his offer was beyond tempting. The attention was nice, especially after her self-esteem had been beaten down the way it had in the past year. Hell, in the past twenty-two. It wouldn't hurt to have someone who spoke fluent French showing her around, either. That he was as attractive as he was just made the deal sweeter.

"Not working so well on you, then?" he asked as she considered him.

"Not so far."

His smile only widened. "Good. I like a girl who's hard to crack." Standing up straighter, he held his palms out at his sides. "Come on, what have you got to lose?"

"I'd say my wallet, but that's already gone."

"See? Low stakes. Listen, you don't trust me." That was an understatement. Was there a man left on earth that she did? "I don't blame you. Devilishly handsome man wanders into a café and buys you a drink without asking? Offers to show you around town? Very suspicious."

"Very."

"So let's make this safe. You said you wanted to see the Louvre? Let's go to the Louvre. I'll show you all my favorites, and then if I haven't murdered you by suppertime, you let me take you someplace special. Someplace no guidebook in the world would ever recommend."

She was really running out of reasons to say no. It was a good plan, this one. They'd be in a public place. She'd have time to feel him out a little more. And if he wasn't too much of a psycho, well, everyone had to eat, didn't they?

Still, she kept up her air of skepticism. She rather liked all his efforts to convince her. "I don't even know your name."

The way his dimples shone when he lifted up one corner of his mouth was completely unfair. Extending his hand again, he offered, "Rylan. Pleased to make your acquaintance."

Rylan. That was unusual. She liked it.

"Kate," she volunteered in return, and with no more real excuse not to, she accepted the handshake, slipping her palm into his. Warm fingers curled around hers, his thumb stroking the side of her hand, and *oh*. The rake. He bent forward as he tugged on her hand, twisting ever so slightly so he could press his lips to the back of her palm.

"Charmed."

"I'll bet you are." But her pulse was racing faster, and the kiss felt like it seared all the way to her spine.

This man was dangerous.

He straightened up but he didn't let go. Sweeping his other arm toward the door, he asked, "So?"

She hummed to herself as she gazed up at him, as if there was any question of what she was going to do. His blue eyes sparkled, like he already knew her answer, too.

"Well." She rose from her seat, feeling taller than usual. More powerful. Maybe it was all the flattery of a guy like this hitting on her. Maybe it was the headiness of making this kind of a decision. Either way, it made her straighten her shoulders and insert a little sway into her hips.

"Well?"

"Lead on," she said.

He didn't let go of her hand. "That's what I was hoping you'd say." With a squeeze of her fingers, he took a step toward the door. "Let's go look at some art."

External pressures aside, she had come to Paris to be inspired by beauty. She could find it on the walls of a famous museum. And she could find it in the lines of this man's shoulders and throat. The latter might not have been what she'd had in mind when she'd set out, but what was a little bit of a diversion?

You couldn't find yourself without taking a couple of side trips, after all.

The girl—Kate—wiggled her hand free as they approached the front of the café. Disappointing, but not really a problem. Rylan reached forward to get the door for her and shepherded her through it with a gentle touch at the small of her back. Following her out onto the sidewalk, he gestured down the street. "It's only a little ways. You up for walking?"

"Sure."

Good. Paris came alive this time of year, with the trees and flowers in full bloom, the sky a brilliant blue. Even the traffic seemed less suffocating now that summer was on the horizon. The influx of tourists made the walkways more congested, but at least the travelers occasionally smiled.

As he led them off in the direction of the museum, she fell into step at his side. He pressed his luck whenever the crush of pedestrians got thick, keeping her close with a hand on her hip, letting his fingertips linger. She fit so well against him, every brush of their bodies sending zips of awareness through him. Making him want to tug her closer in a way he hadn't entirely anticipated.

The whole thing seemed to amuse her, but her efforts to act like she wasn't affected were undercut by the flush on her cheeks. The way she allowed him to keep her near.

Until they paused to wait for a light to change, and she pulled away, turning so she was facing him. "So. Rylan."

A rush of warmth licked up his spine. His name sounded so good rolling off her tongue. Far better than Theodore Rylan Bellamy III ever had. He'd rid himself of the rest of his father's burdens only recently, but he'd shed the man's name years ago. And yet it still made him smile whenever someone accepted the middle name he'd taken as his own. Didn't question it the way his family always had.

Ignoring the ruffle of irritation that thought shot through him, he met her gaze and matched her tone. "Kate."

She looked him up and down. "What's your deal?"

Right. Because this wasn't all just flirtatious touches. He'd asked her to a museum for God's sake, not back to his bed. She wanted conversation. To get to know him.

Just the idea of it made him feel hollow.

He put his hands in his pockets and shifted his weight, glancing between her eyes and the traffic going by. "Not much to tell." Liar. "Jaded expat skulking around Paris for a while. Ruthlessly showing lonely tourists around the city in exchange for the pleasure of their company."

"What makes you think I'm lonely?"

Shrugging, he put his hand to the base of her spine again as the light switched to green, feeling the warmth of her through her jacket as they crossed the street. "You have that look."

"For all you know, I could be here with a whole troop of friends, or my family. My"—her breath caught—"boyfriend."

And there was a story there, a faint, raw note. Temptation gnawed at him to press, to dig to the bottom of it.

But if he went digging into her pain, that gave her the right to do the same.

He hesitated for a moment, then went for casual. "Ah. But then you'd be with one of them, and instead you're here with me."

She didn't contest the point, moving to put a few inches between them as they stepped up onto the opposite curb. Changing tacks, she asked, "How long have you been—what was it? Skulking around Paris?"

"About a year. I wander elsewhere from time to time when I get too bored, but a man can do a lot worse than Paris."

"And what do you *do*?"

Nothing. Not anymore. "I pick up odd jobs from time to time," he hedged. The things he had to do to get at his money felt like a job, sometimes. "But I don't have a lot of expenses.

Buying intriguing women coffee doesn't put too much of a dent in the wallet."

"Hmm." One corner of her mouth tilted downward.

"You don't like that answer?"

"I'm sure there's more to it than that."

Perceptive. "Sorry to disappoint."

"So, what, are you staying in a hostel or something?"

There he hesitated. "Something like that." After all, the bed was the only thing in the place that felt like his. "Is that where you're staying? A hostel?" It would be the most logical choice, if she were worried about money.

"Yes."

"Which one?"

She actually rolled her eyes. "Like I'm telling you that."

"Fine. I'll just wait to find out when I walk you home."

"Is that a threat?"

"An offer. One I hope you'll accept." He leaned in closer and caught a whiff of her hair. Vanilla and rose. Sweet and warm. It drew him in, awakening something in his blood. "Because I would love to"—his lips brushed her ear—"see you home tonight."

She gave a full-body shiver. Flexed her hands at her sides so her knuckles brushed his thigh. Inside, he crowed.

Then she crossed her arms over her chest and took half a step to the side. A twitch of disappointment squeezed at him. But he wasn't fooled.

He laughed as he let her have her space. Resistant though she might be, she was warming up to the idea. He didn't have any worries.

He bumped his shoulder against hers. "And what about you? What's your 'deal'?"

"Not much to tell." It was a clear imitation of his own response, and she narrowed her eyes for a second before shrugging. "I'm from Ohio, but I went to school in New York. My mom sends me paranoid emails, asking me if I've gotten mugged yet once a week."

He winced. "At least you'll have something to say to her this week, then?"

"Yeah." She frowned, patting her side as if to touch the purse that wasn't there. "Four years living in this sketchy part of Brooklyn, and I come to Paris to get robbed." She dropped her gaze away from his. "Mom warned me about it, too, you know. Told me Paris was full of thieves."

Her expression was growing more and more unhappy. God. She really didn't know how to guard her emotions at all, did she? Nothing like the people he'd once surrounded himself with. The ones who would've looked at such naïveté with contempt. Here and now, it sparked a tenderness inside him that was new. He wanted to wipe the frown from her lips—or better, kiss it off. He wanted to know what had put it there in the first place. Neither reaction made sense.

So instead of touching or pressing, he steered the conversation onto safer ground. "Is it just you and your mom?"

"Pretty much. My dad's...out of the picture." And oh, but there was a minefield under there, based on the tone of her voice. She crossed her arms over her chest. "How about you?"

Speaking of minefields...

Before he could try to find a way around talking about the train wreck that was his family, they rounded a corner, and he let out a breath in relief. He craned his neck and pointed. "Look. Those banners up ahead?"

Kate followed his gaze, rising up onto tiptoes. Easily distracted, thank God. "Yeah?"

He reached out to grab hold of her hand and nearly got lost in the softness of her skin. He licked his lips and swallowed. "Come on. We're nearly there."

The crowds of tourists were more overwhelming right around the museum, though not as bad as they would be once July hit. Letting him interlace their fingers, she quickened her pace, falling into step as they weaved their way along the sidewalk. The great walls of the place finally gave, and he dragged her along through the archway.

"Don't we have to go in through the Pyramid?" she asked, sounding breathless, evoking the famous entrance to the museum.

He twisted to look at her and winked. "Would I lead you any other way?"

They emerged out into the stone courtyard. He let go of her hand to throw his arms out wide. *Ta-da.* "Your Pyramid, madame."

Pei's Pyramid. It was a glass and metal structure, located at the center of the courtyard, housing the main entrance of the museum. His mother had always hated it, but he'd never really minded the thing. Besides, it was in all the guidebooks, and in high school French textbooks. Tourists typically wanted to see it.

She stood there staring at the monument for a long moment before scrunching her face up. "That is both so much cooler and so much less impressive than I expected."

Well, at least she was honest. He threw his head back and laughed. "Welcome to international travel, my dear." He dug in his pocket for his phone. "You want a picture?"

"Actually, kinda. Yeah."

"Stand over there." He motioned her to stand where he had a good view of her and the Pyramid. The sky was a bright, perfect blue, and it brought out the red in her hair. Her photo smile wasn't as arresting as her real one, but he'd take it anyway. "Say 'fromage.'"

He snapped the shot, then held it out so she could see. He expected the requisite look of embarrassment all girls gave him when he showed them images of themselves, but instead she simply nodded. "Nice composition."

It made him pause. She had been planning to spend her day sketching, had been swayed by his offer to take her here of all places, so the comment shouldn't have surprised him. But his estimation of her rose. When she looked at something, she looked deeper. Saw more.

The idea of wandering around a museum with her suddenly took on a whole new kind of charm.

He glanced at the picture again before flicking back to the camera app. "Easy when there's a pretty lady in the frame."

She cast her gaze skyward and was just starting to move away when he caught her arm.

"What?"

"One more."

"The one is plenty," she argued.

"One more for *me*." With that, he reeled her in, wrapping his arm around her shoulder. It was a cheap ploy, but he couldn't resist the chance to get her close. Her scent wafted over him again. He took a second to breathe her in, to really feel her against his side before he held his arm out for the selfie, shooting his own best ladykiller grin at the lens.

Her laughter sounded more indulgent than charmed, but

he could work with that. "Does *this* move usually work for you?" she asked.

He pressed the button on the screen to take the shot. "Better than the tour guide offer, even." He snapped his teeth playfully near her ear. "Because this one gives me an excuse to *touch* you."

Making a show of mock-growling at her, he gave her one rough squeeze and let her go. She took only a half step away, but the loss of her left his ribs cold. He mentally shook his head at himself.

Before he could give in to the urge to tug her back in, and without a pretext this time, he turned his attention to the screen. A pang fired off inside him. They looked good together. Like a real, happy couple—the kind he'd been taught didn't exist. Her eyes positively danced, her smile as wide as her face.

And so was his. Not a thing about his expression was forced or fake. The contrast alone made his throat tighten. This wasn't one of the usual selfies he took with girls. Not one of the awful pictures snapped on the courthouse steps. Or the others. The ones from before.

His hands curled into fists, and he had to forcibly relax them.

Shutting that line of thought right down, he turned off the screen of his phone. "You'll have to tell me where to send them later."

Oblivious to where his mind had gone, she raised a brow. "Ah, now I see your game. You want my email address."

"Yes," he said dryly. "It's all been a clever little ploy so I could subscribe you to all sorts of mailing lists for natural male enhancement."

She arched a brow. "Am I going to need that?"

Nicely played. "Not if you take *me* home tonight." He threaded his arm through hers. "Come on. The masterpieces await."

"Are you sure we're still even in the museum?" Kate spun in a circle, looking around in awe. "How can this place be so huge?"

The vaulted archways seemed to soar above her, and the ceilings were almost as gorgeous as the paintings. The whole place smelled of *art* somehow, even though the works were all hundreds of years old, the oils dry and the varnishes cracking. The figures within the canvases glowed with how masterfully they'd been rendered, and something inside of her felt like it was glowing as well.

She'd thought the Met had been amazing, the first time she'd been there. But she'd had no idea. No clue.

She finished her slow circle, coming around again to face the center of the room. To face Rylan. He stood there, arms crossed over the expanse of his chest, gaze hot and heavy on hers, and a tremor coursed its way down her spine.

Then again, she'd also never wandered around the Met with a man like him by her side.

To think, she'd been worried when she agreed to let him take her here. She hated being rushed through museums, and she'd been resolved to take her time. But Rylan had stood by patiently as she looked her fill, had been waiting to take her hand at the end of each set of paintings. Big, strong fingers curled firmly around her palm, and the warm, male scent of him mingled with the wood and polish of the gallery to make her head spin.

Swallowing hard, she checked herself. He was practically a stranger—it shouldn't be so easy to fall into step with him like this. And yet she felt more comfortable with him than she had doing this with any of her other friends. Definitely more comfortable than she ever had with Aaron. Maybe *because* he was a stranger. There was no point pretending to be anything she wasn't. She never had to see him again if she didn't want to. So she had nothing to lose.

Catching her eye, he tilted his head toward the next room, a silent invitation, asking her if she was ready to continue. She nodded, moving into his space again. The heat of his hand seeped into the base of her spine, but she didn't flinch. Ridiculous, how quickly she was getting used to all these little touches. What had it been? A couple of hours?

A couple of *amazing* hours.

They'd seen a bunch of the highlights already. The sweeping statuary of *Winged Victory*, which had been so much bigger and more imposing than she'd expected. Tiny, lovely *Venus de Milo*. And much to Rylan's frustration, they'd even stood in line to see the *Mona Lisa* nice and close. She'd shoved him when he'd asked with that odd mixture of amusement and derision if she was satisfied. She'd known going into it that that particular piece had a tendency to underwhelm, but she hadn't cared. She'd seen it. In real life.

In her head, she was rearranging all her plans for the week she had left in Paris. She *had* to come back and spend a whole day here alone with her sketchbook and her pencils and pastels.

"You are having a total art-geek-gasm, aren't you?" he asked, releasing her so she could get closer to one of the paintings.

At this point, they were in one of the more remote galleries, one he'd insisted they make the time to visit, full of big, classic pieces done up in vivid colors, depicting scenes from legends and myths. None of it was what she'd really come here to see, but she found herself getting lost in them all the same.

She was about to tell him as much when she glanced over at him, and he had that expression on his face again. It made her pause.

She didn't have any illusions that he was here for any reason other than to humor her. He was going above and beyond as far as the amount of time and energy she expected any guy to put into a pickup, but it was still a pickup.

Only, he kept looking at her like this. Like somehow, despite his worst intentions, he was seeing more than just her breasts.

She let a grin curl her lips as she turned her attention back to the walls. "It's amazing."

"It gets even better."

Hard to believe, but how could she resist?

"So the thing that really gets me," he said over his shoulder as he meandered forward into the next gallery, "about European museums is the *scale*."

She followed, craning her neck as she passed through the archway and—wow. He wasn't kidding. The whole room was full of paintings that stretched from floor to ceiling. The canvases must have been twenty feet tall, some of them maybe double that in width.

"Holy crap." In awe, she turned, trying to take in everything. She pointed to a painting at the end of the room. "That one is bigger than my apartment back in New York."

It might have been a tiny studio apartment, but still.

"Don't see this kind of thing in museums in the States, huh?" he asked.

He was standing behind her now, his breath warm against her ear. It felt...nice. But not nice enough to distract her from trying to memorize the images surrounding her.

"I've never seen anything like it, anywhere."

She stepped forward, away from his heat and toward the painting on the opposite wall. He let her go, walking backward to perch on the bench in the center of the room. He sat with his knees spread, his elbows on his thighs. She turned her back to him, but she couldn't help but be aware of him—his presence that felt so unreasonably large in such an enormous room.

"That used to be one of my favorites," he said, gesturing at the canvas she'd been drawn to.

"Oh?" It was arresting, the composition and the arrangement of the figures drawing the eye in. Bringing her hand to her mouth, she read the placard beside it. *"Zeus and Hera?"* She took a step back and tilted her head.

The two figures were seated in a garden, staring into each other's eyes. A smile colored the edge of Zeus's lips.

"They look happy." His shrug came through in his voice.

Really? The king and queen of the Greek gods weren't exactly known for their perfect marriage. How many people had died on account of their fits of jealousy and pique? She furrowed her brow. "Not exactly how I usually think of them."

From behind her, he chuckled. "No. Not usually." He paused, then added, "I think maybe that's why I liked it so much."

She hummed, asking him to elaborate.

"It was just a reminder. No matter how awful things were between them most of the time, they still had their moments. Their good times."

A sour taste rose in her throat. "Doesn't change the fact that he'd knocked up half the pantheon."

If her mother hadn't fallen for all the good times with her father... If the good times with Aaron hadn't blinded Kate...

"And the better part of the mortal realm, too," Rylan agreed, a wry twist to his tone. "But still. I always used to like to imagine that at one point they were like this."

"Used to?"

He chuckled wryly. "We all have to grow up sometime."

They were silent for a minute as she tried to take the whole thing in.

When he spoke again, it echoed in the space. "The first time I ever came here, I was...maybe eight? Nine?" A shade of memory colored his voice. "A few years before my parents got divorced." He cleared the roughness from his throat. "My mother brought me to this room, and I remember finding this picture and not being able to look away from it." He gave a little rueful laugh. "My sister gave me so much shit for ignoring all the giant battle scenes to look at two people who weren't even naked or anything."

Kate glanced over her shoulder at him. That was...kind of a lot of information, actually, considering how evasive he'd been while they'd been trading histories earlier. Turning back to the painting, she cast about for something to ask him more about. Not the divorce—not with the way that topic always brought her own hurts to the surface—though she tucked that away for later. After a moment's indecision, she landed on, "You came to Paris when you were a kid?"

"The whole family did. My dad's work had us doing a bunch of travel."

"What did he do?"

"Finance stuff. Very boring. And a very, very long time ago."

She frowned. "It can't have been that long ago. How old are you?"

"Twenty-seven. Don't try to tell me nineteen years isn't a long time."

He made it sound like a lifetime. For her it nearly was.

"Believe me, it's a long time. I'm only twenty-two."

"That's not so young."

She considered for a moment. "It's old enough."

"Old enough for what?" Suggestion rolled off his tongue.

His flirtation made her bold. "For knowing better than to be taken in by men like you?"

"Men like me?" His tone dripped with mock offense. "Men who take you to beautiful museums." He was off the bench and at her side again, pushing her hair from her face. "Men who want nothing more than to show you their big, huge—"

She made a noise of half laughter, half disgust and shoved him off.

"Paintings! I was going to say paintings."

"I'll bet you were."

"I was." He held his arms out to indicate the whole of the room. "Do you like them?"

And she couldn't lie, not even a bit. She spun around another time, nice and slow, taking in everything. As she twisted back toward him, something inside of her softened. All the innuendo and playfulness had fallen from his lips, and he was simply standing there, waiting for her opinion.

Looking for all the world like he actually cared what it would be.

Impulsiveness took her close to him. "I do." And this was stupid. But she did it anyway—leaned in and pressed the quickest, lightest kiss to his cheek. "I love it. Thank you."

He grinned as she danced away before he could reel her the rest of the way in. "Does that mean you're ready to agree for me to walk you home?"

A little thrill shot through her. How nice would that be? He'd been trying so hard, and she'd enjoyed every minute of it. After months of being on her guard, nursing her bitterness, it was tempting to just let go. To say yes for once. He was funny and smart, charming and gorgeous. She could do a lot worse. But she wasn't entirely sure she couldn't do better.

And besides. She'd never known it could be so much fun to watch a guy work for it.

She started toward the exit from the gallery, a little bounce in her step. "Let's start with you walking me to dinner." Glancing back at him, she smiled at the look of smug satisfaction on his face. "No promises for after."

"I would never dare to assume."

"And it had better be something good." She slowed down so he could catch up, and she didn't bother to stop him when he moved to interlace their fingers. She'd already let enough of her inhibitions go, lulled by the ease of his smile and his touch. Why not accept this, too? Especially when it felt so good. "Off the beaten path. Nothing I could find in a tour guide."

"Don't you worry." A sly grin made his eyes sparkle, and his hand squeezed hers. "I have just the thing in mind."

chapter THREE

"I have to admit," Kate said, licking at her thumb.

It was distracting, watching that little pink tongue. "Hmm?"

"This is not what I expected."

"What can I say? I'm full of surprises."

And he'd had a feeling she would enjoy being surprised like this. Instead of going to whatever cozy, intimate bistro she'd probably imagined her Lothario would take her to, they'd stood in line for almost an hour at the best little crepe stand in Paris and ordered galettes from a man who'd made them right in front of them. Eggs and onions and mushrooms and spinach, all wrapped up in a buttery crepe for her. Ham and cheese for him, and a final one with Nutella and banana clutched in his free hand for dessert. He was still holding out hope she'd let him lick it off her, but it was starting to matter less to him.

He was having too much fun. Ambling around the Latin Quarter. Eating crepes with a pretty girl. He took a big bite and swallowed it down.

"So what *did* you expect?" he asked, nudging her with his shoulder.

"I don't know. You talk such a big game. I was thinking candles, wine. Maybe a table, at least."

"Ooh, big spender."

She gave him a sideways glance.

Sloppy. He'd been giving off all kinds of mixed signals when it came to his finances, and she was too smart by half. He was going to have to be a bit more careful about that if he wanted her to buy into the idea that he was working with a budget.

And he…did. It wasn't a game he'd played before—not with any real sense of dedication. A Black Amex was such a shortcut to seduction, and he'd been leaning on it more heavily than usual this year. Throw a little cash around, and women tended to throw themselves right back at you in return. It was easy, uncomplicated.

But with *this* woman…He'd made the split-second decision to do it differently, and now he was in so deep. Opening up to her, showing her that painting as if she gave a damn about the faint hope he'd clung to as a boy that his parents didn't hate each other quite as much as they always seemed to. And she had. She'd glanced back at him with those soulful eyes that saw so fucking deep, and asked him questions about his life. She'd acted like she cared.

It warmed something in him that had gotten so cold.

Dropping her gaze back down to her crepe, she tugged at the paper it was wrapped in, and a smile teased the edges of her lips. "Just as well." She waved a hand vaguely. "Skipping the whole fancy dinner thing."

"Yeah? You like this better?"

"I do." She took a careful bite and chewed. "But I think you knew I would."

"I had a hunch."

She was the kind of girl more interested in the experience than the cliché. The food over the ambiance. The romance of open air and a warm Parisian night.

"Good hunch."

By the time they'd finished up their entrees, they'd wandered into a busier part of the neighborhood. Colored lights from restaurants and storefronts made the darkness glow, and the pavement seemed to shine, the air buzzing with sounds of life that didn't quite manage to pierce their bubble.

He tossed the wrappers from their crepes in the trash, then took her hand and led her over to a low stone wall that separated a patch of grass from the sidewalk. She'd grown increasingly accustomed to him touching her as the day had rolled on. At this point he was damn near addicted, craving more and more. Releasing her fingers, he trailed the backs of his knuckles over her thigh through her skirt, over the smooth, bare skin at her knee. It sent fire licking down his spine, but he forced himself to pull away. He breathed hard against the simmer of arousal in his blood, but his voice pitched lower all the same.

"Have you had a Nutella crepe before?" He unfolded the paper protecting it. The contents had cooled, but they were still warm enough.

"No, but I've never met a Nutella anything I didn't like."

"You're not about to be disappointed. The funny thing is that they should be the same anywhere. The filling comes from a jar, and the crepe is just flour and milk and eggs. But their griddles must be magic, because"—he tore off the gooey corner of the crepe, the edge crisp, and brought it up toward her lips—"these, my friend, are the best dessert crepes in the city."

"Those are some pretty high expectations you're setting."

"And yet you're still going to be blown away."

Her expression was skeptical, even more so when he tsked her attempt to take the bite from him with her hands, insisting on feeding it to her directly. She rolled her eyes but opened that soft, pretty mouth, and his throat went dry. This was cliché, was so close to the kinds of seductions he'd carried out without thought before, but never with this kind of anticipation. Never with this level of focus on how close they were, this dedication to savoring every sight, every sound. Maybe because he'd had to work so hard for every one of them.

He placed the morsel on her tongue with care, barely grazing the edge of her lip with his fingertips, tempted to press his thumb inside and feel the warmth of her closing her mouth around him. But no. Not yet. He let his hand fall away while his body thrummed.

Gazing straight at him, she rolled the flavor around in her mouth, taking her time about it. Once she was done, she smiled, eyes sparkling. "Okay"—her voice trembled, her only tell that the low intimacy of his feeding her was affecting her as much as him—"that's pretty amazing."

"Didn't I tell you?" He tore off a piece for himself and then another for her.

"You don't have to do that," she said when he offered it to her again. Embarrassment colored her cheeks, and they couldn't have that.

"Of course I don't." He made as if to pull the crepe away. "I don't *have* to share my dessert with you at all."

Except he did. The desire to slip that sweetness between her lips had risen to the point of need.

She narrowed her eyes at him. "Ha-ha."

"I'm not joking. I'll take this and walk away."

She paused for just a second. "No. You won't."

It wasn't said as a challenge but as a statement of fact. Something in his chest gave a little twist. It bothered him, that she was right, but it was offset by a deeper understanding of what they were saying. His throat went rough. "And you're not going to, either." He swallowed hard. "Open up."

A long moment passed as they gazed at each other. She tilted her chin upward before softening her jaw, lips parting gently. He didn't move his hand, but she bowed her neck, keeping her gaze steady as she dipped to take the bit of crepe from him. He watched the way she moved, the bob of her throat, the pink of her tongue as she swiped it across her bottom lip.

And he wanted to tell her a line, something about how Paris wasn't as pretty as she was, or about how he adored her mouth. All the words that came to him were true enough—as true or truer than when he'd said them in the past. But for one time in his life, the delivery felt false.

So he held his tongue as he fed her and fed himself. When they were done, she had a dab of chocolate at the corner of her lips. He brushed it away with his thumb, and her cheeks pinked. She shifted her gaze and shifted her body, looking off to the side as if something had caught her attention, but if there was anything to see there, it'd slipped right past him.

At the moment, all he was seeing was her.

"Was it good?" he asked, leaning in close. He liked the smell of her hair, the soft sheen to her skin. "Was it everything I promised?"

He would promise her a lot of things, if there was any chance she'd believe them. Things about how he could make her feel good. About what he could do with his tongue.

She nodded stiffly. Her shoulders had gotten tense. She looked at him, though, and her eyes held an invitation. He just had to strip a layer of fear from her. Distrust. Whatever was holding her back.

Slipping his hand over the breadth of the stone between them, he placed his palm atop her knee. Edged in close so his breath washed hot across her cheek. "Open up," he said quietly.

His lips brushed the corner of her mouth, and she was sweet and warm, letting him kiss her for just a moment. Just a heartbeat. Then she was turning away, a little stutter to her breath.

The warmth of the space surrounding them shivered, but he closed his eyes and pressed his face against her hair. Pressed another soft kiss to her cheek. "What are you afraid of?"

A huff of a laugh escaped her throat. "I don't know what kind of game you're playing with me."

"No game." He'd played games all his life. Had thought he was starting one with her when he had picked her up, but it didn't feel like one now. He let his voice deepen. "I just *want* you."

She looked away, off into a distance. "And that's the thing." Turning her gaze back to him, she said. "That's the part that I don't understand."

Kate held herself together tightly as those words hung in the air. She could hardly believe she'd said them.

For God's sake. She wasn't a demurring flower or anything.

She knew her weaknesses and her strengths: pretty enough but not a knockout, talented but not so talented she didn't have to work hard. The idea that a guy wanted her wasn't entirely the norm, but it was hardly an alien concept.

Men were good at telling a woman what they wanted to hear. And then turning into something else entirely the second you let your guard down. Her father had done it to her mother—had played with Kate's head, too. Until she'd tried to push herself into a shape that was all wrong, just to please him, leaving her with phantom aches to this very day from twisting herself so hard.

He wasn't the only one. Aaron had done it. And the guy at the bar that once...

Rylan pulled away, brows uneven as he stared at her. He hesitated for a moment, and she was ready for him to turn the charm on even higher. Spout some too-rehearsed poetry, or worse, start quoting One Direction lyrics. But then, instead, he tilted his head to the side and asked, "Who was it?"

Excuse me? "Who was who?"

"The person who made you think every man you came across would use you."

Her breath caught in her throat as memories swamped her. But before she could go too far down that road, she pushed those thoughts from her mind. Laughed him off. "And who made you think you could spend an entire day trying to work your way into a stranger's pants and then ask that kind of question?"

"Touché." He grabbed her hand and held it to his chest. "But you're deflecting. Which means I'm onto something. So who was it?"

Seriously? Was there anyone out there who *didn't* teach a

woman that? "Um. My mom? The US Senate? *Law and Order: SVU?*"

"No." He shook his head. "What was his name?"

That made her pause. When he phrased it like that, she couldn't help it. She'd been burned enough times now, but there were those still-lingering bruises, throbbing hotly in the center of her chest. She dropped her gaze and tried to tug her hand free. "It doesn't matter."

She didn't want to think about her dad. Or about Aaron. About how she'd nearly made her mother's mistakes all over again. She'd been such an idiot. Such a fool.

"Of course it does." He let their hands fall from his chest, but he didn't let go, wrapping his fingers around her palm. Rubbing his thumb into the tender spot in its center where the muscles always cramped from drawing. "Because I'm not him." When she made another move to pull back, he held on even tighter. The heat in his tone abated, a forced casualness taking over. "I mean, sure. You're not from around here. You're only in town for, what? A few days? A week? It's a fling. But a fling can be fun for both of us. I didn't decide to spend the whole afternoon in an art museum or invest the absurd sum of nearly five euros on your dinner just because you were the first girl I happened to lay eyes on."

That made her crack a smile. He ducked his chin, and brought his other hand up to touch the side of her face.

"See?" he said. "That right there. That goofy smile when you like one of my crappy jokes and don't entirely want to admit it? That's why I'm still here."

"Just my smile?"

His gaze darted upward. "And your eyes. I like how they seem to watch everything." He trailed his fingers down the line of her neck. "I like how you give me shit and don't let me get away with anything."

"You like a challenge?"

"A conversation. They're hard to come by with the kind of life I lead."

It hit someplace resonant inside of her. She'd come on this trip all on her own without really thinking about the solitude. How many times had she spent all-nighters in the studio, or locked herself in her tiny apartment for days to paint? Conversation wasn't something she needed. But not being able to have it, being surrounded by a language she didn't understand, even on the radio and the television...it was lonely. And Rylan made her feel anything but.

She faltered for a second. "And if you didn't like any of those things?" She made her tone flippant, to try to hide how much his answer mattered. "You wouldn't still be here, trying to get laid?"

"I might be." His smile was lopsided. Soft and kissable. "But I wouldn't care as much about whether or not it worked." With that, he leaned down and pressed his lips to her hand. He lingered just a little too long, breath warm on her skin. Then he pulled away and rose, tugging gently to help her up. "Come on. Let me walk you to the Metro station."

Her head was spinning as she stood. He'd just basically said he was invested now, but if he was offering to walk her to her train, did that mean he was giving up? For all her resistance, the idea of it made a little bubble of disappointment lodge in her throat.

Maybe she should kiss him. Make some kind of statement that no matter how uncertain she was about this, she wasn't entirely ready for it to end.

Or maybe it was all for the best.

Mind working overtime, trying to sort out the possibilities, she followed him down the street. They walked side by side, hands entwined. When the entrance to the subway loomed, he slowed, stopping to lean up against a lamppost.

Her heart thundered behind her ribs. All her worries about him giving up had been premature, because the way he was looking at her now didn't even begin to speak of resignation. Leaning in close, he cupped her face with his palm, fingers weaving themselves through her hair.

He nosed at her temple, and his breath was warm against her ear. "Invite me back to your hotel."

God, she was tempted. Her bones felt watery, and there was a heat coiling up in her abdomen, flames fanned by the scent of him. By the subtle press of his body to hers. Her chin tilted back, spine arching ever so slightly.

But then her breath caught in her throat. "I can't."

"Why not?" He danced his fingertips up her arm and pressed his lips to the column of her throat.

"I—" She couldn't even remember why. Except— Oh, right. "Can't. Actually can't." Why was her voice so breathy, her skin so sensitive? "Cheap hostel, remember? Roommates."

"All those friends you said you were traveling with?"

"Worse. Strangers."

"Strangers you don't want to know what you sound like when you come?"

Jesus. Part of her wanted to grab him by the collar and pull him down into that subway, just for the heat of that promise.

A promise no man had ever bothered to make to her before. A promise no man had ever managed to fulfill.

His words and kisses were all persuasiveness, like he could

feel her wavering on the point of indecision. "Because," he continued, "this may be a fling." He pulled his lips from her skin, shifting until his face was right in front of her. His eyes burned hot and dark. "But I promise. You will get exactly as much out of it as I will. More, if you're willing to show me what you like."

And god*damm*it. Men broke their promises—they did it all the time, but she wanted to believe this one. She'd had sex only once since she and Aaron had broken up, and it had been awful. Worse than it had been with Aaron even, and after everything... didn't she deserve something good?

Before she could overthink it any more, she reached up. Grabbed him by the hair and pulled him down, taking the kiss she'd been so afraid of a few minutes before.

And it was *worth* it. He tasted like chocolate and sin, the rasp of stubble a delicious burn against her chin. He was still against her for all of a second before he pulled her close, surrounding her with his warmth and pressing forward with his tongue. Scraping his teeth over her bottom lip and accepting everything she offered.

But giving back to her, too. With every push forward, he let her in a little more, until her skin hummed and her breath was coming too fast, heat and need pooling deep inside her abdomen.

This was insane. It was how she'd landed herself in trouble last time. She should disengage, get her breath back, calm the racing of her heart.

But it was also *nothing* like the last time. This man had coaxed her along, patient through every step, his kiss and his million casual touches promising she wouldn't regret letting him in. They'd talked, shared stories. She'd glimpsed more than simple lust in his eyes.

She could do this. This one time, maybe she could have this.

Before she could talk herself out of it, she tore away with a gasp, fingers curled tightly in the fabric of his shirt, breasts pressed to the solid muscle of his chest. "Your place?"

His laugh was pure frustration as he tucked her head against his shoulder, rocking them side to side. "Not a good idea, either, sadly."

Dammit. "Roommates?"

"Something like that." He dipped his head again and kissed her, softer this time but with no less warmth or intent. With one last sweep of his lips over hers, he retreated to rest his brow against her temple. "This isn't going to happen tonight, is it?"

"Doesn't seem that way." She shouldn't feel so conflicted about that. Reason said it was better to wait, but her body said she only had so many days here. She could be laid out on a bed right now, being taken apart the way she'd always imagined the right man could.

Putting his hands on her shoulders, he took a step back, looking at her square on, and there was an intensity to his gaze. One that went straight to the very center of her. "Meet me tomorrow."

"I—" The tick of hesitation caught her by surprise. She had so many things she wanted to see and do and experience in this city. While he was swiftly moving up that list of things, she wasn't ready to ignore the rest of them. "When?"

"When are you free?"

If she took the morning and maybe the early afternoon for herself, she could hit a few sights. Spend some time with a pad of paper and her charcoals trying to capture the light.

Think some more about what the hell she was going to do with her life.

With this man.

"Maybe four?" she suggested, then hedged. "Five o'clock?"

"Four thirty it is." He didn't sound disappointed about it being so late. "You know the Tuileries Garden, right? Back near the Louvre?"

"Of course."

"Meet me there. By our statue."

"*Our* statue?"

He smirked and nodded. "Our statue."

"We've never been there before."

"Nope. But we're going tomorrow." He leaned in and kissed her once more, lightly, on the mouth. "And you'll know it when you see it."

She remembered looking at the garden on her map, before it had been stolen from her. The place was huge, its sculpture legendary. She could spend half the day trying to figure out which piece he happened to be thinking of.

"And you'll know I didn't when I'm two hours late."

"Not going to happen. And anyway, as we're proving tonight"—he tweaked her chin—"I can be a very patient man."

"Ha."

He dropped his arm and turned, but then he paused. "You'll meet me, then?"

She knew the answer in her toes. Her lungs fluttered as she filled them with breath.

This might be insanity. Might be folly of the highest order, and a distraction she couldn't afford. Her smile wavered. Still, she nodded. "It's a date."

chapter FOUR

It didn't seem to matter how long he'd been living like this, or how late he'd been up the night before. Barring the worst kind of jet lag, Rylan snapped awake at seven every morning, alert and blinking and ready for somebody to start barking at him.

Sighing, he forced himself to relax and sagged against the headboard, scrubbing a hand through the mess of his hair. He looked around at his surroundings, at the pale light streaming in through the curtains. The four gray walls and the bookshelves and the sheer quantity of *stuff* he'd managed to accumulate over the course of the past year. There were noises out on the street, but in here it was blissfully quiet. It was just him in the apartment, same as every morning.

Well, most mornings. He chuckled to himself as he slid his palm down his face. The few occasions he did bring someone back with him—the even rarer ones when they spent the night—they usually weren't *barking* at him. Not his scene, thank you very much.

No, his scene was pretty art students, apparently. Pretty art students he could have had in his bed right now, if only he'd been willing to give up the pretense of what kind of life he was leading here in Paris.

Roommates. She'd wondered if he had *roommates*.

He groaned and shook his head at himself. He probably should have just been upfront about things with her. There hadn't seemed to be much reason to, though. She hadn't even told him how long she was going to be in town, but it wouldn't be more than a week. Two at the most. Why rock the boat? She wanted her charming bohemian adventure, re-plete with shitty hostels and smelly, backpacking roommates? He wouldn't spoil it for her.

He wouldn't spoil it for himself. She hadn't known what he had to offer, and she'd kissed him anyway. She'd chosen nor-mal, ordinary him. No one else had ever done that before—he'd never given them the chance to.

Besides. He really didn't want to see the look in her eyes once she knew. He typified everything charming bohemian types abhorred. Shallow, rich, lazy. Hollow.

To distract himself from that whole train of thought, he grabbed his phone from his bedside table. Sure enough, there were a handful of alerts. He scrolled through them with disinterest. A couple of things from his broker, and one from his father's crony. McConnell. He deleted that one without even looking. The one from his sister he gave a cur-sory glance, but really, he shouldn't have bothered. She had only one thing on her mind these days, and it was nothing he wanted any part in.

He wasn't going home, no matter how many guilt-tripping emails and phone calls they all laid at his feet. Not now. Not after…everything.

Maybe never.

With a sigh, he turned off the screen and set his phone aside. He threw off the covers, rolling over to the edge of the bed and levering himself up to sit. He had until late afternoon to get his shit together, and he basically had nothing to do. Still, it wasn't as if he was going to be able to get back to sleep. Resigned, he arched his spine and stretched his arms up overhead, then gave his bare chest a scratch. Flicked his thumb against the ring that hung from the chain around his neck. Finally, with a yawn, he rose and headed over to the wardrobe in the corner, where he plucked out a T-shirt and tugged it on. Between that and his boxers, he was decent enough.

It was somehow even quieter out in the main rooms of the apartment, and not the good kind of quiet. More the kind that had him out in cafés and museums and, well, anywhere else, most days. Ignoring it all the best he could, he made a beeline for the coffee machine and got some espresso going.

While the thing was grinding, he wandered over to the window and looked down at the world below. He liked the look of Paris in that post-dawn glow. The first commuters were already out, grabbing their croissants and heading to the Metro, but the tourists were still asleep, and the air smelled of bread instead of exhaust. It was peaceful.

This apartment was supposed to be peaceful. His mother had explicitly told the designer that. He turned around, though, and forced himself to really see it, and it made his teeth grate. It set his bones on edge.

Japanese screens and modern art and artisanal vases filled with single fake buds had nothing to do with peace. They had to do with showing off.

With creating a nice little space to drag the douchebags you were fucking back to, while your husband was home in the States robbing the company blind.

Shit. Shit, shit, *shit*.

Rylan stormed his way back over to the espresso machine before he could put a hole through something useless and priceless. He poured the coffee into one of the dainty little china cups the place was outfitted with and slugged it down. It was bitter and it burned in his throat and he didn't care.

He needed to get out of there, and not just for the afternoon. For a few days, at least. Maybe for good. He set the cup in the sink for someone else to deal with later and braced both hands on the counter, breathing in deep.

When it struck him—a solution so obvious, so perfect—he couldn't believe it hadn't occurred to him earlier.

Without bothering with anything else, he stalked back to his room for his clothes and his phone.

He had planning to do.

The glare from the sun was almost blinding as Kate spilled out of the cathedral, blinking hard against the sudden onslaught of light. She fumbled at her side for the new bag she'd picked up at a random stall that morning and kept tucked close against her body all day. Winding her way through the crowd milling around the exit, she managed to lay her hands on the cheap plastic sunglasses she'd bought from the same vendor and slid them up her nose. Vision thus shielded, she cast a glance up and back.

Notre Dame Cathedral, real and in the flesh. Well, stone. It was another sight to cross off her list of must-sees, and she was glad she'd made the time to check it out. The stained glass had been as beautiful as promised. The arching ceilings and tile.

It hadn't been as much fun as the Louvre, though. None of the places she'd visited on her own had been.

Frowning to herself, she slipped her way between the clusters of people milling about the square, scanning until she spied an open bench. She made for it and plunked herself down, resting her purse in her lap and looking around. There were so many things to see, so many people to look at, languages to hear. Rylan would probably have had an interesting comment about them all.

Rylan. She'd see him in a couple of hours, provided he showed—and that she could follow his cryptic directions to their meeting spot. Part of her wished she'd gotten his number, that she could ask him to meet up with her sooner. But no. It was better this way. He was good company, sure, but nothing worth getting attached to. Even if he wasn't just after a one-night stand, everything about him screamed *casual*.

It also screamed *confident in bed*. And didn't that send a shiver of anticipation up her spine?

A lonely night in a room with a bunch of other people who'd shared none of her compunctions about having intimate relations around strangers had made her rethink her prudishness from the night before. No, she wasn't usually the type to sleep with people she didn't know, but she was on vacation, and he was gorgeous, and she just *knew*. He'd know his way around a woman's body. He'd live up to the promises he'd whispered in her ear and pressed against her lips.

Later.

For now, she had come to Paris with a purpose, and this

was it. Opening up the main compartment of her bag, she drew out the sketchbook and pencils she'd brought with her for the day. She was still pissed about having lost a brand-new book the day before, but she was grateful, too. Fresh pages could be replaced, if for a small fortune. Near-full books? They were priceless, for the story that they told.

She flipped through the one in front of her for a moment, watching as faces and scenes and still-life illustrations flew by. She'd been slowly filling it over the last couple of years, and she'd been proud of it—proud of all the things she'd made in her final semesters of school.

And yet, looking at it now, all she could hear were the words her mentor, Professor Lin, had said in their last critique session.

"Mastery of every style, Kate. It's an impressive thing." Lin had tapped her fingertip against the frames of her glasses. "But unless you make a style your own...it's all just imitation."

A sour pit opened in the bottom of Kate's stomach. She'd played with so many different styles in this book. There were faithful renderings, near-perfect photorealism. Fauvist color studies and gestures intended to capture movement. Impressionistic smudges decorated a few, and she'd even ventured into abstraction. By and large, they were good, she'd concede. But they could have been done by anyone. They could have been done by fifteen *different* someones.

You had to have a voice in art. A vision.

And that was the quiet secret of this trip, the one she hadn't dared reveal to anybody before she'd gone.

It was her last-ditch hope that she could find a vision of her own. One she could take to graduate school with her.

She had to stop herself from crumpling the page in her grasp. If she couldn't find it, she'd have to settle down. Take the corporate job she'd been so, so lucky to land, and go sit in a cubicle for the rest of her goddamn life, surrounded by gray, fabric-covered walls. She shuddered. Soullessness and stagnation and the only thing her father had ever let her believe she'd be good enough for.

She'd spent her whole life trying to prove him wrong. But deep down inside, sometimes, she believed him.

Not today, though. Not here.

Squaring her shoulders, she skipped past the rest of her completed sketches, turning to one of a handful of bare white pages and lifting her gaze to the city around her. Paris had something so vital to it, an energy and a romance. The city felt like she wanted her paintings to look, and if she could only capture that...

Maybe she'd have something worth fighting for.

Kate's first sign that time had started flying on her was the angle the sun made with the horizon. She sketched it in behind the cathedral's tower, then frowned to herself. Absently, she flipped to her first study, and yup. The sun had been a lot higher then. She went instinctively for her crappy little flip phone, but the thing had kept resetting itself to New York time, and she didn't trust it.

Crap. How the hell did she ask a stranger for the time?

Frowning to herself, she turned to the person sitting on the other end of the bench. "Pardon?" she asked.

The man turned around, giving her a quick up and down before smiling and rattling something off in French.

She'd known this phrase, back a half dozen years ago. "Quelle..." *What*... Shit, what was the word for time again? In frustration, she tapped her empty wrist.

The man laughed. "Trois heures et demie. Three thirty."

"Thank you." She corrected herself. "Merci."

He said something else, but she was too busy stuffing her things into her bag, a little pang of regret beating inside her chest. She'd needed just another fifteen minutes or so to play with that last sketch she'd been working on. Three times, she'd drawn the same basic view of Notre Dame, the first with an eye for accuracy, and the second with a quicker hand. That last one, though, she'd felt certain she was onto something. There'd been a different quality to her line work, a life to the planes of stone. It had felt better than the other drawings. Better than any of her work had felt since she'd graduated.

But she'd have to sort it out another time.

The Tuileries Gardens were only a handful of blocks away, but her sense of direction had never been good, and worse, Rylan hadn't exactly given her a cross street. She might need the whole hour she had left to figure out where she was going and find the statue he'd told her to look for. What the hell had he even meant by that? *Our* statue?

She snagged a Wet-Nap from her purse and took a quick swipe at getting the charcoal dust off her fingers before she stood. With a little nod of her head toward the guy who'd given her the time and a wistful glance back at the cityscape, she slung her bag over her shoulder and headed off in the direction she was pretty sure she was supposed to go.

To her surprise, she even turned out to be right.

Feeling a little more confident, she slowed her pace as she entered the garden. She was smart enough to keep her eyes peeled and her bag clutched to her chest as she combed the pathways, but the bulk of her attention was on any hunk of granite or marble or bronze she happened to cast her sight on. They were all gorgeous, all epic in their scale and in their subject matter, but not a one of them screamed *me and Rylan* at her.

As she searched, despair coiled up tightly behind her sternum. Rylan had seemed so genuine, but if he'd really wanted to see her again, he could have given her something more specific than some twenty square blocks to scour. Or maybe a phone number. An email address. A last name. Anything that might help her out right now.

If he didn't show, or if she couldn't find him...well, it wouldn't be the first time she'd been disappointed by a guy. Not even close. But that didn't prevent it from stinging.

In the distance, the obelisk that marked the western end of the gardens loomed, and she slowed her pace. It had to be four thirty by now. How long would he wait? Was it even worth doubling back and looking for anything she might have missed? Dropping her arms in resignation by her sides, she turned in a circle, looking for anything that might give a clue.

When she spied something even better. Much better.

A single, choked peal of laughter caught in her throat as she spied him, all messy dark hair and clear blue eyes, dressed in a black leather jacket and jeans that fit him to a T. And held loosely in one hand, a rose the color of a garnet.

Rylan.

And behind him was a bronze. A Rodin—it had to be. A bigger-than-life-sized statue of a man and a woman in a passionate embrace.

It was cheesy. Tacky. Swiftly approaching tawdry, even. But as her feet drifted forward, leading her toward him, all the doubt squeezed out of her heart. He'd made her smile so many times in the day and a half since they'd met. He'd made her body come alive, and worse, he'd seduced her with *art*. If that wasn't worth a shot . . . then she didn't know what was.

chapter FIVE

According to Rylan's usual game plan, his expression should have been a sultry smirk. But as Kate approached, a real smile stole over him instead, one that made his lips stretch and his cheeks tight.

Who the hell did he think he was fooling? If he'd been following his typical playbook, he would have taken the girl home last night, and there wouldn't have been a second encounter. A second—oh, Christ, this was a date. Apparently, the rules had all gone out the window the second Kate had been completely underwhelmed by his charm.

She wandered toward him with her hands folded in front of her and a flush to her cheeks that said she'd been running to try to find him. She was a couple of minutes late, and he had to admit he'd been starting to worry. All that concern was evaporating now, though. Her hair was loose today, the long waves of it framing her face and shining in the sun. She still wore tennis shoes, but she'd paired them with jeans that hugged her hips, and a shirt that dipped low in the neckline and that... was smeared with charcoal?

She stopped short a couple of feet away from him, raising a brow and pointing. "Is that for me?"

He'd nearly forgotten the flower he'd bought on his way to the park.

"What, this?" He twirled it back and forth between his fingers. "Nah. Random homeless person gave it to me while I was waiting. Think he thought I was getting stood up and wanted to soften the blow."

"Sorry. I lost track of time." She narrowed her eyes. "Though it didn't help that *somebody* didn't exactly give me the clearest of instructions."

"*Somebody* miscalculates from time to time." With that, he held out the rose and drew her in, tugging at her hand to pull her close. And hell, but he hadn't been playing this up in his head. She felt as good against him as she had the day before—better, maybe.

Today, she hadn't just gone along with his cajoling. Today, she'd decided to come to him. To seek him out.

Swallowing down the fierce, sudden burst of pride within his chest, he darted his gaze across her face. Raised his hand to her cheek and rubbed away a sooty smudge. He found it unaccountably endearing. "Let me guess. Busy day drawing?"

"Yeah. I got a lot done."

"Good." Did she even know how amazing that was? All his wasted days, and she spent her vacation making things. And then she had stopped—had probably run here if her breathing was anything to go by, because he'd asked her to. His heart gave a squeeze behind his ribs, and he cupped her jaw, taking pains not to grip it too firmly. "I'm glad you came."

"Me, too." But she averted her gaze as she said it, like she was embarrassed to admit it.

Dipping down, he brushed his nose against hers, leaving their lips just a whisper's breath apart. She smelled sweeter than the flower he'd brought her, and her skin was softer than its petals. And nearly as red. Her embarrassment grated at something inside him. Here he was, reveling in her choice to meet him again. He didn't like the idea that she was any less pleased by it. Or that she was having second thoughts.

Whatever doubts she might be having, he resolved to cast them off.

Pressing his brow to hers, he grazed his lips against the corner of her mouth. His chest swelled as she let him kiss her. "You look beautiful today."

She relaxed a fraction in his arms, laughing as she curled her hand around his neck. "You're one to talk."

Pride surged within him again. "You like?"

"Yeah," she said, voice uneven and dipping darker. She smoothed her hand down his chest, lighting fires beneath his skin. "I like a lot."

"Good." His looks weren't worth much more than his bank account, but if they'd won him this chance, at least they were something he'd worked for. Something he'd chosen to invest his time in. Without another word, he captured her mouth with his, parting his lips and darting forward with his tongue. Her curves came flush against him as he reeled her in, perfect and soft and lush. *Willing.*

And that was the sweetest part of all. None of her hesitance from the night before clung to her today, and the way she pushed up into the kiss shot like lightning through his veins. Forget the rule book—the long game was worth playing sometimes, even with a tourist.

Surrounding her with his arms, he kissed her hot and hard

enough to put the statue behind them to shame. Just when it hit the point of testing his control, he pulled away enough to free his lips. Stayed close enough to still share air as he let a growl creep into his voice. "I'm really, *really* glad you came."

She looked a little glazed, her red lips full and wet. "Me, too."

And it was so tempting to try to hurry his plan along, but no. Not this time, and not with this girl.

Yesterday, their trip to the museum had started out a ploy to make her trust him enough to invite him to her bed. But somehow, it had turned into the best day he'd had in this long and pointless year. It had been connection and seeing art through this beautiful woman's searching eyes. Seeing himself through her eyes, too. Not the man who'd had all his choices stripped from him, only to be shown the ugly underbelly of the life he'd been told he had to lead. The man who had seen it, and then turned around and run.

He was just a guy to her. One she liked the look of. One she'd invited to take her home last night. One who could make her disheveled and glazed just from a kiss.

His pulse roared. He wanted her like this, naked and laid out for him, all right. But he wanted the rest of it, too. He wanted *more*.

It took an exercise of will, but he managed to take a step back. His breath was still coming too fast, and he had to will his body to calm down as he forced some distance between them. Dinner. They were going to have dinner. And then they could have the rest.

"Come on." Entwining their hands, he reached down to grab his pack off the ground.

"What's that?" she asked.

Condoms and a fresh change of clothes, mostly.

"Nothing." He slung the bag over his shoulder and tipped his head toward the exit of the park. Changed the subject before he could talk himself out of his own plan to not rush this along. "How do you feel about Ethiopian food?"

"It's not French." Her voice quirked upward with uncertainty at the end.

"Astute. But do you like it?"

"Never tried it."

Perfect. "Feeling adventurous?"

She chuckled and squeezed his hand, letting herself be dragged along as he maneuvered them down the path. "I think that's pretty obvious."

And he liked that—the idea that this was an adventure. One that he was leading her into, but that she was taking him along on, too. In a year of conquests, he hadn't tried it this way, not with dates and dinners and kisses in a park. Not even once.

Had he ever, really? With all the fucked-up examples of relationships he'd had to look to, with the games the people in his life liked to play . . .

Here, with this girl who didn't know who he was, though, who would be on this continent for only so long. It somehow seemed worth a chance.

The restaurant, when they got there, wasn't quite as shabby chic as grabbing food to go from a literal hole in the wall, but it wasn't precisely fine dining, either. Tucked into an alcove on a little side road, the place was below street level, the lighting dim but the colors loud, all the walls painted in or-

ange and red and gold. Keeping Kate close, Rylan glanced
around the space, past all the woven baskets on the tables
and the tapestries on the walls. He frowned. Lucille always
worked on Saturdays.

Ah, there she was, slipping out from behind the beaded
curtain near the kitchen. They made eye contact across the
room, and she smiled as she took him in. She raised an eyebrow as she sashayed her way to the front, dark skin gleaming
in the lamplight. "Deux?" *Two?*

It was unusual, he could concede. He typically showed up
alone.

"Deux," he confirmed, guiding Kate over to a cozy table
near the wall. As he pulled out a chair for her, he checked,
"This okay?"

"Sure?" She didn't sound so certain about that, so he leaned
down, cupping her shoulders in his hands and kissing her
cheek.

"It'll be fine. Trust me."

She made a little humming noise as she settled her purse in
her lap. She was pretty protective of the thing today. Maybe
to the point of verging on paranoia, but he couldn't exactly
blame her, considering.

Projecting confidence, he sat down opposite her and swung
his own bag over the back of an empty seat. Turning to face
the table again, he caught Kate eyeing the pack with as much
curiosity as she'd had before.

Good. Let her keep thinking about it.

Lucille dropped a couple of menus on the table in front of
them. "You need a minute to look?"

It was odd. He'd never heard her speak English before.
"Yes, please."

She nodded and slinked away, but not without running her fingertips over the back of his neck. Troublemaker. He shot her a restrained glare, partly in warning and partly to show Kate he wasn't amused.

As for Kate, she didn't seem to know what to think of any of it. She gestured vaguely at Lucille's retreating figure. "You're a regular, I presume?"

"You could say that."

He liked to find little eateries with their own flavors—ones with owners who doubled as waitstaff, and where everyone was family. Walking in a world of strangers, it was nice, having places like that. Places where they knew only one of his names.

Like Kate did.

"So." He flipped open his menu. "Anything you don't eat?"

"Not really." When she reached for the other menu, he put his hand over hers to stop her.

From the look on her face, that might have been a douche move. He shifted, curling his fingers around her palm instead of preventing her from doing her own perusing. "You can take a look if you want, of course. But . . . if it's not too scary, maybe let me?"

"I'm not scared." She could have fooled him.

He shook his head, trying to allay whatever concerns she might have. "The idea here is you order a few different things. They all come out on a big tray lined with bread. Everybody tries a little bit of everything."

"Uh-huh."

Letting his lips slant upward, he rubbed her knuckles with his thumb. "I don't pretend to know your mind, but I have a few favorites I'd like you to try. What do you say?"

And there was that look again, like she was peering straight through him. It should have felt invasive, but it never did. Instead, it left him wondering what on earth it was she saw.

Whatever it was, it must have met with her satisfaction. As if just to check, she asked, "Nothing too spicy?"

"I can do mild."

"All right, then." She nodded decisively. "I'm game."

Good. He squeezed her hand and turned around to catch Lucille's eye. Once she'd made her way back over, he paged through the menu, picking out a variety of flavors for Kate to sample, mixing up the choices of featured vegetables and meats.

"Will that be all?" Lucille asked when he was done.

"Yeah. Thanks." He passed the menus over to her, never letting go of Kate as he did.

Apparently, his message was received. While Lucille smiled at him fondly, she didn't try to touch him this time.

He'd have to thank her for that later. For now, he had more pressing things to think about.

"So tell me," he said, focusing all of his attention on the woman before him. He picked up her hand in his, spinning it around and uncurling her fingers from her palm. Rubbing at the hints of pigment ground into her skin, he grinned. "Whatever have you been up to today that's gotten you so filthy?"

It probably shouldn't have been quite so appealing, the way Rylan could make something sound seductive and serious and ridiculous all at once. Kate laughed, letting him turn over her hand and inspect her fingernails. The warmth of his touch felt nice, and he was just the right combination of delicate and firm.

And no matter what she felt, she refused to flinch or yank her hand away. How many times had she been nervous about the condition of her hands? Wouldn't a guy prefer the girls with the smooth, soft skin and perfect manicures over the one covered in little cuts and ink and glue? If he cared, he didn't give any sign of it. He loosely grasped her knuckles and tugged at her arm, getting her close enough that he could press his lips to the back of her palm.

"So?" he asked, returning their hands to the table.

"N-nothing all that interesting." Her voice came out raspy in a way she hadn't expected, for all that it matched the jumpy, keyed-up feeling in her chest. The tingling in her breasts. "Just some sketching."

His face lit up at that. "Can I see?"

"It's nothing fancy." The temptation to pull her hand from his grew, but for entirely different reasons.

She didn't like showing anyone her stuff—not if it wasn't finished. Hell, she was kind of squirrelly about it even when a piece was done. It wasn't just insecurity, either. She knew she was reasonably good at this.

But letting someone see your work was like showing them a whole other part of you. And when you didn't even know what your drawings stood for, it was worse. It was showing the other person an unfinished version of yourself. Fragmented and dissolute. The messy insides that hadn't quite formed themselves into the shape of a person yet.

"Come on," he pressed. "I mean, if you don't want to, I understand, but I bet they're great." He tilted his head, looking at her through dark lashes with the most beautiful, clear blue eyes.

"They're not."

"I won't judge."

And he seemed so *interested*. As she wavered, considering letting him have this glimpse inside her head, his eyes shone.

She'd been made to feel self-conscious about what she did so many times and by so many people—her dad, Aaron. Hell, even her mom, sometimes, though she tried to be supportive.

Kate was probably a sucker for letting his eagerness get to her, but it did.

And besides, it was like she'd told herself the day before when she'd given into his entreaties. She didn't know this man from Adam, and he didn't know her. So why not?

Oh, hell. "Fine." Her heart rose up in her throat, her nerves making her fingers twitch. But as she slipped her hand from his, she opened her purse.

She flipped past the vast majority of the pages, not ready to show him quite that much yet. When she got to her first sketch of the day, she frowned. It didn't look any better now than it had while she'd been working on it. But Rylan was peering at her with such keen interest, like he really cared about what she was about to show him, and it was too late to withdraw the offer now.

Fighting for composure, even as her face went warm and the back of her neck cold, she folded the book in half and passed it over.

His gaze dropped to the page immediately as he took it from her. "Notre Dame?"

A little of her unease slipped away. "At least it's recognizable." With its iconic windows, she'd figured it would be. But it was nice to hear all the same.

"Easily." He didn't make any other comment on the quality of the work, and it wasn't until that lack of praise that she realized how much she'd been waiting for some kind of affirmation. Even just the normal, polite sort of approval your average stranger felt obligated to confer. He started to turn the page, then paused. "May I?"

They'd already gotten this far. She nodded, holding her breath.

He examined the next drawing with a look of concentration on his face. "Same basic scene."

"Yeah. I—" Was it worth describing her process to him, when she scarcely understood it herself these days? "It takes a couple looks to figure out where I want to go with it."

Another glance at her for assent before he flipped to the third and final piece. She sucked in a breath as he held the page out at arm's length and pulled it back in, gaze moving over it.

When her resolve cracked, she forced an exhalation and wet her lips with her tongue. "I didn't quite get to finish that one." With weak humor, she explained, "Had to go and meet someone."

His only response was a twitching at the corner of his mouth. Finally, after what felt like forever, his eyes darted up. "I like it."

"You do?"

"Very much." He checked the surface of the table before setting the sketchpad down with the drawing facing up. He tapped the corner of the paper. "This one especially."

And just like that, she was glad he hadn't jumped to say he liked them right away—that he had taken his time and considered each one. It made the compliment more meaningful, made it seem like he actually meant it as opposed to saying so just to be polite.

"Yeah." She let out a sigh, the shaky anticipation of opening herself up to him melting away. Her tongue, tied up in knots this entire time, suddenly loosened, and she leaned across the table, angling herself closer to him. "I felt like I was kind of getting somewhere with that one. Wish I'd had a little more time to finish it."

"You'll go back."

"If I have a chance."

"You'll go back," he insisted. He thumbed the corner of the page. "You know what sets this one apart?"

She wanted to laugh. "That it doesn't suck?"

"No. The others aren't bad. Only there's not as much...*there* there. You were drawing what you saw. But in this one, you were drawing it the way you wanted us to see it. Through your eyes. It's subtle." He slid the sketchbook over to her. "But it makes a difference."

Humming to herself, she turned the page around so she could see it right-side up, and he had a point. It wasn't just a famous church staring back at her as if from a postcard. The big, round window at the center connected to the pointed arches and the tops of the towers, which connected to the sky and to the ground, coming together to give a sense of warmth. Of wholeness. She'd been starting to interpret. To pull it all together and make an image you could *feel*.

Notre Dame. Our lady. A woman standing free and on an island all her own.

Rylan smiled and pointed at the picture. "It's paying off. You can't love what you don't know, and you can't draw like that unless you love."

He wasn't wrong, but she'd never heard it put that way.

How would it be to draw him? She'd never been the best at portraiture, but she could imagine it now. Spreading him out and having him pose for her. Naked, perhaps. He'd be beautiful, and with enough sketches...It would be dangerous.

It was the road to falling in love.

She closed the cover of the book and returned it to her bag. "How do you know so much about art?"

A shadow crossed his eyes, but it was there and gone in an instant. "I've always appreciated it. Never was much good at it myself, though."

Before she could inquire any further about that, the woman who had taken their orders appeared beside the table again. Kate refused to shrink at her presence, opting instead to look up at her and smile. But she couldn't help glancing at Rylan when the lady put her hand on his shoulder as she set a basket on the table in front of them. "Your food is almost ready."

"Merci," Rylan said, not reacting to the proximity.

So Kate wouldn't react to it, either. She'd known what kind of person she was getting involved with. His easy intimacy with beautiful waitresses wasn't anything she shouldn't have expected. It was a good reminder, even.

The nervous patter of her pulse settled down into a low simmer as the woman walked away, leaving them alone again. Looking only at Kate, he lifted the top of the basket, releasing a thin cloud of steam and revealing tightly rolled rows of little towels. He picked one up, tossing it from hand to hand as he cleaned himself up. Setting it aside, he reached for another and looked to her. "May I?"

Oh. "Okay." She held her hands out, only for him to take one gingerly into his palm. The cloth was damp and hot as he swiped it across her fingers with practiced ease.

She swallowed hard. She'd known what kind of man he was, and yes, it came with flirty waitresses. But it also came with this—a relaxed air and a skill with his hands. Deep in her belly, a coiling heat burned and flared.

He'd know what he was doing with her body, if she let him have his way with her. And maybe that was worth the insecurity and the casualness of the encounter. The whole idea was frightening and exciting and new.

And it struck her. If he pressed—and he would—she *could* take him to the hostel with her. There was nothing stopping her but her own inhibitions. The reservations she'd earned over the past couple of years about sex and intimacy and love. Who cared about her roommates, with their quiet groans and creaking bedsprings? Or about how sex had always gone for her before.

Who cared if you could trust a man when you were only going to sleep with him once?

A partner like him—it was something she'd never had, never been sure she even wanted. But maybe it was something she deserved the chance to try.

At that very moment, he looked up at her, and it was like the room shifted. He had no idea that her whole conception of how things might progress between them had changed. He must have sensed that something was different, though. His lips parted and he gave her a lopsided smile. "What?"

"Nothing."

Shaking his head, he rubbed the cloth over the creases of her knuckles one more time before balling it up and putting it aside. "There we go. All clean."

"They weren't all that dirty before."

"But now they're cleaner." He kissed the back of her hand before letting her go.

And just in time. Their waitress cleared the towels and the basket from their table, exchanging them for a circular platter big enough to hold a pizza. As promised, it was lined with some sort of bread, with more rolls of the stuff laid out along the edges. Topping it were servings of things she couldn't begin to identify. They were colorful and different, and filled the air around their table with a hundred scents she'd never encountered in her life.

A dark hand appeared above the tray, pointing at each little area in turn. "Chicken, beef, potatoes, vegetables, lentils, greens." The waitress looked between them for approval.

Rylan nodded, grinning at her, and said something too quickly in French. Her reply was equally incomprehensible, and he laughed, shaking his head.

As the waitress walked away, Kate looked at him with curiosity. "What were you two talking about?"

He unrolled a napkin and placed it over his lap. "I told her it looked wonderful, and she told me to let her know if you chickened out and wanted a sandwich."

"Hmm." Kate grabbed her own napkin, then glanced toward the waitress. "She forgot our silverware."

"No, she didn't." He chose a piece of bread and tore a section off, using it to pick up some of what looked to be the chicken. "See?"

Oh. Suddenly, cleaning their hands made a lot more sense.

It was awkward, but she ripped a bit of the bread and tried to follow his example. It wasn't as messy as it looked, but it wasn't particularly neat, either. "You know," she said, "my mother always told me never to order French onion soup on a date because you'd make too much of a mess. Turn the guy off."

Rylan looked as dapper licking lentils from his fingers as he ever could have in a fancy restaurant sipping champagne from crystal. He laughed. "Well, you officially have my permission to order whatever kind of soup you want to in the future. No need to impress me." He popped his handful into his mouth, then swabbed the corner of his lips with his napkin. Shrugging, he said, "I like a girl who has an appetite. I like things that taste good. I don't think enjoying things is a turn-off. Much the opposite."

He looked at her expectantly. The whole time he'd been talking, she'd still been sitting there, gripping her sauce-soaked bread between her fingers and her thumb. Oh, well. Nothing for it. She took a bite and widened her eyes. The bread was spongy and just a little bit sour, the meat tender and flavorful. It was like nothing she'd ever had before, rich and sweet and delicately spiced.

"So?"

"It's good," she said, and it shouldn't have been such a surprise.

"Here." His smile had deepened into something unaffected as he tore off more bread and scooped up some of the vegetables. He brought it up to her mouth in offering. "Try this."

It was so like what he'd done with the crepe the night before. Except instead of in the open air of the city, they were in a cozy little restaurant, no prying eyes but for the other

patrons and the waitress, and Kate had nothing to hide. Not
from any of them. She dipped her head and took the morsel
from his hand. His eyes flashed dark, and a little thrill ran
through her as he let his fingertips linger, stroking a slow
curve along the bottom of her lip.

She swallowed, holding his gaze.

"I like that, too." The way he touched her and looked at
her and gave her exotic, foreign delicacies to taste.

His throat bobbed as she licked her lips. "Aren't you glad
you trusted me?"

And wasn't that the question of the evening? Of the trip,
even?

She hesitated. But she couldn't deny the truth. "Yeah. I am."

"Well, then." He prepared another bite for her and brought
it to her mouth. "Here's to trying something new."

chapter SIX

It was such a cliché—the ennui that settled in on a person when there wasn't anything he wanted. Rylan had resigned himself to being a certain number of clichés. The jaded expat, the casual skirt-chaser. The lone wolf, hiding from the people who reminded him of who he'd been and what he'd walked away from.

Apparently, it was time to add another to the list.

How long had it been since he had wanted something—someone—so badly? Women fell into his bed. They amused him and pleasured him, and he made them feel good in return. But they left the next morning, if not the moment they were done. They didn't get into his head. Not like this.

As he and Kate spilled out onto the alley, though, her hair hung loose around her shoulders, and her eyes were bright, the long, pale column of her throat so smooth. He didn't know if he'd ever seen her look so beautiful, and he *wanted* her. Desired her with a power that hadn't possessed him in this long and lonely year—and that was what got him. His time in Paris had never struck him as lonely before. He'd never felt bored. But here, with this woman, on this night, all his diversions seemed to crumble beneath his feet.

And he couldn't help himself. Before they could turn the corner onto the main street, he grabbed her shoulder, feeling high on good food and good company and the warmth of a beautiful girl. Emboldened, he turned her and pressed her up against the stonework of the outside of the restaurant. His heart surged behind his ribs as he closed his hand around her shoulder and crowded her up against the wall, chest to chest and mouth to mouth. It'd be so easy to sweep in and claim her the way he'd been longing to—

Alarms went off inside his head, and he stopped himself cold. This was too much, was the complete opposite of how he'd been working so carefully to coax her along. He darted his gaze up to her face, prepared for fear.

But no.

She put her hands on his chest, and her eyes were big and dark. She skimmed her tongue between her lips as her fingers latched on to his shirt. Ready for it.

Relief flooded him, washing away the final traces of his restraint. He tipped forward, pulse thundering as she opened to his kiss. *Fuck.* She tasted of sex and spice, and he wanted to taste her all over—the ripe swells of her breasts and the slickness between her legs.

He dared to let his hand drift up her rib cage, right to the point where his thumb brushed the outer curve of her breast. When she pulled away to gasp for air, he kissed his way across her cheek, burying his face against the sweet scent of her hair. He fairly growled, "You're not going back to that hostel alone tonight."

Laughing, she dropped her head against the stone, lifting one of her hands to run her fingers through his hair. "My roommates had sex last night."

"Yeah?"

"Yeah." She pulled him to her lips and kissed him even more deeply.

It made him burn hotter, imagining her there, alone in a narrow, rented bad, listening to the noises other people made as they came. He edged his hand up higher on her ribs, asking between kisses, "Did it turn you on?"

She squirmed, but her hand on the back of his neck didn't relax its grip at all. "It was embarrassing."

"Not answering my question."

"Maybe. A little."

All his plans receded in his mind, making way for a whole new set of dirty fantasies. He pulled back enough to see her face. "Did you want to put on a show? While we watch them put on theirs? Is someone a little bit of a voyeur?"

"No." But her cheeks were flushing. "No, but I'm not afraid to. If they don't care, then I—I won't care, either."

And he could read it in her eyes and in her breath. She was simply waiting for him to ask.

The words were on his tongue, right on the cusp of spilling out. If he kissed her throat and sucked her ear. If he pressed his hardness against her hip and told her to take him home, she would. He could lay her out on those borrowed sheets in the dark and take her apart. In muffled moans and whispered instructions, he'd touch her and find out how she arched and what she'd shout. Press inside and take what he wanted, no matter who was listening, lying in their own beds on the other side of the room.

It would be so. Fucking. Hot.

But after, they'd be sleeping on a single bed, and the shame of it all would stay at bay only so long. She'd squirm, or maybe outright ask him to go, and no. He'd just awoken from his haze. This thing was temporary, but he wouldn't doom it to a single night.

No. His plan was better.

He gripped the hem of her shirt in his fist and squeezed his eyes closed against the arousal that was growing too sharp, making it almost hard to think. "What if I had a better idea?"

"Hmm?"

She was lost in it, too, and he had to separate them. It took too much of his will to pull a half step back and put some air between their bodies. He did it, though. He put his hands on her shoulders and looked her in the eye.

"Neither of us likes where we're staying, right?"

"No." Her brows furrowed. "But—"

"So what if we pooled our resources?"

"I don't understand."

And he had to be careful how he worded this. "Money for two bunks at hostels. Add it together, and it pays for a real hotel." He slid his hand lower to stroke the hollow of her throat with his thumb. "A private room. Private bath." He dipped in closer so he was speaking in her ear. "I'd make love to you on a big fluffy bed, and then in the shower. Put my face between your legs against the counter. And you could scream as loud as you wanted to. No one to hear. No one to see how many times I make you come."

The moan that poured out of her at that sent sparks skittering down his spine.

She was shaking her head, but her eyes were glazed, and

she parted her thighs to let him slide a knee between them. "Already paid for tonight."

"So this first one's on me." He drew a line up her cheek with his nose. "If you don't have the best night of your life, you can go back to your tiny bed and your roommates tomorrow. But you won't." Nipping at her jaw, he let his voice go rumbly and dark. "I'm very, very patient. I don't let up until everyone is...*satisfied*."

Her resolve was faltering. "You have a place picked out?"

"Reserved and everything. Five stops on the Metro." A perfect place on a quiet street, nice enough for his tastes but not so fancy as to make her uncomfortable or put the lie to all his not-quite truths. "Clean white sheets and a little balcony and a bakery down the street. I'll buy you a chocolate croissant in the morning and eat it off your hip."

Her laugh was like bells, her hands gripping him in a way that told him she wouldn't let go. "Well, if there's chocolate involved..."

"Anything you want." And God, he really meant that.

She shifted, nudging him back so she could look him in the eye. "And if I do have the best night of my life?"

"Then I'll give you more of them." He swallowed hard, surprised by the fervency in his own voice. By how much he wanted this. "As many as you can stay for. They're all yours."

For what felt like centuries, indecision colored her features, bright white teeth flashing as they dug into the corner of her lip. It was all spread out before him—her hesitation and her need. Her body was coiled so tightly, and he wanted nothing more than to give it what it clearly craved.

Say yes, he chanted in his mind. *I'll be so good to you.*

But there was so much uncertainty there, too. Inhibitions

he'd do his best to peel away, but it would take time. Time and a leap of faith.

He held his breath.

Finally, *finally*, she pushed off the wall and lifted up onto her toes, dragging him down for a softer, briefer kiss. His heart did the strangest things inside his chest; he had no idea how much he'd been counting on her to say yes. This kiss didn't taste like yes. He didn't know what it tasted like, and the uncertainty set him on edge. People didn't say no to him, not about things like this.

She dropped down and released his lips, but before his worry could take over, before he could pull her back in and state his case more ardently, she threaded her hand through his.

"All right," she said.

The clouds parted in his mind. That was it. What he'd been waiting for.

Kate wasn't sure what she'd been expecting when Rylan had told her he'd gotten them a room for the night. Really, nothing would have surprised her, and as long as they hadn't been sharing with any patchouli-scented backpackers, she would have been content.

She was more than content.

The room wasn't overdone, but it was nice. Tasteful. Crisp, clean white sheets, just like he had promised, and red draperies framing the doorway that opened out onto a tiny little balcony. Cream-colored walls decorated with a big mirror and classic-looking paintings. A little desk with a chair and a rose-colored settee.

Rylan had excused himself to the restroom, so she was left standing there alone, taking it all in. Trying to calm her nerves. She ran her hand over the headboard, and then the corner of the nightstand. What looked like an intercom was set into the wall to one side of the bed, and she stooped to examine it more closely. When she pressed one of the buttons in the center of it, static crackled, followed by faint strains of music. Édith Piaf. A radio. A radio with five stations, and she moved through them, smiling as the old chanteuse gave way to quiet jazz, then an American power ballad from the eighties. And then a...polka? Shaking her head, she turned the thing off and faced the room again.

But all she kept coming back to was the bed.

She shivered, crossing her arms over her chest and working to force her anxiety down. Neither of them had made any pretense about why they were here. When he was with her, though—when he was kissing her mouth or smoothing his hands down her hips, it all made sense. When she was alone, all she could think was that she had no idea what she was doing. The entire venture was a terrible mistake.

The air in the room suddenly felt too warm, and she crossed to the opposite wall. It took a little bit of fiddling, but she got the doors out onto the balcony to open. Fresh air poured across her face, bringing with it the sounds of the city below, and she closed her eyes as she stepped out onto the landing. She set her hands on the railing and bowed her head.

She was going to do this. She wasn't going to freeze up, the way Aaron always accused her of doing. It was going to be fine.

She opened her eyes, and they stung. Why had Rylan left her alone with nothing to do but *think* for so long?

The sound of running water from within had her fighting for her composure, but she hadn't quite found it yet by the time Rylan's footsteps announced his presence. She stiffened without meaning to, unable to stop the way she flinched at a warm hand on her arm.

Rylan was silent for a moment, and it gave her time to breathe. Without crowding her, he stepped out onto the balcony, his chest not quite touching her back, his palm shifting to settle at her waist.

"Nice view," he said, lips close to her ear.

"Yeah." She hadn't really taken it in yet, too busy letting her nervousness get the best of her. Eager for the distraction, she refocused her gaze on the world beyond their little room.

Sure enough, it was pretty. Much prettier than what she'd been able to glimpse through the tiny alley-facing window in her room at the hostel. They were only a few stories up, but that was high enough in a city like this. She looked out over the quiet street, at the shop fronts and stones and pavement, and then higher, toward the skyline in the distance, twinkling with lights against the gathering dusk.

He chuckled softly, sweeping her hair to the side. Pressing a kiss to the quivering skin of her throat. "I didn't mean the city."

And somehow, it was so like their first conversation in the coffee shop. Part of her was still adrift as her mind raced ahead to what would come next, but a different part sighed in relief as she got a little of her footing back. Relaxing her grip on the railing, she tipped her head to the side. "That line work on most girls?"

"It's not a line."

"Uh-huh."

She could hear and feel his smile. He sidled up a little closer to her, moving slowly, as if to give her time to tell him no. When his body made contact with hers, something in her melted by a fraction, and then another, and then all at once she remembered why this had felt so easy before. With warm lips and just the barest hint of teeth, he took a nip at the lobe of her ear.

"It's not a line if it's true."

How many times had she fallen for a man insisting he was telling the truth?

Taking a chance, she released her hold on the railing, and he wrapped her up in his arms. Kissing down to where her neck met her shoulder, he let his hips meet her backside. A whole other kind of tremor made its way through her body, a heat so intense it seared. He was hard. On instinct, she shifted her hips away, but he didn't let her go.

As if he could sense the root of her anxiety, he murmured, "We don't do anything you don't want to do."

She laughed and curled her hand around his forearm where it draped beneath her breasts. "It's not a matter of want."

"You want me to touch you?" His fingertips played with the hem of her top, and there was so much *promise* there.

Her breath stuttered. "Yes." She squeezed her eyes shut tight again. "Only—"

His fingers and lips both paused. "Hmm?"

"I just—I don't do this much."

Slowly, he pressed another kiss to the side of her throat. "What? Have sex?" His lips drifted higher. "Or let yourself be seduced by a man you just met in the most romantic city in the world? Because if it's the latter, I can't say I'm shocked."

Her laughter this time was easier and sadder, all at once. "I've gone all the way with exactly two people, and one of them was a pickup, and..." She didn't really want to think about it. "...and that wasn't much fun."

She'd been into it enough, but they'd both been drinking, and it had all started moving too fast. When he'd gotten her onto all fours, she hadn't been ready, and it hadn't been horrible. But that was the best she could say.

The way Rylan held her shifted. It was still loose enough that she could get away at any second if she wanted to—she didn't doubt that. But there was a possessiveness there. "If I *ever* make you feel like this 'isn't fun'—" He cut himself off and took a slow, deep breath before restarting. "I will never take anything from you that you don't want, or before you're ready to give it. There is nothing I want to do tonight but give you pleasure."

She couldn't help the twinge of doubt. "Nothing?"

"Nothing." He swallowed. "It'll be torture, but I'll walk away right now if you tell me you're not interested." At some point, he'd pulled his hips back, but now the long line of him pressed against her rear again, not insistent or demanding at all. Just there. "Make no mistake about it. I want you. Badly. But that's all secondary to what you want. If you never touch me but still let me make you come..." Trailing off, he ran her hand down her side. "I promise I'll be satisfied."

She opened her eyes. What was this man doing to her?

Even with Aaron, sex had never been *fun*. He'd had a good enough time, but she'd never managed to get him to understand what she needed him to do. He'd never asked.

And now Rylan was offering her all these things... And she wanted them. So much.

"I want to touch you." Her voice came out whispery and low. "Only—can we . . . can we take it slow?"

"As slowly as you want. I have just one request."

Her stomach sank. "Oh?"

Taking a partial step back, he turned her around until they were standing before each other, eye to eye and face to face, and his gaze was burning. "Please. Kate."

"Yes?"

"Please tell me you'll at least let me taste you."

chapter SEVEN

Kate's breath caught in her throat. It wasn't that she'd never had a man do that before. Aaron had tried a few times. It had been warm and wet, and mortifying. Mostly mortifying, though.

She'd never been so close to giving in and faking it already as she had been, lying there, waiting for him to get bored.

Heat rising in her cheeks, she played with a button on his shirt for something to look at. "You don't have to."

"I don't have to do anything." He ducked, giving her no choice but to meet his gaze. "And neither do you. But I want to."

She shrugged. "It's just never done much for me."

"Then whoever was doing it wasn't doing it right."

"And you think you'll do better?"

"I know I will." With that, he took her by the hand and made to lead her off the balcony. "Come on."

As she followed him into the room, he paused to close the door, drawing a pair of sheers over the glass but leaving the heavier draperies open. Squirming inside and uncertain what else to do, she faced the bed and took a deep breath.

He came up behind her, encircling her waist with his arms, just like he had out on the balcony. "Is this all right?"

"Yeah."

Apparently, he was starting everything on established ground. "And this?" He smoothed her hair out of the way before kissing a longer, wetter line down the side of her neck. The soft scrape of teeth against delicate flesh made it all the better, and some of the stiffness left her limbs.

"Yes."

He moved so slowly, sliding his lips across her skin. With one arm holding her flush against his chest, he brought his other one up. Warm fingertips dragged across her throat and along her collarbones, lingering there before drifting lower. He swept them down the valley of her breasts. At her navel, he turned his hand over and retraced the circuit, again and again, until the thrumming in her abdomen felt like a smoldering glow. She relaxed her arms. Let her head fall back against his shoulder.

"See?" His voice was a low rasp. "Isn't that nice? Don't you like it when I touch you?"

She did, and the pit of heat flared, something clenching deep inside. "Yes." And she should be touching him, too, shouldn't she? She reached to wrap her palm around his thigh.

But he *shh*ed her, brushing her overture aside. "Later, if you want. For now, just let me."

It wasn't easy, but an instinct she'd thought had been burned out of her wanted to do precisely that. To give over and give in. She dropped her arm back to her side and took him at his word.

His hand drifted to her hip. Her breath hitched. On the

way back up, he barely skimmed the apex of her thighs through her jeans, and a sound passed her lips.

Two minutes ago, she'd been so nervous about him coming anywhere near her, and now she was losing her mind, all but whimpering at a teasing glance across her sex.

Murmuring words she couldn't hear against her neck, he skated his hands up and down her body, flirting with but never quite making contact with the places that were slowly starting to strain for it. When another, breathier sound of desire escaped her, he groaned, pressing himself tighter against her spine. Letting the line of him sear its way into her, until she was liquid, yearning for his touch.

He didn't have to ask a question. She closed her eyes and answered it. "Yes."

"Good girl."

It should have been cold water on her flame, but somehow it was anything but. She wanted that praise again, wanted that soft, gravelly voice telling her she was exactly what he wanted her to be.

Sucking the lobe of her ear between his lips, he rubbed the hem of her shirt between his fingertips, transcribing what he was going to do and giving her room to tell him no. Her breath went shallow as he rucked the fabric upward, skimming warm fingertips over her abdomen. He didn't push it all the way up, though. Pausing with her breasts still covered, he ran the corners of his knuckles around the outer curve.

"Can I?"

She nodded minutely, arching forward and holding her breath.

He didn't grab or squeeze at her as he finally let his hand traverse the center of her chest. She exhaled shakily with the relief of his gentle touch, pleasure simmering with the graze of his thumb across her nipple, the pressure of a broad palm encompassing the full swell of her breast.

He nudged at the hem of her top again, and she lifted her arms. He stripped her out of it and let the material fall to the floor before molding himself to her spine again, running his hands more freely over bare skin. Electricity seemed to trail behind every touch, winding her up higher and higher until he dipped into the cup of her bra, brushing the hard, naked nub at her peak, sending crisp and white sparks branching. Panting, she turned her face into his neck, and he held her, even as he was cupping her more firmly, sliding his hand in deeper beneath the satin.

"No one ever took their time with you, did they? Never got you screaming for it before they tried to get theirs, huh?"

She'd thought she'd gone slow before, but it had never been like this. She wanted to twist all the way around inside his grasp. Open her legs and wrap them tight around his hips. She felt so empty and hot and *soaking* with how much she wanted this.

"Gonna take my time with you," he promised, gravelly against her cheek. "Gonna take you apart all night, until you're shaking."

"Please."

Her little begging gasp echoed in the room so loudly. Before she could even muster up the presence of mind to be ashamed of it, he was picking her up. Her eyes flew open, a scream forming in her throat as she scrabbled to keep from falling, but then her spine hit the soft surface of the mattress. She looked up, and he hovered over her, on his knees between her spread legs, staring at her like she was something to eat.

No. Like she was something to treasure.

Her breathing sounded deafening to her own ears as he stared down at her, blue eyes pinning her, the sharp point of his jaw and the lines of his cheekbones glowing gold. Without looking away, he undid the buttons of his shirt and shrugged it off his shoulders, then reached over his head to grab the neckline of his undershirt. His face was obscured for a moment as he tugged it off, and she took the chance to glance downward.

A fine trail of dark hair led into the waistband of his jeans, and above that was the smooth plane of his abdomen, lightly defined musculature glinting in the lamplight. His chest was just as sculpted, widening out into the broad cut of his shoulders before drawing the eye inward to the dip of his collarbones and the hollow of his throat.

And there, dangling from his neck, a plain silver chain.

She didn't have a chance to see what was hanging from it as he dropped the ball of cotton to the side. Leaning over her, he grinned, clearly having caught her ogling, but the smirk receded into an expression that was quieter and more intense. Her chest heaved as he perched on his haunches over her, the muscles in his biceps flexing as he laid his palms on her knees. Slowly, looking up at her through thick lashes, he dipped his head. Placed one kiss and then another on the inside of her thigh, trailing upward, and she could hardly breathe. She clenched her hands as his nose nudged the crease of her hip through her jeans.

Oh God, he'd said he wanted to taste her, but would he? Like this?

He lifted up a fraction of an inch to look at her squarely, and her heart was beating overtime, all her nerves firing off at once, every inch of her body concentrated on the space between her legs. He hadn't even really touched her yet, and already she was gasping for breath.

Her whole chest felt like it was caving in when he lowered his head again, and Christ, God, he pressed his lips right to the center of her jeans, right over her clit. She could feel the warm rush of his breath even through the fabric, the weight of that touch pushing her to the point where she thought she would explode just from this.

Light-headed, her belly and her sex alive with heat, she arched her spine. She'd never had a man make her come before, but the feeling was already gathering, an ache that bloomed and spread, familiar and foreign all at the same time.

He pressed a little harder, sending a wave of heat through her, and she tightened her muscles, unable to believe this was really happening. But then he lifted his mouth to look up at her, and he was smirking. All at once, the tension that had been building within her dropped away, and she clenched, restless around nothing. As she groaned in frustration, soft lips pressed to her abdomen, then an inch above her navel, then higher and higher. He kissed the tops of both breasts, dragging his torso through the valley of her legs.

"So," he said, hovering above her, face to face. He held himself up with both hands planted beside her head, his knees between her calves, hips a firm presence against her pelvis, warm and vital and *there* if not yet grinding in. He kissed the corner of her mouth and then the other, sliding the tip of his nose against her cheek. "Is that a yes to letting me taste you?"

And she couldn't stop herself. She laughed, sliding her hands into his hair and letting the thick strands twist between her fingers. He'd gotten her so *close*. She'd probably say yes to anything. "It's definitely not a no."

"I can work with that."

Shaking her head, she tugged more insistently at his scalp, drawing him up her body. Half-naked like this, he was all warm skin and the scent of amber and lust. He lowered onto her, fitting hips to hips, and *oh*, there was that pressure again, right where she wanted it. Letting out a noise of pleasure of his own, he thrust against the cradle of her thighs, and she felt like she was melting as their lips met. The kissing and the weight of him overwhelmed her, making the air too thick and her lungs tight.

He dragged his lips along her jaw to her ear. "Do you think you're wet for me?"

She wasn't sure she'd ever been slicker. But the words, so easy for him, wouldn't come to her mouth. With a sound that was half whine and half hum, she put her hands on his back, running them over hot, smooth flesh, then lower, to the waistband of his jeans, trying to urge him on.

It was encouragement enough. He kissed the shell of her ear before sucking at it. "Bet you'll be so sweet." Encompassing her hip with his palm, he ground into her harder. "Think you're ready for me to find out?"

She was ready for anything. If he wanted—if he really wanted, she'd let him have it all, misgivings or no. He'd taken such good care of her body so far. Who was she not to trust him with it now?

He lifted his hips and pressed his brow to the pillow beside her head, breathing fast and shallow against her hair. Everything inside her tensed as he shifted his hand, sliding it along the top of her thigh.

When the heel of his hand connected with where she was desperate and aching, she nearly screamed with the relief of it.

"That's right," he murmured. "God, I bet you're soaked. You're burning up, aren't you? Just waiting for me to take you over."

"Please." She was shocked to hear the plea fall from her lips. "No one's ever— I'm—" *Close. Scared.* It was hot and vulnerable, shaking apart like this inside a man's arms, letting him see all these pieces of her as they broke, their hidden facets exposed.

"Shh." He made his way to her mouth again, kissing her softly but with no less heat. "I've got you."

But his reassurances didn't soothe anything at all. Her legs were stiff with how long she'd been tensing, waiting to fall, but all his rubbing at her through her jeans only made her need coil tighter without any of that sweet unfurling of release. If she could just get her own hands on herself...

For one hysterical second, she thought about faking it, the way she'd been so tempted to in the past.

But then he was kissing down her body, undoing the fasteners of her jeans.

"What are you—" she started, but it was a stupid question.

"Tell me you don't want this." He had the side of his face mashed up against her stomach, his long fingers parting her zipper. Brushing against the fabric underneath.

She didn't want to pretend to come. She didn't want to lie.

He turned, burying his mouth and his eyes against her skin. "You're aching for it. I can *feel* it. God, let me do this for you."

What was left for her to do but nod?

As if he'd been dying to do it, he tore her pants down her

legs, cursing in frustration when he got to her shoes. Somehow he got them shoved off, and they bounced across the carpet to the other side of the room, followed by her pants, and then he was hooking fingers into the lace at the hem of her panties.

Shooting one last glance up at her, he peeled them down.

Naked but for her bra, she felt even more uncomfortable and vulnerable. Weird and cold, and her breath was shaking as she tried to close her legs. He wasn't having any of that, though.

More tenderly than she would have imagined, he parted her thighs. Put his palm to the place where her leg met her torso.

The first swipe of his thumb over the length of her slit was a bright burst of pleasure, almost like pain, it was so sharp. Her leg jerked, and she reached to try to still his hand, but then he shifted, getting his fingers into the mix. They were softer as they spread her open, and she forced herself to breathe. To relax.

And then he moved in with his tongue.

"Oh *God*." It was warm and wet, like she remembered, but instead of just spelling out his English homework, this man moved around. He touched and licked, across the less sensitive side of her clit and then at the point where everything was too intense.

Then he found the right spot, and her whole abdomen went molten.

"Rylan—"

Without shifting from her sex, he reached up for her hands. Put one in his hair and grasped the other one tightly, and it gave her something to hold on to. A way to be grounded when words had left her, everything had left her. Everything but the sweet pulsing and the building wave.

Over and over, he lapped at her, through each false start, when she was so close she swore she could taste it, only to have it slip away and leave her panting and frustrated. She whined and clutched him tight, probably pulling too hard at his scalp, but he hummed and dove in more hungrily, nuzzling and kissing, licking and sucking.

Tensing hard, she pushed into his touch, into the eager heat of his mouth, and it was there—*right there*. Warm fingers pressed against her opening, then just inside.

Her eyes snapped open, and her whole body arched, and she reached—reached—

"Rylan—"

God, it wasn't a wave. It was a tsunami and relief and this crashing, incredible, pulsing oblivion. She shattered, over and over again, swearing out loud and groaning his name, and just wanting him to keep her right there. Against his tongue and his kiss and this trust. This promise.

That he had fulfilled.

When the fire and blackness and flesh-ripe taste of fruit inside her mouth collapsed, she opened her eyes, twitching at the few last laps he took across her clit. She drew her hand from his hair and, too sensitive, nudged at his head to try to get him to stop. Pressing upward with his fingers, he placed one more kiss to her sex before pulling away. Another aftershock rocked through her, only to be followed by a dull emptiness when he withdrew.

Rising up onto his knees, he was a vision, all bare skin to his waist, lips and fingers slick from what he'd given her. He dragged the back of his wrist over his mouth, and she whimpered. For a second, he closed his eyes, tilting his head upward as if he were appealing to a deity. When he looked to her again, his gaze was burning, a hunger so intense it sent a lick of misgiving curling up her spine. She moved to close her legs but he was still between them.

"You have no idea how sexy that was," he said. He ran his hand down his torso, skimming it over the bulge in his jeans, and something inside of her clenched down again.

She'd do something for him. He'd probably want to be inside of her, and she could do that. If he insisted. It was only fair.

But as he looked down at her, he seemed to recognize the uncertainty tugging at her heart. He hung his head a little, shifting forward, moving to put one knee to the outside of her hip while the other one stayed planted firmly between her thighs. His thumb and forefinger played at the button of his pants. "I want to come so bad."

"Yeah. We can—" She reached forward to help him.

He shook his head. "Not until you're ready, beautiful."

Still, he pulled at the fastener and lowered the zip. She watched, frozen, in a bizarre kind of fascination as he slipped his hand inside, groaning loudly as his wrist disappeared beneath the waistband.

And he was going to— Oh God, he was. Through the fabric, his hand moved, and she shook her head.

"Want to see."

She'd never witnessed a man touching himself before, and the idea made her tingle, even as sated as she was.

He didn't ask if she was sure. Everything about him was glazed with arousal, and he was looking straight at her as he pushed his pants and underwear down around his hips. Pulled himself out.

And it shouldn't have been so *hot*, but there he was, muscles standing out in stark relief, gaze black with lust, and his cock— She sucked a breath and pulled her lip into her mouth. He was flushed, long and thick, glistening at the tip with fluid.

"See how hard that made me?" he asked, voice husky and dark. "Eating you out. You taste so good, and the noises you make—" He cut himself off with a moan as he took a long stroke down his length with his palm. The foreskin retracted back, revealing more of the head. He took his other hand, still wet with her, and slipped it around the shining skin at the end, leaving it slicker. "*Fuck.*"

In a punishing rhythm, he thrust his hips into his fist. She lay there, frozen in a sort of fascinated awe. Groaning long and deep, he threw his head back, squeezing out more liquid from his slit.

And it looked *good*. His pleasure looked amazing, sexy and gorgeous in a way she'd never fully understood before.

Hardly thinking, she extended her hand, slipping her fingertips over the head of his cock. The flesh was hot and achingly hard. "Let me—"

Before she could finish the offer, he gasped out a sound like he'd been punched, his body a tight bow, mouth open. "Kate, Kate, I—"

His come flowed over her hand, spattering down onto her hip in white streaks that felt like possession. She never would've expected it, but in that instant, being marked that way made a dark flare of satisfaction awake beneath her skin.

"God*damn*," he groaned, taking a couple of last, slow pulls at himself before sliding free of his own grip. His damp fingers entwined with hers, and he squeezed. "Sorry. Didn't mean to get you all messy."

"It's okay."

Something in her chest turned over. Because it was. She didn't mind.

She hadn't been a virgin when she'd met him. They hadn't had sex. But as she lay there, his body between her legs, her flesh wet with him . . . it felt like she had done something for the very first time.

Like she would never be quite the same as she had before.

chapter EIGHT

Rylan was wringing a washcloth out in the sink when he happened to look up. The bathroom was a little cramped, to be honest, but it was clean, the big plate-glass mirror over the vanity smoothly polished.

The man staring back at him from inside of it looked like he'd just had the best fuck of his life.

Balling the washcloth up in his fist, he ran his other hand through his hair, settling it down from where it had been standing up on end. Kate had done a number on him in that respect, tugging hard at his scalp—almost too hard in the moment right before she'd arched and screamed and pulsed against his tongue.

Just thinking about it made him lick his lips. He'd slept with more than his share of women, but he couldn't think of any that had gone to pieces quite like that. He probably had nail marks all up and down his shoulders and his neck.

He'd been the first to make her come. And it had shown. God. She'd been wound up, and toward the end there, even he'd been starting to doubt if it were possible. She hadn't seemed a stranger to the little death—and wasn't that an image? The idea of her getting herself off? But either she'd been psyching herself out or he had lost his edge. Either way, she hadn't asked him to stop, and she'd been so *into* it that he'd had to keep going, drunk on the sound of her moans. She'd clung to the edge for what had felt like forever, and when she'd finally let go...

He hadn't even gotten inside her, and it had been one of the most intense sexual experiences of his life.

So intense, he hadn't wanted to ruin it by pressing for something she'd clearly been uncomfortable with. Sex had been off the table, but he'd been so worked up. He'd thought it would take maybe a dozen strokes of his hand.

In the end, it had taken exactly one of hers.

Spent as he was, his cock gave a little twitch of interest inside his boxers. Which reminded him of what he was here to do.

Making a face, he got himself out and cleaned up the best he could. Not that he'd really made much of a mess of himself. His breath caught short at the image, seared into his mind, of his release on Kate's pale skin. He hadn't taken her, not yet, but that twisted animal hindbrain of his had enjoyed what claim he'd managed to stake.

A claim that had to be getting pretty damn uncomfortable by now.

He set the rag aside and ran a fresh one under the tap, as hot as he could stand, before squeezing it out and folding it up. He turned, stepping forward to face the open door leading onto the main room.

Kate lay there still, all creamy skin and the tumble of her hair against the white of the sheets. She was looking right at him, and for the first time all night, he felt self-conscious.

"You watching me?" he asked, putting on a smirk as he leaned against the doorway.

"You're not the only one who can appreciate a view."

It wasn't ego stroking, and that was what made it hit him so squarely in the chest. He worked hard to look good—it was one of the only things he had to put effort into these days. It was nice to be appreciated. But it was also somehow something more.

The wryness to his smile melted away, leaving a curve to his mouth that felt entirely too genuine, and he'd curse himself later for being such a softie. But there wasn't much to do about it now. Shaking his head, he crossed the room to her, sitting down on the edge of the bed at her side. She was still wearing that pretty blue lace bra, and it cupped her tits so perfectly. Made the soft pillows of the tops of them look all the fuller and more inviting. Resisting their temptation, he bent to nudge the sheet from where she'd draped it across her hip, leaving it high enough to hide her cunt without dragging through the puddle he'd left on her skin.

At the touch of the washcloth to her abdomen, she hummed. "Warm," she said.

"Figured you'd like that."

"Yeah."

Once he'd wiped it all away, he bowed to press his lips to the hollow beside her hip. Planting his hand on the bed, he dropped another kiss on her navel and one on the top of each breast. He bypassed her lips, though, leaving a final one on her forehead.

He rose, pushing off to head to the bathroom.

"Thank you," she said.

He paused. "You're welcome?" It was an odd thing to say, right in that moment.

Apparently, she heard his confusion. "For everything. That, with the washcloth. It was nice. And...before. You were really patient with me."

The insecurity dripping from her voice stopped him in his tracks. Forget the nasty rag in his hand. He rounded back toward the bed, dropped a knee to its edge, and probably with too much fierceness, insisted, "You do *not* need to thank me for that."

What he really wanted to do was ask her what kind of assholes she'd been sleeping with. When you got a girl to be with you, you made damn sure she came, with your mouth or your fingers or your dick, and if she wasn't cool with that, then by her own damn hand. Fuck anything else. And when you got a girl dirty, you sure as hell cleaned her up. Took care of her.

And just like that, he wanted to deck any guy who *hadn't* done any of that for her before. She deserved better. So pretty and smart, so giving.

For a second, he squeezed his eyes shut, forcing himself to calm down. Sure enough, when he looked at her again, she had a wariness to her expression, and no. That wasn't okay.

He cupped her face and leaned down, covering her mouth with his as gently and as sweetly as he could. "It was a pleasure," he promised. "Every single moment of it. A privilege."

He slid his hand down her neck before pulling away.

On his way back to the bathroom, he flexed his fingers at his side, still feeling the warmth of her skin against his palm. More often than not, he went to bed with a woman once, and then he moved on. But he hadn't been lying. She'd been beautiful in her pleasure, and it had been a privilege to give it to her.

A privilege he hoped he'd get to have again. At least once.

The man in the bathroom mirror stared at him, and he didn't know who he'd been fooling. He hoped he could have her a lot more times than that.

As many times as he could before she left.

While the water was running in the other room, Kate took the opportunity to quietly freak the hell out. She'd only ever done the one-night stand thing once before, and that had been completely different. The guy had come to her place, and as soon as he was done, he'd left her there, sore and confused and desperate for a shower.

Nothing about this encounter seemed to be heading in that direction.

Still, sharing a bed with a guy wasn't something she'd done a lot of. Rylan had told her explicitly that he'd gotten the room for the both of them, and they could split the cost for the rest of the time she was in town. It didn't seem likely he was going to duck out, or that he expected her to. But what was she supposed to do now? It wasn't that late, and she was way too jazzed to sleep.

Glancing over at the big hiker's backpack he'd left against the wall, she scowled. He could have given her a heads-up about this whole plan of his. What she wouldn't give for some fresh underwear and a T-shirt to change into now. Chewing on the inside of her lip, she played with the strap of her bra. She'd been wearing it all day, and the underwire was digging into her uncomfortably. She'd like to take it off, but...but then she'd be naked.

She rubbed the heel of her hand into her eye. He'd had his face between her legs, and here she was, worrying about him seeing her boobs.

"You wanna borrow a T-shirt or something?"

Somehow, she'd missed the sound of the tap shutting off. She turned, grateful, to find him standing in the doorway to the bathroom again.

"Yeah, actually. That would be really great." She considered for a second. "I mean, we're—we're in for the night, right?"

"Unless you have something in particular you want to do."

"No." Her legs still felt like they might turn to jelly. Staying in sounded like a good idea.

He rummaged around in his bag for a second before tossing her a plain black undershirt. "You want a pair of boxers or something, too?"

She thought about it for a second before nodding. It would be better than nothing. Way better than the pair of panties she'd just about soaked through.

"They're clean." He passed over a crisp blue cotton pair. "Promise."

"Thanks."

"Do you mind if I—?" He gestured at the jeans he hadn't bothered to refasten, hanging loose around his hips.

She didn't want him to be uncomfortable. And really, it was only fair, wasn't it? He'd seen an awful lot of her. She should get to at least catch a glimpse of his legs. "It's fine."

He sat on the edge of the bed to tug off the shoes and socks she somehow hadn't realized he still had on, followed by his pants. Stripped down to his boxers, he was even more attractive. Maybe because he was so comfortable in his skin. His gorgeous, smooth, golden-colored skin.

He smirked as he looked over at her, and she dropped her gaze from the lightly haired musculature of his calves. The man was a figure painter's dream, an anatomy lesson waiting to happen, and she was dying for the chance to draw him.

"You okay?"

"Yeah." She raised her gaze from the sheets and fiddled with the clothes he'd given her.

"Want some help?" Playfully, he ran a finger under her bra strap, then drifted down to tug at the hooks and eyes. "I'm really good at these."

She bet he was. She shook her head at him and held her hair out of the way. "Sure."

He popped the fasteners in a single deft movement. She twisted away from him as she pushed the straps off her shoulders, exposing her breasts, still bashful even after everything.

God but she wished she could let that go. That she could quiet the voice in the back of her mind that kept whispering all these doubts, about her looks, her talents. About what she deserved. She shivered, flashes of memories crowding in around her, feeling tiny and worthless, and none of it had been fair. It wasn't fair for it to be coming back to her now.

She'd taken this huge chance on this man, and it had paid off in spades. So why couldn't she just relax and enjoy it?

Even as she obsessed, Rylan sat there behind her, solid and present and real. He ran his hand down the line of her spine, a whisper-light touch that chased a little of the chill away.

"Pretty," he said, leaning in, pressing his lips just once, quickly, to the center of her back.

She caught the word and tried to hold on to it. To believe it. "Thanks."

He eased off then, giving her space to pull his shirt on over her head. The fabric smelled like him, clean and warm somehow. Comforting. Without lifting the sheet from her hips, she got his boxers on, too. They were big on her, but not too bad. The man had a lean, trim waistline.

"Better?"

"Yeah," she agreed, pulling her hair free from the collar of his shirt. "Much."

"Good." With that, he flopped himself down on the mattress, head on the pillows and legs straight in front of him, one ankle crossed over the other. He held his arm out in invitation.

One she was only too happy to accept. Pulling the covers halfway up, she curled into him, resting her head on his shoulder and letting her hand fall across his chest. He was so warm, and he smelled so good. What had she been saying a minute ago about it not being late enough to go to sleep?

They lay there in silence for a while, him combing his hand through her hair while she danced her fingertips over the lines of definition across his abdomen and chest. It was strangely comfortable.

Until she ran the edge of her nail along the chain draped around his neck. It was a series of little interlocking links, and there—hanging from the center of it was…a ring? Gold and silver with a row of tiny diamonds down the middle. Large enough that it was probably a man's. His fingers stilled in her hair when she touched it.

"What is it?" she asked.

His hand settled over hers in a firm but gentle grip. She let go of the ring as he guided her to rest her palm against his belly instead.

"Nothing." His throat bobbed.

"Nothing?"

"Just my father's wedding ring."

Oh. A hundred questions raced through her mind, but it was invasive, wasn't it? If Rylan was wearing the ring around his neck, his dad was probably gone. Dead or disappeared, or—

"Is he . . ." She trailed off.

Rylan scoffed, apparently hearing what she wasn't sure if she should say. "He's in prison."

Oh.

Another dry chuckle escaped his lips. "The man spent his whole damn life telling me what to do. Imagine my surprise when I find out what he's been up to all these years." A flicker of pain—of betrayal—creased his brow.

"I'm sorry."

He shook his head. "It doesn't matter. I've made my peace with it."

Like hell he had. Everything about him was bristling.

Letting go of her hand, he trailed his fingers up his chest to tap the edge of the band. "He gave me this a long time ago. Right after the divorce. He took it off the second he got back from the lawyer's office and he . . . he made as if to throw it away."

She hummed in invitation, willing him to go on.

Remembering her own father, and how he had thrown them all away . . .

Ever so slowly, he resumed his stroking of her hair. "I asked if I could have it. And he laughed." Bitterness shadowed his tone. "But he still gave it to me."

She stayed there, quiet, waiting for more, but he didn't speak again.

It was the tiniest glimpse. She could imagine it, a younger, wider-eyed Rylan looking up to this hulking father figure. From the sound of it, only to be let down over and over. An ache pressed at the center of her ribs, a sudden need to know more.

The words were right there, compelling her to ask, but before they could escape, she bit her tongue. She hardly knew this man. They'd shared a couple of nights together, and she liked him. A lot. But he didn't owe her anything. Not his history and not his confidence. Not if he didn't want to offer them up to her.

From the stiff set of his jaw, she had a feeling he'd already given more of each than he usually did.

A different instinct crept over her as she stared at him. Not to push, but instead to give him something in return. She considered for a long, silent moment. Then with forced deliberateness, she relaxed her posture, returned her breathing to normal. Stroked the stretch of skin beneath her fingertips, keeping them far away from the shiny glimmer of that ring.

"I haven't spoken to my dad since I was twelve."

Some of the tension bled out of his shoulders. "That's a long time."

"Yeah. Well. He was... not a nice man." That wasn't even the half of it. He'd left her with this mess in her head, this tiny piece of herself that always said she wasn't good enough, didn't deserve what she did get, was never going to make anything of herself... She swallowed hard. "Not to me and not to my mom. He..." *Manipulated us. Made us think we couldn't stand on our own two feet and then...* "He lied to her. For years. Cheated." That was an offense anyone could understand. One she could explain without tearing herself apart. "Not exactly the kind of thing you get over quickly."

Or at all.

Rylan chuckled, rubbing his thumb across the back of her palm. "Fathers, huh? They fuck you up."

She shivered. "You can say that again."

She loved that he had said it. He couldn't possibly understand with how much she'd kept unspoken. But for one shimmering instant, it felt like he did.

They lay there, gently touching and holding each other in the quiet of that space. It was tentative, a shaky intimacy built on half-formed confessions and the barest hints of their histories. But it felt good. Safe.

After a minute or two, he let out a breath and squeezed her shoulder. "So." A brightness crept into his tone, a false levity. Letting go of her hand, he reached over to the nightstand for the remote. "You had a chance to try French television yet?"

The fuzzy closeness of the moment shivered, but it didn't shatter.

She turned her gaze toward the screen as it came to life on the other side of the room. "No. I haven't."

"It's an experience."

As he pressed a button, the sounds of fast-spoken French filled the room, and she frowned.

"Do they have English subtitles?"

"Don't worry." He pressed a kiss to the side of her temple. "I can translate."

He flipped through the channels for a bit before he found

something that must have appealed to him, and he set the remote down at his side, shifting to hold her hand again. True to his word, he murmured his interpretation of the dialogue into her ear, his voice deep and warm. She let it wrap around her the way his arms did.

And if she couldn't keep her gaze from flickering to the bit of gold between his collarbones, well. At least she did her best.

chapter NINE

"So." Rylan tapped his razor against the rim of the sink before dipping it under the stream of water again. "What's on your agenda for the day?" He smirked at himself in the mirror. "Besides checking out of your hostel and grabbing your things, of course."

"Of course." Kate's eye roll was audible in her voice. So was the sound of the sleep in her eyes. The hint of a yawn. Not a morning person, that one.

She'd slept in later than he'd thought she would, while he'd blinked his eyes open at the crack of dawn, same as usual.

Well, not quite the same as usual. Most mornings, restless energy plagued him, only he didn't have an outlet for it anymore. He stalked around the apartment or went to the gym or read the business section of the paper, reminding himself even as he did that it didn't concern him anymore. Today... today, there'd been Kate, face soft with sleep. Somehow, just watching her had been enough to calm him. Tracing the line of her throat with his gaze. Gently brushing his knee against her soft, bare thigh.

From the main room, the sounds of her moving around filtered quietly over the running of the tap. He frowned and gripped the handle of the razor tighter.

It was killing him, knowing she was right around the doorway getting dressed while he was standing here, naked but for a towel and the chain around his neck. Still damp from his shower. Half-hard at the thought of what she might be up to out there.

Scowling, he tipped his chin up and swiped the razor across the tricky spot beneath his jaw. He'd promised to be good and not look. It was the only way she'd let him open the damn door to let some of the steam out so he could see his own face in the mirror well enough to shave.

He ran his finger over the damp patch of new skin, feeling for any stubble he might have missed. "Seriously, though. What do you want to do today?"

"I'm not sure. I picked up a new guidebook."

He scoffed. "Which you obviously don't need since you've got me."

She continued as if he hadn't spoken. "Which I haven't had a chance to look at yet. So I guess I should sit down somewhere and go through it at some point."

"Waste of time," he muttered under his breath. Louder, he said, "But what do you *want* to do today?" He considered for a second. "How long are you staying, anyway?"

"My flight home is on Friday." It was Sunday now. They must have both been doing the math in their heads, because just as he was thinking it, she announced, "So, another five full days, including today."

Plus the two they'd already had. Seven nights in total. He could work with that.

Finishing up, he rinsed his razor and set it aside. "Well, you're not going to get as much done today as you might like. Hazard of traveling in Catholic countries."

"Yeah. But there will still be some places open, right?"

"Sure." He turned the tap to full blast and cupped some water in his hands before splashing it over his face, cleaning away what was left of the foam and hair. He dried off and patted on some aftershave, then tiptoed toward the door to sneak a peek.

Except he'd *promised*. Groaning at the conscience he'd apparently grown overnight, he slapped his hand over his eyes. Pitching his voice, he asked, "Can I come out yet?"

"Um. Yeah."

Finally. Grinning in spite of himself, he stepped around the corner to find her perched on the edge of the bed, fingers worrying the strap of her bag, which was sitting beside her. She was wearing last night's jeans, but she'd stolen another of his shirts. He raked his gaze up and down her form.

There was just something so damn sexy about a woman in a man's shirt. The thing was two sizes too big on her, but the way she'd tied it off, her waist looked tiny, her breasts and hips fuller. Worse, she'd only buttoned it partway up, leaving this swath of skin across her collarbones exposed, this hint of cleavage. His throat went dry, his cock giving a twitch of interest that he didn't even bother to try to hide.

All day long, he'd have to look at her like this. See her draped in his clothes. How the hell was he supposed to stand it?

"What?" she asked, pulling his attention from her chest back up to her face. She arched a brow.

He smirked, unashamed to be called out. The way she acted, she could stand to be the subject of some open ogling.

"You're wearing my shirt," he said.

A flicker of uncertainty passed across her eyes, but she lifted her chin and looked at him head-on. "Is that a problem?"

"Only if you expect me to keep my hands off you today."

She flushed, but it was with a pleased little smile playing on her lips. "I wouldn't expect you to keep them to yourself entirely."

"Good." He stalked over to her and bent to place a hard, fast kiss to her lips, hooking a finger into the gap of the shirt and peeking down it. *Delicious.*

Swatting his hand away, she shook her head. Her smile didn't fade, though. "Go get dressed."

"Well, that's no fun," he muttered, but it was getting late. He made his way over to the corner where he'd dropped his bag, considering for a second as he leaned down to paw through its contents. It was slim pickings for five days, especially with how freely she was borrowing from him, but he'd make do. Plus, she probably wouldn't notice if some more clothes magically showed up. He could sneak off to the apartment at some point if he needed to.

Unself-consciously, he dropped the towel from around his hips and shook out a pair of boxers. He was standing with his back to her, and he delighted in the little sound she made as his ass came into view. When he was pretty sure she'd looked her fill, he stepped into his underwear, then picked out a pair of pants. After pulling on a shirt, he sidestepped to check himself over in the mirror on the wall, running a hand through his still-damp hair to mess it up a little.

"Would you like to hear what I had in mind for our outing today?" he asked.

She hesitated. "You really don't have to spend all this time with me. I wasn't expecting..."

Of course she wasn't. He didn't like the note of insecurity in her disclaimer, though. He half twisted around. "Do you not want me to?"

And that wasn't an immediate no forming on her lips.

Huh. He faced the mirror again. "You can have the day to yourself if you want." Annoying, because he'd thought his plan was pretty good, and he wasn't particularly fond of the idea of spending the day alone. Not when there was someone interesting to spend it with.

"I want to get some more drawing done," she said after another brief pause. "But it doesn't have to be today. What were you going to suggest?"

He'd been starting to think she'd literally never ask.

"Well." He fixed the collar of his shirt, then turned around. "Since you're a tortured artist and everything." With a little spring in his step, he threw himself onto the bed, landing on his stomach with his head by her side, his elbows braced beneath himself. The mattress bounced around as he settled, and he laughed at her yelp of surprise as she was jostled. Sneaking in under her arm, he pushed the hem of her—*his*—shirt up and planted a smacking kiss to her side. "What do you say we head up to Montmartre?"

Tugging the shirt back down, she gave him a playful shove. He let her go and twisted around, clambering to sit beside her on the bed, close enough to catch the echoing sweetness of her scent.

"Montmartre, huh?" She reached up, threading her fingers through his hair.

"Sure. See some of Picasso's old haunts, steep ourselves in

what's left of the whole turn-of-the-century art scene. Drink some absinthe. You know, like artists do."

She smiled, a real, nice, genuine smile. "That's actually a really great idea."

"Of course it is. I came up with it." He nipped his way down her neck, sliding an arm around her waist.

Laughing, she leaned into him, and suddenly it wasn't just silliness anymore. They fit together so nicely like this, and his throat got tight.

"Plus," he said. "It's beautiful. All set up on the hill like that. You can walk to the very top, and there's Sacred Heart Basilica. All these gorgeous stained-glass windows. And the view from up there? You can see all of Paris, spread out at your feet."

"Sounds amazing."

"It is."

He wanted to show it to her. Wanted to show her a lot of things, and as he held her closer, it was a little too easy to imagine they were any ordinary couple, heading off to explore the city together.

Dangerous, entertaining thoughts like that. They were only fucking, after all—and they hadn't even gotten around to doing that yet.

Retreating slightly, he cocked one eyebrow in a leer. "Unless you'd prefer to stay in today."

"Nah. Tempting as you are"—she unwrapped her hand from around his neck, sliding it lower, fingertips lingering for a second at the chain where it crossed his collarbone—"daylight's burning. And there's plenty of time for that later." Her voice wavered, and her thumb stroked lower, drifting closer to his father's ring. "Right?"

Instinct had him grabbing her hand, but his rational mind stopped him from pushing her away from the ring. Instead, he lifted her knuckles to his lips, kissing each one in turn. "Plenty," he agreed.

Five more days, he reminded himself.

The golden band against his breastbone felt like a weight.

Five days was more than enough.

Kate didn't think she would ever get enough of Paris.

Rylan was barely hiding the bemusement on his face as she all but skipped along at his side, her hand wrapped around his elbow. She *loved* Montmartre. How much time had she spent studying all the people who had lived and died and loved and painted here? Pablo Picasso and Henri de Toulouse-Lautrec. Renoir and Degas and Van Gogh.

So much must have changed since their time, but the whole place had this feeling to it, like you could picture someone whipping out an easel and a set of paints at any moment. She and Rylan had had brunch in the kind of dingy café she'd always imagined artists sipping coffee in—not one of the fancy ones near the museums down by the Seine. Ducked into little shops and even taken cheesy selfies in front of the Moulin Rouge, and she was bursting. She just wanted to set up shop and draw hungover people in black clothes, smoking cigarettes and talking, forever.

And always, in the background of every one of those scenes would be Rylan. Rylan with his self-satisfied smirk and his fake frown. He liked to stand aside and watch her have her fun, scowling at it all, but she saw through him. He was having fun in spite of himself.

It was sort of strangely adorable. Like a cat who didn't want to admit he loved being petted.

"Okay," she said, putting down a hat she did *not* need to spend any of her dwindling resources on. She tugged at his arm as they set off down the sidewalk again, nudging him until he took his hand from his pocket so she could intertwine their fingers. "You've indulged me all day."

"Really? I hadn't noticed."

She was ignoring that. "So now what do you want to do?"

Suggestiveness colored his tone. "I can think of a couple of things."

She could think of a couple, too. Montmartre had kept the lion's share of her attention today, but it had taken effort not to slip into daydreams about how patiently he'd touched her the night before. Images of those big hands on her breasts and framing her hips. The warm lapping of his tongue...

Blinking, she squeezed his hand harder. "Things you want to do *in Montmartre*," she clarified.

"You're not narrowing it down much."

"Be serious."

"Well, that's no fun." He eyed her legs, but not in quite so suggestive of a manner. "Your feet too tired yet?"

They were, a little, but considering how much walking she'd been doing, that was basically to be expected. "Not too bad. Why?"

He gestured up the hill, and she squinted against the brightness of the sky. "It's a heck of a climb, but it's worth the effort."

She considered. "That's Sacred Heart up there, right?" A big, old, famous church. That didn't sound like something that would be particularly enthralling for him.

"Yup."

"Why do you want to go there?"

"Isn't it on your list of things to see?"

"Yeah, but I asked what *you* want to do."

"I told you." He wasn't looking at her. "I want to show you around town."

"Which you've done. A lot of. There must be something you'd like to do for you."

His mouth settled into the lines of a frown, and he didn't answer for a solid minute. Finally, just when she'd been about to start needling him, he offered, "It's got the best view in the entire city. If we're this close already…" He shrugged. "I'd like to see it. And I'd like to see *you* see it."

"Oh."

And it wasn't lost on her, that half his entertainment really did seem to amount to watching her taking in the city he'd clearly come to know so well. She couldn't pretend she entirely understood it, but she wasn't going to question it anymore.

"All right," she said, looking to cross the street in the direction of the hill. "Let's go."

He yanked her back, chuckling at her as he led her farther down the way. "Lesson one about navigating any European city. The shortest path between two points is never a straight line."

"No?"

"Nope. Gotta go this way."

She was glad he knew where he was going, because by the time they reached the steep stairs heading up, she was out of breath and completely turned around. He slung an arm around her shoulders, tugging her close as they avoided a couple more aggressive street peddlers, deflecting them with his body language and a short burst of annoyed-sounding French. It made a warmth grow in her chest, to have him looking out for her like this.

Working to keep up with him as they ascended, she asked, "How did you get to be such a good tour guide, anyway?"

"Dunno. Just had a lot of time to learn my way around the city. Figured out what my favorite places were and decided to share them." His voice trailed off before he could mention how many people he had shared them with.

And it was funny—she didn't have any illusions that she was the first one he'd given this tour to. He'd taken her to places that had seemed tailored to her tastes, but he was clearly pretty practiced at this whole thing. Hell, he'd basically admitted that his shtick had served him well with women in the past.

Still. Her gaze drifted to the center of his chest, where the drape of his shirt concealed the ring he wore around his neck. Maybe the hitch to his voice as he'd told her about his father had been a part of the act, but she didn't think so. This time they were spending together was only temporary, and she was far from unique. But she had *some* claim on him. Something that set her at least a little bit apart from the rest.

That thought made her bold.

"You know." Glancing at him out of the corner of her eye, she tested the waters. "You never did tell me what brought you here."

He hummed, frowning, and subconsciously or not, picked up the pace at which he climbed. She quickened her own gait, hooking her hand into his belt for something to hold on to.

"What brings anyone to Paris?" he asked after a moment, shrugging and dropping his arm. "Great city, good art, better food. I already knew the language, so I figured why not?"

"Those are all good arguments for Paris," she agreed. She could have let it go there, but she couldn't help pushing. "But you're not from here."

"Nope."

God, this was like pulling teeth. Why the freedom with his story last night and this brush-off today? "So where are you from?"

"New York, originally. The city."

"Is that where your family still lives?"

He shot her a look she couldn't quite decipher. "You know full well my dad's not *living there* anymore."

Yeah, she did know that. Not exactly the most sensitive way she could have phrased it. "Right." She cleared her throat. Tentatively, she prompted, "And your mom...?"

He let out a short bark of a laugh that sounded pained. "Who knows? Could be in New York. Could be in Argentina or Shanghai, for all I know."

Casting a glance over his shoulder, he sped his pace even more as they passed a clump of slow-moving tourists, and dammit all. This hill was *steep*, and his legs were a hell of a lot longer than hers. The bastard didn't even seem out of breath.

"Jesus," she finally said, giving up. She let her hand slip from his waist as they hit another set of stairs, not even caring that the family they'd just passed would now have to get around them. Her thighs burned, and she grabbed her chest, winded. "What the hell are you running from?"

All at once, he froze. And she almost missed it. The way

his eyes widened and his mask of casual flirtatiousness evaporated, leaving this wretched, surprised expression. Betrayal and hurt, and...she didn't even know what. As fast as it had appeared, it retreated, and he blinked a couple of times, brows furrowing. "Excuse me?" he asked.

What the hell? She just wanted to know why he was walking so damn fast, and...

And then it struck her all at once. She'd been needling him and needling him, and without even meaning to, she'd tripped right over the truth.

He was here, in Paris, thousands of miles from home, avoiding her questions about his life *because he was running away*. From what, she couldn't guess, but from something. Something big.

She swallowed hard, and her voice cracked. "Literally. I meant, literally."

"Oh."

The grin she'd been waiting for made a valiant attempt at surfacing on his face but ultimately couldn't quite seem to manage it. Looking away from him, she put her hands on her knees, hunching over to take a few good deep breaths. Silence hung over them, low and sticky like the air felt after their uphill jog. When she dared glance up at him again, he was leaning against a railing, arms crossed in front of him.

And clearly determined to ignore everything he'd unwittingly revealed in the last few minutes.

"You good?" he asked. And he didn't sound distant, precisely. Just guarded in a way he hadn't been. It felt more like the show he'd been putting on that first day, picking her up and buying her coffee and trying to be so debonair.

Trying and succeeding.

She nodded, standing up straight again. "Yeah. I'm fine. So long as you don't do your Road Runner thing and take off on me again."

"I'll try to restrain myself."

Ignoring the group of people currently passing them, he held out his arm to her, and she slipped her hand into the crook of his elbow. He felt warm and solid and dependable.

It was deceiving. How many times had her mother told her—you could never really trust a man. Especially not one that could do better than you. She swallowed hard. It didn't matter how open Rylan seemed sometimes. This was a man who wasn't telling her everything.

Arm in arm, and at a much more reasonable pace this time, they set off up the hill again. They talked idly about the things they passed and how far it still looked to the top, but it was superficial, allowing a wide berth around whatever they'd nearly stumbled into a few moments before.

She kind of hated it.

Finally, after what felt like forever, the stairs gave way, and he steered her to the right.

And suddenly her feet didn't hurt and her lungs didn't burn. "Wow," she murmured absently.

"Told you."

He hadn't been lying. The basilica itself stood off to the side, but it barely fazed her, because they were on the top of the world, the sky was blue, and all of Paris lay beneath their feet.

"Come on."

Taking her hand, he wandered through the crowd, somehow managing to find a clear place against the railing to look out over it all. Urging her to stand flush against the fence, he stepped in behind her, hooking his chin over her shoulder, his chest warm against her spine.

"Do you have a camera?" she asked. If she'd known this was going to be so spectacular, she would have insisted on going to her hostel first so she could grab hers.

"Don't worry about it." He shook his head and held her closer. "We'll worry about it later. For now, just enjoy it."

Her breath caught in her throat. She wanted some images to remember this moment by, but also to use as references for paintings she might do someday. But what was the point of remembering a moment she was too busy recording to be a part of?

She needed to soak this in.

Fact was, she had a lot of things to worry about. Between the progress she'd been hoping to make with her art and the decisions facing her as soon as she got home and all these twisty-turny feelings Rylan was awakening in her... her head and heart were more than full with troubles.

But then something happened. He rubbed her hand and stroked his fingers up and down her side, the steady rhythm of his breathing making the noise of her thoughts and the rest of the world die down. Just a little bit. Just enough for a warmth to replace them. For her to give in to being surrounded by so much beauty.

They stood there together a long, quiet time before he squeezed her close and pressed his lips to her temple.

"There are a lot of reasons why I'm here, in Paris." His voice was gruff, but it was honest. "Not all of them are the best reasons. But what matters—what I prefer to think about—is that I am here. In this moment, in this spot." He bent to place a soft, more lingering kiss against her cheek, then whispered beside her ear, "With you."

Just like that, the wariness she'd donned like armor mere minutes ago faded away, his words worming their way past her defenses. She didn't even care that it was a line. It didn't sound rehearsed. It sounded true.

And in that instant, that was all that mattered to her, too.

chapter TEN

Rylan was a bastard. First, for misleading Kate about where he came from in the first place. Second, for being so damn evasive all afternoon—for keeping his cards so close to his chest every time she asked him about his past. He'd given enough away already, but the details she seemed so eager to ferret out of him were getting too real. This had become a vacation for him, too, a respite from the tedium he'd settled into. A chance to not have to think about all the things he'd left behind.

Third and finally, he was a kinky motherfucker of a bastard for what he was about to do right now.

"Come on," he said, guiding her with a hand at the small of her back. They'd reversed their trip up to the top of Sacre Coeur and were down in Montmartre proper again, which she had loved. But she hadn't seen all of it yet.

"Where are we going?" She laughed, a high, warm sound that he was glad to hear again after everything had gotten so serious there for a bit. She'd better still be laughing when she saw where they were going next.

"You'll see."

It was a subtle transition, the way all the kitschy shops and little cafés gave way to the area's red-light district. The first couple of places they passed with dildos in the window, she didn't even seem to notice.

But then her steps slowed and her eyes narrowed.

"Rylan," she said, all warning.

Damn, he was a bastard. And this was going to be way too much fun.

"You know what brought Toulouse-Lautrec to Montmartre, right?"

"This isn't funny."

"Whores, dancing girls. It's part of the experience."

"Rylan!"

"What do you think the Moulin Rouge was? A nursery school?"

"That's not why I wanted to come here."

"I know it's not." He pulled out the trump card he'd been saving. "But you did ask me—repeatedly, if I might add—what I was getting out of this trip."

"I'm not going into a—a *brothel*."

He put on an expression of mock offense. "Of course you're not." They'd started moving forward again in spite of her misgivings, and—perfect. He stopped and put his arm out, gesturing to just the place he'd been planning to bring her. "You're going into a sex shop. Totally different."

"I don't want to—"

"But I do." He leaned in close, and she might be angry, but she didn't flinch away. "I want to buy you a present, and then tonight I want to show you how to use it." He let his arousal at the thought seep into his voice. "I want to find out how many times you can go before you beg me to stop."

She drew back, and her face bloomed tomato red. But she put her hands on her hips, a defiant set to the angle of her chin. She looked around. Made sure they were alone before she choked out, "I know how to use a—a—" She lowered voice comically. "A *vibrator*."

Well, color him surprised. "You do?"

"Of course I do." She glanced over her shoulder again, looking uncomfortable but in a different way. She leaned closer, still keeping her voice down. "I *told* you. No guy has ever managed to. You know."

"Make you come?"

God, he could feel the heat coming off her face from here. But her silence was her agreement. "So..."

"So?"

"*So* a girl has needs."

"Never doubted it." He'd been pretty sure she knew what an orgasm felt like, considering the way she'd arched into his touch and bucked against his tongue. Just the idea of her reaching between her legs and sating that ache had him hardening. The image of her doing it with a little mechanical assistance had him ready to pull her into an alley right here and now.

But he had patience. Not much of it, but enough.

He raised an eyebrow in challenge. "What I doubt is that you have any idea how to tell a man what those needs are. Which is why"—he stepped to the side and opened the door to the shop—"we are going to practice."

She looked from the open door to him and back again, but her feet seemed glued to the ground. After what felt like an eternity of indecision, her flush deepened to the point where he was actually starting to worry she might blow. But just when he was half expecting her to go running for the Metro without him, she crossed her arms over her chest. "Fine."

With that, she stormed into the store, and damn. He liked it when she got all fired up. Chuckling to himself and shaking his head, he followed in after her and let the door fall closed behind them.

Inside, the place was well lit. There were some racy images on the walls, and all the shelves were lined with books and DVDs and toys, but it wasn't the typical place people imagined perverts in trench coats sneaking into to find material for jerking off. Only a handful of people were browsing, but more of them were women than men. Hopefully, that would set Kate at ease.

He picked up a basket and nodded at the girl behind the counter before wandering over to where Kate was standing, eyeing a display of glass dildos.

"Pretty, aren't they?" He picked up a bulbous one with red swirls and put his lips close to her ear. "Wonder what this one would feel like inside of you?"

She squirmed. "Sounds cold."

"It would be." He set it down. "But that's half the fun." Grabbing one still in its packaging, he placed it in his basket.

She put her hand on his arm. He opened his mouth, ready to argue for why this was a good idea, why he'd love to rub this up and down her slit and watch it slip inside. But in the end, all she did was lift it out and replace it with a slimmer, purple one.

He practically swallowed his tongue. "Good choice."

She hummed, walking past him to keep looking around.

While she was doing her own perusing, he grabbed a bullet that looked interesting and considered picking up some lube, but that seemed a little presumptuous. Maybe next time.

When he caught up with her again, she had the package for a mini-wand-type thing in her hands.

"Find something good?"

She startled but didn't lose it on him again. She added it to their purchases with a shrug. "Travel-sized version of one I know I like."

"Smart thinking." He gestured at the rest of the store. "Anything else that gets your motor running?" Speaking of which, they had to stop for some batteries, too. "Handcuffs? Whips? Porn?"

"No, thank you."

Fine by him.

Up at the front counter, he paid for everything in cash, keeping his open wallet out of her view. He waved her off when she tried to contribute. "It was my idea," he insisted.

"Fine. But I'm getting dinner tonight."

He rearranged his mental list of places he'd been thinking about suggesting for the evening. "Fair enough." He twirled the box for the wand she'd picked in his hand. "And then, after, *dessert* is on me."

Kate stood before the mirror in the hotel room. *Their* hotel room. She swallowed hard, watching the way her throat moved in the foggy glass.

Except for a towel, she was naked.

After they'd gone into that store of his, they'd had a simple dinner, then swung by her hostel to check her out and grab her things. They'd been banal enough activities, but static had crackled in their air between them with every step, anticipation a hot, heavy thing in the hollow of her abdomen.

The previous night, she'd had a sense of where things might be going, but tonight, the whole way back, she'd *known*. He would strip her clothes off and put his mouth to her skin. Run those warm, careful fingers of his along the swells of her breasts and hips, dip them into the secret places she rarely showed to anyone. Her whole spine tingled, lit up with an equal mix of nerves and thrill.

He'd probably expect to have sex tonight. After he'd been so patient with her yesterday, how could he not? She still wasn't so sure how she felt about letting him do that to her, but had been psyching herself up for it as they'd walked through the door.

Before he could start turning her to mush with little kisses up and down her neck, though, she'd broken away, insisting on a shower. Alone. If he was planning to be putting his mouth on her again—especially *there*, she wanted to be clean for him. And besides, she'd needed time to get her head on straight.

She'd stayed under the spray for as long as she'd dared. It still hadn't been enough.

Picking up her brush, she focused her attention on the tangles in her hair. Her chest and face were flushed from the steam, and little beads of water still clung to her throat and the tops of her breasts. Setting the brush aside, she pushed the damp strands of her hair behind her shoulder. Grazed the tips of her fingers over her clavicle, letting her own touch linger.

Her anxiety was high, but she couldn't deny it. She'd never felt so *sexual* before. She wanted this. And she just had to trust: If she were in Rylan's hands...somehow, she'd be all right.

Before she could change her mind, she opened the door to the bathroom and walked out.

Rylan sat on the bed, elbows braced on his knees. He'd stripped off his jacket and his button-down, leaving him in an undershirt and jeans. Behind him, the covers had been turned back and a handful of pillows had been arranged as a cushion against the headboard.

His head snapped up as she emerged from behind the door-frame, and his gaze raked up and down her body. He licked his lips. "Feel better?"

"Yeah. Much." She fought to keep her hands at her side. Not to reach up and fidget with her towel or hold it more securely across her breasts.

"Good." He rose and strode forward to meet her, stopping shy of pulling her into an embrace. With one hand, he traced the edge of her face, then down over her shoulder, to the place where the towel gapped over the center of her chest. He didn't pull at it, though. Didn't move to reveal her any further. "You look edible."

A full-body shudder moved through her. "You look good, too." He always did.

And there was that smirk. "Go." He gestured to the bed. "Lie down."

He stroked her cheek again, then moved toward the chair near the entryway to pick up the bag from the sex store. Her face heated, but she didn't comment. As he took their purchases with him to the bathroom, she turned to face the bed, ignoring that he was washing them up and probably filling them with batteries.

She still wasn't exactly sure what he planned to do with those things. She hadn't been lying when she'd said she had some experience with them. Her roommate her junior year of college had spoken about her vibrators rhapsodically and had been shocked when Kate had confessed to not knowing anything about them. At the time, she'd been involved with Aaron, so she hadn't really thought much of it. He hadn't ever succeeded in getting her off, but they only spent the night together a few times a week. She'd been able to find time to...attend to her needs when he hadn't been around. But the idea of actually going so far as to procure sex toys had felt a little too much like admitting defeat.

After he'd fessed up to everything—after she'd walked away—defeat had pretty much been the order of the day.

Her first attempt at ordering a vibrator would probably have been comical if it hadn't been so mortifying. After going back and forth on it a hundred times, though, she'd finally settled on one and clicked "buy" before she could stop herself. The thing had come in a plain brown package a few days later, and when her roommate had been gone, she'd locked the doors and turned on some music. And proceeded to have the best orgasm of her life.

Until last night.

Combining Rylan's unnatural understanding of her body and the power of a couple of double A's very well might kill her. Still, it was with reluctance that she clambered onto the bed. Her small, carefully chosen collection of little mechanical friends wasn't something she talked about, much less shared with anyone else. She kept them hidden in pouches, tucked under pajamas and respectable novels and anything else she could toss into her nightstand drawer to make sure no one would ever find them. Rylan might act like they were no big deal, but to her, they'd always been a shameful secret—like the idea that she ever touched herself at all.

In the other room, the sound of the water running cut off. Showtime. Keeping the towel wrapped around her, she settled herself gingerly on the bed, pulling the sheet up to her waist. Was it too awkward to lie back against the mound of pillows he'd created? Should she have dried her hair?

Before she could obsess too much or work herself up, Rylan reemerged from the bathroom. "Comfy?" he asked, tilting his head to the side.

No. "Yup."

The corner of his mouth crept upward, showing just how little he believed her, but he didn't call her on it. Instead, he crossed the room to her. Pushing the covers down partway, he spread a towel on the mattress beside her, then laid out the things he'd decided they should buy. Everything about his demeanor was practical and casual, as if this were something normal people did every day.

Her breathing sped a hair faster. Maybe this was something *he* did every day.

"Hey."

She looked up at him. Felt the warmth of his touch against her bare arm, and it helped relax her, pulling her down from the edge of neuroticism she'd been in danger of going over. The best she could, she pushed her worries and fears aside. Yes, this kind of stuff made her nervous and embarrassed. Yes, Rylan had a lot more experience than she did. But that was okay. He knew what he was getting into. And through everything they'd done together, he'd never seemed to mind having to take the lead before.

Letting out a long, deep sigh, she put her hand over his and gave him a weak smile. "Sorry. Just nervous."

He leaned in to kiss the point of her shoulder. "Don't be. Only good things are going to happen here."

Right. It was hard to believe after all the ways she'd been beaten down, but Rylan hadn't given her any reason not to trust him yet. "Okay."

"Here." He nudged at her. "Scoot forward a bit."

She rearranged herself at his direction, only realizing as he climbed onto the bed that he was maneuvering to sit behind her.

"Aren't you going to—?" She cut herself off.

"Hmm?"

He had taken off his socks and shoes, but other than that, he was still basically dressed.

"I—" God, why was this all so hard for her to talk about? "I don't want to be the only one who's naked."

He laughed, but not in a mean way. He ran a fingertip along the edge of the towel where it stretched between her shoulder blades. "You're not naked yet."

"I might as well be."

"Fine, fine." He tugged his undershirt off and stood to take off his pants. He still had his boxers on, though, as he settled in behind her again.

"What about—?"

"In a minute." Once he'd gotten himself arranged, he pulled her in against his chest. She sat in the V of his legs, awkwardly reclining with her spine to his front, unsure what she was safe to lean against. He made a little groan when she tried to relax into him, and heat seared through her. There he was—the hard line of him pressed against the small of her back. "See?" he said, rubbing his hands up and down her arms. "If I take everything off, I'm going to be right there." He tilted his hips forward, dropping his voice. "And I don't think either of us is ready for that."

She certainly wasn't, but feeling him there, knowing he was erect and so close—it made a fresh, new wave of heat roll through her body. His chest was broad and firm beneath her, his hands so sure in their strokes. He smelled good and sounded good, and she had him for only so long, but he was here for her. He wanted *her*.

With a quivering breath, she closed her eyes.

"That's right," he said as she relaxed. "That's beautiful."

Drawing his fingertips in expanding circles, over her arms and up her torso, across the naked swaths of skin above the cover of the towel, he leaned in. His mouth was hot and wet against her neck, and he had to know what this was doing to her. As she slowly lost the tension she'd been carrying, a new one settled in its place, but instead of nerves, it was all desire. Her skin felt like it was humming, unnaturally sensitive to every stroke of his hands and lips. Between her legs, a deep ache settled in, liquid flowing, making her feel warm and ripe and glowing.

"That's perfect," he murmured. "Let me make you feel good."

She didn't know how long she lay against him like that, letting him touch and trace. When it started to become too much, she shifted, pressing her thighs together, but it didn't help. He made a sound low in his chest and, pausing for just a second, let his hands drift lower. Through the towel, he caressed her breasts and her sides, then down. Gliding warm hands over her hips and the tops of her thighs, but bypassing the needy center of her. After a few passes, her attention all seemed to be focusing there, the one place he refused to touch, and a worry flickered deep in her belly.

Would he make her say it out loud? Make her ask, or worse, beg?

A gasp of a whine escaped her lips, and it made him press harder, cupping her with more eager hands.

All at once, it struck her—he wasn't the only one who could move here.

As if her arms had suddenly come unfrozen, she reached one up, tangling her fingers in his hair. She craned her head to the side as she pulled him down, and when their lips met, it was with a crush of heat and need. He parted for her, pressing forward with his tongue and letting hers in beside it. He tasted like sex, and he made her *feel* like sex, heady and powerful and reeling.

Breathless, she pulled away for air, but it was only to have her lungs seize in her chest. His index finger played over the stretch of skin right above where her towel was tucked, teasing at the terry cloth.

"Can I?"

He sounded as lost in this as she was, as turned on and wanting. She tilted her head up, stretching her neck to sip from his lips one more time. Her heart thundering against her rib cage, she released the kiss and moved so she could look into his eyes.

Her voice seemed to echo in the room. "Yes."

chapter ELEVEN

It was all Rylan could do to keep his movements even and slow, building up the anticipation as he unwrapped Kate like a gift. She'd been so squirrelly about letting him see her really naked the night before, and those hints of uncertainty still lingered in the way she braced herself.

Fear had no place in his bed. He was going to have to teach her that. Again.

Leaving one hand on her cheek to keep her angled toward his mouth, he worked the other one under the fabric of her towel. The cloth gave way with the slightest nudge, going loose across her breasts, and he closed his eyes as he nipped at her lips. He was hard as diamond against her spine, and he needed to pace himself if he was going to make this good.

It was the work of a moment to get himself back under control. Gently, carefully, he peeled one side of the towel away, and then the other. Her breathing picked up as he revealed her. With the lightest touch, he traced his fingertips through the valley of her breasts. Her skin was so smooth, water-warm from her shower, a delight against his palm as he let it graze across her nipple. A high-pitched little noise leaked from her lips at the touch. He left her wanting, though, drifting lower, down the soft planes of her abdomen.

Just before he reached her cunt, he paused. She'd been so wet last night, so sweet against his tongue, and he wanted to feel that again. But he had a game plan for tonight.

He let his other hand slide from her face, teasing the line of her throat before grazing lower. Overlooking the way she tensed, he parted his lips from hers, opening his eyes and shifting to look down the length of her body where it was splayed out before them.

The sheet lay across her thighs, barely obscuring the sweet, dark triangle of her pussy from his view, but the rest of her was entirely on display. And what a sight it was.

Her breasts weren't large, but they were soft and round, her nipples a dusky rose, hard and pointed where they peaked. He drew his hands back up her body to cup the fullness of those curves.

"Do you like that?" he asked as she shivered.

She nodded, but was squirming. Uncomfortable, and he had to remind himself that he was trying to show her something here.

"Has anyone ever done this before? Given this much attention to just touching you?"

"No."

"Idiots." There were treasures here—pleasures so much greater than a quick come in a warm hole. But here was the real question. "Did you ever ask them to?"

She laughed, and it was a sad thing that made his frustration boil even hotter.

"You've been sleeping with idiots," he repeated. He kissed the shell of her ear, wet and slow. "Here's the trick. You can get a man to do all kinds of things. But you have to tell him what you want."

Uncertain silence met him at that. It was no surprise, but it still bothered him.

"Come on," he said, more taunting. "You never miss a chance to give me a hard time. What's holding you back now? You can tell me you want me to suck on your tits." He said it as crudely as he could think to, and the way her throat moved, the way her spine pressed against where he was still so damn hard for her confirmed that it had been the right move. "Or touch your cunt."

Her hips tilted forward at that, and she shifted, like she was trying to cross her legs, and no. There wasn't going to be any of that. In a deft maneuver, he hooked his ankles over hers, holding her open.

"Don't close up for me now," he murmured. With a last stroke of his thumbs across her nipples, he dropped his hands to her thighs, running them up and down the smooth flesh, nudging the sheet lower with every pass until he could see everything. He edged higher, slipped his fingers along the creases where torso met leg, so close to where she wanted him—so close to where he wanted to be.

"Why are you so afraid of this?" he asked.

"Not afraid." She could have fooled him. Her voice shook with it.

"No? You could barely even admit to me that you'd gotten yourself off before. Still can't tell me what you want me to do to you." And he was getting into dangerous territory here, he knew. "Those other men. The ones who never made you come. Could you tell them what to do?"

She shook her head, but there was something anguished about it. "This isn't as easy for everybody else as it is for you. Girls, we—" She cut herself off.

"What?" He gave her a second to finish her thought, but when she didn't he could guess where she was going with it. "What? You don't want to seem easy? Or like you know what you're doing? Well, let me assure you." He dragged his hands all the way up her body again, over her breasts and then down to hover once again above her cunt. "There is nothing sexier than a woman who knows what she wants. *Nothing.*"

"But—" The words sounded choked. "I can't."

Couldn't what? Talk about it?

And then it occurred to him—the most brilliant idea he'd ever had. His cock throbbed at the thought of it. He moved his right hand to put it on top of hers. Lifted them both and brought them to her thigh.

His throat bobbed. "Can you show me?"

Kate felt all the blood drain from her face.

She was so tangled up—on a knife's edge of arousal, confused and mortified, and he was challenging her in all these different ways. In her head, she knew she should be fine with this. A woman should stand up for herself, should stick up for herself in bed and anywhere else.

And deep down below that, she was a writhing mass of insecurities and shame. She didn't want to have to ask for things. Asking meant opening yourself up to being told no, to being told you weren't good enough, didn't deserve it.

God, there was that voice in her head again. The one that had haunted her all her life.

Only Rylan spoke over it, drowning it out. He pressed her hand closer to the center of her need. "I want you to show me what you like."

He chased away one kind of doubt, leaving her with just the one.

She didn't know how to let him see her like this.

"But—" She curled her fingers into her palm, resisting. "You know how to—" *How to make me come.*

He'd done it last night. Why was he putting her through this?

"Yeah, I do. And I could do it right now, but I'd rather do this."

"Why?"

"Why?" He skated his other hand down her thigh. "Because it turns me on. Because I still have things to learn for the next time I eat your pussy out." He exhaled, breath hot against her ear. "Because I want you to be able to do this for the next man you meet who wouldn't know his way to a woman's clit if he had a map."

Of course. She was only here for a handful of days, and then she'd never see him again. She'd known that from the very start, had actually seen it as a positive. As an excuse to let go. And yet to hear him put it so plainly took her breath away, a sharp sudden pang.

She pushed the thought away, but it wouldn't loosen its hold. No matter how little time they had together, right now he was here. With her.

And she wanted nothing more than to be closer.

"Can we..." She twisted, craning her neck to look at him. He gripped her hip, as if trying to stop her—as if he thought she were trying to escape. "The towel," she said. Trying to explain.

If she could feel the heat of his skin, maybe it would ground her. Keep her in the moment, this tiny pocket of time when it was just him and her.

"Of course."

She gulped. "And your boxers?"

"You sure?" he asked after a brief pause.

She considered it. Yeah, she was certain. "Yes."

"All right."

She sat up and away from his body long enough for them to get the towel out of the way, and for him to tug his underwear off. When he pulled her back against him, into the cradle of his thighs, all she could feel was warm, firm flesh beneath her, and it made her pulse hotter. The wiry hair of his legs and chest tickled her. And the smooth, silky line of him, bare and damp against her spine lit her up from the inside.

"Fuck," he said, a low breath against her ear as she settled against him. "Someday..."

Her breath caught. "Someday what?"

"Someday," he continued, grasping her wrist, curling her fingers and bringing them, this time, unerringly to her sex. "When you're ready..."

The first brush of her own hand against her folds was electric. God, she was soaked, and it was such a relief to finally get some pressure there, where she was slick and hot and aching.

Still, something deep inside of her told her this was wrong. She tried to pull her hand away, but he gripped her palm, and when she didn't delve any deeper into her pleasure, he took the initiative. Fingertips covering hers, he slid them around in the liquid, sending a low, rolling wave of pleasure up her spine.

With his other hand, he cupped her breast, teasing at the peak, and she gasped. She'd never known her nipples were so sensitive, but he'd spent so much time working them up before. There was a rawness to the sensation now as he twisted and squeezed. The scrape of a nail across the tip had her shifting her own hand against her sex, needing something, anything to push against her clit.

"That's right, beautiful." His voice dropped a level as he praised her, and that made a whole fresh wave of need surge through her.

God. What was she doing?

Unable to take it anymore, she let out a sound that was half a sob as she started touching herself in earnest. It felt good—it felt amazing.

And then he was *talking*. "Someday," he resumed, still caging her hand against her sex, still pulling sparks of desire from her breast, "when you're ready, I'm going to strip you down, just like this. Open you up and put your legs over my shoulders. I'm going to lick you out for *hours*."

Damn. Oh, damn. She rubbed harder at her clit, losing herself in it.

"But I'm not gonna give you my fingers. Not gonna give you anything to fill that ache inside. Leave you all empty and coming around nothing until you're dying for it. Do you want that? Do you feel how bad you want to be filled up?"

She *did*. It was a hollow deep inside, and she didn't want to come like this, no matter how close she was.

"Yeah," she groaned.

"Don't you want something in that pretty little pussy while I lick you?"

"*Yes.*" So badly. She pressed harder, fingers working furiously against herself even as she shied away from the abyss that was yawning at her feet.

His hand dropped from her breast, and all she could hear was the slick sounds of her body, embarrassing, horrible, but it felt too good. She couldn't stop.

Not even when he took her other hand in his. Wrapped it around something long and cool and smooth.

"What—" She snapped her eyes open to see the glass toy they'd purchased there inside her grasp.

Another new level of mortification rose up, choking her, but it didn't matter. She wanted it. Wanted him to make her feel like this.

"Come on," he urged. "It's gonna feel so good. It's gonna *look* so good. Don't you know how pretty this is going to be inside of you?" At her shaky exhale, his voice deepened further. "Can't you feel how hard I am, just thinking about filling you up?"

Her focus shifted in an instant, forgetting the toy and the thrumming need in her own sex, because, God, yes, he was. His cock pressed into her back, unyielding in its desire. Long and thick, and she could have that. Inside her. All she had to do was ask him for it.

She bit off a curse, not even resisting when he curled his fingers more firmly around hers, solidifying her grip on the glass. Bringing it down to that sweltering need between her legs. And he was the one to press it just between her lips.

Making her. He was making her do this, even though she was willing, and that idea lit a match of need so hot it burned.

Fingers twitching, she helped him aim it, getting it directed into place.

"Do you want me to fill you, sweetheart?"

She clenched her eyes shut tight. "Yes."

The glass felt even colder as it pressed inside, and her body opened, welcoming it, and she moaned aloud. The emptiness was gone, even though it wasn't what she really wanted. Cold and fake, and she longed for hot flesh. For his weight on top of her, pushing her into the mattress. Making her take it.

His voice was liquid sin against her ear. "Someday. Before you go. Before I have to give you up." She whined, that sharp edge of a pang cutting into her again at the thought. But he kept her close, his own breath catching as if it pained him as much as her. He clutched her tight. "After I've made you come a hundred times with my tongue, I'm going to lay you out. And I'm going to be so hard for you. Just *aching* for this sweet little cunt."

He flexed his hips against her backside, sliding roughly against her skin, and letting out a shaking groan of his own.

"Just the way you're fucking yourself with this," he said, thrusting the toy inside. "I'm going to fuck you. I'm going to get so deep inside you."

"Please—"

He pressed something else into her other hand, and she was so far gone it took her a second to recognize the vibrator they'd bought. Breathing hard, she curled her fingers around the handle. With a flick of his wrist he turned it on, helping her to get it right against her clit.

Everything in her leapt to life. It was perfect, hard and rumbly and turning the sweet pulses of pleasure into something overwhelming in their intensity. Together, they bore down, to the point where she wasn't sure who was doing what, only that she was so close and needed to get there. Needed—

He thrust the toy into her harder. His voice needy and rough, "I can't wait to come inside you."

She held her breath. Tensed every muscle and pressed her face into his neck. Pushed down harder with the toy, and—

Her climax tore through her, dark and vibrant all at once, sweeping her along into a cocoon of ecstasy she'd never imagined before. Her throat hurt, and there was scream-ing, his name and God's, and her whole body sang as she arched, head dropping back. Wave after wave, and he held her through it all.

After what felt like eternity, the pulses started to dim. She fumbled, trying to turn the toy off, and eventually she man-aged. His hands had shifted, one still keeping the glass held deep within her, while with the other he grasped her hip, and— Oh.

His breath was still coming in harsh rasps as he pulled her more tightly against him. His hot length slipped and skidded over her skin, and her belly dipped. Maybe he'd take her like this someday, her on his lap. He'd be buried deep inside of her, helping her ride him, touching her clit and her breasts, and she *wanted* that.

She reached a hand back, grabbing his hair as she twisted, pulling him down into a fiery kiss.

"I'm going to—" he panted.

Against her mouth, he groaned, and everything went slick against her spine. Deep within, she throbbed, aftershocks trembling their way through her as he came on her skin, painting it with his release.

For a long moment, he stayed there, trembling and tense, pulsing weakly as he clutched her close. Finally, he sighed, lips going slack. He pulled away, kissed her temple and eased the body-warm glass from her sex.

It left her feeling empty, but not unpleasantly so. How could it, after what he had given her?

After what he had shown her how to do?

And yet, as he held her, wrapping both arms around her chest, he was the one to murmur, "Thank you."

Shaking, she curled her hands around his forearms. Wonder pounded through her, the way arousal had moments before.

"No," she said, the words choked. "Thank you."

chapter TWELVE

Another day, another museum.

Rylan gazed at the painting in front of him, trying to come up with something insightful to say about it. His mother had given him some of the language to talk about art, but he was drawing a blank now. Of course. If only he'd known back when he was a kid that he was actually going to need that kind of stuff someday.

He snuck a glance to the side. After more than a little cajoling, Kate had consented to spend the day with him again. It burned him that he'd had to dangle a visit to the Musée d'Orsay in front of her to get her to agree. He was pretty sure he'd paid for the pleasure of her company in orgasms the night before, but apparently, that wasn't valuable enough of currency for her. What she really wanted was Monet and Van Gogh.

He didn't mind, exactly, but there was still something petty niggling at the edges of his thoughts. Like he was torn between loving how she got so *into* all this modern art stuff and being annoyed that she was scarcely paying attention to him. He frowned. Even more annoying was that her preoccupation bothered him at all.

She was staring at a different piece, her head tilted to the side, and he could just about *see* all the art history knowledge running through her head. She took a small step back and into a beam of light streaming in from the window. It made her hair glow, and God. He really *really* wished he had something intelligent to say.

He straightened his shoulders, shaking off the plaintive, insufferable tone to his own internal monologue. Ridiculous. His mother wasn't the only one who'd taught him anything, and there was more than one way to get a conversation going. His father had instilled in him that much.

People loved to talk about the subjects that interested them—whether or not the people they were talking at knew a goddamn thing.

Biting the bullet, he sidled over to stand beside her, and nudged her with his elbow. "So. Teach me about art."

Tearing her gaze from the painting she'd been staring at, she raised an eyebrow at him.

Right. Because she always saw through him.

Speaking slowly, voice colored by both distraction and skepticism, she asked, "What do you want to know?"

He shrugged. He had to do better if he wanted her to actually talk to him. "Everything. Teach me about..." He squinted at the placard on the wall. "Eugène Boudin."

The thing that killed him was, he did actually want to know. Maybe not about Eugène Boudin in particular, but about why she looked at the picture the way she did. What drew her in about all this Impressionism and Cubism and Fauvism?

"Funny." Her tone was desert dry. "The man who paraded me around the Louvre showing off his favorite painting is looking for an art lesson now?"

"I'm serious." More serious than he'd realized a couple of minutes ago. And besides . . . "I may know the Louvre pretty well, but—" The next words took him by surprise. He cleared his throat to hide his pause. "Mother never really cared all that much for this place."

If she caught his hesitation, she ignored it in favor of her incredulity. She flung her arm out as if to encompass the museum as a whole. "Who doesn't care for *this*?"

She had a point. The building was gorgeous, with warm light pouring in from all the windows, and the statuary and paintings were undeniably masterpieces.

He shrugged, sorry he'd brought it up. "It was still the 'new museum' when I was a child. Mother was more interested in showing us the classics."

She'd appreciated modern art as much as any cultured woman of her social status should. Hell, she'd let that interior designer fill her apartment with the stuff. But it was the work of the old masters that made her seem alive.

Made her eyes light up, the way her husband and children so rarely seemed to manage to.

Of course, what Kate latched onto after all of that was " 'Us'?"

"Me and my brother and sister." The Bellamy children. Something in the back of his throat tasted sour.

She pursed her lips. "I didn't know you had siblings."

"We're all scattered. Doing our own things." He'd scarcely spoken to either of them since the trial.

"Let me guess. You're the oldest?"

"Guilty as charged."

"You were probably super bossy, too."

That made him grin. "There I plead the fifth."

"Uh-huh." She leaned in closer to inspect a corner of the painting, and he half thought she'd decided to drop it. But then she turned to him, arms crossed over her chest. "You never volunteer anything, do you?"

He frowned. "Excuse me?"

"Every time it's your turn to talk about yourself, you answer questions. Barely. But you never offer anything."

Her accusation took him off guard.

He'd volunteered plenty, their first couple of days. He'd shown her that painting and told her about his childhood visits to the Louvre. About his father's ring.

He'd volunteered things he'd never volunteered before.

And besides. "This all started with *me* asking *you* to tell me more about what we were looking at."

It had started with a question he hadn't even cared about until it had come out of his mouth.

"But it evolved into us talking about your family. Or at least me trying to."

She wasn't wrong, but nothing about it seemed fair. "So you can be evasive and I can't?"

"I wasn't being evasive. I was just trying to figure out what you wanted."

"To get to know you." He spat it. "Is that such a crime?" He heard what he'd said—heard the hypocrisy in it about a second after it was out in the air. He tried to backtrack, spinning wildly. "That's not the same thing at all. Stories about dead artists versus my whole..." *Clusterfuck of a family.* He was practically pleading now. "It's not the same."

"If you can't tell me anything about who you are, then what are we even—" She cut herself off, eyes shuttering. He'd never seen her so pissed off before, and a ball of dread formed in his stomach when she waved a hand at him and turned, heading toward a sculpture on the other side of the room.

It left him alone, standing there beside a fucking Eugène Boudin, watching her walk away from him. An instinct surged up, telling him *fine*. If she wanted to be like that, what did he care? It was only a matter of time until she walked away in any case. If not now, in the middle of a museum, it would be in a matter of days, disappearing behind airport security, never to be heard from again.

But…but…

Fuck.

Forgetting the people surrounding them, he jogged across the gallery. Came up behind her and took her shoulders in his hands, spinning her around until they were face to face. She gazed at him expectantly, like everything that would happen after this point revolved around what he said now.

Maybe he should cut his losses and go. There were a hundred other women just like her, tourists on their own in a beautiful city, waiting to be shown a good time.

Only none of them were her. None of them would see through all his lines or make him work so hard for it. None would come to him so innocent and yet so fiery. She was the one he wanted to give up his empty days to walk around museums with, and take to quirky restaurants, and kiss and touch. The one he wanted to spread out naked on his bed.

"My name is Rylan Bellamy," he said, and it was the truth.

But like everything he'd told her this week, it was only a partial truth, and the part he didn't say burned. He'd been going by his middle name since college—had settled on changing it the day his father sent in his acceptance letter for him. As if choosing his name were any kind of substitute for choosing his fate. He hadn't offered the rest of it to anyone in years.

But now it rose up in his throat, that monstrosity he'd been saddled with at birth. That weight that had been placed on his shoulders, that had determined his path for his entire life.

Theodore Rylan Bellamy III.

Somehow, withholding it from her felt like a lie.

He darted his gaze up to her face, searching for any sign she'd caught him in it. But her mouth was a flat line, her eyes impassive and impatient. She was still waiting. He needed to give her more.

Right. She'd been asking him about his family.

He took a deep breath. "I'm the oldest of three children. My sister, Lexie, is three years younger than me. She's finishing business school, and she's going to take over the goddamn world someday." She really was. Lexie, the spitfire. If she'd only been a son...Instead, his father had gotten him. Him and..."My brother, Evan, is the youngest. He's a junior in college, and no one knows what he's going to do with his life, but he—" He cut himself off at the pang in his chest. Because Evan was the real disappointment of the family, and yet..."He's like you. And my mother. He loves art, and beautiful things."

And that's why Rylan had always fought so hard to protect him. To keep him from being stuffed into the same airless box that Rylan had.

He'd made sure his brother had a choice.

Kate's mouth had dropped open, like she hadn't been expecting any of that. It hadn't hurt to give it to her, though. All at once he wanted to take back the myriad half truths he'd told her and start anew.

But the idea of it had him reeling, suspended on a tightrope and ready to fall. She'd walk away for real if he did.

That didn't just hurt. It ached, and in ways he wasn't prepared for it to.

Something inside of him lurched, reversing wildly to pull him from the precipice. All the lessons he'd had drummed into him about holding his cards close to his chest, not showing people the tools they could use to ruin you—they crowded in around him. Keeping him safe.

He let her go, drawing his hands to his sides to hook them in his belt. He took a single step back. Squaring his jaw and lifting his chin, he said, "And that's more than I've volunteered to anyone. In years."

Hell, when was the last time he'd given away his last name?

There was danger in all of this, but he stood there beneath the weight of her scrutiny. She'd effectively asked him to let her get to know him. If what he'd offered hadn't been enough, that wasn't his fault. Not now.

After what felt like an hour, she closed her mouth, and her posture softened. She reached out a hand, crossing the space he'd put between them, and the air seemed to shiver as the distance shattered and fell.

Her hand on his was cool and small and soft, but it was a relief. The one she placed against his heart even more so.

Gazing up at him, she smiled, real and tentative. "Thank you."

His throat refused to work, so all he could do was nod.

"Come on," she said after a moment. She nodded her head toward the hall. "I don't have a lot I can tell you about Eugène Boudin. But I hear they have an incredible collection of Cézannes?"

It terrified him, just how good that invitation sounded. Twisting his wrist, he moved to intertwine their fingers, swallowing past the tightness in his lungs. "Lead the way."

The strangest mixture of excitement and nerves bubbled up behind Kate's ribs. Rylan's palm was warm against hers, and he followed her so willingly.

She'd challenged him. Called him out for the evasiveness that had been making her feel more and more disposable with every aborted conversation. And he'd chased her down and told her things. Not much, but enough.

And now he wanted to listen to her talk about art.

She was falling into something entirely too deep with this man, giving him more and more of her trust, despite the way her head screamed at her not to. But as they wound their way through the galleries, dodging other patrons and nodding at security guards as they passed them by, she gave in to it. She felt incredible and in control and *alive*. Consequences were things she could worry about later.

Finally, they reached the part of the museum she'd been thinking of. She skidded to a stop in the center of the room and looked around. Landscapes and still lifes and even a portrait or two lined the walls, all created from thick, short brushstrokes on canvas. All portraying *something* she'd been trying to figure out but had never quite managed to pull off.

She turned her head to look at Rylan and found him eyeing

her expectantly. A moment's doubt rocked her, making her come up short before she could really launch into anything.

"You sure you want to hear me talk about this stuff?"

"I asked, didn't I?"

He had, but she couldn't quite believe he really meant it. "Just, I get carried away."

"If you do, I think I can manage to get a word in edgewise."

Now that was something she did believe. Gathering up her confidence, she nodded to herself, then gestured around at the paintings on the walls. "How much do you know about any of this?"

He tipped his head side to side. "As much as anyone whose mother took them to the Louvre when they were a kid?" At the look she gave him for that, he shrugged. "A little. No formal education, but I know who Cézanne was." His mouth pulled to the side. "Sort of."

She chewed on her lip, considering. He really didn't need a full-on history lesson here, but he had asked . . . "So, there were always schools of art, right?"

"That's what I've been told."

She ignored that. "But for ages and ages, it was all basically realism. Lots of variation inside that, and different styles, but for the most part, people used art to capture what the world looked like. There weren't cameras, so you needed some way to make your castle look pretty. Or to document things."

"Makes sense."

And wow, but it was a good thing he hadn't asked for that full-on history lesson, because she was taking some serious liberties here.

"But then things changed," she said. She glanced around

at the rest of the room. None of this was based on her own formal education, which, truth be told, was a little lacking in the art history department. But she'd sat through enough lectures, looked at enough slides. Drawn enough studies of other people's works. "It's not really formally linked to the camera, but I like to imagine it was. When you don't need these painstakingly done renderings just to remember someone lived or that something happened, why have them at all? Why make art?"

Rylan's smile was low and wry. "To express the inner workings of your poor, tortured soul?"

She laughed, a little breathless with it. "Yeah. Basically. That's what it finally became, when it wasn't needed anymore just for documentation." She lifted one shoulder up before setting it back down. "It didn't make sense to pay a painter to take three months to do what a photographer could do in a day." She connected her gaze with his again. "And it didn't make sense to replicate something a lens could do, when as a person you were so much more."

There was a warmth to the way he looked at her then, and she squeezed his hand before glancing away. "So people started mixing it up. Making it personal. Impressionism brought in all these crazy colors and left in all the brush-strokes the old masters would have blended in. They let you see the artist in the art."

And that had always been the place where she'd struggled so much. She'd never known what to let people see.

She still had her father's voice in her ear, telling her there wasn't anything in her *worth* seeing.

Beside her, Rylan nodded. "So it's more about the interpretation instead of just about what they saw."

He'd said something similar before, hadn't he? That one time she'd showed him her sketchbook?

"Yeah," she said.

They stood there for a minute before he raised their joined hands and gestured at the images surrounding them. "What made you want me to look at these pieces in particular?"

It was hard to put her finger on. "I don't know. This is technically Postimpressionism, and it's just...it's my favorite, I guess. Things started getting all blocky, and he was playing with..." She stumbled, looking for the right words to describe what it felt like Cézanne had been trying to do. "With the shapes of things. Deconstructing the forms. But it was all still real, you know? That's clearly a rooftop"—she pointed at one picture and then another—"and that's a man."

"A funny-looking man."

"But a more *real* man for all that he's impossible." The idea suddenly gripped her, fervent in a way she couldn't quite explain. "You're seeing what he looked like and getting this idea of who he was, or who the artist thought he was." The thick strokes of paint split the man's face into planes, hinting at where Cubism was heading without quite getting there. They broke him up. Disassembled him, and put him back together, more whole than he could have been if he'd been rendered any other way.

"I don't know," Rylan mused. "I see Cézanne's style more than I see a personality. Am I seeing who the subject was or am I seeing who the man behind the easel wanted him to be?"

"Hard to tell, isn't it?"

He let go of her hand, but it was only to shift to the side, moving to stand behind her and wrap his arms around her waist. With his lips beside her temple, he asked, "What do you want me to see?"

And she didn't know if he meant as a tour guide, showing him the works that had moved her in the past. As an artist in her own right, or as a—whatever she was to him, sharing his days and his bed in this finite slice of time they had.

Something shaky fluttered inside of her, but she pushed it down, folding her hand over his. "I guess I'm still working on that."

chapter THIRTEEN

Rylan set the key to their hotel room on the table beside the door with a heavy hand. The quiet slap of plastic on wood echoed more loudly than it had any right to. Kate had entered ahead of him, and she stood with her back to him, gazing out the window as she lifted her bag over her head, sending the loose tumble of her hair falling across her shoulders. His mouth went dry.

In the past wasted year, and in all the time before, he'd chosen his conquests for a variety of reasons. Most he'd liked the look of. Drawn to full breasts or sultry lips or legs that went on for miles, he'd introduced himself. Turned on the charm and flashed his credit card around.

And then there was this woman. She was beautiful enough, but she was smart and funny and she saw the world in a whole different way than he ever had—talking about art like it could save the world. She was trying to *do* something with her life, and if they'd met on another continent, in another universe, he would have run screaming from the way she made him feel.

Love was a weapon. People used it against you to get you to do things you didn't want to do, to steal from you. They took it and they threw it away.

But this wasn't love. This was a few days of connection. This was lust, for her mind as well as her body, but lust all the same.

He wanted her so much it hurt to breathe.

"Come here."

She turned at the sound of his voice, and the low roughness of it took even him aback.

"Come here," he repeated.

She quirked one eyebrow up, but as she twisted her hair between her fingers, she did as he'd asked, advancing on him. She'd taken off her shoes, and God, even her feet were dainty and lovely, and the lines of her legs from under that skirt made him even harder.

As soon as she was within reach, he struck, reeling her in and pulling her tight against his body. He'd been so patient with her the past two nights, and part of him was aching to take what he really wanted. He could bend her over the mattress the way he had so many girls before, and shove her skirt up and—

"Rylan?"

Torn from the fantasy, he looked down at her. She pressed a hand against his chest, not quite pushing him away but not far from it, either, and while there was arousal in her gaze, there was something else, too.

Fear.

The same fear he'd cursed other men for daring to put on her face.

He closed his eyes and filled his lungs, once, twice, then

made his mouth and his hands both soft, holding her instead of gripping her. "Sorry. Just—" The emotion he'd felt, standing in the middle of a museum, listening to her as she described why an image of a man reading a book had moved her so deeply swept over him. A helpless smile stole over his lips. "You look so beautiful when you talk about the things you love."

Her cheeks bloomed, and she glanced away, but he wasn't having any of that.

Taking hold of her chin, he tilted her head up, all gentleness in his motions. He darted his gaze between her eyes. "You are," he insisted. "The whole time you were talking, I wanted to..."

He'd wanted to stay there, listening to her forever. She was the exact opposite of him, full where he was hollow, caring so deeply while every choice he'd had stripped from him had fed a growing, gnawing apathy. Her vibrancy was shaking his soul to life.

But he couldn't say that. Without the words to describe how she was confusing everything, he showed her the best he could, dipping down to capture her mouth. He'd wanted to do that, too, in the museum. Wanted to kiss Monet and Degas and Picasso from her lips, until they were nothing but brushstrokes and canvas and air.

Deconstructed, precisely the way she'd said. And reassembled by an artist's knowing hands.

Feeling like he was the one being taken apart, he gripped her more tightly, with none of the possession of a few moments before but with an intensity that he couldn't quite explain. She held him right back, though, curling her hand around his nape and threading her fingers through his hair.

He took control of the kiss, trying to push all these thoughts she'd been awakening inside of him into the possession of his mouth.

She made him *feel* things, dammit, in places that had been so cold and empty for so long. Made him want to be *better*.

He swallowed down the lonely throb that thought evoked in him—the undeniable knowledge of all the ways he was lacking, especially now.

He'd left all of his responsibilities behind, had discarded the life he'd been forced into after his father's bullshit had been exposed. He'd been directionless ever since. But here, with her, he had a purpose. Clutching at her hips, he crushed her closer to his chest, bending his will to the warm pleasure of contact. The needy thread of desire pulsing just beneath his skin.

She moaned and opened wide to him, letting him lick into her mouth. The scratch of nails against his scalp set the low burning inside of him thrumming hotter, and everything came into a sharp kind of focus. He wanted inside—wanted to fuck and touch, and be touched, but more than that he wanted to *give* her something.

With his heart hammering and his own need a dull, dense ache, he walked her backward toward the bed. He pressed on her shoulder until she sat, and then he dropped to his knees. Her legs fell apart with the barest of prompting. Dragging both palms up the curves of her calves, he licked his lips. Looked up at her for permission as he skimmed his hands up her thighs, rucking her skirt up higher. When he slipped his fingertip along the elastic of her underwear, her breath stuttered in her chest. The fabric was damp and hot, the perfume of her cunt a soft presence in the air, one that made him even harder.

He slid his thumb along the center panel of her panties as

he stared into her eyes. "This. The whole time you were talking about art. I wanted to do this."

"What?" She'd dug one hand into the hem of her skirt, clenching it in a fist so tight her knuckles paled. "Get between my legs?"

But it had been more than that. He shook his head and leaned down, kissed one knee. Then higher, on the inside of her thigh. With his lips still pressed to her flesh, he curled his fingers into the waistband of her underwear. Cast his gaze up the length of her body. "To thank you." For so many things he wasn't ready to say aloud. So instead he lifted his chin and smirked. "For teaching me about art."

"Oh, really?" Her words and tone were all skepticism, but she lifted up when he prompted, letting him tug her panties down. He eased them over her feet and spread her legs again, holding them wide with his hands on her thighs.

"Really."

He'd wanted to thank her for letting him see what she was seeing when she looked at ancient paintings, for helping him understand what she was trying to do in her own battered sketchbook.

For giving him this week and all of its diversions, and making him talk about himself, if only a little.

"Well." It came out like a sigh. She was uncomfortable. Twitchy and nervous, and her thighs kept pressing against his hands as if she were trying subtly to close them. None of it was as bad as that first night, but he still wanted to shake her—to remind her that only good things were going to happen here. Her throat bobbed. "You're welcome?"

"You can't say 'you're welcome' until I've finished with my thank you."

"You weren't done?"

He raised his brows. "Believe me. You'll know it when I'm finished with you."

He hadn't even started yet.

With that promise in the air—with the scent of her driving him mad and with his ribs ready to burst, he slipped his fingers along the soft, pink folds of her. He held them open and ducked his head, transcribing his actions, looking up into her eyes before taking a first gentle lick.

Just like the first time, she was all sweetness and musk and the salt-sweat taste of sex against his tongue. She wasn't as desperate—he hadn't worked her up as hard, but he was cresting on his own desire, and he dug in, unreserved and unabashed. He worked teasing circles over her clit and then dipped down to lick inside. Her fingers wound themselves into his hair, finally letting go of the hem of her skirt, and he shifted the fabric higher. There was still something so illicit to it, though, even if he'd lost all sense of shame so many years ago. He knelt there, completely dressed, with his head up a girl's skirt, eating her out on the edge of a bed. It was juvenile, and it was beneath him. And it was *fantastic*.

The noise she made when he pressed his fingers inside had his hand digging into the tender flesh of her thigh, his eyes closing as he sucked her clit between his lips. She'd shown him how and where to touch the night before, had taken the buzzing end of that vibrator and pressed it just—

Her knee jerked up, a sharp shock of impact against his shoulder, and her moan was the most uninhibited he'd heard. He caught her leg before she could do more damage, throwing it over his shoulder and swiping harder with his tongue, curling his fingers, trying to match the way she'd angled the glass as she'd thrust it home.

She jerked hard at his hair, and fuck, it hurt, but in the best way. She tried to let go, starting to stutter out some kind of apology, but he grabbed her hand and put it exactly where it had been.

He parted from her flesh just long enough to glare up at her. "Don't you dare hold back."

Not after all the progress they'd made, not when she was finally starting to give him exactly what he'd wanted.

Even if it wasn't anything like what he thought he'd been looking for when they'd first begun.

It didn't take long after that. As if a spell of her own inhibitions and all that ingrained doubt had suddenly melted away, she gave in to it, pressing her hips forward. He gave her another finger beside the first two, filling her up the way that someday—God, he hoped, someday—he was going to do for real. Kissed her clit wet and sloppy, lapping up the slick taste of her, and when she finally tensed, he locked in. Didn't change a thing, kept pressing and pressing, circling right where—

"Fuck!"

Her walls clamped down around his fingers, thick waves of pulses squeezing him tight as she arched backward, the hand in his hair yanking hard, sending a shock of pain and need straight down to the roots.

And he was dying for it. Was desperate to rise up over her and get himself right up in all that slick, shove himself home and take what he wanted.

Except before he could even ask—before she could give him that *look* again, the one that turned all thoughts of his own pleasure to ash and dust, she was urging him upward.

He parted from her sex, tugging his fingers free, and then she was kissing the wetness from his lips.

"You're welcome," she said. It was breathless and harsh, needy in a way he'd yet to hear from her.

And practically before the syllables were out, she was shoving him over. Getting him onto his back on the bed, and straddling his hips, and he was so ready he could scarcely think to slow things down.

But he didn't have to.

Before doubt could creep in, she put his hand where he was aching for her and cupped him oh so perfectly through his jeans. Her face was flushed and mottled, her hair a mess, and she was beautiful.

She rose up over him and said, "Now it's my turn to thank you."

Kate's body was still pulsing with aftershocks and she was kneeling there, bare beneath her skirt with her hand on a man's cock. He'd made her come, and it had been so *easy*. In these few short days he'd stripped her of her inhibitions, and without them, she'd had nothing left to do but spread her legs and hold on to his hair and let him.

And she was so grateful it hurt.

She didn't have any condoms—she hadn't come to Paris planning for any of this—but she bet he did. Ignoring the taste that lingered there, she kissed his mouth and closed her eyes. She planted one hand beside his head while with the other she worked at his fly. These past few times, she'd scarcely touched him, and he'd seemed fine with that, but it was time.

Fear closed the back of her throat, but she pushed it down. God*dammi*t all.

She was sick and tired of her own hang-ups, of letting the past taint the present the way she always did, in her life and in this bed. This time, sex would work. It had to work.

A little of the fog of orgasm cleared as she got her hand into his boxers, curling it around hard flesh. He was big, but she was as ready as she'd ever be. It probably wouldn't hurt. And she'd be glad she had, later. When she was back in New York alone, remembering the only man who'd ever made her feel like this, and he was here, doing whatever he'd done before he'd decided to do it with her.

A noise of distress fought its way past her throat.

"Hey. Hey."

A warm hand cupped her jaw, edging her away. She sat back, and he grasped her wrist, stilling it against his flesh. His eyes were dark with need, and he was hard in her grasp. She gazed down at him, confused. "What?"

He shook his head. "You seemed a little..." He trailed off, but she could hear the words, and her skin felt hot. *Frigid, scared, stiff.* He stroked his thumb against her cheek, and his voice went softer. "I want you. So much. But we only do what you want to do, and if you're not ready..." He shrugged, but he let go of her wrist, sliding his hand up her arm to her shoulder.

God, this was so frustrating. She wanted to be ready. He'd made her feel so good, and if she was ever going to love sex, it would be with him.

Except, in the end, a voice in the back of her mind whispered *no*.

Forget the fear of physical pain.

Her heart clenched just looking at him. The sharp corners of the jaw that had drawn her in in the first place, and then the things she'd come to love about him since then. The wavy, dark strands of his hair and how they stood up on end once she'd had her hands in them. The subtle cleft of his chin.

The depths behind the piercing blue of his eyes.

He was beautiful and wounded, kind and gentle and so guarded that when he let her see even a fraction of himself, it took her breath away. Already, she felt too much. If she let him inside of her, if he made it as good as he had promised to...

Her ribs squeezed so tightly it ached.

If she let this happen between them, how would she ever stop herself from loving him?

The answer pulsed its way through her chest: She couldn't.

She couldn't go through with this.

He must have seen her decision slide across her face, because the questions around his eyes smoothed away. He pulled her down for another kiss. "It's fine." The words washed warm against her lips. He grinned. "I may die a little, but it's fine."

And she couldn't help it. She laughed. "I wouldn't want that."

"A little death never hurt anybody."

She chuckled at the pun, unsure if it had been intentional or not, but then it didn't matter anymore, because his mouth was warm and soft, the kisses tasting of heat, and of a fire barely banked. His hands traversed her spine and sides, slowly coming to rest on her hips. A shiver moved through her. Her body hummed with satisfaction, but want still pulsed through her veins.

She wanted to give him *something*.

With her eyes closed, she parted from his mouth to kiss down the line of his throat, rasping her teeth against the stubble on his jaw. It was rough, his skin salty and male, and the little spot of boldness in her grew.

"Kate..." He threaded his fingers through her hair, neither pushing her up nor down so much as holding on.

There was something more than want or need or even boldness going on here. Something like power.

Her reservations slid away as she undid one button of his shirt and then the next. There was still the cotton layer of his undershirt beneath it, but she kissed her way along the center of his chest regardless. When she reached the bottom of his rib cage, she shoved the fabric up. His abdomen was firm and smooth. She nosed the lines of muscle, flicked out the tip of her tongue to taste the flesh beside his navel.

With a deep breath, she pushed aside the open denim of his jeans.

His fingers tightened against her scalp. "You don't have to."

She looked up the length of his body, and God, his eyes. The sensation of power in her hands swelled. "Do you want me to?"

He threw his head back, exposing the line of his throat, huffing out a sigh of laughter that sounded pained. "Fuck. More than anything." He looked at her again, lifting his other hand to draw a fingertip along the edges of her lips. "Your mouth would look so good around my cock."

Her heart felt like it skipped a beat, and even sated as she was, her sex throbbed. She lowered her head, resting her brow against his hip.

Then, before she could stop herself, she tugged the waistband of his boxers down.

She'd seen him before. Touched him and let him come against her, but being so close was another thing entirely. He smelled like sex, and he felt like silk beneath her fingertips, searing hot and wet at the tip. When she skimmed her thumb down the length of him, the foreskin shifted, uncovering more of the dusky flesh beneath.

Sated as she was, a tickle of arousal moved through her, and she was tempted to dive right in. To find out what noises he made when she was the one bringing him to the edge. But he'd been so patient with her, had taken the time to find out exactly what drove her mad.

She barely recognized her own voice, deepened by lust, as she asked, "What about you? What do you like?"

"Your hands on me." His breath cut off when she curled her fingers around his base. "Fuck." As she took a slow stroke up the shaft, his eyes slipped closed, his head tipping back. "Everything you're doing feels good."

He looked amazing like this, the tendons in his neck straining, abdominals tensing.

Heat spread through her. And suddenly she *got* it. Why he looked at her the way he did, why he seemed so desperate to touch her and make her come.

A hot spark of understanding lighting off inside her, she tightened her grip, and fluid beaded up at his tip.

"Everything you're doing feels *really* good," he revised, biting back a groan.

Triumph echoed behind her ribs, but it wasn't enough. She wanted more.

She let him go, drifting a hand over his thigh. She felt too hot all over, while at the same time prickles of cold dotted her skin.

She dropped off the bed and sank to her knees between his legs.

His moan was loud this time as she took him in the circle of her fist. "Whatever you want to do," he said, sounding earnest, and like it was killing him not to tug her down and guide himself between her lips.

So she turned it on him. "What do you want me to do?"

He cursed aloud, fisting his hands into the bedspread beneath him. "I wanna fuck your mouth."

Lightning blazed through her abdomen and up her ribs. How would that feel? Part of her remembered exactly how it felt to be used that way, but this was different. Rylan was different.

Rylan would make sure it was good.

Still, she shook her head. "What do you want *me* to do?"

"Lick it." There was no hesitation. "Right at the head—yeah." A noise punched from his lungs when she did just that. "Fuck, that's perfect. Get your tongue all over me. Nice and wet."

He tasted like salt, marred by a hint of bitterness, but the warm feeling in her sex and in her chest more than made up for it. He put one hand on her shoulder, light and stabilizing. Just heavy enough to ground her to the earth.

His thumb stroked over her collarbone. "Now open up. Let it slide inside. That's it. *Oh.*"

She knew this part. But it had never felt so good to her before. The way his hips flexed and the noises he made all fed the fire deep inside. Taking a deep breath, she wrapped her lips around the solid flesh, taking him in.

"Jesus. Looks better than I thought it would." His other hand came up, fingertips soft against her lips where they were stretched around him. He stuttered out a long breath as she took him farther. "Fuck *looking* good. You feel...oh shit...wet and warm..."

She remembered this—the weird shame of his praise and how it turned her on in spite of herself. She squirmed, pressing her thighs together.

"You like sucking me?" he asked.

Desire burned through her as she popped off long enough to nod.

His fingers tightened on her shoulder. "So good..."

He trailed off, letting silence fill in around them, pierced only by the soft, slick sounds of her mouth on his flesh. By his breathing and by how much she liked this. How much she loved it.

"Move your hand," he urged.

And she loved that even more. The motion was easy, a wet glide as she followed her mouth with the tight curl of her hand, up and down. His hips rocked up into it, not enough to choke her. She followed his pace, and she was lost in it. Wanted so much for him to—

"Baby—" he started. The muscles of his legs were coiled, his abdomen tight, and the way he sounded..."I'm gonna—" His fingers threaded through her hair, a light tug of warning as his voice cut off, the desperation in it making her burn.

She stayed right on him. Let the first hot pulses coat her tongue, swallowing what she could. When he twitched and pushed her off, she swiped her wrist across her mouth and he *growled.*

"Holy hell, Kate." He hauled her up bodily, sitting up as he got her on his lap. He kissed his own release from her mouth, practically devouring her as he slid his hand back under her skirt.

No easing in this time, thank God. His thumb pulsed over her clit, and she was too sensitive—he'd just made her come with his mouth, but when his fingers pushed inside, she all but sobbed against his lips.

"Beautiful." He broke their kiss to stare right into her eyes, his lips parted, gaze fiery as he worked her faster, pressed deeper.

Her climax shocked her with how suddenly it came over her. Hot liquid boiled inside, and when it burst, she dug her nails into his skin. Buried her face in his neck and screamed.

All she could think, as he held her, was that she'd never known.

Twenty-two years old, and two partners under her belt, and how, how, how had she never known?

chapter FOURTEEN

Sunlight filtered through the gauzy curtains over their window. They must've forgotten to pull the heavier shades the night before.

Just as well.

Rubbing the sleep from his eyes, Rylan turned over in the bed. Kate was still asleep, her hair mussed. She'd insisted on wearing a tank top and some pretty, lacy panties to bed, but the way the sheets were tangled around her, he could almost imagine she was naked.

God, her skin was so smooth and soft. His morning arousal gave a little twitch, and he reached down to adjust himself inside the boxers he'd resigned himself to keeping on for her. All she'd had to do was give him that *look* as he'd been undressing.

All she ever seemed to have to do was give him a look, and he was doing a whole host of things he normally never would.

That should probably be bothering him more.

She made a little sound in her sleep, snuffling and burrowing her face against the pillow. She was resting on her side, twisted away from him, the sheets tucked under her arm and rucked up across the middle of her thigh, leaving her long, bare calf exposed.

He didn't want to wake her, but he couldn't resist. Propping himself up on one elbow, he reached his other hand out, skimming it along her shoulder and pushing her hair aside. A huff of a sigh escaped her lips, but she barely stirred, so he shifted closer.

His chest fit to her spine like they'd been made to lock together that way, and he set his lips to the side of her throat. Trailing a line of soft, sucking kisses along that sleep-warm skin, he let his erection graze her rear and swallowed the groan the contact pulled from him. If they were fucking already, he could pull the panel of her panties to the side. Be buried in all that nice, slick warmth. Take her nice and slow, rocking them to a sweet morning peak.

If they were fucking.

He breathed his want into her skin and grazed the backs of his knuckles down her arm. She hummed, finally showing signs of life as she let him entwine their hands.

"What time is it?" she asked.

"Early." He had no idea, honestly. All he knew was that she was beautiful, and she felt so good against him. He could stay there all day, kissing her and trailing his hands across her skin.

But Kate had other things in mind. Lifting her head, she glanced around. "Ugh, it's after eight," she said, flopping back down and covering her eyes with her arm.

That had him looking for the clock, too. He never slept so late. Sure enough, though, the bright red numbers read 8:17.

Huh.

He shrugged, then resituated himself on his stomach, his hard-on pressing into the mattress as he held himself over her, dipping to kiss her cheek and her ear and her chin. "Day's a-wasting?" He peeled her hand away from her eyes.

But what waited for him wasn't the easy flirtiness he'd been hoping for. Instead, there was actual anxiety. "Yeah, actually. It kind of is."

"Nothing opens until nine anyway. So we grab croissants to go. No harm done." He leaned in to kiss her mouth.

She let him, for a minute, but all too soon she was pulling back. "We should get up."

"I like getting down better."

"Ugh, do you ever stop?"

"Not if I can help it."

She was a mess of mixed signals, body melting beneath his kisses even as she was pushing him back. She half sat up. "Do you want first shower or should I?"

"We could share."

He'd love that. She was always putting her damn clothes back on. Even when she let him get her naked, it was never for long. In the shower, he could touch her all over. Wash her back. Maybe warm her up enough to let him get his hand or his mouth between her thighs.

Or maybe not, considering the look she was giving him.

"What?" he asked. "I hate to waste water, is all."

"You hate to waste an opportunity to get me undressed."

"Waste is a sin in all its forms."

Rolling her eyes, she put her hand right in his face and shoved him away. Apparently, she really meant it this time. She got her legs under her and clambered off the bed, heading toward the bathroom.

"Kate—"

She closed the door behind herself before he could say anything further.

Well, great.

He lay down again on his back, staring up at the ceiling. The light on his phone was blinking, but he didn't want to deal with any of the shit that could be waiting for him. The people from his father's company. McConnell, with his casual updates that fulfilled his duties while making it perfectly clear he'd be happy if Rylan stayed away. Or Thomas with his even worse entreaties to return and set things right. His sister. God, Lexie was the worst. He missed her fiercely, but the only thing she could talk about these days was how much he was letting her down.

He was letting them all down, but they could rot. He'd given them enough. Someday maybe they'd understand that. Until then, they could all wait another goddamn day—or another year. He stretched an arm out to flip the screen over so he wouldn't have to look at the alert.

In the other room, the water for the shower turned on, and he clunked his fist against the headboard. His morning wood had subsided a little, but it wouldn't take much to get it going again. Just thinking about Kate standing underneath the spray, soap bubbles clinging to her curves...

"You coming?"

He startled, sitting up all at once. Somehow, he'd missed the door opening again. And there she stood, leaning against it, invitation written all over her face.

"Hopefully I'm about to be," he mumbled under his breath.

He tossed the sheets off and launched himself out of bed. A handful of strides, and he was on her, picking her up and spinning her around. When he set her down, it was with one hand coming to cup the back of her neck, pulling her into a long, filthy kiss. She didn't fight him this time, so he reached for the hem of her top and pushed it up.

"What's your hurry?" she asked as she let him lift it over her head.

"Told you. Hate to waste water."

"Uh-huh."

Her underwear and his followed quickly enough. His erection pressed against the soft skin of her abdomen and he groaned. "Come on," he said, tugging her toward the shower. "Before I have to eat you out on the countertop."

"Is that supposed to dissuade me?"

He didn't even know.

Somehow or other, they managed to get the shower curtain shoved aside. He climbed in, barely letting go of her as he dragged her in after. Around them, the water threw up little licks of steam as it beat down on their skin, and it was perfect.

It got even better when she reached between them and got a hand around his cock.

"Fuck." He bit down harder on her lip than he'd meant to.

"Okay?" she asked.

"So okay."

He kissed her and kissed her, curling his hands around her tits. All slippery with water, they fit just right in the palms of his hands, and they pebbled up nice and hard when he stroked her nipples with his thumbs. She made the best little noises, too, and what had been starting to look like a letdown of a morning was positively rosy once she got a good rhythm going.

Letting go of one of her breasts, he felt around blindly behind his back until he connected with a bar of soap. He grabbed it and lathered it up, then wrapped his hand around hers. "A little tighter," he urged, and *fuck*, yeah. "That's right."

He rocked his hips, fucking into their fists, and with the soap it was all easy and slick. He clutched her close, mouth open against her temple, urging her faster and faster until—

The feeling came all the way from his toes, drawing his balls tight before exploding forward in a rush. He might have blanked out for a second, and his knees wobbled. He threw a hand out to brace himself against the tile.

She laughed as he twitched. He was shockingly sensitive in her grip as she pumped the last of it out of him. When he couldn't take it anymore, he stilled her wrist, shuddering as she dragged her palm over the head before letting him go. He rubbed his fingers over hers, smoothing the mess away, then caught her face in his hands.

He kissed her, soft and grateful. "What brought that on?"

"You seemed like you needed it."

Kind of an overstatement, but he wasn't objecting.

She turned her face away, looking down and kissing his chest. He wrapped her up in his arms and squeezed her tight.

"Can I return the favor?"

She shook her head. "Maybe tonight."

Disappointing, but not exactly a surprise. Loosening his hold, he pressed his lips to hers. "Definitely tonight." He paused before he let her go; considering what she'd told him about her sex life before this, he wanted to make sure. "You know you didn't have to do that, right? Guys can't *actually* die of blue balls."

"I know." She still wasn't quite looking at him, but there was a sly smile spreading across her face. A new, different one from any he'd seen on her before. "I wanted to."

"Okay." He kissed the top of her head and pulled away.

He set down the bar of soap he'd somehow managed to hold on to through it all and perused the collection of little bottles lining the built-in shelf. When he found one that said shampoo, he picked it up and poured some into his palm.

"Didn't you bring your own?" she asked.

"Yeah. But this isn't for me. Turn around."

She leveled him with a questioning look but did as he'd asked. Her hair was wet enough from the time they'd spent messing around. With gentle hands, he started working the shampoo into it. The slowly forming suds smelled sweet. Not overpowering. Just nice.

"I love your hair," he said quietly.

She shivered.

He took his time, massaging her scalp, giving her the attention she'd given to him sexually, but in a different way. Taking care of her like this...it made something in his heart feel raw.

He dropped his hands and shifted to put his back to the tile. "You can have the water."

She gave him another, different look, then snuck past him, tilting her head down into the spray.

The water made the soap cascade along her curves, soft white washes of foam caressing pale skin. His body was still ringing with satisfaction, but looking at her made him want to start things all over again.

To distract himself, he plucked his own shampoo off a different shelf. Working it into his hair with brisk efficiency, he turned his mind to other things.

"So I was thinking," he said.

"Hmm?"

"How do you feel about going to Versailles today?" Girls tended to like all the frilly décor and dresses and things. Not that he took many women there. It was a bit of a trek, after all. But he wouldn't mind a train ride into the country with her.

She twisted around, grabbing a little bottle of conditioner to work into her hair. "I don't know."

He was getting into the idea now, though. He could take her around the castle, then they could grab a nice dinner somewhere outside the city. Get some fresh air. Walk around, hand in hand, like a couple of romantics.

It'd be different. Nice.

"I think you'd like it. It's a weekday, so the crowds won't be too bad."

"I just—" Her tone made him come up short.

Shampoo threatened to drip into his eyes. He wiped it away with his wrist. She sighed, rinsing the conditioner out of her hair before trading places with him again so he could scrub at his own.

His eyes were still closed, and her voice only barely rose over the pounding of the water.

"I was thinking maybe I'd head out and do my own thing today."

Oh. "Oh."

"I mean, I've only got three full days left, and I haven't gotten nearly as much drawing done as I'd planned to. I've still got all these things to figure out before I go home. And I've been having fun with you, but..."

She trailed off, but he could fill in the blanks. He was a diversion. A distraction. She had other things to worry about.

The whole thing made him feel sort of hollow.

Holding his tongue, he took a little longer under the spray

than he really needed. She had limited time here and a lot to do, but he had limited time, too. Limited time with her. Limited time to spend not bored and alone and spinning his wheels.

When he couldn't pretend to have any more soap in his hair, he sighed and turned around. "Fine. No problem."

Her expression was hopeful in a way that just squeezed the emptiness harder. "You sure?"

"Yeah. Whatever you need to do. We can hit Versailles tomorrow." He hesitated, working to sound nonchalant. "If you have time."

"We'll see." She had a mesh pouf in her hand and started working a softly scented lather over her chest.

He flexed his hands at his sides. Then gave up. Keeping his distance was fucking stupid, especially in a five-by-two-foot tub.

"Here. Let me."

He reached out and took the sponge from her, grazing her skin as he did. She consented, flipping her hair out of the way and turning so he could soap her back. He traced the sloping lines of her body with an intensity that surprised even him. Memorizing.

"The thing is——" She cut herself off, and he paused, surprised. "With wanting to go work on some art stuff today."

"Yeah?" He returned to sliding the sponge along her curves.

"Remember how I came here to *find myself?*" Her inflection held the same self-mocking lilt to it as the first time they'd met. When she'd admitted to being an artist and a dreamer, and had begun to wrap him around her finger.

So he echoed it, too, his smile wry. "It's a romantic notion."

"But it's actually true." She turned, and he let his hand drop to his side. She took the sponge from him and bent to soap her legs. When she straightened up again, determination colored her expression. "I got accepted into an MFA program."

His brows rose toward his hairline. A master of fine arts? That was a pretty big deal. "Wow. Congratulations."

Pride warred with demureness in her tone, making her voice pitch higher. "At a really good school, too. At Columbia. In New York, so I can keep my apartment and everything."

"So what's the debate?"

"I didn't want to put all my eggs in one basket. So I applied for a bunch of jobs, too. And I got offered one of them right before I left." She hesitated before adding, "At an ad agency. Entry level, but it would pay the bills."

"Well, that's great, too." Insane that she would even be considering it when she had a chance to pursue what she obviously loved, but great. He guessed.

She pointed toward the water, and he shifted, making room for her to trade places with him. As she stepped beneath the spray, the lather twisted and ran, sliding in foaming sheets along her form, and his throat went dry.

She rinsed herself off in a way that must have been designed to torture him, then hung up her pouf and sluiced the water from her eyes. "I can't do both, is all. I have to decide."

"Is it really that much of a decision?"

"Yeah. Just the biggest one ever." She twisted her knuckles. "So this whole trip—it was supposed to be about finding inspiration, or discovering myself, or whatever. But it's about deciding some things, too."

He couldn't hide his confusion anymore. "But you love art."

She made a snorting sound. "I love eating, too."

"But you *love* art." He wasn't letting that go.

"Love isn't always enough, you know. People don't make a living painting."

It sounded like she was parroting back someone else's words.

He shook his head. "*You* could."

She dropped his gaze, and he reached out, putting a hand on her shoulder and the other on her waist.

"You could," he repeated.

She leaned in and kissed his chest, then rested the side of her face there, inviting him to put his arms around her. "Guess I still have to prove that to myself," she said.

He held her close and bit his tongue.

She had no idea how lucky she was, having the opportunity to decide. Once upon a time, he would've given anything for that chance. Instead, there'd been his father's college and his father's company and his father's entire fucking life laid out in front of him. Even when he hadn't hated what he was doing, he'd had that hemmed-in, caged feeling pushing on him.

And here Kate had all these options. All these dreams.

He wouldn't be the one to stand in the way of her choosing to follow them.

"Okay." He pulled away enough to press his lips against her temple. "I won't pretend I'm not disappointed, but I understand."

"You sure?"

"I'm sure."

He let her go, then reached for his bar of soap. Moving quickly, he lathered it up and spread the suds across his chest.

When she spoke again, it was tentative. "Any idea what you'll do today?"

"Not sure." He hadn't really planned on having a day to kill on his own. "Catch up on some things I suppose." He probably had a lot of emails to delete. That would take at least ten minutes.

"Will you spend it here?"

He slowed the motions of his hands. "Do you want me to?"

She shrugged, then stepped aside so he could get under the spray. "I don't think I'll be gone the entire day. I could meet you when I'm done? Maybe relax a bit before dinner."

He'd like that. "Sure." He ducked his head under the water. Once he'd slicked his hair from his face, he said, "I'll head back here by late afternoon?"

"Okay."

A few hours, cooling his heels by himself. That was practically nothing.

It would feel like nothing, after. When she was gone for good.

He didn't want to think about that now. He finished rinsing off and sluiced the water from his eyes. Despite the curls of steam, she looked cold, standing near the back of the shower. He held out a hand in invitation. "Come here."

She came without resistance. Pulling her flush against his body, he opened his mouth against hers, drinking her in. He closed his eyes. And held on.

chapter FIFTEEN

Kate had let herself get way, way too comfortable with Rylan doing all the work on their adventures together. It gave her an uneasy, restless feeling, realizing how much she'd come to rely on him.

She mentally shook her head at herself. Well, not today. Today, she sat in her seat on the Metro on her own, watching the signs go by. Navigating the system and the language barrier all by herself.

Part of the appeal of foreign travel was finding your way around, after all. Immersing yourself in a whole new place, hearing different words in different tongues. She'd been missing that part of the experience, letting him do all the talking for her.

She'd gained another kind of experience, though. Her cheeks flushed warm as she tried not to think about the things they'd done these past few nights. It had been good. Really good. But that wasn't the point right now. It didn't matter how much she'd been enjoying herself—sex wasn't going to help her figure out her *life*.

And nothing was as easy as Rylan made it out to be.

Her stomach did a twisting set of flips as she recalled his reaction to her grad school dilemma. He'd made it all seem so simple. She loved art, so therefore she should go for it, give it her all. Risk everything. The very idea of it was terrifying.

And thrilling. She'd never gotten that kind of support before. Had someone stand up to her father's voice in her head, telling her that drawing was a waste of time. *She* was a waste of time.

The twisting in her stomach turned into a hard, painful clench.

Rylan's words had made her feel better about considering taking this chance. But they were just a few words, after years and years of being made to feel like she wasn't enough. Sure, Rylan's opinion was the one she wanted to believe. But she still had to prove that she was worth this chance. At least to herself.

Before long, her stop came up, and she rose, clutching her bag close as she made her way off the train and up to the surface.

Of course, that was where she really had to start paying attention.

With her mental map firmly in grasp—and her paper one tucked away so she didn't look like too much of a clueless tourist—she headed north, keeping an eye out for the things that looked familiar. More than once, she half turned to point something out or ask a question. To grab Rylan's hand.

She rolled her eyes at herself as she crossed the street. Stupid. She'd left him behind not only because she needed some time to herself—which she did.

But also because she was embarrassed to admit that she was going back to someplace she'd already been.

Her very first day with him, she'd sworn she'd find some time to go back to the Louvre, but as her time in the city had flown by, it hadn't been the old, grand paintings in the museum that had called to her to visit them again. Instead, it had been the city itself. The version of it that Rylan had shown her. The top of the hill where he'd challenged her to open her eyes.

And she had. And what she'd seen had been beautiful.

Montmartre was just as bustling, the climb to the top of Sacred Heart just as arduous as she remembered. But somehow, when she finally reached the top of it, the view of rooftops and skyscrapers and the swath of city spreading out before her toward the horizon was even more incredible. The feeling of lightness in her chest more expansive.

Winding her way through the thinner weekday morning crowds, she found a spot at the railing near where they had stood together Sunday afternoon. It was earlier in the day, so the angle of the sun was different, but she could work with that. She picked out a place to sit a few feet away and pulled out her tools, planning ahead in her mind. Graphite on paper to start with. Then if she liked where that was going, she had some other options. Colored Conté crayons or charcoal. A cheap little set of watercolors. Concentrating, she decided on a composition and dug in, sweeping her pencil across the page.

Twenty minutes later, she had a fair representation of the scene. She held it out at arm's length and looked at it, frowning. Accurate, but not emotive. It didn't give any sense at all of how it felt to *be* there, looking out across the Paris skyline.

Frustrated, she flipped the page and started again, attacking the scene with more fervor this time, laying down bolder lines and deeper swaths of shading. Trying to pour the light and air and scent of Montmartre into her page.

Her piece of charcoal snapped in half within her grip, and she blinked furiously against the blurring of her vision as she stared down at what she'd done. Her eyes prickled harder, and her breath got short. Shit, this one was even worse.

She wanted to fling the whole damn sketchbook off a cliff. Who did she think she was kidding? This was high school–level work; she'd be laughed out of critique for it. She'd be laughed out of grad school.

And there was that voice again.

The worst part was, her dad had almost never told her to her face that she wasn't good enough. He'd said it with his frowns and his disappointed sighs. His absolute disinterest when she tried to show him something.

He'd said it to her mother. Maybe he'd thought she couldn't hear, or worse, maybe he hadn't cared. She'd been right in the next room. *She's wasting her time on that crap. Like hell I'm paying for lessons. She's gotta grow up sometime...*

Maybe it was time to grow up. To give up.

She dug her nails into her palms, sharp enough to snap her out of it. No. No way in hell she was giving up. She'd spent the last ten years overcoming that kind of thinking, working to banish that doubt. It hadn't been easy, after she and her mother had finally left, but it had been good. There'd been no more tiptoeing around a quiet house, afraid to awaken a sleeping beast. There'd been a tiny apartment full of love, and there'd been her mom, telling her she could do anything. Be anything.

Just like Rylan had this morning. Rylan, who'd taken it for granted that of course she could make it in the New York art scene. Rylan, who barely knew her and who believed in her.

She swiped a clean part of her wrist across her eyes. She was better than this. She could *do* better than this.

Turning the page, she took a deep breath and closed her eyes.

In her mind, she was back there on that Sunday afternoon, on this very hill and on the footsteps of this very church. Rylan stood behind her, his chest broad and solid against her spine, his hands warm on her skin. He'd kissed her neck the way he seemed so fond of doing—the way that made her shiver and turn to mush.

She'd felt something more than just in awe of the city at the time. Tired from the climb, and close to someone who was interesting and beautiful and who treated her like she and her pleasure were precious. She'd felt... *connected*. To Paris. To her own life and breath.

To a man with more secrets than she had time.

That wasn't the doubt she needed right now.

If he were here, he'd be sitting right beside her. Quiet and supportive. Reading or playing with his phone, making random comments as they struck him. But he'd be patient. He'd let her see the city the way he knew and loved it. He'd let her make something of what she saw.

She opened her eyes again, and the cityscape in front of her seemed to resolve itself. Without looking, she traded her pencil for a stick of soft, ephemeral vine charcoal and started sweeping out the world in broad strokes.

Once she had the basic shapes sketched in, she eyed the work she'd done. She was calmer now, better able to look at it with an analytical eye. It needed more bulk. More weight. She fumbled for the little tin of powdered charcoal she'd made fun of herself for bringing at the time. It was such a mess, but when she dipped her fingertips into it, the sootiness of it felt *right*. She smeared it onto the page, using the hard pressure of her strokes to show the crevices and depths between buildings. A light blush of it to hint at the wispy expanses of clouds in the sky.

Darker, more permanent compressed charcoal now. Finer lines. Her fingers started adding in other things, too. Spindly intimations of connections between rooftops and streets, anchoring the sky to the earth. Tying her and it and the lover she could almost *feel* behind her back together in one rough portrait of a place. Of a time.

Of herself, from beyond the page.

Finally, she set her stick of charcoal aside. Her shoulders were stiff and her left foot was half-asleep, but in her lap, she had a drawing. She regarded the image for a long, long time. Relief broke over her like the dawn.

When she looked up at the city again, she smiled.

There was something *wrong* with Rylan. His incessant pacing brought him face to face with a wall again, and he groaned before turning around. Putting his back to the plaster, he covered his face with his hands.

Late afternoon. He was supposed to meet Kate back here at the room sometime in the late afternoon, and here it was, barely past two and he was wearing a hole in the carpet waiting for her.

But what else was he supposed to do? He'd gone for a run,

then stopped by the apartment to swap out some of his dirty clothes for clean ones. Had lunch in a café and caught up on the business papers. Deleted emails and voicemails from his inbox.

On a normal day, he'd read a book or watch a movie or maybe cruise for pretty girls beneath the Eiffel Tower, but none of that appealed right now. He just wanted Kate to get home already so he could ask to flip through her sketchbook. Tell her she was amazing, and that she was insane for even considering turning down a chance to pursue her art for real. Take her to dinner and then turn all his charm to getting her naked with him again.

He dug the heels of his hands into his eyes.

What the hell had he been doing with his life before this week?

He'd just about finished another circuit of this stupid, tiny room when his phone buzzed in his pocket. He pulled it out, hoping like hell that it would be some kind of diversion.

His sister's face stared back at him from the screen, and his thumb froze over the button to either accept or ignore the call.

They'd spoken a couple of times in the year he'd been away. It'd been a while, though. The last time, she'd been relentless in her insistence that he come home. He hadn't picked the phone up since.

He surprised himself when he did today.

He stared blankly at the screen as Lexie's voice, distant but there, came across the speaker. "Teddy? You there?... Teddy?"

God, he hated that nickname. Forget that he didn't even go by Theodore anymore, that he'd shed his father's name nearly a decade ago. But he brushed it off and raised the phone to his ear. "Yeah." He cleared his throat. "Hey, Lex."

"About time I got a hold of you."

Something about her tone grated his nerves. His hackles rose, and just like that, instead of annoyed and bored, he snapped into annoyed and defensive. "What do you want?"

Her eye roll was almost audible. "Nice to hear your voice, too."

He sighed. Took a deep breath. It wasn't her fault she sounded like their mother and talked like their father—all clipped sentences, all too fast. Even as children, it was like they hadn't spoken the same language sometimes. And somewhere along the way, they'd lost the dictionary.

"Sorry," he said, scrubbing a hand over his face. "How are you?"

"Same as usual. Busy." She was always busy. "You?"

"About the same as usual, too."

She made a huffed sound that got across exactly what she thought about that. "I'm sure bumming around Europe is terribly taxing."

She had no idea. He dropped his hand and rapped his fingers against the wall. "Listen, I don't mean to be a dick, but seriously. We both know this isn't a social call."

"It could be."

"It isn't." It hadn't been. Not since he'd turned his back on the mess their father had left for them, the mess his father had told him was his destiny. Not since he'd walked away.

She hesitated for a second. And then dropped all pretenses. "You still haven't gotten back to Thomas about the new board. He's been trying to get in touch with you for months."

Ugh. "Try a year."

"I don't know what you're running from——"

Yes, she did. She knew all the pressures, all the expectations, because they'd both been forced to deal with them. She'd emerged from the crucible a workaholic, desperately driven to prove their father wrong about her. While Rylan . . .

He'd worked himself to the bone, rising to the top, just the way their father had demanded. And yet with every floor he rocketed past, the walls had started to close in until he couldn't *breathe*. When the bottom had fallen out . . .

He'd looked down, only to see nothing but air underneath him, and he hadn't been willing to spend another minute in that fucking box, trying to live up to the expectations of a criminal, of a man who had ruined lives and ruined everything they'd worked for. Even their family name had become a *joke*.

So he'd gotten out, and if his sister couldn't see why he wasn't willing to get back in . . .

He curled his hand into a fist and worked his jaw. "I'll come back to New York when I'm ready to."

"And when will that be?"

If the pounding in his heart and the cold sweat on the back of his neck were anything to go by, not for a while. "I don't know."

A long couple of seconds passed. "We've only got a few months left before the board becomes permanent. If you don't step up, McConnell stays at the helm, and you know Dad trusted him as far as he could throw him——"

Rylan straightened his spine and widened his eyes, incredulous. "And I'm supposed to care about who *Dad* trusted?"

"Look, I know you're still angry."

"Damn right I am."

"But it's your company now! I'm not old enough to take

over, but you are. If you give a shit about our family, about anything—"

"If Dad had given a shit about our family he wouldn't have fucked it over in the first place. He wouldn't have fucked *us* over, he—" He snapped, shoving the side of his fist into the wall, and fuck. He hadn't let himself get so worked up about this in a year. He forced his fingers to unclench, forced his lungs to expand and contract. Between them, in the space above the center of his ribs, his father's ring hung from its chain, searing like a metal brand against his chest.

Why the hell had he answered the phone in the first place?

When Lexie spoke again, her voice was measured in a way that made the hairs on the back of his neck stand up on end. "You care. You pretend you don't. You fuck off to Europe to avoid all your responsibilities. But. You. Care."

He'd cared too much.

He laughed, and the sound was shaky in his throat. "You always did like to believe the best about everyone."

He tore the phone from his ear, ignoring whatever else Lexie was trying to say, hanging up before he could dig himself in any deeper. When he'd blanked the screen again, he stared at it for a long, aching moment, until his vision flipped and he wasn't seeing the empty screen but instead was staring at his own reflection in the glass.

After all the shit he'd given Lex about her voice. He had his father's face and his mother's eyes. Had their faithlessness and their morals, and every single thing he'd come to resent them for.

He turned his phone over so the dull plastic case was facing him. Then tossed the damned thing on the bed before he could throw it through the window.

chapter SIXTEEN

Kate was practically walking on air as she stepped off the elevator on their floor. She'd filled her sketchbook. Finished it. Images of Montmartre and Sacred Heart and the view from the top of the hill. Little cafés and giant cityscapes, and for the first time, there was this *certainty* buzzing through her veins. The drawings were good. More than that, they were her.

She couldn't wait to tell Rylan how well her day had gone. To see that conviction in his eyes when he told her she could do this after all.

At the door to their room, she rucked her shirt up and reached into the security wallet she still kept strapped around her waist. She grasped the keycard between two fingers and slipped it into the door, pausing long enough for the light to flash green before turning the handle and striding through.

"Hey!" She dropped her bag on the bed and skipped across the carpet. Rylan was at the little desk in the corner, his back to her. She tugged at the chair to spin it around. But when she saw his face, she paused, drawing her hand back. "Are you okay?"

There was something haunted to his eyes—a weariness she'd caught a glimpse of in the past, but not like this. Shadows under his cheekbones and a tightness to his jaw. A coiled anger, an old anger.

For the briefest fraction of a second, he reminded her of her dad.

She blinked and it was gone, but she was already backing away. He reached out, wrapping his hand around her wrist before she could retreat any more. With what looked like effort, he twitched the corners of his mouth upward, but it wasn't a real smile. She knew what those looked like on him now.

"I'm fine," he said. The sharpest edges of his expression bled away, but now that she'd seen them, the signs of his agitation were everywhere, in the corners of his eyes and the set of his lips. His thumb stroked across the bone of her wrist. "Sorry. Was just thinking about some things."

"Things?" She arched her brows, but something inside her was shaking. She fought to push it down. To joke with him the way she normally would. "Like what? Torture?"

He laughed at that, and it made a little of the tension in her shoulders ease. "Close."

Touching his face felt like a risk, like pushing past some kind of boundary. She did it anyway, wary, half expecting him to flinch. He did, a little bit, but allowed the contact. She swallowed to try to slake the sudden dryness in her throat. "Really, though. You okay?"

"Fine."

She almost believed it.

He turned his neck, shifting to press a kiss to her palm,

lips lingering there for a long moment. He closed his eyes. When he opened them again, they seemed clearer. He let go of her wrist to settle both hands on her hips. "How about you? How was your day? Get everything done you wanted to?"

She took a deep breath, the tremor inside of her melting away.

The dark look in his eyes might have echoed an expression she'd seen before, one that had haunted her for years. But it had only been an echo. Her father. Aaron. Any of them. Their bad moods didn't end with them getting a hold of themselves and focusing on how she was doing.

She was safe here.

She slid her palm down past his neck and collarbone to rest against his heart. "It was good. I drew a lot."

"Yeah? Can I see?"

A nervous flutter fired off behind her ribs, but she nodded.

Slipping out of his grasp, she headed over to the bed. She opened her bag and pulled out her book, planning to flip it to the work she'd done today, but before she could, he plucked it from her grasp. He sunk down to sit on the bed and opened to the very first page.

It wasn't just nerves anymore, beating inside her chest. "There's a lot of old crap in there."

Old crap she'd put so much time and energy and dedication into, and letting them be seen like this...It was like letting him see all the unfinished edges of her. A work in progress, and he'd already witnessed her naïveté in other situations. In his bed and with her hands between her legs.

She fought the instinct to rip the book from his grip.

Oblivious to how she was churning up inside, he turned the pages slowly, gazing at each with an appraising set to his jaw. Her face went another shade warmer with every amateurish imitation of another artist's style, every mistake in perspective. Every sketch that betrayed exactly what a mess she was and how little she knew.

"Really." Her voice was rough. "Some of those are ancient."

He lifted up a single finger and shook his head, asking her to be quiet without saying a word.

She resigned herself to her fate. Picking at her fingernails, she moved to sit beside him, close but not quite touching. He'd told her he liked the couple of drawings she'd shown him before, and he'd expressed such confidence in her ability to hack it in grad school. But he hadn't really known, then, had he? He hadn't seen enough to make that kind of statement, and the idea that he might take it back now, after having seen more, made her stomach clench. It hardened further about halfway through the book, when the quality of the images changed. That had been about when she'd started thinking about what she was going to do after college, a hundred futures spinning out in front of her. Grad school and office jobs. Huge risks and life sentences.

And then the image she'd drawn the day Professor Lin had pulled her aside. Told her that if she didn't define herself, she'd never make it as an artist. That she'd never sell.

He paused, hand hovering at the corner of the page.

"You were angry," he said. It was the first comment he had made.

"Scared," she corrected.

"I can see that."

He flipped past the pictures she had already shown him from the day she'd sketched outside of Notre Dame, and then he was looking at the first one she'd done today. His brow furrowed, and he turned his head to look at her. "You went back to Sacred Heart?"

"Yeah?" She didn't mean it to come out like a question, but it did.

The way he was staring at her, it was as if he could see right through her. He didn't look angry or exhausted anymore, not the way he had when she'd come through the door. But he didn't look like the confident, oversexed guy she'd taken a chance on, either.

His gaze held for a moment that felt like it went on and on. Then he lifted a hand, the tip of it stained gray from the charcoal on the edges of her sketchbook. He cupped her cheek and leaned in. The kiss, when it came, was a simple, chaste press of lips on lips, but there was a weight to it. An unspoken moment of connection, of understanding. She'd seen what he'd seen on that hilltop. Had tucked it away and treasured it, and when she'd most needed to recapture some sort of inspiration, some impetus to *make* something with her hands...

That's where she'd gone.

He let her go, drawing back, but the heat of his gaze lingered even as he returned his attention to the page. He flipped to the next and then the next, and she held her breath. This was the one she'd felt so good about, after her first set of false starts. The one she'd done with the memory of his presence flowing from her fingertips, imbuing every stroke and shade with life.

Ghosting his fingers over the dark, black marks, tracing without touching or smudging, he followed the swooping arcs she'd mapped onto the paper. For a long time, he stared at it.

Finally, he started moving through the pages again. She

watched from over his shoulder, her breath coming more easily now. These pictures didn't give her that cringing feeling
she got looking at her own work sometimes. She was proud of
these. When he reached the last one, he flicked back through
them, stopping on the one she'd drawn from the top of the
hill.

"These are incredible," he said.

The urge to demur stole over her, even as she flushed with
the praise. He'd believed in her before, and he believed in her
now. It pushed away the doubt that always plagued her. Made
the spark of her inspiration ignite. "I was just playing with
something. An idea." She pointed to the web of lines he'd
been drawn to before. "Tying everything together."

"It's great. Really." He shifted to look at her. "It's really,
really great."

And what could she say to that?

He shook his head, as if he could sense her discomfort at
taking a compliment. "I love the way you see things. And
these . . . Not that the rest of your stuff wasn't good, but the
stuff you did today. It's something different."

Her lungs felt tight, a warmth and an excitement fit to
burst behind her breast. These images had *felt* different. Still,
it hadn't just been her and her skill. "It's the city. Paris. It's
beautiful."

"No." There was such certainty to his voice. It stopped her
cold. "It's you." He shook his head. "I don't know how you
can possibly even consider not going to grad school for this.
You've got this . . ."

He trailed off. *Don't say talent, don't say talent.* People always
said that, and she hated it. It demeaned all the work that went
into what she did.

His mouth curled up into a soft, sad smile, and suddenly he wasn't talking about her future anymore. "It's how you see things, Kate. In these pictures, the ones you made today... It's like I can see through your eyes."

And there was an aching note now. She glanced up to meet his eyes.

All the edges of him were on display again. Not as jagged as before, not as tired. But they were there, and it struck her: She had no idea who this man was. What had happened to him to put those shadows in his eyes. How he felt or where he'd come from.

She wanted to, though. Desperately.

His gaze burned. As if he could hear her thoughts, he closed the book. He grazed a single fingertip along her temple beside her eye.

And then he asked her, "How do you see me?"

The strangest part was, it sounded like he actually wanted to know.

She blinked, once, then twice. With trembling hands, but with a surety she didn't know how to name, she reached for her bag and the supplies that it contained. For the fresh sketchbook she'd picked up on her way back to the hotel.

Because she had wanted this. From the very first time she'd laid eyes on him, she'd been itching for this.

"I don't know." She turned it to the blank first page. "But I'd like to find out."

Rylan glanced between Kate's face and her hands. What she was offering was clear, and it was what he'd asked for, wasn't it?

God, but his mood was twisted right now. He wanted to

be here, enjoying their last couple of days together, but after Lexie's call, all he could think about were his shirked obligations. His mother's face and his father's betrayals and everything he was missing back home. Everything he'd run away from.

All he could see was his own reflection staring back at him, and it was ugly. He didn't even want to look into his own damn eyes.

And there was a part of him, an angry, sullen piece of his soul, that wanted Kate to draw him. He wanted to look at himself through her pretty brown eyes and see the same callousness and apathy he'd been accused of so many times this year. To see it all confirmed would be a relief almost—a sign that his decision to sit here wasting his life alone was as good a choice as any.

He set her sketchbook aside before he could crush the pages with his grip.

He wanted her to draw him. And he wanted her to see something in him worth holding on to.

"Okay," he said finally, mouth dry and palms sweating. He managed a vague half smile. "What should I do?"

"Just get someplace comfortable. Sitting in that chair maybe. Or lying down?"

"Whatever you want."

She looked away, cheeks flushing.

That was interesting.

He ducked to put himself in her line of sight, quirking one eyebrow up. "What do you want?"

"Well, we—" She fidgeted, fussing with the binding of her sketchpad. It seemed to take her actual physical effort to meet his gaze. "We could do a figure drawing."

"Which means?"

"Drawing your"—she gestured vaguely at his torso—"*figure*."

It struck him all at once. "You want to draw me naked?"

She fake-smacked him with the book. "Well, it sounds dirty when you say it that way."

"It sounds dirty if you say it *any* way."

"It's not." A seriousness bled into her tone. She lifted her chin. "You're—you're beautiful. All the muscles, and your jaw and your . . . you."

Some of the ugliness that had been festering in his heart all afternoon melted away.

She shrugged, looking down again. "You are," she insisted. And she was so brave. He'd never given her enough credit for that. "The first day I met you, part of why I took that cup of coffee was your—your jaw. You were like a statue, and I wanted to get to look at you a little longer." Twisting at her knuckle, she bit her lip. "And then I got to touch you, too, and see you without your clothes, and you're just— I'd like to. If you'll let me."

Finally, she glanced up again, and his breath caught. Gears turned over in his mind, words rising up to the surface, but for once in his life, he couldn't seem to get them to spill forth.

Her face fell. "Or not. If it makes you uncomfortable, or . . ."

And what could he do? He reached out before she could turn away from him, putting a hand on her face and holding her steady as he leaned in for a kiss. Her lips were so sweet, made all the more so by the foreign warmth inside of him he couldn't seem to tamp down. And why should he?

Pulling back from the kiss, he touched his brow to hers.

"I think that's the nicest thing anyone has ever said to me."
When she scoffed, he insisted, "It is."

Sure, he'd gotten compliments before. He'd had people—
women—tell him he looked good. But this was something
else altogether.

So he tried to treat it with the respect it deserved. "I'd be
honored."

It wasn't a line and it wasn't a lie. He pressed his lips to
hers once more, then backed away.

"You want to do this now?" he asked.

"Sure. I mean, I've got all my things."

They had a couple of hours before they typically wandered off in search of dinner. He couldn't think of any
reasons to delay.

"Okay." He nodded and stood, setting his fingers to the
collar of his shirt.

And it was strange, wasn't it? The still-racing beating of
his heart and the desert of his throat. He'd gotten naked in
front of more women than he cared to count. He wasn't shy
about his body. He'd worked hard for it and kept it in the best
possible condition. It wasn't as if he'd ever been shy in front
of Kate. Hell, just this morning, he'd been wheedling to *try*
to get his clothes off in front of her. So why was this giving
him pause?

Behind him, she was fussing with something or other. He
snuck a glance over his shoulder and spied a neat little row of
materials arranged across the desk. Turning around again, he
took a deep breath.

Tucking his thumb into the placket of his shirt, he slipped
each button through its hole, then shrugged the fabric off. He
actually took the time to hang it up, and cursed at himself

in his head. Stalling. It was ridiculous—why was he stalling? He tore off his undershirt and dropped it to the ground. Took off shoes and socks, and unfastened his belt. Biting the bullet, he shoved his jeans and his boxers down as one and stepped out of them.

He turned to Kate with as much bravado as he could muster. All he had to do was make a dickhead comment about his—well, his dick, and everything would be fine. Normal.

But he met her gaze, and fuck. There was a warmth to it that was more than simple aesthetic appreciation.

Alarm bells sounded off like klaxons in his mind. He slept with tourists, with women passing through. He'd disappointed enough people, and he didn't have anything to offer a nice girl. It was better to stay unattached. Free.

But in a few short days, this girl had wound herself around him, and there wasn't any point denying it. He'd sunk his teeth in, too.

When it was over, it was going to bleed.

Right now, though, she was still *looking* at him like that. Any pervy joke he would have made died in his throat.

"Where do you want me?" he asked.

"Lie down." She gestured to where she had turned down the bed.

He let her direct him until he was positioned how she wanted him, with a handful of pillows propping him up. One arm extended toward her and the other bent under his head. Legs splayed out across the sheets.

"Perfect," she said after a moment, and she sounded as hoarse as he felt. "Do you think you can hold that for a while?"

He shifted in minute ways, but the discomfort he felt wasn't physical. "Yeah. I think so."

"Let me know when you need a break."

"Sure."

He lay there in silence for a long minute as she arranged herself in the chair, getting her sketchbook settled in her lap and selecting an instrument to draw with. And then, as far as he could tell, she just *stared* at him.

He had to turn his gaze away.

The *skritch-skritch* of pencil on paper told him she'd started working, and he had to fight the instinct to fidget all over again. *Relax. Calm.* He sank into the bed the best he could.

But no matter how deeply he breathed or how hard he focused on letting his mind drift, the simple truth was there.

He'd been naked a thousand times before. But he'd never felt it.

Not like this.

chapter SEVENTEEN

There was a certain kind of focused, aware calm that settled over Kate when she was really in the zone. Staring at the excess of riches laid out in front of her right now, though, she wasn't focused. She wasn't calm.

But she was aware.

Incredibly, brilliantly aware of Rylan's lips and eyes, the tousled mess of his hair and the stubble on his cheeks. He had the most gorgeous shoulders, taut with muscle without being bulky, and his biceps and forearms were sleek and strong. She'd always loved the feeling of his hands on her body, but she'd never truly taken in the shape of them before. Long fingers and blunt nails. The lines of tendons flexing underneath his skin.

And then there was the rest of him. With the subtle twist she'd made of his body, the crest of his hip stood out sharply, shadowing the hollow beneath it, pointing to the dips and curves of his abdominals. Solid thighs and well-formed calves. Hell, even his ankles and his feet were pretty, and she could scarcely catch her breath when she let her vision encompass the whole of him.

He wasn't hard, which was possibly the weirdest thing. She'd seen him in various stages of erectness, even seen him gently deflating in the aftermath of orgasm, but completely soft like this was new. She couldn't help the way her gaze kept being drawn back to it.

She'd touched that part of him. Had him on her tongue and in her hands and pressed up against her spine as he moaned into her ear.

And now it was hers to look at. As much as she wanted to.

With less than steady hands, she adjusted her book in her lap. She'd already done a quick couple of gesture sketches of him, waiting for him to settle. Tension lingered in his limbs, though, and she frowned. He wouldn't be able to stay still for long if he didn't relax.

"Do you want to stretch or anything?" she asked. "Get a drink?"

He blinked a couple of times, chest rising and sinking more rapidly. "Yeah, actually." He sat up in slow increments, rolling his shoulders and flexing his feet.

Just for something to do, she stood and grabbed him a bottle of water.

"Thanks." He took it from her and twisted off the top, lifting it to his mouth and taking a couple of careful, measured sips before setting it aside.

In the time she hadn't been looking, he'd pulled the sheet up to his waist. Part of her wanted to tease. He'd seemed so confident in his own skin before, but now there was a self-consciousness to him.

It was just so…unlike him.

She picked at her thumb, unable to stop staring at the drape of the cloth across his groin. "We don't have to do this, you know."

"I know." He looked down. "I'm fine."

"You sure?"

"Yeah."

"All right." She returned to her chair and picked up her pencil again.

After another minute of twisting and stretching, he shoved the sheet away and settled back against the pillows. The pose wasn't quite the same as the one she'd directed him into earlier, but that was almost better, honestly. What it lacked in drama it made up for in the way he eased into it, some of the stiffness from before bleeding away.

It was even more beautiful, and something in her heart stuttered.

"Is this okay?" he asked.

She looked up to find him gazing straight at her. It took a couple of tries to get the words to form. "It's perfect."

Flawed and perfect. *Just like you.*

She swallowed, forcing herself to relax her grip. She traced all the lines of his body in her mind one last time.

Then she turned the page and began.

It was easier, this time, to quiet his mind. He lay there, splayed out on the sheets, bare but for the chain around his neck.

He should have taken it off, probably. He hadn't thought to at the time, and with the way she was sketching away, at this point it seemed too late. Sometimes, he wondered why he wore it at all.

The scratching of her pencil on the paper settled over him, and he drifted along on it. He didn't want to throw her off by staring into her eyes, so he varied his gaze between her hands and the window and the ceiling above his head. Maybe he should have asked if he could pose with a book, or if they could turn on the television, only...

It didn't seem right, did it? He wanted to know how she saw him. She should see him with his attention undiverted.

And more, there was an energy to it. A humming static to the air surrounding them, moving from her to him and back again. This was intimate.

This was exposure.

Trying to hold still, he sucked the inside of his cheek between his teeth and bit down hard.

Maybe this was how she imagined it would be, letting him inside of her. He'd let it go; every time she'd squirmed or looked uncomfortable at the idea, he'd been quick to back off. But for the first time, now, he thought maybe he understood it. He felt vulnerable, lying there naked for her inspection. It wasn't sexual at all, but that was *why* it was so difficult for him. Sex he was good at. This—being open like this. It was something different, something he didn't quite know how to do.

He unclenched his jaw before he could draw blood. If he told her how uneasy he was, she'd probably say that they could stop again. But he felt like he was on the cusp of a revelation. If he could find a way to work through this, it would mean something. To him and to her.

The person he had been a handful of days ago told him it would get him in her pants at last. But a newer voice said that didn't matter. Whether he got off or not didn't *matter*.

If he made it through this, and if she saw in him something worth seeing...he'd earn her trust.

How much that mattered to him made him tremble.

For a long moment, he closed his eyes, focusing on the sounds of marks being made on paper. Then he shifted his attention. He relaxed his toes and his calves and his glutes. Breathed air into his fingers and his arms. Quieted the beating of his heart.

He looked again to find her staring at him in a way that made him feel not exactly vivisected, but...

Seen.

She smiled at him uncertainly, and he answered with the slightest of shakes of his head.

He let his gaze go soft and aimed it at the gauzy curtains framing the doors out onto their balcony. He gave himself over to it.

And as she kept on drawing, he felt like, somehow, deep in the empty parts of him, he was getting everything he wanted in exchange.

Kate looked down at what she'd drawn and blinked. She tilted her head from side to side and shifted her legs. Rylan had taken two more breaks in the time she'd been working, but she had scarcely moved except to reach for different materials.

Now, it was like coming out of a fog, the haze of creation receding as she examined what she'd wrought.

And it was...good.

Really good, and she didn't say that lightly. She knew better than to let herself get carried away. Ego was an ugly thing on an artist. But this was more than good. It was *right*. Exactly what she'd been going for when she'd set out to capture this man.

Holding the pad at arm's length, she regarded it more critically. She'd gotten the shape of his nose, had left some of the details of his features vague while still suggesting the parts that needed to be seen. She'd captured the pride and the self-assuredness, but between those lines, the rest of him bled through.

Vulnerability. Anger. Hurt.

There was something coiled to the man she had drawn, and the lines she'd penciled in to anchor his form to the sheets only accentuated it. He looked like he was waiting. She didn't know what for—or if he knew, even. But there was anticipation in the cant of his hips and the rigid set to his limbs. His pose spoke of relaxed ease, but it belied a readiness to walk right off the page and out of frame.

She tightened her jaw. She'd gotten that much right at least.

Shifting her gaze back to Rylan, she let the low ache that had been building in her chest all week come to the forefront. She had two full days left in Paris after today. She was the one who was going to leave. And he was going to let her.

"You okay?" His voice surprised her, interrupting the quiet that had descended on them.

"Yeah." She nodded, pulling her thoughts back to the here and now. "I'm fine."

"You sure?"

"Definitely." She tapped the corner of the page with her nail. "You good for a few more minutes?"

"Sure."

Putting the low curl of dread aside, she examined her work one more time. Made a couple of careful marks, darkening shadows and sharpening the appearance of a particular jut of muscle. She swept her gaze over it again, comparing it with the reality of the man in front of her. The drawing was as finished as it was going to be.

But she wasn't *done* yet.

Hoping he wouldn't mind, she turned the page, taking care not to smudge the work she'd just completed. She shifted in her chair to get a slightly different angle as she studied his face.

It wasn't only dread filling her belly now. It wasn't quite affection, either, though there was some of that there, too. It was deeper and warmer, and it hurt inside her chest.

Looking at him *hurt*.

So she channeled it.

With quick strokes, she tried to get down on paper how he made her feel, all twisted up and uncertain—like she was the one on display, exposed, even though he was the one stripped bare for her to see. Roughly intimating the shapes of his features, she focused on his eyes and his mouth, taking them apart into lines and shapes, distilling them into something she could understand.

But the end result didn't help. It was a portrait of the same mystifying, beautiful, inscrutable man, and she wanted to crush the paper in her hands.

A fresh page and another try, and another and another, but none of them put her any closer. Frustration made her blood hot. It wasn't the same angry, self-despairing aggravation that had nearly overtaken her up on Montmartre. It was knowing the solution to a puzzle lay just out of reach, and watching an hourglass about to run out of sand. She only had so much time.

To find herself, sure. But also to get some kind of grasp on what was happening to her, here, with him.

She turned the page once more. On the bed, he was getting restless, either because he'd gone too long without a break, or maybe because he could sense her distress. She had to calm the heck down. Now. Before it was too late and she'd lost her chance.

She took a deep breath and set down her charcoal, trading it out for a hard-leaded pencil. This time, she approached the page with all the quiet she could summon to her mind and her nerves and her hands.

Soft brushes of the graphite across the tooth of the paper. A hint of an outline. And then more line work. More and more, tracing around and across the planes of his face. The eyes she adored and the mouth she had kissed, and the man she . . .

A deep pang made her breath catch.

She didn't know Rylan. She didn't know him at all. But she knew his wit and his secrets and the careful way he'd touched her body. Brought her pleasure. Showed her around *museums* for God's sake. Opened himself up to her like this . . .

She sketched in the curve of his lips, and the last piece of the puzzle slipped into place.

She loved him.

It was written so clearly across the page—couldn't have been more clear if she'd spelled it out. Love shone from the curve of his cheek and the fall of his hair and the tender softness of his earlobe. So many tiny details, and he was going to see.

God, he was going to want to look at this and he was going to know everything.

Beyond her tunnel vision, he stirred, the rustling of sheets a low murmur of a sound, lost beneath the roaring in her ears and of her heart. Warmth on her shoulder, then blunt fingers making a dark contrast against the snowy white of her page as they tipped the book down.

It broke the spell.

She dropped the book, looking up. With the sheet draped around his waist, Rylan stood in front of her, concern twisting his frown. "Kate? You went all"—he waved his hand at her—"pale. You sure you're okay?"

She wanted to laugh.

No. She was the furthest possible thing from okay.

She'd burned her savings on an idiotic trip to Paris. Had gotten her purse stolen and had spent her days ignoring the work she'd come here to do because a *man* was paying attention to her. Was taking care of her and charming her and teaching her all sorts of things she'd never known her body could do.

So like the sad, naïve idiot she was, like her mother's daughter, she'd fallen for him. And she knew it. Without a shred of doubt, she knew.

He was going to break her heart.

She sucked in a breath like she was drowning. If the outcome was a forgone conclusion, what the hell was she doing here? She should grab her things and run back to her nice, safe hostel with its awful roommates and communal baths.

Or she could dig her feet in. There wasn't anything to lose.

If she wanted anything from him, she should go for it. Now. While she still had the chance.

chapter EIGHTEEN

If it hadn't been so scary, it would have been hilarious. Because, seriously, Rylan had driven plenty of ladies out of their minds with his cock.

But he'd never done it quite so literally before.

He stood there, wrapped up in a sheet, trying to pull Kate out of whatever sinkhole she'd fallen into. She stared at him, emotions breaking like waves across her face. Humor and anguish and resignation. One by one, they all ceded until there was only resolve.

"Kate?"

"Do you want to see?" She flipped to the first page of her sketchbook and held it out like an offering. She was still looking at him so strangely, and he wanted to shake her. To make her snap out of whatever had taken hold of her.

But in the end, he just nodded. "Of course." Extending his hand to accept it felt like stepping out onto a ledge somehow. He curled his fingers around the binding and paused, a whole new kind of apprehension taking hold. This entire thing had started when he'd asked her how she saw him. He was about to find out. But did he really want to know?

With a flash of false bravado, he cleared his throat. "You didn't make me ugly or anything, did you?"

"You tell me."

Her tone stopped him cold, because there was dread there. Christ, what the hell had she drawn?

Unable to put it off any longer, he took the book and sat down on the edge of the bed.

The first picture told him very little. It was a series of quick sketches—no detail. Just the outline of his body. He raised an eyebrow at the suggestion of his *anatomy* in one of them. But he really wasn't learning anything here. The second page was much the same, but the third...

His breath stuttered in his chest, and he jerked his head up. She was watching him look at her work, worrying her knuckles and chewing on her lip. The instinct to tell her it was amazing welled up in him. The whole thing—it was incredible. But he knew better than to spit those words out before he'd thought about it. He dipped his head again, studying the image of his own nude body, splayed out across pale sheets.

The likeness alone was remarkable, but there was more to it than that. It didn't just resemble him. It *felt* like him. Like the man he looked at in the mirror every morning, only better. If he'd questioned how she saw him, this was the answer.

She saw him too fondly. In a light he didn't deserve. From the scraps of his messed up, cobbled-together life, she'd made something beautiful.

All that time he'd spent secretly convinced that if you took away the trappings—the money and the clothes and the name—he'd be nothing. He'd taken them all off for her. Since the moment he met her, they'd all been off. And this was what she'd seen.

"It's good," he said at long last. "Like the one from Montmartre." He gazed up into her eyes. "Your perspective is all over it." It made him *feel* things, just looking at it. Things he still wasn't sure he was ready to feel.

Her expression didn't lighten any. "Keep going."

He frowned, peering down again. He wanted to keep studying this one. There were treasures inside of it. All the detail of musculature and fabric and space.

"Keep going," she insisted.

He shook his head, hesitating. If that was what she wanted...

His stomach flipped as he turned the page. She'd gone back to quicker sketches, not quite as vague as the first ones had been, and she'd narrowed in on just his shoulders and his face.

But the images were angry. Frustration bled through the marks. Some of the portraits looked just like him, while others only held the faintest resemblance.

What had she told him about Cézanne the day before? That he played with the shapes of things, making them more real by making them wrong?

It put him off balance. Did she think he was a monster? A puzzle to be figured out?

"One more," she said.

He turned the page, fearing the worst.

Only he shouldn't have.

The drawing staring out at him through the page wasn't like the others. But that didn't put him back on solid ground.

If anything, he listed further in his mind, because this one wasn't angry.

This was unbearably, achingly sad.

"Kate—"

"This is how I see you."

God. It was a web of delicate lines, silvery wisps of pencil marks. The image they created was a perfect likeness, only it evoked the exact opposite response in him as the last one had. It opened a new pit in his stomach. He wasn't so noble or so . . . so unapproachable. He was just a guy. Flawed and scared sometimes. Irresponsible and inconsiderate and so many other things his sister and his father and all the men who ran their company would have called him.

"I don't look like this," he said, quiet and unsteady.

"To me, you do."

He huffed out a wry little ghost of a laugh. "You're too kind to me."

"I'm not. You're just . . . you're gorgeous." She hesitated, as if waiting for him to say something more. When he didn't, she took his hand, lifting the sketchbook from his lap and setting it aside. Her voice was more restrained. "Thank you for letting me do this. You didn't have to, and it meant a lot to me."

"It's no problem."

"No. It was. This was hard for you."

That was an understatement, but the best he could, he shook it off. Still reeling from the vision she had shown him of himself were he a better man, he looked down at their hands. How they intertwined, her dainty, soot-stained fingers against his larger ones. His were stronger, but they were clean. They made nothing, they did nothing.

Except touch her.

When he met her gaze again, her eyes were dark, her full lips parted.

As he watched, she rose up higher on her knees, sliding a hand into his hair and pressing her lips to his. An intensity colored the edges of the kiss, an intent. He tried to give himself over to it, to the warmth and to the taste of her. But in the back of his mind, he was fixated on what she had made of him, and he didn't deserve it.

He didn't deserve the way she lifted her own shirt over her head, baring all that soft, beautiful skin. The way she unbuttoned her jeans.

It struck him all at once what she was doing. His body, already primed by her closeness and his nakedness, went instantly, shockingly hard.

"Kate—"

The look in her eyes as she pulled back left him no doubt. He swallowed, throat working against a tightness that didn't make any sense.

She slid her palm down his chest to rest over his heart. "I want this."

She couldn't possibly want it as much as he did.

And yet, for all his experience, there was something inside of him that trembled. "You don't have to."

"I know I don't." Her fingers splayed out wide across his ribs, and she looked at him with eyes that were so deep. So bold, where before they had always held fear. "Do you want me?"

His mouth went dry. "More than you know."

Gaze steady, cheeks warm, she said, "Then please. Rylan. I'm ready."

* * *

He hadn't seen it.

Even when confronted with the most obvious, incontrovertible evidence of how she felt, Rylan had let it slip right past him. The whole time he'd been staring at the lovesick drawings she'd done, he'd had those ghosts in his eyes again, and her heart had hurt. For her and for him.

There'd only been one other way to let him know. One way to satisfy the emptiness that came with the thought of holding back from him now.

It hadn't been a hardship, beginning to match his nakedness with hers. They'd been together like this enough times by now. It hadn't even taken much to offer him what she knew he'd always wanted. After all: This wasn't that one-night stand she'd had that once. Rylan wasn't drunk, and he'd proven he wasn't selfish. This wouldn't be painful. It would probably feel good.

And she'd get to keep it. Later, after she'd left him and gone back home, she would always have this to look back to.

Rylan's throat bobbed as he covered her hand with his, pressing it harder to his chest. He flicked his gaze from her eyes to her breasts to her hips and back. "Are you sure?"

Just like he had considered her drawings before rendering a verdict, she gave it the thought it deserved. Nothing in her heart wavered or changed.

Then she pulled her hand free of his. Reached back to unhook her bra and let the straps slide down her arms and hoped that was answer enough.

Dropping his gaze to the hollow of her throat, he placed a fingertip there and traced it through the space between her breasts, down to her navel, where he stopped. He looked her in the eyes again. "You change your mind and you tell me. Anything that makes you uncomfortable. If anything I do, if I touch you wrong or…"

She took his hand and brought it to the gap where she'd undone her jeans. He licked his lips and nodded. Together, they pushed the denim off her hips, taking her underwear with it. She grasped the sheet he'd draped across his waist and set it aside.

And then they were naked. Together. She shivered, because it was different this time, with her offering him everything. Knowing how deeply he'd affected her in this handful of days.

Refusing to be frightened, she shifted, edging closer to straddle his hips. It trapped the hard length of him between their bodies as she curled her fingers around his neck and pulled him into a kiss. She opened her mouth, and he slid his tongue inside, letting out a choked sound of desire as he wrapped his arms around her. God. He felt so good like this, so warm and solid and protective. With one broad palm between her shoulder blades, he folded the other around her hip, sliding it down to cup her backside before gliding it along her thigh. Her breasts were pressed against his chest, the tips tingling as they rubbed against firm flesh.

She got lost in it, melting into him, an ache of need growing soft and hot and wet within her sex. With long, lush kisses that went on and on, he kept her close, and how had she ever doubted that this would be how sex would feel with him? Safe. Like nothing could hurt her—not even him.

She shifted her hips against him, and he moaned into her mouth. He pulled back from her lips, dropping to suck kisses across her neck and jaw.

"How do you want this to go?"

"I don't know." She let her head fall to the side, just wanting him to keep doing what he was doing. She gripped his shoulder tighter as he scraped his teeth against her throat. "However you want. Whatever you—"

He *shh*ed her. "I'll take care of you."

God, how had he known that was exactly what she needed him to say? The heat building between her legs bloomed anew as he lifted her, twisting them both until she was falling into the mattress. He shoved aside the mound of pillows he had rested on while she had sketched. She grabbed at him when he moved to pull away.

"Just a second," he promised.

She shivered without his heat, but she didn't reach for the covers. It felt strange to be lying there nude while she waited for him, except—except this had to have been how it had felt for him. For a couple of hours, he had laid himself out for her, entirely exposed.

The least she could do was wait a couple of minutes and not be afraid.

He'd retreated to the foot of the bed, and she furrowed her brows in confusion for a second before he picked up her sketchbook. How could she have forgotten it was there? With absolute care, he closed it and put it on the desk in the corner, turning back to smirk at her. "Wouldn't want it to get messed up."

Then he padded over to his bag and unzipped one of the little pockets on the side. He palmed something, and she frowned, confused until she realized what it had to be.

He set the condom packet on the bedside table before coming to sit on the edge of the mattress beside her. He looked her over, and she tried not to fidget or wilt beneath his gaze. With the softest touch, he ran the backs of his knuckles down the length of her side, tracing the curve of her breast and the dip of her navel. The swell of her hip.

"What I would give to be able to draw right now."

Her lip wobbled, and she couldn't take it anymore. "Come here," she urged, intertwining her fingers with his and tugging him down.

He came willingly enough, rolling to lie beside her, his front flush against her thigh. As he gazed down at her, a warmth overtook her, and for a moment, she could pretend. This wasn't a brief foray into intimacy, and it wasn't just her who had gotten attached.

He let her have her moment. His expression still achingly soft, he shifted forward to kiss her again. It was all the soft motion of his mouth on hers and the heat of his body against her skin.

And then it was more. As he licked into her mouth, he danced his fingertips across her abdomen, lower and lower. Each pass had the restless feeling inside her growing, and she shifted, trying to curve into his touch. She ran her hand up and down his arm, wanting to coax him and not wanting to ask.

When he finally slipped his fingers into the swelter of her sex, she whined, and he smiled, and she wanted to smack him or kiss him or . . . or more.

She panted against the soft roll of pleasure he wrung from her. "I thought we were going to . . ."

"We are." He shifted to kiss the corner of her lips, her chin, her jaw. "But not until you're dying for it. Gonna make you so wet for it, Kate." His swallow and his breath against her ear made her pulse. "And then. Only then, when you're ready to scream. When you're slick all down your thighs. That's when I'll know you're ready." He scraped his teeth against her lobe. Pressed the searing flesh of his own desire to her hip, and she shuddered. "Not a moment before that."

She closed her eyes against the feeling.

No wonder no other man had ever succeeded in making her come. None of them had ever approached it like this. Like a privilege and a job, and something they'd achieve if it were the last thing they ever managed to do.

He was good to his word, too. With careful fingers, he took her apart, two of them inside and pressing just exactly where she needed them, his thumb moving in tight circles against her clit. All the while, he kept his lips on her skin, kissing and sucking and *biting*, and when he teased her nipple with his teeth, she twisted hard. Trembling with the electricity shooting between her breasts and her sex and the heat that was rising to a boil, she shifted onto her side, reaching for him, wanting him closer before this feeling consumed her and turned her to ash, but he kept her still.

"You're there, aren't you?" He pulled his fingers free, and she threw her head back, gritting her teeth. "How does that feel? Does it leave you empty and needy and shaking?"

"Yes, God, yes."

Before she knew it, he was on top of her, two hands planted on the pillow beside her head, and the soaring crest of oblivion she had been hovering on fell away, leaving her reeling. The tip of his erection dragged, hot against her hip. She reached down to grasp it, to get that silky flesh in her palm, but he tilted away. Put his face right into her vision, and, God. His eyes were so dark, the intensity of it overwhelming, and perfect, and maybe she wasn't the only one in this.

Maybe it wasn't just her, feeling like everything had changed.

He put his hand on her face. "Tell me," he said, voice rough.

And the words almost slipped out. *I love you. Don't leave. Don't let me go.*

She came to her senses just in time. When he didn't stop her, she curled her hand around his hip. Lifted the other to touch his face.

"I want you." It felt like it took all of her breath, and it might as well have. The force of his kiss stole anything else she had left in her. He dropped down, rocking the hot, thick length of him through the valley of her thighs in an intimation of what he was going to do, so close but not quite there, torment for them both for an instant.

And then he was in motion. He rose up onto his knees and grabbed the condom, tearing it open and getting it rolled on before she could move to try to help. When he held himself over her again, she spread her legs and braced herself.

But all he did then was kiss her. Kiss her long and slow and wet, until she was dizzy with it, until all she knew was his mouth and his embrace and this gaping need inside of her, just waiting to be filled.

This desperate place in her heart, where he had already managed to fit himself, long before she'd invited him in.

When she slid her hand even lower to grasp the solid curve of his rear, he groaned and repositioned his hips. The blunt head of him nudged against her sex, but she didn't tense. He'd promised he'd take care of her.

He looked into her eyes. "You're so beautiful," he said.

The first breaching felt huge, but it didn't hurt. Not even

close. A long, gentle glide inside, and she closed her eyes at the fullness of it. The completeness when his hips met hers.

And then he did something no one else had ever done. He pressed his lips, soft and gentle and chaste to each cheek, even though he was *inside* her.

"You okay?"

She fluttered her eyes open to find him so close, mouth hovering just above hers. "Yeah." Because she was. "More than."

"Good." His lips twitched as he rocked deeper into her, and he stifled a little groan. "Because you feel *incredible*."

"Yeah?"

"Oh, hell, yeah." With that he covered her mouth with his, pulling backward with his hips while surging forward with his tongue, and it felt like a complete circuit. Like she was possessed by this man, and she never wanted to be anywhere else.

With gentle strokes, he pressed into her. She fell into his rhythm like she'd fallen into everything else with him. Each thrust ground him hard against her clit, building that warmth again in her abdomen. She held on tight, clutched him closer and tilted her hips, seeking that pleasure.

"That's right, baby," he murmured. It was less a kiss now and more simply breathing the same air. Being locked up tight inside this tiny bit of space where he was hers and she was his. "Take everything you need."

She closed her eyes and dug her nails into his back, straining, focusing until—

It was just a warmth at first, a soft curl of a promise in the base of her abdomen, but she grabbed on to it. Held on to Rylan and pressed her face to his throat as she whined. Each roll of his hips made the feeling grow. She gripped him harder, moving him against herself, against that hot brightness and pleasure just above where he was filling her. Bucking her hips up into him until it was all searing heat—light and darkness and a rush of nothingness, taking her under and down, and she was afraid she'd shake apart.

But he was there. Holding her together and crushing her close, murmuring in her ear.

It was all she needed to let go.

Her climax crashed down on her in a crescendo of feeling and need. Her voice and her body all shattered as she breathed his name over and over again, and God. To do this with someone who meant so much, to feel the hot breadth of him as he buried himself inside of her.

Only once the fog began to fade did he rear back. She looked up at him, and he was staring right at her, eyes open and cheeks flushed. He took another half dozen long, hard strokes in and out of her, and then he was arching. His mouth dropped open, and the groan that fell from his lungs shook her. His whole body trembled, and her heart twisted.

He was so beautiful in his pleasure. Felt so right inside her body and in her arms.

How was she ever supposed to let him go?

Rylan collapsed over top of Kate, scarcely remembering to catch himself and not force her to take all of his weight. For a minute, all he could do was lie there, breathing into the pillow. Fuck. He was still inside her, still twitching, and he had to squeeze his eyes shut tighter.

Because he'd had sex before. He'd had a *lot* of sex before, but not like that.

And wasn't that just Kate, though? She put him in these situations he thought he knew inside and out, and she made them different. More.

He shuddered and lifted himself up. He didn't need to be thinking things like that. As he got his elbows underneath himself, she stroked a hand up and down his spine, pulling a shiver from someplace deep inside of him. Her face was flushed and glassy, and her legs were folded gently around his hips. A warm rush of tenderness lit the center of his chest. He leaned in closer, stroking his nose against hers and then kissing her mouth, nice and soft. The way a girl should be kissed after letting a guy get that close to her.

She tasted so sweet, and the curl of her thighs around his waist had another round of aftershocks racing through him. He could have stayed like that the whole night.

With a groan and a last little sucking nip at her bottom lip, he pulled himself away. "Back in a sec."

He made his way to the bathroom, feeling less than steady and trying to keep that to himself. Dealing with the condom was the work of a moment, but he dawdled anyway, washing his hands a lot more thoroughly than he usually did, just for something to do while he got himself put together.

Turning off the tap, he dragged one damp hand through his hair, pushing it back from his face. As he did, he caught a glance of himself in the mirror.

Instead of shaking his head and moving on the way he usually did, he straightened his spine and forced himself to really take it all in. Not the sex hair or any of that, but not the shit he usually noticed, either—the too-deep cleft of his chin or the slant to his nose, or the bits that reminded him a little too much of his dad. It wasn't easy, staring at himself that way. No matter what he did, he couldn't conjure up the things Kate had drawn and seen. Was it really any use?

He dropped his gaze and grabbed a towel, drying his hands off as he walked back into the main part of the room. He furrowed his brow when he caught faint strains of music.

And then he stopped, everything in him just kind of going quiet at once.

Kate was sitting on their bed, facing the headboard, a loose sheet tucked under her arms and wrapped around her chest and hips. The crisp white of the cotton against her pale skin made it look all peaches and cream, and he swallowed hard. She was fiddling with a panel on the wall. He'd noticed it before but hadn't really paid it any mind.

The sounds on the air resolved themselves in his mind.

"Édith Piaf?"

She twisted, looking at him over her shoulder, and she was so beautiful he could hardly breathe. The soft curve of her smile cracked his heart. "It's a radio. All it plays is this really random old stuff."

And she looked so charmed.

"Yeah?"

"Yeah." She beckoned him over. "Come here and listen."

His feet didn't seem to want to move. For a second, he could only stand there, staring at her.

If he could draw, he'd paint her in ivory and pink and umber, looking exactly the way she did in that instant. Preserve her forever, to look at when he was old. Just like this.

But he couldn't.

"Rylan?"

"Sorry." He tossed the towel he'd been using in the vague

direction of the bathroom door. Unglued his feet and walked himself over to the bed.

He sat behind her, wrapping his arms around her waist and burying his face against her hair. Vanilla and rose, and layered in with it, the sharpness of his aftershave. The faintest notes of sweat and sex. His throat felt tight, and his heart was pounding too hard.

She put her hand over his. "You okay?"

"Yeah." He breathed her in, memorizing her scent. *Their* scent, all tangled together. "I'm fine."

"You sure?"

Lifting his head, he pressed a kiss to her temple. It was probably too intense, probably lingered too long. When he could, he nodded. "Absolutely. I'm just…happy."

She laughed, a soft, ringing sound. "Good. Me, too."

His heart felt like it was pressing against his ribs, but what could he do? He bit the inside of his cheek and cast his gaze skyward, then gestured at the radio, drawing attention from the way he'd been completely, utterly disarmed. "Does it play anything else?"

She paged through the handful of stations, each stranger than the last. The whole time, he held her, watching her and listening and trading comments about the selection of songs.

And it was another thing he'd heard of in the past—one he'd thought he'd done before. But really. He'd never known what *basking in the afterglow* meant.

Not until now.

chapter NINETEEN

"I can't believe we're doing this."

"What?" Rylan shot her a cheeky smile. "You've never had room service before?"

She tossed her napkin at him. "Not what I meant."

Honestly, she wasn't sure she ever *had* had room service. It was always so expensive. But Rylan had insisted, and at the time, her legs hadn't felt up to working. Even now, an hour after he'd turned her to jelly, her whole body was still thrumming, a warm glow of satisfaction radiating from the very center of her.

Yeah, staying in for dinner had been a good call.

Still. "Eating dinner in bed. Naked." She cocked her brow at him. "This is something you do all the time?"

He was sitting opposite her on the bed with their dinner plates between them. Somehow or other, they'd managed to split the sheet so it draped over his lap with enough left over for her to tuck the other end under her arms. All the important parts were covered, but it still felt illicit. Obscene.

Sexy.

Shrugging, he took a bite of his sandwich and chewed. "It's not exactly a first. But I wouldn't go so far as to say I do it all the time."

That dip was coming in her stomach. The little lurch that happened every time he reminded her that she was one of many.

Only then the corner of his mouth curled upward. "Can't say it's ever been this much fun before, though." He wiped his fingers on his napkin before reaching out to drag the back of a knuckle down the bare length of her arm. "Or that the view has ever been so good."

The anxious dip turned into a flutter. She dropped her gaze to stare at her own sandwich. He did this to her every time. Made her feel like she was special, when really she was just one of the herd.

"Hey." He gave her a second, then hooked his finger under her chin to tilt her head up. "Where did you go there?"

"Nowhere." She tried to smile.

Those piercing blue eyes stared back at her. "You're a terrible liar."

"Don't have a lot of practice, I suppose."

He cupped her face and swiped his thumb across her lip. "Good. I like you like this. All fresh-faced and innocent."

She shook her head. Kissed his thumb before batting his hand away. "Says the man who's been doing everything in his power to corrupt me."

"Not everything." His eyes twinkled. "But a lot of things." His grin receded as he poked at what was left of his pile of fries. "Haven't pushed it too far, I hope."

It didn't quite lilt up as a question, but she heard it as one all the same.

And she could do this. She could talk about the things they'd done. There didn't have to be any shame to it—even if something cold and uncomfortable threatened to unfurl in her lungs. "I—I don't regret anything. If that's what you're asking."

"It's something a guy likes to know." His one shoulder quirked upward and then settled back down.

"I don't regret it." She put more conviction into the words this time, because she didn't. No matter the heartbreak that was bound to come. It had been…amazing. Like nothing she'd ever experienced before. She was glad she'd get to hold on to that. "You were really good to me."

He made a little huffing sound and tore at the bread of his sandwich. "I am never going to stop being angry about the fact that anybody ever *wasn't* good to you. If you—" He cut himself off, fingers clenching into a fist before he relaxed them. "I hope you never let anyone treat you like that. Not ever again."

Right. The little dip in her stomach was back, twisting her insides up. He was talking about the other men she'd sleep with, after she left.

"I won't." It sounded too solemn, but there it was. Out on the air between them.

She'd promised it to herself once before, but it had been an abstract then. Now she knew how good she could've been getting all along. How terrible the bad had been by comparison.

"Besides." Her voice threatened to crack, and was she really going to do this? "There were only a couple of other guys," she blurted. "Before."

Apparently, she was.

Rylan paused. "Yeah?"

She'd told him that much their very first night. He'd prodded her then, clearly wanting her to tell him more about them, but she'd shied away. Now, though... She'd let him inside of her, had given up the one thing she'd been the most afraid to. She could give him just a little bit more.

"One was a hookup," she said, testing the words on her tongue. "I don't think I even got his name."

A month after things between her and Aaron had fallen apart, her friends had decided that enough was enough. They'd told her it was damn well time for her to pick herself up. Get back on the horse. Move on.

So they'd taken her to a club and bought her drinks all night. She'd caught a guy's eye, and she'd been so starved for the attention, she'd let him dance in close behind her. And when he'd asked her if she wanted to get out of there...

"I was...drunk. Not so drunk that I don't remember it or anything, but enough that I was maybe not making the best of decisions." She focused hard on picking at the crust of her bread so she didn't have to meet his gaze. Or show that her hands were trembling. "He was...fine. But he'd been drinking, too. Everything moved way too fast." She shrugged. "And when he was done, that was kind of the end of it."

It'd been the end of her interest in sex. Right up until she'd met Rylan.

"Asshole," he said, quiet but intense. It made her shiver.

But it also made her want to tell him everything else. She wanted him to hear it all, to know it all. She hadn't done anything wrong. But God. What she'd let herself become. How little she'd accepted for so long. It made her gut twist and clench, made her throat ache, even after all this time.

"The guy before that...Aaron." She gave up on her dinner. She'd more or less had enough of it anyway, and just thinking about this made her stomach turn to stone. She pushed her plate away and curled her hands together in her lap. "He was my first. First really long-term relationship, you know? I'd dated here and there in high school, but nothing serious. Definitely not anybody I'd...have sex with."

Rylan made an encouraging noise.

She drew her knees in close to her chest, hugging them tight. "He was smart. A business major. Really practical and driven." Goal-oriented was how he'd put it. The exact opposite of her with all her dreams about galleries and art. "Took me on nice dates and stuff." She paused when Rylan put his sandwich down, something in his gaze darkening. But he didn't try to interrupt her, so she soldiered on. "After a couple of months, he started wanting more, and I did, too." A dark chuckle bubbled up in her throat. "I was a twenty-year-old virgin, you know?"

Part of her had been terrified, as much by the relationship as by the sex. Her parents' marriage had been less of an example and more of a cautionary tale, and she'd carried the metaphorical scars with her for years. Still carried them, really.

Another part of her had just wanted to get it over with.

"He wasn't awful in bed or anything, but when he...did stuff, it never worked. I'd get turned on, and we...had sex. But." Her tongue had gone all twisted up, and her face felt hot, her neck cold. Why couldn't she just *talk* about this stuff? "I couldn't come."

"What?" Rylan looked at her with confusion, a displeased furrow coloring his brow. "He never fingered you or ate you out?"

The heat on her cheeks deepened, flowing down her chest. God. He said it like it wasn't dirty or weird or wrong at all.

Maybe because it wasn't.

"He did," she said. "Sometimes. It just didn't do anything for me."

"And you never took things into your own hands?"

Her laughter choked off with the force of her embarrassment. "Until you made me, I didn't even know that was something I could do in front of a guy." Not without him thinking she was a slut, or a pervert. Or who knew what else.

He'd finished up his sandwich by then, and he leaned over, the sheet sliding off his lap as he twisted to set his plate down on the floor. Sitting up again, he scooted closer to her, letting their bare legs brush beneath the covers. "Kate." He coaxed her to unfurl herself and took her hand in his, the skin warm and vital and strong. "I told you. There is nothing in this world sexier than a woman feeling pleasure."

A lump formed at the back of her throat. Because he really meant that, didn't he? He'd shown her as much with every kiss and every touch, had told her in a dozen silent ways, and this wasn't the first time he'd said it out loud.

"I mean it." His voice grew in its fervency. "You deserve someone who makes you feel amazing."

It was the *deserve* part that hit her like a punch to the chest. She shook her head without even meaning to, this automatic denial.

He squeezed her hand tighter. "You are beautiful and sweet and so fucking talented. You deserve—" He cut off, a flash of bitterness flitting across his face, but it was there and gone in a second. "You deserve someone who can give you everything."

Someone like you? The question pressed at her tongue, but she swallowed it whole. Nearly choked on it. Because he had. He'd given her this unreserved support, had shown this faith in her. And here in this bed, he'd taken care of her in a way that no one ever had before.

Because he thought she was worth it.

Her lip wobbled, her breath coming harder as the realization crashed over her, and she tried to tug her hands back, to get herself under control. She'd already accepted that she'd fallen for him, but what he was saying here, this kindness in the face of her sad history—it just made it hurt even worse. Her face crumpled, and his eyes went wide.

"Kate?"

She shook her head, but her voice wouldn't work. "I just—"

An impossible, unbearable warmth wrapped itself around her heart. She closed her eyes against it, but in the next breath, he was shifting across the bed, pulling her bodily into his arms, and the heat inside her went supernova. It burned through her, changing her.

Something that wasn't quite a sob broke past her lips, and he held her tighter. She swabbed at her eyes, but it didn't help. God, this was awful, breaking down on him, and because what? He'd been nice to her?

Muttering quiet assurances into her hair, he rocked her back and forth. "You're okay, baby."

But she wasn't. She was extraordinary.

A new kind of light seeped into her heart.

He treated her this way, gave her his time and his body, opened her up with such patient, tender care, because he thought she deserved it.

"I just—" she tried again. She opened her eyes, and the

world was still upright, the ceiling and the floor still exactly where they were supposed to be. It was her that was floating. The tear that escaped her felt like it glowed. "I didn't realize how badly I needed to hear that."

He practically forced the breath from her, his arms squeezed around her so hard. "I'll tell you every day," he said, and he didn't even bother to correct himself. To put a time limit on it. "You deserve the entire fucking world, Kate."

She didn't have to ask him if he meant it.

And that was it. The whole rest of the story came rushing out.

Burying her face against his chest, she said, "It wasn't just the sex with Aaron." He hadn't been outright abusive or anything. It hadn't ever gotten that far. But... "He started out so nice, but he put me down in all these subtle little ways." The shame of it all crept up on her again, that she'd tolerated it for so long. Had fallen into the same damn trap. "Like these offhanded remarks about how I dressed or the classes I took or what I was going to do after I finished college."

When you're still waiting tables and I'm on Wall Street...

"And it just got worse and worse, until I was believing it." She'd always believed it. "That he was better than I was and I was lucky to have him." That she didn't have any right to expect more of him. More affection or more time. More patience with her body.

Rylan's voice was murderous. "He's lucky I don't know where he lives."

"I could tell you," she said weakly. If it would get Rylan to come to New York, he could beat up as many asshole ex-boyfriends as he pleased.

"Don't tempt me."

She bit her lip. "When I found out he was cheating on me..."

Rylan's huffed-out breath was almost a growl.

And it was that—his fury on her behalf—that gave her the strength to tell him the rest. "There was this part of me that was ready to forgive him, because it was probably my fault." She'd been bad in bed, not attentive enough. Not good enough for him. "Until I remembered, until I realized..."

It was all hitting her again. A dizzying kind of pain and a stab of regret.

Rylan stroked her hair, patient. He was always so patient with her.

"It was the same damn thing that had happened to my mom."

Her crazy, wonderful, amazing mother, who had given up her own dreams to put her husband through school. To raise a daughter who'd come too young, and she'd never complained. Not until...

"My dad did the same thing, only it was so much worse." He was so much worse.

The tiny insults and the idea he'd given them both that they'd be lost without him. Scatterbrained creative types who always messed things up. Who made him so angry sometimes...

But they'd stood strong. He'd gone on to some other woman, and they'd been just fine all on their own.

Kate hadn't learned her lesson, though.

"After I found out about Aaron, I called my mom, crying, and she reminded me how guys just... change sometimes. They start out great and then there's this whole dark ugly other side to them."

It had been like turning on a light. She could suddenly see all the little ways she'd been broken down over the year she and Aaron had spent together. She'd dumped him the very next day, swearing she'd never let the wool be pulled over her eyes again. Her self-esteem might have taken another beating, but she'd promised herself it was the last time she ever accepted so little from a man.

And then Rylan had come along. He'd shown her what she'd been missing.

"My dad did it to my mother, and Aaron did it to me. They started out so nice and then they turned into these assholes, and I..." She could say this out loud. Thanks to Rylan, she could. "I deserve better."

She'd found it. Right here.

But Rylan's throat bobbed, and his hands went still, the little caressing motions he'd been making against her spine suddenly stopping. For a long moment he said nothing, and she sat there.

Bare for him the way that he had been for her that afternoon. And waiting. Waiting...

He sucked in a long breath, then let her go, his gaze burning as he took her face between his hands and kissed her. Her cheeks and her brow and her eyes and finally, finally her mouth. Drawing back he swore, "You do. You deserve the best." He hugged her again, and it was the warmest embrace she'd ever known.

For what felt like forever, she shook in his arms, letting him soak up the old, lingering hurt that had been weighing her down for so long. He murmured vague apologies into her hair, and she let him.

She felt more warm—more *loved*, sitting there, naked and

held by a veritable stranger than she had in her entire time with Aaron. Maybe her entire life.

"You know what?" she said, once she'd gotten her breath back.

"What?"

"I wish it had been you." Christ, she did. "That you'd been my first. That you'd shown me how—how *incredible* it could be."

How differently would things have gone with Aaron, with that random one-night stand, if she had known? Would there even have been anyone else? If she could've had Rylan first? If he'd pushed away all the damage her father had done with careful hands and kind words.

If she could have kept him?

He made a little *shh*ing sound, stroking his hand up and down the bare stretch of her spine.

She buried her face against his neck. "You just—you make me feel really safe, you know?"

Like she could let go. Like she could touch and be touched. Like she was worth it.

"Yeah," he said, clutching her close. "I know."

Aiming the remote at the TV, Rylan clicked the volume down to almost nothing. For the past half hour, he'd been slowly softening his voice as he narrated the romance taking place in French across the screen. But Kate's breaths had finally evened out. As the television went quiet, she snuggled in closer but otherwise didn't stir.

He left the screen on as he lay there with her. The pale blue light washed across her skin, making her face seem to glow. Her head was resting on his shoulder, her hair soft between his fingers. Beneath the sheet, all of her nakedness was pressed to all of this.

And he didn't deserve this. Not the tiniest fraction of it. His heart squeezed, and he had to pull his hand back from her hair, had to cover his mouth with his fist to keep the grunt of distress from falling from his lips.

This whole time, he'd been sitting around, feeling morally superior to the jackasses who had dared to touch her and not make her come. God. When she'd told him the rest of the story, it had felt like the floor was falling out from underneath him.

Like the moment when his father had been subpoenaed. When Rylan's eyes had been opened.

He was just like his father in so many ways. Since birth, people had been telling him that. Every step of the way, he'd been groomed to fill the old man's shoes, and it had chafed. The path that had been laid out for him, each decision he should've gotten to make on his own already predetermined. But it had been worth it. His father was a paragon, a monument, everything a man could hope to be. Everything Rylan was supposed to be.

When Kate had talked about her dad, her ex, those men who had seemed to be so good and who had turned out to be dark and ugly...

That day in his father's office, when the doors had burst open and the agents had filed in.

Dark and ugly. Those words didn't even begin to explain it.

Suddenly, all his father's faults had been laid out. His charm was his philandering, his business sense his greed. Aggression turned to cruelty and callousness, and Rylan had seen them all. He'd seen them in himself.

When Kate saw them in Rylan. When she found out who he'd been in line to become...

His lungs squeezed so hard he could scarcely breathe.

When she found out he'd been lying to her all along.

He bit down into his knuckle, trying to force the bile back into his throat.

Rylan hadn't lied to Kate. Not once had he said something explicitly untrue. But that wouldn't save him. He was just as bad as her asshole of an ex, as her dad. The ones who'd made her look at a man who was extending his hand and believe he was a threat.

Rylan was that threat. He was a liar.

And he hated himself even more than he had before.

A shiver ran through him. Kate shifted, and he froze. All she did was slide her knee across his thigh, though, letting her hand rest higher on his chest.

She trusted him.

Fuck. He curled his hands up into fists, digging his nails into the meat of his palms, but it didn't help. A good man would wake her up right now and tell her everything. He'd let her make her own decisions. He'd watch her walk away.

And Rylan just... *couldn't*. Her face would crumple, and it would kill him. She'd been so skittish when she'd met him, and the idea of putting that fear in her eyes again made him want to take every single thing back. Every word and every touch. And he would never do that. Not in a million years.

What was he supposed to do?

Except be as good to her as he could.

They only had another couple of days, and if he could keep his conscience quiet, he could spend those days with her. He could shower her with all the affection and care she deserved.

Then at the end of it, she'd go, and she would never have to know. She could keep *some* kind of faith that maybe there was a guy out there who wouldn't screw her over.

He couldn't decide if it was the most selfish plan or the most selfless one he'd ever had.

Her body gave another little restless twitch, and his heart ached. But he didn't wake her. He didn't let the confessions welling up inside his chest pour out.

His decision had been made.

He'd do what he had to do. He'd stay quiet, and he'd adore her the best he could. He wouldn't hurt her. Not any more than he had to.

Picking up the remote again, he turned the television off, bathing them both in darkness. With a murmur, she turned over, and he followed, fitting his front to the curve of her spine. He buried his face against her hair and wrapped her up inside his arms, closing his eyes and breathing her in.

But sleep didn't come to him for a long, long time.

chapter TWENTY

Rylan blinked his eyes open to an early morning glow seeping in through the curtains. Blearily, he closed his eyes again. He'd never been good at getting back to sleep, but if he could just roll over and kick his feet free from the covers, he might be able to.

Beside him, Kate gave a soft moan, and just like that, a layer of fog cleared from his mind. The two of them were still spooned up together, though by some mercy, he'd managed to end up with a few inches of air separating his dick from her ass. Not that it helped much. She was sleep-warm and slack against his chest, their fingers intertwined beside her head, her breasts pressed softly to his forearm where it draped across her ribs.

His morning arousal gave a little kick, and he shifted his knees forward, sliding his shin against the back of her calf. Her skin was so smooth, felt so good against his own.

His guilt from the night before crowded in on him, though. He closed his eyes and fought the tide of want pulsing through his veins. He started to tug his arm back, but she stirred, humming and squeezing his hand. He swallowed, ready to pull away when she half turned over and snugged her ass against his hips.

Lightning flooded through him.

"Kate," he groaned, and it was strained even to his ears. He extricated his hand from hers and gripped her hip, trying to keep her still. Not pressing forward, no matter how much he was dying to, just in case she wasn't okay with this when she woke the rest of the way up.

"Hmm?"

God. She was still moving against him, probably completely unaware of what she was doing.

His voice came out raspy and low. "You're killing me." He tried to scoot away, but to no avail.

Fuck this. He shook her this time. She was all pliant and warm, stretching her arms and craning her neck and feeling so fucking sexy against him he could hardly handle it.

And then all at once she froze.

Yeah. That wasn't a gun pressed to her rear.

"Sorry," he mumbled, releasing his grip. Maybe she'd let him get away from her now. He could go rub one out in the bathroom. Or maybe take a cold shower. *Something* to keep him from losing his fucking mind with how much he wanted her.

From taking something he didn't deserve.

"No." She sounded more awake now. Reaching back, she curled a hand around his thigh, preventing him from going anywhere, and goddammit all. He wasn't made of stone.

He wrapped his arm back around her, stroking the underside of her breast and mouthing at the smooth skin of her shoulder. "Baby." He shook his head in warning. "You're playing with fire here."

"You haven't burned me yet."

She had no idea.

He squeezed her tight, fighting against the instinct to roll his hips, but it was a losing battle.

Sliding her hand higher up his leg, she pushed into his touch, and he gave up. He cupped her breast. Let himself enjoy the soft flesh pressed all along the length of him. She made a little contented sound and craned her neck. Lifting up, he caught her lips, kissing her deep and wet. She tasted like sleep and sex, and she was moving with the gentle rocking of his hips now, rubbing her thighs together.

And he'd come to a resolution last night. He'd decided to keep the status quo intact, keep all the ways he'd misled her to himself, and there'd been a good reason for it. Sure, it gave him two more days to enjoy all the light she shone into his life. But it let her hold on to this as a good memory, too. It afforded him another chance to treat her with all the care and kindness she deserved.

He could do that. He could take this pleasure for himself. And give it back to her every way he knew how.

He closed his eyes. Dropped his voice even lower as he succumbed. "Are you wet for me?"

Her only answer was a breathy whine and a shifting of her legs, and yeah. Every time he'd spoken to her like that, she'd squirmed and acted all uncertain about it, but her body'd never had any doubts at all.

Growling, he scraped his teeth against her neck. "Guess I'll have to find out for myself."

With one last tweak of her nipple, he slipped his hand down, over the smooth plane of her abdomen to the tops of her thighs, and to that soft, sweet place between.

"Oh, baby," he groaned, turning his face into the pillow. "You're soaked. Were you having naughty dreams?"

"Maybe."

What he would give to see inside her head. Barring that, he slipped his fingers over slick flesh, dipping two just inside to get them nice and wet before sliding them up to tease at her clit. She squeezed his hip, digging her nails in.

"Feel good?"

"Yeah." She moved against him, thighs parting for his exploration, teeth scraping against his bottom lip. "Do you have another condom?"

He had a whole box. Pulling his hand away from her cunt, he grabbed her wrist. Put her own fingers right where his had been, because that was okay. She had to remember that she could do that. "Keep yourself warm for me."

She must have been pretty far gone or still a little bit asleep, because there wasn't any of the reluctance from the other night. She just curled in on herself, the motions of her fingers on her flesh sounding soft and wet in the quiet room, and fuck. He could stay there, listening and watching—maybe tasting—all day.

He huffed out a breath and tore himself away. The rest of the condoms were where he'd left them in the pocket of his bag. He tore one off from the strip and opened it up. Wrapping a hand around himself, he gave a few rough tugs at his cock before rolling the latex on, then stalked back to the bed to wrap himself around her.

She hadn't stopped touching herself. He was dying to get inside, but he made himself slow down. With his knee, he nudged her top leg forward, making more space for him to get at all that sweetness. He ran his fingers along hers, through the slickness and across her clit, then down. She took two fingers easily, clenching around them, tight but not too tight. Wet and unbearably hot.

"Can I?" he asked.

"Yeah, God. Come on."

Fuck, she was close already, and what a change that was from the first night. It made a warmth that had nothing to do with sex burn through his rib cage. She was so open now, so trusting. So willing to let him see her pleasure.

It was beautiful.

He drew his hand away, reaching between them to grab a hold of himself and guide his tip into place. He groaned aloud at the easy slide into her body, and it punched a noise out of her that made him even more desperate for it. When he was all the way in, he wrapped his arm around her and bit down hard at the meat of her shoulder.

"You feel so good," he managed.

"So do you." She moved to shift her hand away, and he shook his head.

He grasped her wrist before she could get too far, bringing her fingers back to the place where they were joined. "No. Don't stop."

"But you're—" She honestly sounded confused.

"Fucking you," he finished for her. "Yeah, believe me, I know."

"So..."

"So keep touching yourself."

"You don't want to..."

He wasn't sure where she was going with that, but he shook his head all the same. "I want to fuck you while you finger that sweet little clit. Can you do that for me, Kate?"

The moan that wrung from her was a twisted mix of mortification and arousal, and it made him start to rock his hips, unable to resist the temptation to move within her. Even those short strokes had him clutching her tighter, and yeah. He wanted her mad for it. He wanted her to *remember* this.

"Can you?" he asked again. "Can you make yourself come on my cock?"

"Yeah." It was high-pitched breath of a word.

And it was all he needed to hear.

He drew back farther this time before driving back in, running his hand up and down her side. He'd always loved having sex spooned together like this—the proximity and the heat of it, all the access it afforded to a girl's clit and tits.

Here in the dim light of dawn, in this bed, with this girl, it felt even more intimate. Having to stay wrapped up tight against her back matched his mood in selfish ways. He wanted to be close. Wanted the freedom to touch her skin and kiss her ears and shoulders and neck. He wanted to give her the best sex she'd ever had, so she'd never be afraid of it again. He wanted to give her everything.

A haze of slick wanting and motion blurred his vision as he sped his hips. It was a mix of technique and instinct, and the way she seemed to bring out the best in him. He blanked his mind to the crescendo of sensation, holding out, trying to push her over.

She panted when he rubbed her nipple between his fingertips, and it only got louder when he dragged his hand up to her face and ran his thumb across her lips. It was dirty and perfect, and he pressed the pad of his finger between her teeth, only to have her suck on it hard.

"Oh, that's beautiful," he murmured. He tugged free of her mouth and rubbed wet fingers across the peak of her breast.

She twisted and fucked herself back onto his cock, hand flying between her legs. It had his balls tensing, ready to shoot, but he closed his eyes and gritted his teeth.

"Come for me. Squeeze me. Let go, Kate. Come all over me, make me come, give it up and—"

She cut him off, crying out his name, and fuck. Fuck, fuck, *fuck*, it felt even better than he'd thought it would. He sped his strokes, shifting his hand to hold her by the hip. Giving into the heat and tightness of her, the feel of her all against his front. The smell of sweetness and sex, and just *her*.

"God, Kate—"

His whole world went dark as he released himself into her, fucking forward with a few last strokes until the sensitivity got to be too much. Buried within her, he stilled, just trying to fill his lungs. After a long few breaths, he forced his fingers to uncurl, petting her flank and hoping he hadn't grabbed her hard enough to bruise.

It would be just one more thing to feel guilty about, if he'd left any marks on her skin.

As gently as he could, he wrapped his arm around her, tucking her close. They lay there together like that in silence until he started to go soft. Wishing he didn't have to, he drew back, slipping from her warmth and pressing his lips to the point of her jaw.

Before he could get any farther, though, she twisted around, lifting up a hand to touch his face, tugging him down again to meet her mouth with his. It was a soft kiss, a serious one.

He pulled back after a long moment. "You okay?"

"Yeah."

He opened his mouth to ask if she were sure, but what right did he have to press? "Okay." He leaned in for another kiss before drawing away, rolling over to the edge of the bed. Keeping his back to her, he scrubbed a hand through his hair and rose.

The sex had been amazing, and he'd done right by her. He'd given as much as he had gotten. That was the line he had to walk, these last two precious days with her. He'd hold his tongue, and he'd be so, so good to her.

Then at the end of them, he'd let her go.

"So," Rylan called from the other room. "You ready to hear my awesome plan for the day?"

Kate's hand tightened around the bottle of ink she'd been returning to her bag. In theory, she was out here getting dressed while Rylan shaved, but then she'd gotten distracted by her art supplies and by thoughts of where she might like to go to sketch this morning. His question stopped her cold.

She already had plans for the day. Good plans.

Plans designed to distract her from the twisted-up mess that had become her feelings for Rylan.

Laying herself out for him the night before had left her feeling so much lighter. She'd let him into her body and her heart and even her mind, and it had been amazing.

But it made the reality of letting him go even more impossible to bear.

"What's that?" she asked, setting the ink aside.

Kneeling beside her suitcase, she fished out the cleaner of

her two pairs of jeans. She ducked behind the bed, checking she was out of Rylan's line of sight before sucking in her stomach and tugging them on.

"Remember how I tried to talk you into going to Versailles yesterday?"

Damn, she did remember that, now that he brought it up. She frowned, pausing with her hands at her waistband.

The simple truth was, she didn't want to go to Versailles. Sure, the history of the place was appealing, but everything she'd read said it was overpriced and overcrowded. It wasn't the kind of history she was interested in anyway.

"Vaguely," she said, shaking out a shirt. She shrugged. It wasn't *too* wrinkled.

In the bathroom, the water ran, the sounds of the razor clinking against the porcelain telling her he was almost done. By the time he joined her in the main part of the room, she'd gotten the shirt on and her wet hair combed out. She tried not to stiffen when he came up behind her and put his hand on her hip.

If he noticed the tension in her body language, he didn't point it out. Instead, he wrapped his arms around her and rested his chin on her shoulder. His body was so warm. It sent a shiver through her.

"I've been thinking about it some more since then." He rocked them gently side to side. "Imagine it. Train ride out into the country. Big old fancy rich guy castle. Dinner at a little château somewhere, away from all the traffic and noise. It'll be romantic."

That was the last thing she needed. He'd swept her off her feet with the most casual of gestures. If he actually *tried* to woo her, she didn't know how she'd survive it.

She let that doubt creep into her voice. "I don't know. I only have today and tomorrow left."

It hurt just thinking about it.

"I know," he said, more serious than she'd expected. "Which is why I want to show you the best time I can. Before you go."

God. Did his voice sound as wistful as she felt?

Scolding her overeager heart, she squirmed her way out of his embrace. "Rylan..."

"You don't have to if you don't want to." He shrugged, but his smile didn't reach his eyes. "I just thought it would be nice."

He turned around and padded over to his bag, dropping the towel when he reached it. The view of him from behind was as good as from the front. Maybe better. She got lost for a second, staring, remembering herself only once he'd pulled his boxers up to cover his rear.

She snapped her gaze away, taking a couple of steps backward to fall into the chair beside the bed.

"It's just..." She worried the inside of her lip between her teeth. She couldn't tell him that she didn't want to go to Versailles; he'd just come up with another, better plan. Admitting she was afraid to spend more time with him wasn't really an option, either. Which left... "I told you all the stuff I have to figure out this week. With grad school and art and jobs and stuff."

"And I told you. You'd be crazy not to pursue what you love." He looked at her over his shoulder as he shook a pair of jeans out, his tone all matter of fact. "And what you're amazing at."

"It's not that simple."

"Why not?" He stepped into the pants and tugged them up, fastening them before turning around.

Where should she start? "It's just...not. I'll have to take out loans if I go to school, and then am I ever going to be able to pay them off? Am I just wasting my time?" Surely he had to understand that. "I have friends who did the grad school thing and ended up at ad agencies afterward anyway, but two or three years older and saddled with these massive piles of debt."

"They aren't you."

She snorted. "You make it sound so easy."

"Then let it be easy." He hopped up onto the bed and stalked across it until he was on the opposite edge, right in front of her, their knees close enough to touch. He held out his hands, and she slipped hers into them. His eyes looked so sincere. "Listen. If you really think another day of working in your sketchbook will help you figure out your future—where you should be, what you should do..." His throat bobbed, and there was another layer of meaning, one she couldn't quite grasp. "Then that's fine. Do it."

"I just..."

"But," he interrupted her. "I think you already know what you want to do. It's just battling with what you're afraid you *should* do." The stroking of his thumb across her knuckles paused, a wrinkle appearing between his brows. "What you think other people expect you to do. And all the time in the world spent thinking about it isn't going to change that." He shrugged, expression clearing. "In which case, come take a trip with me. Let me show you some pretty things and try to make out with you in inappropriate places." Squeezing her hands, he smiled. "Choice is up to you."

He had no idea which choice was killing her the most right now.

Regardless, she wasn't ready to admit defeat quite yet. She drew her hands back and let out a long sigh. "Let me finish getting ready and think about it, okay?"

He didn't seem to like that answer, but he nodded anyway. "Fine."

By the time she'd dried her hair and gotten her makeup on, she wasn't feeling any better about things. She planted her hands on the counter and stared into the bathroom mirror. Raising her voice so he would hear it, she asked, "Versailles is really expensive, isn't it?"

He popped his head around the doorframe, fully dressed and looking infuriatingly perfect. "My idea. My treat."

She frowned. "How can you afford this?"

"Don't worry about me. I can handle it." He put his hands on his hips. "Just make a decision, Kate."

Putting his insistence on treating aside for a moment—she was going to have to find some way to pay him back before she left; no chance she was letting him bankrupt himself for her—she pulled her mouth into a sideways frown, regarding herself again in the mirror. Weighing her choices. In her peripheral vision, she could see his reflection, too, though.

He looked so ready to be disappointed.

And who was she kidding, really?

"Oh, what the hell." It felt like throwing caution to the wind, like ditching class. And knowing you were probably going to get caught. She pushed the sinking feeling in her stomach aside. "I can always draw from photos when I get home, right?"

The corner of his mouth ticked up. "Yeah?"

"Sure. Why not?"

She could think of a hundred reasons, but really . . . he was right. She knew what she wanted to do, with her life and with him. What she *should* do, she could worry about later.

And for the moment, she could almost forget about the consequences, as the biggest, broadest smile spread across his face. Brilliant and handsome, and all of it raining down on her. He darted forward and picked her up by her waist, spinning her around. "You won't regret this."

She tried to echo his grin.

She really, really hoped that was true.

chapter TWENTY-ONE

Okay. Rylan *may* have overbuilt this in his head a little.

With a sinking feeling in his stomach, he caught Kate's eye and tipped his head toward the next room. She crossed her arms over her chest and nodded. They weaved their way past the horde of Korean tourists between them and the next doorway.

They were coming up on the most famous parts of the entire damn palace, and Kate had yet to crack a smile.

A couple more rooms and another tour group later—Japanese, this time, he was pretty sure—they spilled out into the lushest set of quarters yet. Dimly lit but glowing all the same, the bedroom was all bright gold draperies and gleaming wallpaper, every inch of it embellished by *something*, be it a fleur-de-lis or a curlicue or a sun. Hell, even the fireplace was lapis lazuli.

This was it. Louis the XIV's fucking bedroom, the centerpiece of this whole place.

He turned to Kate, hoping for something, anything. "So?"

"It's . . . cool?" The corners of her mouth twitched up, but he knew when he was being humored.

Fuck.

Curling his hands into fists, he tried to see the place through her eyes. It was sumptuous and lavish and dripping with wealth.

And it was useless. Hollow. Just like him.

Beside him, she made an impatient noise and stepped around one of the tourists in her way. He followed her, reaching out to grab her arm. She started, like she hadn't been expecting him to touch her, and his chest hurt.

He could fix this. He would fix this.

"Hey," he said, leaning in close. "Do you wanna get out of here?"

She looked at him in confusion. "Do you?"

"I don't know." He didn't care. So long as she smiled.

"You were the one who wanted to come here, weren't you?"

"I wanted *you* to come here. And you don't seem to be having a very good time."

He paused as a little white-haired woman tried to sneak between them. He barely managed to restrain himself from yelling at her to go around—couldn't she see they were having a moment here? Ugh. Shaking his head, he motioned toward the next room and tugged Kate along as he headed off. She didn't put up any protest, so she couldn't have been too invested in the stupid Sun King.

Of course the next room wasn't any better than the last one had been, so he kept charging past everyone. They were missing all the most well-known stuff, but he didn't care. Finally, he hit the end. He stormed down the set of stairs, only to have her wrench her arm back.

"Slow down," she hissed. She was taking the steps at half the speed that he had been, and it was a reality check.

Restraining himself from saying anything or from rushing her any further, he stayed one pace behind her until they were back in the courtyard, breathing the fresh air.

She rounded on him. "What got into you back there?"

He shrugged, looking at the building behind her. "You looked miserable."

"I told you this isn't really my thing."

"I know, I know." God, he knew. "I'm sorry, okay, this was a shitty idea."

"It could have been worse."

"How?"

The corners of her lips flirted with a grin, and it was like a weight coming off his spine. "There could have been a Russian tour group in there, too?"

He barked out a laugh. Swiping his hand across his brow, he shook his head. "Look, I wanted to show you a nice time." He'd wanted that so much. "But apparently I mucked that up."

For the first time since they'd gone into the palace, she stepped into his space. Put her hands on his chest and waited for him to look at her. "You didn't muck anything up. No, this hasn't been my favorite trip we've taken, but no one's perfect."

"This was a really long ways from perfect."

"Everywhere else you've taken me has been."

He didn't want to let go of the tension he'd been holding on to—the irrational panic, because they had so little time left, and he'd wanted to make the most of it. But when she pulled him down into a kiss, he couldn't help it. His shoulders dropped, and the rigidity of his spine melted.

"I'm sorry," he said after a minute. He spoke over her when she looked like she was going to interrupt. "Not just for talking you into coming here." He grabbed her hand and held it in his. "But for pouting like a four-year-old when you looked like you weren't enjoying yourself."

"Apology accepted." Lifting up onto tiptoes, she dragged him down to kiss his nose.

He felt so much calmer now. Letting her go, he gestured at the palace behind them. "Do you want to try to get back in there? Walk around the gardens? Anything? Or do you just want to go?"

"Were our tickets time-stamped?"

If there was one thing his family had taught him, it was how to talk people into letting him do what he wanted. Sometimes it took a greased palm, but that wasn't a problem. Still, he fished out his wallet and flipped it open, thumbing through the billfold for the tickets. He examined them for a second. "I don't see anything that says we can't go back in."

He looked up from the tickets to find her brows furrowed, and her gaze was on— He snapped his wallet shut.

The back of his neck sprung out in a cold sweat. This whole week, he'd managed to remember to pay cash wherever they went, and in small denominations, not wanting to flash around his Amex or the amount of paper money he typically carried around. He'd opened his wallet up under tables or behind the cover of his jacket or his sleeve. He'd been so damn careful about it. And now here he was, flipping the thing open in the clear light of day and right under her nose.

His pulse raced. *Play it cool.* Hanging on to the tickets, he slipped his wallet into his pocket. "So? Want to brave the crowds again?"

She just kept staring at his hands.

"Kate?"

She shook her head, snapping out of it. "Huh? Oh, um. Nah.

Though, I guess I wouldn't mind looking around the gardens? It's such a nice day, and we came all the way out here."

He had to stifle a sigh of relief. He still couldn't quite escape the feeling that she'd seen through him, but until she brought it up, he sure as hell wasn't going to. With a smile, he held out his arm for her to take. "Lead on, my lady."

She slipped her hand into the crook of his elbow readily enough. But there was something contemplative to the way she kept glancing at him as they walked. Like she was looking at him just a little bit too closely.

Lots of different credit cards looked the same.

Kate reminded herself of that on a loop, every time the niggling bit of suspicion tickled at the back of her mind. She didn't even know what a Black Amex looked like—how would she? But if it was as literal as it sounded... Well, then what else could it have been?

She snuck a peek up at him. They'd walked a decent stretch of the gardens around the palace now—hopefully enough of it to make him feel a little bit better about things. She was just starting to think about broaching the idea of heading back to the city.

He stopped her with a hand on her arm before she could turn around. "Hey." He pulled out his phone with his other hand. "Remember this trick?"

With that, he tugged her in, tucking her under his arm the way he had outside the Louvre on their very first day together.

Something nervous fluttered in her chest. "When you convinced me to take a selfie as a flimsy excuse to get your arm around me?"

"Yup. Say cheese."

She smiled the best she could, but as she did, she was looking at his phone. It was a new model. Fancy. Expensive.

She shook the thought from her head once he'd taken the shot. He let her go and flicked back to see if the picture had come out all right. When he found it, he smiled, turning the phone to show it to her. "We look good, right?"

They did. Tense but good. She nodded.

He twisted his phone around to get both thumbs on it, holding it as if to type. "You never did give me your email address, you know."

She did know that. "Oh. Right."

"Do you not want the pictures?" He raised an eyebrow.

"No, I do." It made her nervous for some reason. As if giving him a way to contact her crossed a line. Ridiculous, considering all the other lines they'd merrily waltzed past without a second glance. Fighting down the fidgety feeling, she rattled it off to him.

He typed it in and nodded. "Ta-da. Sent."

"So now I've got your address, too."

"Yup."

She hadn't checked her email since she'd left the hostel. She should probably make a point of doing that soon, just in case. Without really thinking about where she was going, she started walking again.

"So." He fell into step beside her. "Anything else you want to see here?"

She hadn't particularly wanted to see anything here in the first place. "Not really."

"May I make a suggestion?" His usual cockiness had simmered down a notch. It sounded like a real question.

"You may."

"I say we catch a train back to Paris. Have dinner. My treat."

He'd offered to treat enough times this week. She'd practically lost count.

She was counting again now. "You don't have to do that."

"I want to." He nudged her shoulder with his own. "Come on, let me apologize for... this." He waved his hand around.

This. Which he had also paid for.

Her heart was in her throat. "What did you have in mind? Dinner-wise?"

Shrugging, he steered them toward the main gates. "I haven't taken you to a real French restaurant yet. What do you say? Escargot? Cassoulet? Foie gras?" His voice lilted up, his flawless accent kicking in.

The one he'd acquired following his parents around Europe when he'd been a kid.

God. The itch of a suspicion turned into a tide of realization, her heart thumping hard against her chest. All that stuff about hostels and splitting the cost of a hotel room—had it all been a trick? If so, she'd fallen for it. He must think she was such an idiot.

"Can we just head back to the hotel first?" She needed to get her legs back under her.

Concern crossed his features. "You okay?"

"Yeah."

But when he tried to put his arm around her again, she couldn't relax into it.

All day long, ever since she'd slipped out of his bed this morning, she'd been thinking she had to protect her heart.

Maybe she should have been protecting more than that. Maybe she should have been protecting it from the start.

chapter TWENTY-TWO

Rylan managed to wait until the door of their hotel room was closing behind them before he rounded on her. And shit, he could actually feel his father's boardroom training taking over. Making him keep his distance. Making his face hard.

Just like his dad, when Rylan or his siblings or his mom had disappointed him.

What the hell else was he supposed to do, though? Kate hadn't exactly refused to touch him the whole way home, but fuck if it hadn't been the longest train ride of his life. Her, sitting right beside him, hand held loosely in his until she took it away to fidget with her nails, her hair, her bag. She forced him to reach for her when he wanted to touch her again—never offered contact herself. The entire time, they'd spoken maybe a dozen times.

Regret was eating at him, but it was slowly shifting into something angrier. He never should have pressured her into spending the day with him. He definitely shouldn't have suggested Versailles.

He should have put the tickets someplace other than his wallet.

It didn't seem like it could be that simple, but she'd gotten all closed off right after he'd flashed the damn thing in front of her. He didn't need to be a detective to figure it out.

He closed his eyes and curled his hands into fists, taking three deep breaths before staring across the room at her. Last night, everything had seemed perfect. And now it had come to this.

Fuck it.

"Say it." He tore his jacket off and tossed it in the corner with the rest of his things. "Whatever you're thinking. Just say it."

She'd been facing away from him, rummaging through her bag, but at the harsh sound of his voice, she shoved the thing aside, sending it clattering to the floor. The violence of it startled him, and his heart squeezed as she set her hands on the edge of the desk. Dropped her head and drew her shoulders up.

"Who are you?" She didn't look at him until the question was out of her mouth, and even then, she didn't turn. Just twisted her neck to gaze at him with dark, sad eyes.

His heart rose up into his throat. "What do you mean?"

The whole thing was choking him, the irony making it hard to breathe. Yes, he'd hidden the details of his life from her. But in these spare handful of days, he'd shown her all these other things. Parts of himself that people who knew a lot more of the facts had never seen. Parts he'd never shown to anyone before.

"I mean," she said slowly, "who are you?"

"You know."

"No." Her mouth drew into a tight line. "That's the problem. I don't."

For a moment that felt like an age, he stood there, waiting for the blow.

Finally, Kate turned around, her gaze level. Her voice quiet but strong. "Let me see your wallet."

And there it was. Not a physical impact, but a punch to the gut all the same. "Kate..."

Negotiate. Dodge around the subject. Turn the tables.

She held out her hand. "Give it to me."

He tried to joke, "If you needed money, you could have just said—"

"That's not what I need. That's the last thing I want from you." Her throat bobbed, and her eyes were far too bright. "Don't you know that?"

There wasn't any negotiating with that—with the way she was looking right through him. She'd seen his heart; all these days and nights, he'd showed it to her again and again. But she didn't want that. She wanted the shell.

And it was all his fault. He'd set himself up for this right from the start.

"I can explain everything," he tried, but she shook her head.

"Just let me see."

He wished he'd gotten a chance to kiss her one last time.

Resigned, he reached into his pocket and pulled the damn thing out. Really, if she'd been paying attention, just the brand and the suppleness of the leather gave him away. A hundred tiny details all gave him away, from the watch he'd been wearing that very first day to his patterns of speech to the shape of his father's ring. But she hadn't wanted to see. Hadn't wanted to hear.

And now he had to tell her the truth.

"It's funny," he said, handing his wallet over. The world seemed to shiver, a low sense of vertigo making everything sway. "I told you my last name when we were at the Musée d'Orsay. You didn't flinch."

"Should I have?"

"A lot of Americans do."

She opened the billfold and counted out the five hundred odd euros he had left in there. Then with unsteady hands, she pulled out the Black Amex. The membership to the VIP fitness club attached to his mother's apartment building. Each card as damning as the last, and when she looked up at him, her expression was bereft.

"Theodore Rylan Bellamy the third," he said, like he were introducing himself for the first time. It was a weight lifting off his shoulders and an anchor sinking him to the bottom of the sea. "Firstborn son of Theodore and Felicienne Bellamy."

She repeated the name, pronouncing it slowly, recognition a distant but approaching hollowness to her eyes. "Theodore Bellamy."

"I'm surprised you don't remember it, if you go to school in New York. It was in all the papers last year. He embezzled half the earnings out of Bellamy International." He couldn't help grasping the ring through his shirt. "Within five years, it went from one of the biggest IPOs of the decade to a cautionary tale."

Her gaze followed the motion of his hand as he tightened his grip on that little slip of gold. "Your father who went to prison."

"Currently starting the second of a fifteen-year sentence."

"I don't remember—" She cut herself off. "I was in school. I didn't pay that much attention to the news."

"There's not much more to tell. Well, unless you skip to the gossip pages. Then there's his society wife who was having dalliances with half the young men in Europe. She had her own assets, so when Dad went away, she started over again. Somewhere. I imagine she's doing well."

"And your assets?"

"My father lost almost everything, but we each had trust funds predating the crimes. The courts couldn't touch them."

Looking faint, she sunk down to sit on the edge of the bed and dropped her head into her hands. "Trust fund. You have a trust fund."

Of course that was what she keyed in on.

"I never lied to you, Kate." Spoken aloud, it sounded just as empty as it had when he'd thought it in his head the night before.

She look up at him, eyes blazing, and *fuck*. Apparently, it sounded even worse than that.

And then she laughed, the sound ugly and wrong and bordering on hysterical. "No," she choked out amidst it all. "No, of course you didn't. Stupid me just made assumptions about you being a normal guy. Stupid me suggested you'd been staying in as terrible of a hostel as I was."

"I should have corrected you."

"Damn right you should have. Crap." She buried a hand in her hair and tugged. It looked painful—made him want to cross the room to her and stop her, or soothe the ache with his touch. "Shit, you must think I'm such an idiot."

"No. Not at all." He went so far as to reach out, but she recoiled, standing and stepping back, putting as much space between their bodies as the room could afford.

It was a slap in the face. One he deserved, but one that

took him by surprise. It hurt even more when she wrapped her arms around herself.

Her expression was lost. "You lied to me. I trusted you, and you lied to me. After everything I let you do, after everything I told you last night..."

"I wanted to tell you..." His excuses and his plans seems so pathetic now.

She shook her head. "With that kind of money, you can have anything, do anything you want. Stay at the nicest place in the city. And yet you're here."

"I thought you'd be more comfortable—"

"What? Someplace cheap?"

This was all spinning out of his control so fast. "Someplace..." The word stuck in his throat. "Normal."

Because that was what he'd been stealing here, what he'd been squirrelling away in this pocket of time. The chance to be *normal*. To have a normal life instead of having to be...him.

It had been exactly the wrong thing to say.

"Normal." The corner of her lips twitched downward. "Ordinary, right?"

She was the furthest possible thing from ordinary. "No!" He planted his feet, raked his hand through his hair. "You're twisting everything I say."

"Because you lied." She said it so quietly. "I asked you who you were, so many times, and you lied."

"Not about the things that mattered."

Something in her eyes broke. "But they were things that mattered to me."

And what could he say to that?

He wasn't sorry. She never would have touched him had

she known, and he wouldn't give up what they'd had for all the money in the world. Even with how much this hurt right now. He wouldn't give it up.

"Tell me how to fix this."

Shaking her head, she looked away. "I don't think you can." She swiped a hand under her eyes and turned, picking her purse up off the floor.

Reaching for her suitcase.

Everything in him screamed. She wasn't really leaving. Not without giving him some kind of a chance to make this right. "What are you doing?"

"Packing."

"And where are you going to go?"

"I don't know. Back to the hostel. A different hostel. I don't care."

"No. No way."

"I'm sorry, but you don't get to tell me what to do."

His throat ached. "You're really going to throw this all away? Just like that?"

She twisted to look over her shoulder at him. "Throw what away? This was never going to last." And there was something bitter there. "Even if—even if you hadn't...It was a fling. I live in New York and you live here. Even if I were in your league—"

"Don't you ever say that." He steamrolled right over her. She could say a lot of things, but she could *not* say that.

"Please," she scoffed. She looked away again, but not before he saw the redness in her eyes. "I'm this naïve, broke art student, and you're..."

The word came out before he could stop it. "Lost." With her, he'd felt found for the first time in months. In years. "You weren't wrong, that day in Montmartre. When you asked me what I was running away from. I may have more resources—"

"And more experience, and all these..." She waved her hand, flustered. "...moves. Your pickup crap."

"My pickup crap never worked on you."

She shook her head. "It worked so much better than you ever would have imagined. I just pretended it didn't because—"

He gave her a beat before asking, "What?"

"Because I knew you were going to break my heart."

God.

"Kate..."

"No." She grabbed the couple of things she'd spread out on her nightstand and shoved them into one of the pockets on her bag. "It doesn't matter."

Two could play at that game. "It matters to me."

She snorted, clambering over the bed to avoid touching him on her way to the bathroom. The second she stepped away, he headed over to her bag and started taking things out again. She came back, her toiletry and makeup bags in her hands, and glared at him.

"I'm not letting this go without a fight," he promised. "After everything. All the places we went, and the..." His gaze drifted to their bed. The one where she'd let him strip her bare. Let him taste her and touch her and put himself inside her. He squeezed his hands into fists. "After everything we've done together." His heart dropped another inch. "After I posed for you."

He'd shown her his fucking soul, and now it was all worth nothing to her? Because he'd told a couple of little half truths?

She paused, breathing slower, and for a brief instant, he

let himself harbor a hope. She surveyed the tiny space where they'd touched and kissed, and dammit, made love.

And then she gave him the most watery, awful smile. "Maybe it's better this way."

"Better?"

She stepped around him, placing her things into her bag. Swallowing hard, she grabbed his hands, and it felt so fucking good just to have her touch him. Right up until she took the shirt he had balled up in his fist and pried his fingers away.

She repacked it, along with the other items he'd removed. "If this had gone on—if I'd left feeling the way I felt yesterday..." Her voice cracked, and just the sound of it had his own eyes burning. "I would have held a torch for you for-ever. I always would have wondered."

He would never, ever stop wondering.

"And now?" He barely dared ask.

She zipped her bag, and it sounded like the end of the world. "Now I can go home knowing it was never meant to be."

He took a step back. She was done. Really, truly done, and he didn't have any more illusions about changing her mind. Besides, it wasn't right. He'd told her, that first night she'd let him make her come: Anything she didn't want to happen—he would never force it. That hadn't just been about sex.

It was her choice. He could respect that. He *had* to respect that.

She raised the handle of her suitcase and turned toward the door.

Oh, goddammit. Fuck decorum and fuck respect. "You know," he said, stopping her. "The only reason I didn't tell you the truth right off the bat." It was a weakness, admitting this. It rankled, but who cared? He'd already given her everything else. "It wasn't to deceive you, or to seduce you."

She paused.

It was his only chance.

"You were beautiful, and smart, and you saw right through my bullshit." He took a deep breath. "And I thought—I thought you saw something more than just that superficial stuff. Like you *wanted* to see more than that. And I wanted it. I wanted it so fucking bad, though I didn't know it at the time. The idea that a girl might like me not because of my name, or who my parents are, or because I've got some money." Because of all the things that had been beyond his control. His lungs felt hollow in his ribs. "I wanted you to like me for who I was."

"Oh, Rylan." Her gaze met his. "I would have liked you for who you were regardless." The corner of her lip wobbled. "But you were the one who wouldn't show me who that was."

He had to look away.

When he turned to her again, her eyes were glassy and her cheeks splotched, but her shoulders were back. She lifted her chin.

"You told me—" She cut herself off and started again. "This morning, you said you thought I already knew what I wanted. I just had to stop worrying about what I *should* do and go for it. You're right. You were right about me." She shook her head. "I hope you figure out what *you* want, Rylan. I hope you can be honest about it, at least to yourself, when you do." She shot him a shaky smile. "Because I'm not the only one you've been lying to this week."

With that, she let go of the handle of her suitcase and came over to him. She put two hands on his shoulders, but he knew what this was.

The kiss when it came was hard and angry and sad. It tasted like good-bye.

"Don't go," he said, sounding broken to his own ears. "If you want me to leave, I will, but stay. Take the room." *It's yours anyway.*

With a wistful little smile, she said, "I like to pay my own way."

And that was it.

She made it all the way to the door before he gave in and stopped her one last time. It was fucking masochistic, dragging it out like this, but he couldn't let this one thing go unsaid. "I never lied about how amazing you are." There was more, too, about how he hoped she pursued her art and her dreams, because she was so damn *good*. She made the world a more beautiful place.

But before he could reopen his mouth, she said, "Neither did I." She didn't look back.

The door opened and closed behind her. It sounded like a death knell. All the energy going out of him at once, he collapsed into the empty chair in the empty, empty room.

Just like that, she was gone.

chapter TWENTY-THREE

Oh God.

Kate just barely made it to the elevator bay before she broke down, smacking the button over and over while the dam burst inside her. She heaved out her first rough sob while still mashing at the button, waiting for the freaking doors to open. She had to get this under control—there could be someone in the lift, Rylan could decide to chase after her, hell, a maid might stumble by—but it wasn't any use. She'd managed to hold it together that whole time in Rylan's room, and now it was all crashing over her.

She'd walked out on him. He'd lied to her, had been pretending to be someone he thought she'd like. The entire time, when he'd touched her and when he'd told her she deserved more. It had all been one big lie.

The doors of the elevator slid open, revealing an empty car, thank God. Dragging her suitcase along after her, she stepped in and pressed the button for the lobby, letting out a whole new fresh torrent of tears with the closing of the doors.

Alone in that contained space, she shuddered and buried

her face in her hands. She'd loved him so much. It had been too soon to feel so strongly, but she had. None of it had been real, though, and she'd been such an idiot to let him in in the first place. More of one to fall so fast and so hard. He was probably laughing at her right now.

Except she'd seen the look on his face. The devastation. He was a damn good actor, she knew, but was he that good? Did she care?

The elevator dinged as it arrived at the ground floor, and she scrubbed at her eyes. As if that would help.

She had practical things to worry about. She needed to find a place to stay for her last couple of nights. Rylan probably wouldn't come looking for her, but there weren't any guarantees about that, so she needed to find a different hostel than the one she'd started out in. He had her email address, but no other contact information for her. She was probably safe.

She shoved her hair back from her face and squared her shoulders before stepping out. The little details—the ones she'd somehow managed to ignore every time they'd strode through here in the past—stuck out to her like sore thumbs now. Gilded edges on mirrors and a marble bust beside the door. Thick draperies and gleaming tile. Of course this place cost more than he'd said. Lying *liar*.

Shaking her head, she marched up to the desk and dug through her purse until she found her keycard. She placed it down on the counter and slid it across to the woman standing there.

Who of course asked her a question in French.

Shit. She'd gotten way too dependent on Rylan handling all of their transactions this past week. She blinked a couple of times, all her high school French flying out of her mind, deserting her.

"English?" she asked weakly.

"But of course. Are you checking out, mademoiselle?"

"No. No, I—the other person I was staying with. He can keep the room." It was his anyway. She bit her lip. Maybe she should offer to pay her half of the bill for the past few days. As if there was any chance she could afford it. "It's just me who's leaving."

"I see." She took the keycard and fixed her with a sympathetic look, and Kate wanted to melt right into the tile and disappear. "There is a water closet." She pointed to the left, down a hallway, then gestured at her own face. "If you would like to freshen up, I can hold your bag."

How much of a mess did she look like?

She nodded. "Thanks." She rolled her suitcase to the end of the desk, where the woman tucked it under the counter.

Her cheeks burned as she rounded the corner to the bathroom, hauling the door open and stepping inside. At least there wasn't anybody else there to witness her humiliation. She stepped up to the mirror and took a good, long look at herself.

It was worse than she'd thought.

Her eyes and nose were red, heartache written across every inch of her. In despair, she grabbed a wad of paper towels and ran them under the tap.

The goddamn gold-filigree tap.

God*damm*it.

She squeezed the sodden mess in her fist and threw it away, turning off the tap and running to lock herself into a stall. Her head hit the back of the door, and her eyes blurred and burned. Hot tears made tracks down her face. Their room had been just as nice, the fixtures had shone just as brightly.

She felt so *stupid*, and not just for missing the signs.

Her mother's voice kept coming back to her, telling her that people weren't always who they said they were. Kate hadn't learned from her mother's mistakes, and now she hadn't even learned from her own. After her last breakup, she'd sworn she'd learn to stand on her own, that she'd never let anyone lure her in with pretty words again.

Rylan's words had been pretty all right.

Another choking sob tore itself free from her throat. He'd made her feel special, and so she'd let down her defenses, convinced that he was *different*.

She took a deep, shaking breath and blew it out, opening her eyes. She tore off a couple of handfuls of toilet paper and wiped her eyes and blew her nose.

This time, she'd learned her lesson. Letting people in was a mistake, believing any of the things they told her to get her in bed. It was all a mistake.

One she was never, ever going to make again.

Rylan wanted to throw something. He eyed his phone, the lamp, half the contents of his suitcase. Reared back and started to take a swing at the wall itself but drew himself up short.

He could see the headline in the gossip page: BELLAMY HEIR TRASHES HOTEL ROOM. He didn't need that shit.

He didn't need any of this.

Threading his hand through his hair, he gave it a good

hard tug and turned around to look at the fucking empty room he'd been left with. She'd only stalked out a few minutes ago. If he ran he could catch her. For a few euros, the doorman would probably be happy to tell him which way she'd gone.

But no. Fuck, no. He'd already made his case. He'd stopped her ten times on her way out. Nothing he could say would change anything. It would probably just make things worse. He couldn't go after her.

He couldn't stay here, alone, either.

Jaw gritted, barely restrained violence still thrumming through his limbs, he gathered up what little of his stuff he'd let get strewn across the room and shoved it into his bag. Out of habit, he opened all the drawers and checked the closet. Even lifted up the bed skirt—

Only to find a book there.

A sketchbook.

Fuck.

It suddenly seemed impossible to breathe through the tightness of his chest. He flipped it open, and he had to close his eyes. Had to stop himself from crinkling the paper in the stone of his fist.

They were the pictures of him, of course. A dozen pages of his face and his eyes and his hands. All of him, spread nude across that bed.

He'd shown her so much. He'd hidden things he shouldn't have, but his ribs were clawing at him with the anger boiling in his chest.

Well, fuck her. Fuck that and fuck everything. He grasped the pages in his fist and moved to tear them out and—

And he couldn't. It was all he had of hers.

Faltering, eyes hot, he closed the book and laid it on top of all the other crap in his bag. He'd find a way to get it back to her. That would be the right thing to do.

With that, he zipped up the bag and slung it over his shoulder.

He took the stairs down to the lower level. When he slid his card across the counter to the woman at the desk, she raised one eyebrow and asked, "Vous partez?" *Are you checking out?*

That had been his plan, but…"Non." He'd booked the room through the end of her stay.

And he might be livid with her now, but if she couldn't find someplace else…she could always come back here. He wouldn't take that option away from her.

The woman furrowed her brow as she scanned the card. "Une clé nous a déjà été rendue pour cette chambre." *I've already had another key returned for this room.* She looked up from her screen, and the expression on her face was damning.

Kate had dropped her key off when she'd left. It made him even angrier, that she would have left herself without recourse. What if she couldn't find someplace? Her options had to be limited on her budget, and hostels sometimes sold out.

"Oh." He blinked a couple of times. Dammit all. Refusing to be judged, he asked to add another name to the reservation.

Kate wouldn't come back. Her pride wouldn't let her. But if she had to…he'd make sure she was taken care of.

It was too little too late. But it was all he had left that he could do.

* * *

Of course the only open bunk was a top one, smack-dab in the middle of the room.

Kate put her bravest face on. She was lucky to have found a place to stay, and to have been able to afford it. Forget that it had no privacy, or that she was probably going to fall and break her neck if she had to go to the bathroom in the middle of the night.

She shook her head and rolled her suitcase up to the wall beside the bunk. She was lucky to be here, and it was only two nights. Two nights alone in a tiny bed, sharing a room with five strangers.

But it was fine. The best she could have hoped for, considering.

Grabbing her purse, she climbed the ladder up to her bed. At least the ceiling was high enough that she could sort of sit up without bumping her head. Sighing, she dug through her bag until she found her travel guide. It was already well into the evening, so there wasn't much point going out, but she could figure out what to do with the rest of her trip. Not everything was lost. She had one more day here in Paris, and she had the freedom to spend it any way she wanted to. No negotiating about when to meet up with anyone for dinner. No smoldering, pleading eyes staring at her. No gorgeous man entreating her to stay in bed.

Just her and her sketchpad. Exactly how she'd wanted it to be.

But it wasn't what she wanted anymore.

The idea of exploring museums on her own hurt her heart. Eating meals in cafés alone, reading a book when she could be snuggled up in bed, watching weird TV while listening to the translation being whispered, warm against her ear. It all *hurt*.

The cover of the book blurred as her vision went damp. She'd had so many ideas about what this trip would be, and all of them had been wrong.

She had one more day to see everything left she had to see.

And all she wanted to do was go home.

The door to the apartment banged against the wall as Rylan slammed it open. Shoving the thing closed behind him, he dropped his bag in the foyer and stormed into the kitchen.

The mess he'd left behind had all been cleared away, but the foul, stifling feeling in the air still lingered. No cleaning crew would ever be able to contend with that. He laughed darkly at himself.

Reaching up into the cabinet, he pulled down a highball glass. The good liquor was stashed behind the bar in the living room. Seemed a pity to waste thirty-year-old scotch on a mood as poisonous as the one he was choking on right now, but that was the benefit of his life, right? His stupid, pointless life.

Gripping the glass, he headed to the bar, not bothering to turn on the lights. He'd left the curtains open, so Paris's glow was seeping in. He popped the top off one of the crystal decanters and poured himself a couple of fingers. The whiskey went down nice and smooth as he knocked it back.

He slapped the glass down on the top of the bar, then braced his arms and let his head hang.

A week. He'd had one fucking week with Kate. After

spending a year essentially alone, it should have been nothing. A drop in the bucket. But it had been everything.

One week had been all it had taken to make the rest of his life look so hollow.

He raised his head a fraction, and his gaze focused in on the vase sitting on the corner of the bar. It was pink porcelain. Probably cost a fortune.

He *hated* the fucking thing.

He hated all the time he'd spent staring at it, hated the color of it, hated the idea that his mother—his *mom* had left it here along with all the other things she didn't need. Left it here to rot.

The violence that had shaken his limbs at the hotel came rumbling back with a vengeance. Before he knew what he was doing, he'd picked the vase up and drawn his arm back. And he put all his force and all his anger into hurling it as hard as he could.

The vase hit the wall with a crash, shattering into ruin. A rain of jagged porcelain shards, crumbling into the carpet, and fuck. Just *fuck*.

He'd made such a mess of everything.

"Was that really necessary?" a voice asked out of nowhere.

He jerked his head up, flailing his arm to the side, getting his hand around a stray corkscrew that'd been left out. A figure was sitting up on the couch—the very one he'd just flung a vase over. Pulse rocketing, he reached behind himself, feeling along the wall for a light, flicking it up when his fingers connected with the switch.

He blinked hard against the sudden brightness, willing his vision to adjust. Once it had, he gaped. Set the corkscrew back down on the counter.

What the hell?

"Lexie?"

His sister arched her back, letting out an enormous yawn. "Long time no see, brother dearest." She paused for a minute and sat up straighter. She blinked, then cocked her head to the side. "Dude. You look like shit."

chapter TWENTY-FOUR

"Seriously, what happened to you?"

Rylan wanted to bang his head against the table, but he managed to restrain himself. Barely. "Could we maybe focus first on what the hell you think you're doing here?"

"What"— Lexie looked around innocently—"in the dining room? Where else am I supposed to eat my dinner? Midnight snack? Is it closer to midnight in this time zone? I'm not sure."

He rolled his eyes.

Once he'd more or less recovered from the heart attack she'd given him by showing up in his living room, he'd stormed off to the bedroom he'd been using as his own to wash his face and try to get himself under control. His sister had apparently taken advantage of the pause in conversation to order take-out.

Now she sat at the big, fancy dining room table he never used, dark hair tied in a knot on top of her head, bright pink pajamas making his already sore eyes hurt.

He gestured toward the croissant and lox and fruit she'd

unpacked from the brown paper sack it had arrived at their door in. "Who even delivers croissants?"

She shrugged. "Beats me. Jerome can get you anything you want, though. Night or day."

"Jerome." The concierge down in the lobby. "How do you know Jerome?"

She gave him a look like he was an idiot. It wasn't an expression he'd had directed at him in a while, but it was painfully familiar. "Mother and Evan and I killed an entire summer here one year." She waved a hand at him. "But you wouldn't remember. You decided to stay at Exeter or something, I think."

Of course he had. He'd taken any excuse he could get not to go home back then. "You were, what? Fifteen?"

"Fourteen."

"And Jerome was getting you anything you wanted, huh?"

"Within moderation." Her eyebrow twitched upward. "Some things I preferred to handle internally."

Rylan really didn't even want to know.

He gave her a second as she tore off a piece of croissant, topped it with a bit of the salmon, and popped it into her mouth. The noise she made was borderline obscene. "You cannot get a croissant like this outside of Paris."

Of course you could. There were five places he could name in New York alone. "Lex," he finally said, out of patience. He'd come back here to lick his wounds, dammit, not deal with his sister. "What are you doing here?"

"Well, I was trying to take a nap, right up until you decided you didn't like Mom's interior decorating."

He didn't take the bait. "Aren't you supposed to be at school?"

She rolled her eyes. "I graduated two weeks ago. If you read your email you'd know that."

"So, what, you decided to celebrate with a trip to Paris? Here to find yourself or something?" The question came out sneering, but it threatened to strangle him.

"Ha-ha. Not all of us have time to travel for pleasure, you know." She stabbed a bit of her fruit, then set her fork aside, narrowing her eyes as she stared at him. "Look, Thomas has been trying to call you. I've been trying to call you. The one time you actually pick up, you brush me off within about three seconds. It's been a year, Teddy."

"Don't call me that."

"I'll call you whatever I want. Family gets to do that."

He snorted. "Family."

"Yup. Like it or not, that's what we are."

"And we're supposed to, what? Band together and pick up the pieces our disgraced patriarch left for us?"

"Basically."

"Well, I don't want to." He rose from his seat, feeling too caged in there at the fancy table in this ugly, fancy room. Feeling too caged in this conversation. Rubbing a hand over his face, he paced over to the wall, then flipped, putting his back to the plaster. "I wash my hands of the whole damn thing."

"You washing your hands of me and Evan, too?"

"Evan doesn't give a shit about any of this."

"He will, someday, when he wakes up from the hippy dreamland he's living in."

That *hippy dreamland* being art school. Anger rose up in Rylan's throat. "Why do you always have to dismiss what he wants to do with his life?"

"Because it's not a real life! He should be part of the family business—"

"Not everybody wants to be you!"

Fuck. First it had been Kate, thinking about throwing away her passion because of whatever imaginary pressures she was facing to conform, and now it was this. It had always been this.

It had always been Lexie, striving so damn hard to be their father. Only their father hadn't wanted a daughter for a CEO. He'd wanted a son. Evan had been too sensitive—too drawn into other things.

So Rylan had been the one to step up. He'd done what he had to do, for the family and the company, and for Lexie and Evan, too. Fighting for Lexie's right to a seat at the table. For Evan's chance to study whatever he wanted to at school. Fighting for everyone except himself, and he was tired, goddammit all.

He was done.

He glanced up at Lexie to find her staring at him, face stricken.

"Fuck it," he mumbled under his breath. She'd never understood anyone who hadn't had her drive.

He was almost to the door before she spoke.

"I don't want anyone to be me." Her voice was unusually soft. Just a little bit shaky.

He didn't turn around, facing the hall as he said, "But you expect us all to want the same things you do."

"I don't. I just want you to care."

"Well, I don't. Not anymore."

"Just because Dad got caught—"

"He didn't just get caught. Christ, Lex, don't you get it?"

All the things he never talked about—the things he never even let himself so much as *think* about—were rising up, sticking in the back of his throat and dripping poison into his gut.

She threw her hands up. "No! I don't, okay? I don't get it. The whole thing made you so damn butt-hurt—"

"They took everything." Fuck, fuck, *fuck*. He smacked his fist against the archway of the door and closed his eyes, pressing his brow to the back of his hand. "I gave my whole fucking life to Dad's ambition." His breath went short, his lungs tightening. "It was all I had, okay? Dad's name and Dad's company and Dad's dirty money, and the name's worthless now. Our family is worthless. The company is in ruins. All I have left is the money."

He'd thought there'd been something else there. With Kate, when she hadn't known who he was or what he brought to the table. She'd looked at him like he was something more.

But in the end, after she'd found out...

It still hadn't been enough.

He squeezed his eyes shut tighter and gritted out, "Without it, I'm nothing."

A long beat of silence followed, deafening even over the roaring in his ears.

"Teddy..."

He cut her off right there. Pushing off the wall, he opened his eyes and squared his shoulders. "If you're still here in the morning, the coffee's—"

"In the jar next to the fridge."

"Right." He took another step forward.

Her voice followed. "You're not nothing."

"Sure."

"And you know you can't run forever."

He clenched his hands into fists and kept walking.

Only in the silence of his room, with the door closed, did he whisper, "Watch me."

Kate knelt beside her suitcase the following morning, gathering her things as she got ready to head out. Her heart still ached every time she let herself think about what had happened the day before, but she was done with that. *Done.*

She'd given into the temptation to be a self-pitying lump the night before, but this morning, Paris was her oyster. She was going to do all the things she'd been too caught up in her whirlwind romance to take the time for. There were a couple of sights she still wanted to see, and she was getting back to the Louvre if it killed her. All she needed were her pencils and charcoals, maybe that lonely little bottle of ink. Her new sketchbook...

Her heart pounded in her chest as she turned the contents of her suitcase over a second time. Her sketchbook.

It wasn't there.

The metal structure of the bunk behind her creaked as one of her still-sleeping roommates turned over in her bed. Kate bit her lip. She felt like a heel to be making so much noise, but she needed that book. Professionally if nothing else. Those sketches she'd done had documented the new style she was developing. She could've used them for reference for when she wanted to—

She stopped herself, an ugly bubble of laughter getting caught in her throat.

For when she wanted to what, *draw* him?

And suddenly, she wanted to do just that. Not the lovesick paintings she'd imagined she'd labor over while she nursed her broken heart, but angry ones. She wanted to take him apart, lay him out with furious brushstrokes and flay him to pieces with a palette knife. Expose him as a liar and a thief and—

A thief.

A new, colder rage slipped like ice into her veins. Did he *steal* her book? He would've had the opportunity. While she'd been in the bathroom, when he'd started to unpack her stuff in an effort to get her to stay. He'd already stolen her secrets and her story and her body. Taking her art would've been just one more violation.

Maybe he'd done it to get her to contact him. He was so good at saying all the right things. He'd lured her into his bed once already, and he'd been damn close to convincing her to stay and hear him out yesterday. Maybe this had all been another trick to rob her of her time, or convince her to let him fuck her again before she left.

Maybe she should do just that.

He had told her that she deserved pleasure and sex, and clearly he knew how to give it to her. She could get in touch with him and ask him if he'd found her sketchbook and go back to the mansion he probably lived in and get him to put his mouth on her again. Take what she wanted from him this time.

And then leave. Go home with all kinds of lessons learned.

About what she could ask for in bed and what happened to her when she let it become more than that. More than just sex.

But no. Crawling back to him after everything she'd said—she wouldn't give him the satisfaction.

She couldn't afford to take the risk. Rage might be fueling her blood right now, but her heart was still too tender. Too bruised. She didn't trust it enough.

It—and she—needed time to harden up before she tried getting close to anyone again.

Hands shaking, she repacked her suitcase and stowed it, then checked over her purse. She'd swing by the hotel where she and Rylan had stayed on the off chance that housekeeping had found her book. That she'd just left it there by mistake.

If it wasn't there, she'd write it off as a loss. She'd put it behind her.

She'd move on.

Lexie was still there when Rylan woke up. She'd traded the pajamas for one of her usual ensembles, a black and white and pink top with jeans she'd probably paid a grand to have look like they'd been casually worn in. She'd done her hair and makeup, too, though he had no idea who for.

He stopped at the threshold of the living room to blink the sleep from his eyes.

Jesus, when had she started to look so much like their mother?

Scrubbing at his face, he stumbled past the couch where it looked like she'd decided to crash for the night, pillows and folded-up blankets stacked up neatly on the floor beside it. He mumbled out a low grunt of a greeting as he passed her.

"You seem chipper."

He grunted again and poured himself some coffee. Lexie must have made it earlier. At least having her around was good for something.

It was early yet. By his own ridiculous standards, he'd slept in the past few mornings with Kate, but waking up alone had apparently reverted him back to his usual habits. And he was exhausted.

"What're you doing up?" He poured some cream in his coffee and took a sip.

"Jet lag is a bitch. I got a nap in, but that was about it."

"You could have used one of the bedrooms."

"You're in the one I always used to stay in. And Mother's room..."

Yeah. That was the last place he wanted to sleep, too.

"There's always a hotel."

"Like the one you've been staying at the past few days?"

That woke him up. "Excuse me?"

"You left the bill on the entryway table. You still have the place for another night, you realize."

"That's not for me." Not anymore.

"And the duffel bag by the door is just one you keep full of dirty laundry all the time?"

He didn't have an answer for that. Flipping her off was close enough, though.

"Very mature." She turned off the TV and crossed the room to him, empty coffee mug in hand. "You know, you never did tell me what was wrong last night."

There wasn't much point denying that something had been bothering him. The shattered vase in the corner kind of gave him away. "I don't want to talk about it."

"Ooh, it must be good, then." She refilled her cup and put her back to the counter. "Come on." Her voice went teasing. "I can braid your hair and you can tell me all your secrets."

He gave her an appraising look. She was trying just a

little too hard here. But then again, she also decidedly wasn't pressing him about going back to New York to save the company. Or giving him shit about his outburst from the night before.

So he went with it, letting the one corner of his mouth curl up. "The hair-braiding thing only ever worked on Evan and you know it."

She hummed in agreement. "He had such nice hair, before Dad made him cut it off."

"It's probably grown back by now."

"It was still short the last time I saw him."

"Which was when?"

"Six months ago, maybe? He came and stayed with me for Christmas."

While Rylan had stayed here, staring out a window at a Paris that was lit up like a tree.

"Teddddyyyyyy," she whined. "Tell me."

The name and the question made every hair on the back of his neck stand up.

"It's nothing." He gripped his mug tighter. "Just—just a girl."

"I knew it!"

"Please."

"What's her name? What does she do? Is she French? I bet she's French."

"It doesn't matter." He set his mug down before he could break it. "She's gone now." He put his hands on the counter and faced away from her. Fuck, this hurt to admit. "It's over."

He tried to remind himself: It had been over before it had begun.

* * *

Kate hesitated, standing at the base of a set of white marble steps. It was one of her very favorite parts of the Louvre. Above her loomed *Winged Victory*, the huge statue she'd seen with Rylan that very first day, when he'd taken her here to try to earn her trust. This was the path they had taken. Just a few more twists and turns and she'd be back in the rooms where he'd charmed her, looking at beautiful, enormous paintings. Waxed philosophical about Greek mythology and told her about his family. If any of that had even been true. Bitterness welled up at the back of her throat.

But then she hesitated. His tales about the rich, socialite mother who'd taken him to art museums when the family visited Paris on business—they fit with the confessions he'd made once she'd figured him out. So maybe not every story he'd sucked her in with had been a lie. Just the majority of them.

If only she could go back in time and *shake* her former self. Open her eyes and save herself so much heartache. All the signs had been there. She was the idiot who'd refused to read them.

She dug her nails into her palm. And he'd been the asshole to let her believe what she wanted to.

She was blocking up the flow of traffic, standing where she was. Sighing at herself, she changed direction and headed away from the stairs, back toward the gallery she'd just been through. There were entire sections of the museum they hadn't made it to. She was going to hit as many of them as she could.

This was what she'd come to Paris for in the first place, after all. Not to have some torrid love affair, or to fall head over heels for a beautiful, tousle-haired, blue-eyed boy.

A rich, lying, confused, sad man.

She was here for art and beauty and culture. To find her muse, and she'd found it all right. She'd happened upon a whole new style of drawing that she was going to take home with her, and into whatever was next for her life.

She didn't need him to make the art come to life. Didn't have to conjure the feeling of him at her spine to get her drawings to come out right. She didn't.

She wouldn't.

The next morning, Lexie slammed a briefcase down on the coffee table.

Rylan looked at it for a long second, then turned his attention back to his phone. "Nice. But I prefer black leather. Brown snakeskin is a little feminine."

"You asshole."

"Yes, dear?"

It was pointless, but he tapped the refresh icon on his email again. When nothing happened, his throat threatened to close on him.

There were so many things he'd never asked Kate about. He didn't know where in New York she lived or what her parents' names were. He knew she'd gotten into Columbia for graduate school, but he didn't know if she'd take the offer, and if she didn't, he didn't know where she'd end up working.

He knew that she was leaving the country today, at some unspecified time, on some unspecified flight. He hadn't expected her to contact him, and the same restraint that had kept him from running after her when she'd walked out of their hotel room had stopped him from sending a message of his own.

But she was leaving. Soon. It already felt like she was a little bit farther away.

Lexie shoved the briefcase closer. "These are all of the reports you're legally entitled to as Dad's proxy."

"Wonderful. I needed some kindling."

"Goddammit, Teddy."

He snapped his head up. "I told you not to call me that."

"And I told you to come home." For a second her mouth wavered, real emotion in those cool, distant eyes.

It made him pause. "Lex..."

"Please. I can't do this without you. Legally, I'm not allowed to." She took a deep breath and dropped her arms to her side. "I don't want to do this alone. Dad built this company from nothing. It's all we have left."

"He should have given it all to you."

"Yeah." She said it unironically. "After the way you flaked, he should have. But he didn't." She looked him right in the eye. "Please. Rylan." Her voice shivered as she gave in and used his actual name. "I know he fucked you over. Him and Mom, both. They fucked us all over, up, down, and sideways. But we can make something of it."

"Like what?"

"A life? A family?" Her half attempt at a smile crumpled. "I don't know. Maybe it's a stupid idea. But it matters to me. And you being okay matters to me, too."

He leaned back against the couch. "I'm always all right."

"No. You're not." She crossed the room to the bag he'd

somehow failed to notice her packing. She put on her jacket and lifted the handle of the suitcase. "I told you before. You can't run forever."

"Is that a challenge?"

"A fact." She shook her head. "I can't tell you what to do. Obviously. But I'm worried about you. I'm mad at them, too, but I want to make something of what they left us. If you change your mind..."

"You'll be the first to know."

"Please, Rylan. If you won't leave with me today... the next board of directors meeting is in a few months." Her expression went pleading. "It's our last chance."

His chest constricted, his throat catching.

One of the emails he hadn't replied to had warned him they were coming up on the date. Ninety days out from the sentencing, the now provisional board had taken over, with a one-year mandate of stewardship. Once that year was up, the Bellamy family had a final chance to restake their claim, and then that was it. Everything his father had built and destroyed—everything he himself had helped build...

He'd get to watch it all be swept away. A silent shareholder with a front-row seat to witness his legacy as it burned.

He should have laughed. Should have been delighted to watch it go.

But there was something. This quiet voice in his heart, one Kate had awoken.

It told him he was better than sitting here idly. He could make something of his life.

He pushed it down and returned his gaze to his phone. He could go back there, all right. But if he did, his life would never be his own.

With a sigh, Lexie rolled her suitcase across the carpet to
him. Bending at the waist, she dipped to press a kiss to his
cheek. "Come home. Help me fix this."

He grabbed her hand and squeezed it.

But he couldn't promise her any of that.

Letting go, he said, "Have a safe trip back, Lex."

Something in her face fell. She turned around without saying anything else.

He didn't watch her walk away from him, luggage in hand.
He'd had enough of that to last him a lifetime this week. Instead, he buried his gaze in the screen of his phone.

And he hit refresh. Again.

Kate heaved out a sigh as she plunked herself down in the
lone free chair at the airport internet café. Around her, people were moving, wheeling around their tiny suitcases and
checking their passports. She tucked her own boarding pass
and travel documents into the front pocket of her purse, her
security wallet relegated to the bottom of her carry-on at
last.

With an hour and a half left before her flight took off, and
her gate only a flight of stairs away, she let herself relax. It
hadn't been easy, getting herself packed up and checked out
of her hostel, or carrying her things down to the Metro, or en-
during the long ride out to Charles de Gaulle. But she'd done
it by herself, and now it was over.

Her trip was over.

She wiggled the mouse to dismiss the screen saver. A window popped up, asking for her payment information before
it'd let her log on and actually use the thing. She hesitated.

She wasn't unwilling to spend the couple of euros, extortion-ate though the price might be. But she wanted to get her head on straight before she started burning time.

She'd come here for a reason. Both to Paris and to this café.

Swallowing hard, she rummaged through her bag and pulled out her sketchbooks. She flipped through the one she'd finished, forcing herself to really acknowledge the progression in the images flicking past her. More than a year's worth of drawings, more than a year's worth of trying to figure out who she was.

When she got to the one she'd done from the top of Mont-martre, she ran her thumb across the bottom of the page. It was good. Really good. A nice capstone to all the other styles she'd tried on over the past year—one drawing done in a style that felt like her own.

She'd *found* something that day. The whole trip was worth it, just for that. No matter how much the rest of it hurt.

Refusing to dwell, she closed that book and opened up the one she'd started yesterday. She'd filled a dozen pages with studies of statuary in the Louvre, and views of the Arc de Tri-omphe and the Seine. They didn't have the same quality to them as the ones she'd done before things with Rylan had fallen apart. But that was okay. She could recapture that with time. After a few days alone to lick her wounds.

Nodding to herself, she turned back to the computer screen and entered in her information. Once she was in, she opened up a web browser and fired up her email. She glanced at the clock, giving herself exactly five minutes to indulge herself.

The snapshots Rylan had sent her took a few seconds to load, and she watched the screen with her heart in her throat.

When they appeared, the sight of them was a punch to the gut. God. That first day, with the two of them outside the museum, him looking so debonair, her with a smile that seemed about to crumble right off her face. Brittle and wary. She'd had no idea what she was getting herself into.

And then their last day together, when she was a whole different kind of miserable.

He looked… fragile in this picture. Like he knew, and had accepted it, and was waiting for the blow.

Well, she'd delivered it. He deserved even worse for how he'd used her and lied to her and betrayed her trust. But at least she could hold her head high. She'd figured him out, and this time she hadn't hesitated. She wasn't her mom, and she wasn't her old self, either.

She deserved better. And she was finally starting to demand it.

As much as part of her wanted to forget their whole time together, that was one thing she could be grateful for. Rylan's voice had joined her own in drowning out her father's. He'd told her that her artwork was amazing, and it hadn't just been simple praise. He'd really looked at the work she'd done, and with a considering eye. He'd always taken a moment to think before making his pronouncement.

He'd told her that it was she herself who was special. Her way of seeing. The pieces of herself that she let bloom across the page.

He'd told her she already knew what she wanted to do.

There were still a couple of minutes left of the five she'd budgeted for wallowing, but she minimized the window with the images, returning to her inbox.

It only took a moment to pull up the messages that had

been haunting her this entire time. She brought each one up in a new window and arranged them side by side.

Grad school or a real job. Risk or safety. Dreams or security.

She'd come to Paris chasing a dream. She'd followed a different one, one about love and sex and the ideal of a man who might treat her with honesty and care.

That one had turned out to be a fantasy.

But the other one...

Rylan might have been a fantasy. But he'd told her some things she'd needed to hear.

Without another thought, she clicked on the message from the admissions office.

She typed out her acceptance with shaking hands. This might be crazy, but if she didn't take the chance, she'd regret it always.

Her reply declining the job offer was even quicker and easier to write. Once you knew what you were doing with your life, everything seemed to flow.

She hit send on both messages, then closed the windows.

Before logging out of the terminal, she brought up the photos of her and Rylan again. Every moment since she'd left him, she'd been torn between wanting to punch his teeth in and wanting to contact him. She didn't know what she'd say, but things felt somehow unfinished between them.

Just in case, she checked her inbox one last time. Her chest deflated when there wasn't a message from him. A tiny part of her was still hoping for some kind of overture, some kind of apology.

Just as well.

With her time on the computer running out, and with only an hour until her flight, she took one last look at his face on the screen. She was still angry, but there was more there, too.

She pressed her fingers to her lips and then grazed them across the screen.

"Thank you," she whispered. "You asshole. For everything."

She ended her session and gathered her things.

It was time to leave Paris—and Rylan—behind.

chapter TWENTY-FIVE

Three months later

The stool next to Rylan's made an ugly, scraping noise as it was dragged against the floor. He furrowed his brow. He hadn't thought he'd been quite that unaware of what was going on around him. But shit happened. He looked up from his paper to take in the girl settling herself in beside him.

Smooth, caramel-colored skin, tight curls. One of those weird teardrop-shaped bags.

Shorts. Converse.

He folded his paper over and shot her a halfhearted grin, feeling a little sick at himself as he did. God. It was like muscle memory or a reflex, the way he flirted. No wonder he didn't come across as the kind of guy to trust.

The girl smiled back and held up her hand to try to get the bartender's attention. The man came over and glanced between the two of them.

Rylan tapped at his own empty glass. The man looked at the girl expectantly as he reached for Rylan's whiskey.

"Anglais?" the girl asked. *English?*

Fuck it. Rylan was bored. Holding up a hand to stall the

bartender, he turned to her. "Allow me. What would you like?"

She raised an eyebrow. "Red wine. Dry. Local would be nice."

Rylan knew just the thing. He rattled off her order to the barkeep. While the bartender was pouring, Rylan held out his hand to the girl. "Rylan."

She took it, her grip warm and firm. "Naya."

"Nice to meet you."

"You, too."

Her wine appeared in front of her. Dropping her hand, Rylan plucked his own glass off the bar and held it up. She clinked obligingly and they each took a sip.

It was a promising start, if a tired one. There were more than enough free stools at this particular bar this early in the evening. She didn't have to pick the one right next to his. He didn't have to buy her a drink. And yet she did and he did.

A handful of months ago, he'd have considered it ideal. Now it was just another way to pass the time.

"Traveling by yourself?" he asked. Creepy as conversational openers went, but he didn't really care. This wasn't going anywhere.

"Nah. My girlfriends ditched me for a club. Not my speed."

He hummed and took a sip of his drink. "And what is your speed?"

"Quiet bars. Dark, mysterious strangers." Her elbow nudged his, and God. A handful of months ago, he'd have considered this a *dream*.

Today, he shook his head, grinning wryly. "What else?"

At least the girl could take a hint. She shifted her arm

away. But she didn't pick up her drink and go. "I don't know."
She shrugged. "Art museums, I guess."

She said it so casually, as if they were just another thing
she'd get around to while she was in town. Not the way Kate
had said it, voice warm with reverence. Like those shrines to
old, dead masters were exactly that. Sacred.

Still, he lifted his gaze, his flagging interest recaptured.
"Yeah? Which ones have you been to so far?"

"Hit the Louvre today. Musée d'Orsay is on tap for tomorrow."

Rylan twisted in his seat to face her more fully. "You're
going to love it. They—" He paused, the back of his throat
suddenly dry. "They have an amazing collection of Cézannes."

"I'll be sure to keep an eye out for them." Her gaze raked
him up and down. "And what's your speed?"

Nope. Not happening. He shook his head. "Don't worry
about me." He turned his glass in his hands, feeling that tight
ball of wistfulness unfurling in his chest. "I'm just a guy."

Just a part of the scenery.

He didn't know why he was still here.

He slammed his fifth glass of whiskey down.

She pulled out her sketchbook.

He ordered another.

"Whoa, you okay there?"

Rylan listed in his chair, frowning unhappily at his empty
glass. "I'm fine," he lied. "Just fine."

The girl paused, lifting her pencil from the paper.

Squinting, he tilted his head to the side. "You know who you remind me of?"

"Who?"

His smile felt like it would break. Just like his ribs.

Just like his heart.

He opened his mouth to answer—

Rylan woke the next morning to the sound of his phone. His head throbbed dimly, and vague flashes from the night before skipped through his mind as he struggled to sit up, reaching for his nightstand where he always plugged the damn thing in. Only it wasn't there—

Only it wasn't even his bed he was lying in. Jesus, he'd passed out on the couch again. A quick pat-down of his pockets and he found his phone. Holding it up to his face, he saw his sister's name. Mashing the button to ignore the call, he tossed his phone aside. With a groan, he lay back down.

He hadn't forgotten about her fucking board meeting, thank you very much. As if he could forget that the whole future of the company was riding on him tucking his tail between his legs and letting himself get sucked right back into the life he'd finally escaped. The one full of mandates and guilt trips and his father always breathing down his goddamn neck. High-stakes negotiations with clients and business partners, wining and dining, and the blood-heating rush of adrenaline, of power when you got what you wanted.

The satisfaction of a job well done.

He thunked his head back against the arm of the couch and instantly regretted it. A shock of pain burst through his skull.

Wincing, he squeezed his eyes shut tighter and gripped the top of his head.

See? Why would he need his old life back? Here, he had an uncomfortable designer sofa. An empty apartment and empty days and an empty fucking heart.

And a hangover from hell.

What the hell had he done to himself last night? He'd dragged himself home at least, but he'd slept in the living room, in his clothes, and he smelled like the bottom of an ashtray.

Like perfume.

Fuck. There had been a girl. An artist. She'd tried to pick him up, and he'd said no. He'd *definitely* said no. He knew how that kind of thing ended now.

Kate had left and Lexie had left, and he had stayed, and he had *tried* to go back to his routine. To his distractions. But no one was Kate.

This girl hadn't been Kate, either.

She'd still tried to draw him, though.

His stomach gave a protesting lurch as it started to come back to him.

The girl had waited until he was pretty hosed before she'd asked if she could do a sketch of him, and he'd tried to decline. But the girl hadn't given up. Eventually, he'd closed his eyes and let her do her worst, and it had *hurt*. Deep inside, in a place that liquor could never touch, no matter how hard he tried, it ached.

Because he remembered that. He remembered being as naked as a person could be, lying back and letting a woman see every part of him. Letting her capture it on a page.

Only to have her walk out the door the very next day.

At some point, the girl had finished. She'd shown him her sketch despite his protests, and it hadn't been like it'd been with Kate. The image staring back at him had looked as ugly as he had felt. In the very center of it had been the gap of his shirt. The glint of his father's ring against his chest.

His hand darted up to his neck, to the chain draped over his collarbones. And it burned. He'd been wearing the thing for years now, and why? When it just reminded him of his father, how he threw everything away. He'd thrown away their mother for being as faithless as he was. Had thrown away Lexie for being a girl and Evan for wanting more, and Rylan...

Bile filled the back of his throat.

Rylan he'd kept, but only the parts of him that served. Anything else Rylan had wanted for his life had been discarded like so much trash. Like he'd tried to discard the ring itself.

Only for Rylan to save it. To hold on to it and wear it above his heart.

Just like that, Rylan was back in his father's office, the day the papers had been signed on the divorce. He'd watched his father rip the band from his finger and hold it over the garbage bin. And Rylan said, "Stop."

The world threatened to swim, and it wasn't the low ripple of nausea or the way last night's bad decisions still throbbed through his brain.

Kate had worked her way under his skin because she'd looked at the world differently. She'd looked at *him* differently.

And the sudden twist of vertigo was him seeing his life in a whole different kind of light.

Clutching the top of his head against the lingering ache there, he shoved himself off the couch and stumbled down the hall toward his room. He caught himself in the doorframe for a second, then made his way to the wardrobe in the corner. He tugged on the handle of the drawer he never let himself open.

Kate's sketchbook was sitting there. Right where it always was.

He reached out a hand for it. Gripping the spine as delicately as he could, he pulled out the book and dropped backward, bracing himself as his ass connected with the floor. He winced at the impact, clasping his head a little tighter before letting go. Crossing his legs, he cradled the book on his lap and brushed his fingertips over the cover. And then he flipped it open. Past the cover where she'd written her name and her address, past her warm-ups, to the image of his body, naked on a bed for her.

Without even really thinking about it, he gripped his father's ring. It stood out in Kate's drawing, the chain darkly shaded against the bare skin of his chest. He'd kept it on him when he'd stripped everything else of himself away, and Kate had rendered it as if it were a part of him. Maybe it was.

Their very first day together, Kate had shown him this little sliver of her world, reminding him of art and beauty and all the things his father had taught him there wasn't room for in his life. He'd wanted to give her something back, and it hadn't even occurred to him at the time, as he'd led her into a deserted museum wing . . .

He hadn't just been showing her a painting he'd once been fond of. He'd been showing her a sliver of himself, from before. When he'd still had hope.

Hope for Zeus and Hera and hope for his parents' marriage. A vain hope, because he knew they both ended in ruin, but still. A hope that maybe, from all that pain and awfulness, there was something worth saving.

He raked a hand through his hair, tugging at the scalp until the ache lit up into a fierce, splitting pain.

Rylan had been so eager to believe the best about his parents' lives, and about the lives of ancient, fictional gods.

But not about his own.

When he'd first gotten to Paris, he'd felt like hell itself was on his heels. The trial had still been fresh, the loss stinging. He'd thrown himself into wasting his life with gusto, and he'd done a damn good job of it, too. The time had flown by, right up until it hadn't. Even then, the restlessness had only driven him to pursue his diversions more intensely.

Until, one day, a beautiful girl with eyes that saw the world in a way he'd never managed to before had walked into a coffee shop. She'd reminded him that there were parts of his life worth not throwing away.

And then he'd done what he'd been doing all year. He'd denied his past. God, but he'd deserved it when she'd left him.

Every day since then had felt like a year. He had no idea what he was doing anymore. Casual sex was ruined; sightseeing and chatting up tourists and exploring the city—they were all ruined.

He flipped to the page where Kate had drawn just his face.

It was such a contrast from what the girl last night had drawn.

It looked like the man he wanted to be.

His vision went blurry, his fingers curling in on themselves. Before he could destroy anything else, he closed Kate's sketchbook and pushed it away across the floor.

Right before she'd left, Kate had told him that he needed to figure out what he wanted. That he had to stop lying. To her, to himself.

Maybe he already knew. Maybe he just had to get past the things that were stopping him, too.

Around him, everything went still. He held his breath.

With unsteady hands, he reached for the back of his neck. He fumbled with the clasp of the chain. One, two tries, and then it was slipping from around his throat.

Nothing happened. No music played, and his life didn't suddenly change, but he felt lighter somehow. Dropping the ring into his open palm, he stared at the dull gleam of it.

Fucking off to France had felt like a way of saying to hell with everything and everyone. His father and all the ways he'd betrayed him; his mother and her distance, her abandonment. But all the while, he'd worn this symbol around his neck. He'd kept this reminder that even in the midst of an awful defeat, there had once, at its core, been something good.

Something worth not giving up on.

He'd done a lot of giving up of late.

He'd given up on Kate, had let her go without a fight.

He'd given up on his life and his family, on the company he'd helped build—and so what if it hadn't been his choice? He was the one who'd let himself be corralled down his father's path.

He was the one who could salvage something from its ashes.

But he'd given up on himself, too.

With his blood roaring in his ears, he took his father's ring, and he set it down. Let the chain that had tethered it to him for years fall by its side, and then he stared at them both on the ground.

It was time to stop romanticizing people who'd been too flawed to save themselves.

There was something worth saving. In his life. In his work. And with the girl who'd opened his eyes to all of it.

With Kate.

It didn't seem to matter how hard Kate tried. Nothing was working.

Her frugality was the only thing keeping her from tossing the stupid canvas in the trash—or better, lighting it up. Well, her frugality and her vague goal of trying to come across as sane to the others in her program. Pulling her ear-buds from her ears, she glanced around the studio. No one else was paying her any attention. Still, she suppressed her groan of frustration as she dropped her brushes in the turpen-tine and covered her face with her hands.

The semester had only just begun, and she was already starting to wonder if she'd made the wrong decision.

No. That was her father talking again.

She mentally slapped herself, pulling the brushes out of the soup and swabbing them off on her wad of paper toweling. Stabbing a little harder at it than was really a good idea for the health of the bristles, but whatever.

She belonged here, dammit all. She was as good as the rest of the students in her cohort, and she'd worked just as hard for her spot. Sacrificed as much, if not more. She was just in a rut, was all. A big Rylan-shaped rut.

Her heart gave a little pang, and she tightened her grip on the paint-soaked towels.

Three months it had been since she'd left him. Since she'd walked away from him and all the amazing, incredible things he'd done for her life and her confidence. He'd made her body and her art come alive. And then he'd torn her damned heart out.

She'd tried to paint him. Tried to process the mess he'd left of her chest in charcoal and oil. Working from grainy cell phone photographs and out-of-focus candids she'd snuck while he wasn't looking, she'd traced the outlines of his face. And every time she'd tried to sketch in those lips or those soulful eyes, she'd just about broken down.

She'd tried to destroy him, in her paintings. Taken him apart in a completely different way from how she had in that perfect hotel room on that perfect afternoon. Sliced streaks of crimson and black through the lying lines of his smile, blocked out the hollow of an eye and scrawled her anger across his ear as if that could make him hear her.

Once or twice, she'd tried to worship him, too. Lovingly rendered the details of his brow line and his jaw. But that hadn't worked for her, either.

She hated him and she loved him, and if she spent another second dwelling on either, she'd never make it out of this mess she'd made for herself. She needed to move on. Maybe she'd made the right decision, refusing to even so much as hear him out, and maybe she hadn't. But she'd made her choice, and she had to live with it now.

And so here she was. Even her pictures of the rest of Paris had been soured by her memories, but New York...New York was home. Intent on embracing what she had instead of mourning what she'd lost, she'd taken her crappy point-and-shoot to all the corners of the city and tried to capture it. The people and the dirt and the beauty of the place. She'd tried to *see* it, the way she'd learned to on her trip.

Facing her canvas again, she sighed. The city street looked dull, the line work she'd been so close to *getting somewhere* with in Paris contrived and stupid and pointless.

She dragged her wrist across her brow.

Then she picked out a brush. Squeezed a little more cerulean out onto her palette and dabbed the bristles into the paint. She closed one eye and regarded the image.

Returning her headphones to her ears, she stepped in closer to the canvas again.

She'd given up on Rylan, but she wasn't giving up on this. Time healed all wounds, and soon enough, with enough hard work, she'd find her muse again.

She'd find her *self* again. Here. On her own. At home.

chapter TWENTY-SIX

Home. Rylan turned the word over in his mind as he stared through tinted glass at the streets he'd left behind some fifteen long, pointless months ago.

At the time, he hadn't given a shit if he ever saw them again. He'd boarded a plane with his proverbial middle fingers up and washed the taste of the trial and his father and his wasted life away with the burn of airline whiskey. He'd left with the clothes on his back and a couple of books in a knapsack, and he wasn't returning with a whole lot more. A single suitcase and Lexi's briefcase.

Kate's sketchbook.

Swallowing hard, he ran his thumb across the cover one last time before tucking it safely back away. He'd have his chance to face that particular bit of smoldering landscape later. First, he had a different set of fires to put out—ones he'd once thought he'd just let burn.

But not anymore.

Smooth as could be, the car made the turn onto Sixth Avenue, and he worked his jaw, leaning forward to brace his elbows on his knees. Closing his eyes, he ran through his talking points in his mind.

It was his first time entering the lion's den on his own, and that alone made his pulse beat faster. If his father were here, he'd be drilling Rylan, checking with him over and over that he understood the plan. Rylan would've stared out the window as he nodded, silently stewing all the while.

He'd put in the time. Earned the degree his father had demanded of him, worked the long hours and sacrificed everything else. The least he could ask was to be trusted to know how to do his job.

There was no one telling him he had to be here now. Well. There'd been Lexie's entreaties and the board's demands, but at the end of the day, this was Rylan's decision.

The first one he'd made about his life in so long.

At last, the car slowed, and he took a deep breath, opening his eyes. There it was. Bellamy International. His goddamn name in big red letters on the side of a hundred-story building, and it made something squeeze in his chest.

No matter how much his father had ruined, this remained. It bore his name, so it was his.

It was well past time he acted like it.

As the driver came around to get the door, Rylan checked his watch. Five minutes to spare. Exactly as he'd planned.

Grabbing Lexie's briefcase, he adjusted his tie and his cuff links. Did up the button on the jacket of his suit.

Showtime. The door swung open. And he stepped out onto the sidewalk not just Rylan, but Theodore R. Bellamy III. And like it or not, he was home.

* * *

The whispers started before he'd made it halfway across the lobby. Tightening his grip on Lexie's briefcase, he ate up the marble-tiled space with long, measured strides, gaze forward. He recognized one of the girls at the visitors' desk and gave her a nod, holding a finger to his lips when she did a double take and reached for the phone. He didn't need to be greeted, and he sure as hell didn't want to be announced. She narrowed her eyes at him but moved her hand away from the receiver. Good girl.

At the executive elevator, he got a whole different sort of a look from the operator. "Mr. Bellamy. We weren't expecting you today."

He raised a brow and stepped into the waiting elevator car. "Good to see you, too, Marcus."

"Didn't say it wasn't good to see you, sir." Marcus pressed the button to close the doors. His reflection in the mirror smiled. "Just didn't know I'd get the pleasure."

"Ninety-fifth floor, if you would."

"Sure thing."

Rylan's ears finally popped around floor eighty-two. When the doors slid open, he gave Marcus a salute. He waited until the elevator was gone before turning around to face the hall.

Because if he hadn't, he might've stepped right back into that car.

Jesus, but it was his dad's tastes personified. Red carpet and dark wood and all the little tricks he swore reminded your visitors that they were on your turf now.

It was the furthest thing from home Rylan could imagine. But considering the closest he'd gotten to having one in the last ten years had been a tiny hotel room on a bread-scented *rue* in Paris, maybe that wasn't saying much.

Squaring his shoulders, he took the first step forward.

By the time he reached the conference room, it was two p.m. on the dot. The door stood all but closed, just a crack of space revealing the room within. Silently, he nudged it wider and peeked inside.

The scene was familiar enough. Spread out around the giant oak table were men old enough to be his father. There, at the head, was that bastard McConnell. Meanwhile, Thomas had been relegated to a seat maybe two-thirds of the way down. Rylan noted a half dozen other friendly faces and a couple of new ones. More than a couple of unfriendly ones, too. He cast his gaze wider, taking in the rest of the room. Behind the board members, in chairs pulled up to but not quite *at* the table, were their bevy of secretaries and PAs, and—

And Rylan had always known it looked bad. But in the past, he'd been at the table himself, not looking in.

Not seeing his crazy, fierce-as-hell sister sitting all alone in the corner of the room, lacking even an old white guy of her own to justify her presence there.

A nonvoting member. That was the status Lexie had been relegated to. The shortsighted assholes. The day she came of age or Rylan figured out a way to work around the charter to get her a spot on the board, they were going to be wishing they'd never pissed her off. Because she was going to *own* them.

Literally.

Only . . . only, she didn't look entirely her imperious self right now. Rylan tilted his head to the side, watching. Her gaze went from her notes to the head of the table, then to the clock and back again. Her chin was lifted high, her posture straight, because she wasn't giving an inch of ground, oh no. But there was something resigned about her. Not even disappointed, but like disappointment were a foregone conclusion. Like she'd already been disappointed so many times before.

But today, she wouldn't be. At least not by him.

Up at the front of the room, McConnell cleared his throat. "What do you say, gentlemen? Time we got started?"

That was probably Rylan's cue to make his presence known, but he smirked as he leaned against the doorframe, folding his arms across his chest. Biding his time. Never let it be said he didn't know how to make an entrance.

"Let's come to order then. Let the record show that this meeting of the board of directors of Bellamy International began at 2:02. Members in attendance include..." McConnell rattled off the names of all the gray-haireds at the table. He swept his gaze around the room, purposely passing Lexie over. "Is there a representative of the Bellamy family?"

And *there* it was. He paused to the count of three, just long enough for Lex to grit her teeth and open her mouth. But before she could get the first word out, Rylan pushed the door open.

"Why yes, there is." He projected his voice across the room as he swept into it. A dozen heads swung around to gawk at him, and he took them all in at once. Caught the split-second of surprise on McConnell's face before he schooled his expression. Caught Lexie's grimace turning into what was, for her, in this room, the closest thing to a shit-eating grin Rylan had ever seen. "Two of them, actually," he said, raising a hand in greeting to her. "Hey, sis."

She nodded back, eyes triumphant but smile restrained. "Theodore."

Ugh. He'd get her back for that later.

Putting a little extra swagger in his step, he headed straight for the front of the room, lifting an eyebrow at the guy who'd been presumptive enough to sit in his seat. The dude went red in the face, a battle clearly going on inside him about whether or not to budge. Thomas added the weight of his stare, and the chair-stealer finally caved. Leaving his PA to pick up his stuff, he scooted a few feet down, and Rylan dropped himself into the open spot.

Opening the briefcase, he pulled out a folder and set it on the table.

Ever since the day his father'd been led away in handcuffs, Rylan had been fighting who he was and where he came from, afraid he'd gone too far in becoming the man his father had wanted him to be. Into a copy of himself. But in that moment, there at that table, he remembered. The rush of it washed over him. He was good at this. He'd trained at it all his life.

He let the energy of confrontation fill him up, and then he banked it. With his posture that of a man completely at his leisure, he leaned back in his chair, twirling his pen and nodding along as McConnell fought to recover his balance and start working his way through the agenda. One by one, the other board members got over his unexpected appearance in their midst.

Right up until he asked his first question. Then all the heads in the room turned as one.

"What?" He pointed to the part of the document they'd been discussing. "I did the reading."

McConnell made a strangled-sounding noise with his throat.

Fortunately, Thomas jumped in before McConnell's eyes could actually pop out of his head. "Mr. Bellamy does bring up a good point."

Rylan swiveled back and forth in his chair as the discussion shifted. Over the course of the next hour, he left the running of the meeting to the people who'd been there all along, but he managed to keep things pointed in the direction he wanted them to go.

The direction Lexie had laid out for him.

He looked over at her as the tide started to turn in their favor, quirking one eyebrow in a silent question. *Good enough for you?*

She made a show of heaving her shoulders as she sighed, but her smile belied it all.

After what felt like about a million years, the meeting neared its close. Just one item left on the agenda.

McConnell looked around the room, and Rylan could see him counting in his head. Well, Rylan had done his counting, too. "As for the matter of reversion of the Bellamy family's controlling interest..." His gaze went to Rylan.

The bastard wasn't sure he had the votes to stay in control. Honestly, Rylan wasn't sure he had enough support, either.

But there was one motion he was sure he could get through.

Rylan cleared his throat and stood. "I'd like to call for a ninety-day grace period before the vote."

Relief fairly rippled through the room. McConnell's shoulders even lowered a fraction. "The motion stands," he said. "Simple majority."

Hands went up in the air to the tune of aye, and Rylan sank back into his seat.

Ninety days. Ninety days to shore up support, to devise a strategy.

To decide exactly how far he wanted this all to go, and whether or not he was prepared to take the helm.

The meeting adjourned shortly after, and Rylan stretched his arms over his head with a sense of satisfaction. There was still a lot to figure out, but he'd taken the first step, at least. He'd shown up. Claimed his place. And declined to let Rome burn.

Standing, Rylan packed up the briefcase, holding off the couple of folks who seemed to want to strike up a conversation by nodding toward his sister. He made his way over to her while she was still finishing her notes.

"So?" he asked. "How'd I do?"

"There's room for improvement." She closed her folio and set her pen down. "But I think you've got potential."

He smirked. She'd begrudged him his father's favor for so long. Even that admission felt like a triumph. "Glad to hear it."

Rising, she crossed her arms in front of her chest. "You cut it a little close there with the timing."

The corner of his lip threatened to twitch up, but he held steady, expression blank. "Sorry. Traffic across the Atlantic Ocean was a bitch."

"Asshole." Her frown held for another few beats. Then all at once, it fell away and she held out her arms.

He stepped into the hug, scooping her up.

"Thanks for coming," she said into his chest.

"Thanks for the push."

He held her close for a long minute. There weren't going to be any big emotional declarations here. Hell, already they'd said more than they usually did. That was how they worked. But all the same, it was apology and forgiveness. Approval and acceptance.

Letting her go, he stepped away.

"So," she started, slinging her bag over her shoulder. "You want to grab a drink or something? Dinner at Ai Fiori's? I can probably call in and get Dad's table. God knows he's not using it."

He jerked his thumb toward the door. "Nah. Just got into town this afternoon, and there are some things I need to do."

"*Pfft.* It's been a year. No one's going to care if you put them off another day."

"But I will."

She gave him an appraising look, and not for the first time, he felt like she could see right through him. After a second, she glanced away and shrugged. "If you say so. You have a place to stay?"

God, he hoped he did. "I'll figure something out."

"Well, if you don't . . ."

He shook his head. "Thanks for the offer, but I think I'm good."

"Suit yourself. Later this week, though, let's catch up. We need to talk strategy going forward for handling all of this." She gestured at the board table.

"Sure." He half turned away, one foot already edging toward the exit.

She stopped him before he could go. "Rylan?"

"Yeah?"

"I'm glad you're home."

His heart did something strange and complicated inside his chest at that word. *Home.* "Yeah."

"It's just—I don't have a lot of people left who I can count on. Who I can trust. It's nice to know you're one of them."

He swallowed down the things he wanted to say to that. Managing the barest excuse for a smile, he touched the outside pocket of the briefcase. Felt the spiral binding of the sketchbook he had placed there through the leather.

The fact that he still had it said he wasn't worthy of anybody's trust.

But he was trying to be.

Nodding, he turned his back on Lexie, on the room as a whole.

At his father's insistence, he'd sacrificed the parts of his life that happened beyond this building, but not anymore. He had other responsibilities, other apologies to make.

He just had to pray that they'd be heard.

chapter TWENTY-SEVEN

"I didn't peg you for a Brooklyn girl."

Kate startled and whipped around, managing to yank her headphones out of her ears and knock over a brush in the process. As she fumbled for them both, she darted her gaze up. Liam, one of the guys from her program, stood behind her, looking way too amused at having caught her unawares. If the streaks of paint on his jeans and in the front of his messy, sandy hair were anything to go by, he'd been in the studio for a while. She must've really been out of it not to have noticed him until now.

As she ducked to retrieve her brush, she smiled. It wasn't that she hadn't made other friends among the students here, but Liam was the one who made a point of saying hi to her, of offering to grab her a coffee when he went on a caffeine run. She wasn't under any illusions. The niceness was probably flirtiness, but that wasn't the worst thing in the world.

If there was one thing she had learned from the mess this summer, it was how to handle a guy who wanted to get in her pants.

The slow flicker of a smile on her lips faded and died. She faltered as she stood back up. This summer...Well, she'd learned a lot of things, and most of them the hard way. But that was fine. Time healed all wounds, after all. The scars Rylan had left on her heart weren't gone yet, but they were slowly closing over, leaving her stronger than she had ever been.

Slowly but steadily, she was recovering.

Now if she could only say the same about her art.

With a grimace, she glanced over her shoulder at the painting she'd been working on. Liam had recognized it at least, so that was something.

"What's wrong with Brooklyn?" she asked.

"Nothing. Well, unless you're talking about Park Slope, in which case only everything." Liam grinned. "But Bushwick is pretty legit." He nodded toward the photo she had tacked up beside her easel. "That's where you took that?"

"Yeah." She'd been scouring a bunch of local neighborhoods, taking pictures, looking for different sorts of architecture, different types of cityscapes. She just couldn't seem to connect to them the way she had the sights in Paris. Trying to paint from them didn't feel the same.

"You're not happy with it?"

She sighed. "It's a process." That was what they all said when they were struggling.

"Maybe you've been staring at it for too long?"

"Nah, I've only been here for..." She wiped her hand on her pants and pulled out her phone and did a double take. How the hell had it gotten so late? "...okay, a *lot* of hours." Maybe it was time for a break. Right on cue, her stomach made a groan of protest. Between covering the breakfast shift at the diner and running to her seminar class and then losing track of time completely here, she hadn't exactly had a chance to eat. Or sit down. Or anything, honestly.

"You definitely need to get out of here." His tone shifted, going just a little bit too casual. "You wanna go grab a bite or something? I know a couple of good places."

The invitation made her pause. She half turned away, swirling her brushes through the turpentine to buy herself a second.

She'd just acknowledged to herself the fact that he might be flirting some thirty seconds ago, so it shouldn't be a surprise that he was making an overture. And yet she hadn't been sure—she still wasn't, honestly.

Lying liar that he was, at least Rylan had been upfront about his intentions.

Whatever Liam was trying for, she really didn't have the energy right now. "Actually, I'm pretty beat. I think I might just head home."

His eyes fell, but if he was too disappointed, he kept it under wraps. "You sure?"

"Yeah. Maybe some other time."

"Okay." That seemed to lift his spirits. "I think I'm going to go." He pointed his thumb toward the door. "But you want me to wait for you? Walk you to the subway? Or whatever."

She shook her head. "It's going to take me a while to get this all cleaned up."

He didn't linger for long after that, and she couldn't decide if she was relieved about it or not.

It was the first time someone had really made a pass at her since this summer, and it had unsettled her more than she would've expected it to. As she went about the work of washing her brushes and wrapping up her palette, she kept replaying it in her mind.

What was the worst that could've happened if she'd said yes? She and Liam were friends, sure, but they'd only known each other a little while. Even if their quasi date had tanked, they probably would've been able to get past it. *She* would've been able to get past it.

Her conviction about that much solidified as she tugged on her jacket and made her way down to the subway.

Being with Rylan this summer had taught her a lot of things. She knew now, in a way she hadn't before, that she had a right to ask for what she wanted, to tell a potential partner what felt good and when he was leaving her cold. Or worse, hurting her. Sex was sex, and love was something else entirely, something that had burned her yet again. She'd gotten too attached too fast.

But she hadn't made the same mistake with Rylan that she had with Aaron. The one her mother had made with her father. At the very first hint of Rylan's deception, she hadn't stayed to hear his excuses or let him sweet-talk her into giving him another shot. She'd packed her bags.

Maybe, just maybe, she could try again with someone else. Learn from this mistake the same way she had from her last one. She could find a guy, be it Liam or whomever, and she could get all the touching and kissing and bone-melting sex she'd had the barest taste of in her week with Rylan, except this time without all the pain. If she guarded her heart, it might even work. She could keep it casual and keep her feelings and her secrets to herself. She could give herself a chance.

Maybe she was ready, at least for that much. For a fresh start.

By the time she finally made it to her stop and trudged the last few blocks home, she'd just about managed to convince herself that this time, really, she was ready to move on. Crossing the street, she dug around in her bag for her keys, only to find the door to her building had been propped open anyway. Ugh. People locked their doors around here for a reason. She kicked the doorstop out of the way before checking her mail and heading for the stairs.

At the top of the second flight, she turned in the direction of her apartment, fumbling with her keys again. Once she'd found the one she needed, she lifted her gaze from them. And froze.

Her knees shook, and she gripped the strap of her bag hard enough to make her knuckles hurt. A half dozen times, she blinked, but nothing about the vision before her changed. It was there. *Real.*

Her worst nightmare and her most infuriating, shameful fantasy.

The figure sitting on the ancient carpet outside her door—the one dressed in a fucking three-piece suit, gorgeous hair a finger-combed mess, jaw as sharp as it had ever been—was Rylan. Beside him was a suitcase.

And in his hands lay her sketchbook.

chapter TWENTY-EIGHT

It was the tiniest sound. The faintest hint of a whimper, but it was as loud as gunfire in that quiet hall. Rylan jerked his head up from his near-meditative consideration of the cracks in the plaster wall in front of him. The ones he'd been staring at for hours now. So long that if it hadn't been for her name beside the buzzer at the door, he might've worried he had the wrong place.

But all that waiting, it'd been worth it. He would've waited the rest of the night if he'd had to, and still would've called it a fair deal.

There she was. Kate. For a minute, all he could do was drink her in. Her cheeks were flushed, her eyes bright and hair a mess. She was wearing the most unappealing, awful, shapeless pair of paint-streaked jeans he'd ever seen, and *fuck*. He wanted her. Not just in his bed and in his arms but in his *life*.

Her name rose to his lips, but before he could so much as get it out, all the words he'd planned, the ones he'd re-hearsed for this very moment, evaporated in his mouth. Moving slowly, as if not to spook a skittish horse, he dusted off his slacks and climbed to his feet. The distance between them pulsed. In the silence, he willed the words to come.

Then finally, quietly, she said, "Rylan."

He nodded.

"You're here."

His face cracked, a smile stealing over him, and he found his voice. "Yeah."

She didn't move, and he didn't, either. Their very first conversation rose to his mind. That first cup of coffee in a bustling French café. She'd been suspicious, and he'd been overconfident, and every single word he'd dragged out of her had been hard-won. A softness crept over him just thinking about it. His Kate.

Well, he could do the conversational heavy lifting here, too. He opened his mouth.

But she cut him off before he could speak. "What the hell do you think you're doing here?"

The soft haze of memory evaporated. The sharpness in her tone and the anger in her eyes slid like a knife between his ribs.

Right. This wasn't a cozy nook in a coffee shop, and they weren't two tentative prospective lovers, feeling each other out. She wasn't the same quietly cautious girl. He wasn't that brazen, bored, angry man.

Her gaze grew more pointed, and his chest squeezed. He would've denied it, if anyone had pressed him on it, but there'd been this piece of him that had clung to the hope that she might welcome him with open arms. Even after everything he'd done and all the ways he'd hurt her. All his illusions crumbled to the ground.

It wasn't quite like being in front of the firing squad of the boardroom, but he found himself drawing up straighter all the same, bracing himself for whatever defenses he might have to construct. Grounding himself.

She wasn't going to throw herself at him? Fine. But he wasn't going to let her walk away this time without hearing him out.

"I..." He worked his jaw. Where did he even start? Gripping the spiral binding tighter, he lifted her sketchbook. "I found this."

Her brows rose. "And? Are all the postal workers in France on strike?" He faltered, but she didn't miss a beat. She let out a harsh, sad bark of a laugh. "I mean, I know the economy is rough, but if billionaire moguls have to resort to taking courier jobs—"

"Kate—"

"No." She lifted a hand up in front of herself, and he stopped in his tracks, held back from the step he'd been about to unconsciously take forward.

Because she was here. Real and beautiful and everything he'd ever wanted and been too much of a fool to keep back when he might've had a chance, and he needed to touch her so badly it ached.

"Kate," he tried again, "you have to know—"

"No, I don't *have to know* anything." If it was possible, her posture went even more closed.

He took that single step forward. Threw his arms wide, ready to throw her sketchbook, too, if it weren't the most important thing he had. "You have to know, I came here for you. To see you. This is yours. I found it in our room after you left. It was selfish of me to keep it for so long—"

"For three *months*. Three months, Rylan. You can't just walk back into someone's life after that kind of time."

"But I've spent every second, every moment of it thinking about you."

She rounded on him, her cheeks flushed, hands curled tightly into fists. "Like I haven't spent it thinking about you? About what an idiot I was for you? You used me."

"Never," he said, and he spat the word. He'd come here to apologize, but not for that. Anger boiled low in his gut, taking up some of the space that had been nothing but regret and hurt. "I didn't take anything from you that I wasn't prepared to give back a hundredfold."

"Except my trust." Her face scrunched up, her eyes shining, and it was the first glimmer of anything except disgust. Her voice wavered. "Except my heart."

His own shuddered. He took a deep breath.

He'd always wondered, deep down where he'd nursed the ache she had left in her wake. To get as angry as she had, to have acted so betrayed. She must have felt something for him. His stunted heart that hadn't dared to feel anything for so damn long had grown three sizes for her, and maybe she wasn't as attached as he was. But she had—she'd cared. At some point.

And fuck guardedness and fuck silence. They'd had enough of that these past few endless months. He edged even closer, hands in front of himself in a gesture of supplication. He licked his lips. "Like I said. Nothing I wasn't ready to give right back to you."

Her eyes snapped wide, her whole body going still, and something inside of him ached. If he could just reach out to her, just bridge this gap. There was something here. She'd admitted it. Something worth salvaging, if only she'd let him.

In the distance, a door on one of the lower floors creaked open and slammed shut. The muffled sounds of footfalls and the jangling of keys. It knocked Rylan out of his trance.

Jesus. They were in a public space here. Anyone could walk by. People in every apartment around them were probably listening in.

He shook his head and leaned forward that final inch. His hand closing around her arm was a jolt of electricity, the warmth of contact that soothed him even as it seemed to set Kate further on edge. He stroked the point of her wrist with his thumb, feeling her tremor through her clothes. He caught her gaze and held it, pitching his tone lower. No one else needed to hear this.

"You told me—before you left. You said I had a lot of things to figure out for myself, and I've been trying. I've been trying so damn hard." Gulping, throat dry, he hauled her hand up to his chest, slotting it underneath his tie, pressing her palm flat to the muscle underneath. To where the absence of his father's ring hung like its own kind of weight.

Did she understand him? He was freer now. He wasn't running away, not from who he was or from the possibility of being known. And he'd never hide who he was from her again.

"There's a lot of stuff I'm still working on," he said, "but there are two things I'm certain of. I'm a better man now. And I'm a better man because of you."

"Rylan..." Her gaze flickered down, to the rise of his chest. To his heart beneath her hand.

"I'm sorry. For everything. But please." He wasn't above

begging. Glancing meaningfully at the doors around them, he pled, "Please just let me come inside. Talk to me."

Her eyes drifted closed, her head shaking ever so slightly, and his stomach plummeted into his knees. But she didn't pull back. "Do you have any idea how angry I am with you?"

"I think I'm starting to, actually, yeah."

She curled her fingers in the fabric of his shirt, and it was so wrong, so inappropriate, but even as he was waiting for the verdict that would send him to the gallows, heat flooded his skin. His sex drive, nearly MIA these past few months, gave a kick.

When she lifted her gaze back to his eyes, it was with a new kind of uncertainty, one he himself had put there, and damn if he wasn't prepared to spend the rest of his life working to take it away.

"Me inviting you in doesn't mean I'm any less pissed."

The sudden rebound of his gut snapping back into place left him dizzy. Relief, pure and simple, felt like the first breath he'd taken since he'd let her go.

"I can work with that."

"I know you can," she muttered.

And it struck him that maybe, just maybe, he had a shot.

Pulling her hand from his chest, she turned toward her apartment. The center of his ribs felt cold without her touch, his eyes sore without the vision of her face as she bent to get the lock. But none of that mattered, because a second later, she was opening the door, and stepping inside, and instead of slamming the door between them, she held it open wide.

She twisted around to look at him and asked, "Well? Are you coming in or not?"

* * *

Never, not in the two years she'd been living in it, had Kate's tiny shoebox of an apartment ever felt so small.

Mechanically, she undid the buttons of her jacket, then dropped her keys into the bowl on the little table beside the door—the one she had literally picked up on the side of the road. All the while, her eyes stayed glued to Rylan's form.

She'd never seen him dressed anything but casually in their time together in Paris, but damn could the man fill out the lines of a suit. Expensive and perfectly tailored, it made him look even taller than she remembered, more handsome. Her eyes burned.

She wanted to give in to the trembling in her hands and in her knees. Run over to him and kiss him and beg him take her, hard, on her bed or on the floor or against the wall. It took all of her restraint not to.

She wanted to slap him.

It was like he sucked all the air out of the room, leaving none of it for her, and her lungs went tight. He took up so much *space*. Moved into it with hardly more than a by-your-leave. Entered it and dominated it, the same way he'd pushed his way into her vacation and then her thoughts and her life.

And, God, but how dare he? Three long months after she'd found him out, after she'd done the hardest thing she'd ever had to do in her life and walked away from him. After she'd spent all this time getting over him—and it had been working, too. She'd been so close.

Now she was going to have to start all over again.

What the hell was he even doing here? What was *she* doing here?

Shaking it off, she set her bag down and hung her coat up. She didn't let herself look at him again as she made her way into her cramped little kitchen. "Anything you have to say can wait until I eat."

"Do you want to go somewhere? I don't know many places in this neighborhood, but..."

"Nope." If someone had told her this morning she'd be turning down not one but two invitations to dinner today, she'd have laughed herself hoarse. Forget that dinner out for once sounded amazing. If Rylan was coming all the way out to the boroughs for her, coming into her home, he could deal with her food. Her terrible, terrible food.

She tugged open a cabinet and surveyed the prospects. She hauled out a packet of noodles with a sigh.

"Are you hungry?" she asked. It'd be a hit to her budget, but she was pretty sure she could spare the seventeen cents to feed a guest.

"I could eat."

She bet he could. She grabbed a second pack and closed the cabinet. "I hope you like ramen."

"Can't say I've tried it."

She dug her fingers into the counter hard enough to bruise. Slow and steady, she forced herself to take a couple of nice deep breaths. She unclenched her hands and turned her head.

He was there. Rylan, the guy who had stolen her heart this summer and then ripped it to shreds. He was standing there, his back to her, in that perfect, expensive suit, with his perfect hair, not even knowing what ramen was. And he was in her apartment, looking at her stuff. Looking at her *life*.

Her vision swam for a second as her focus shifted. She'd tried so hard, on a limited budget and with limited time, to make her home a sanctuary. Dove-gray walls to make a crowded space a cozy one, her friends' art on display, an eclectic mix of things she'd found at flea markets and rummage sales all over the city giving the place character.

And it all looked so cheap.

If she'd known he was coming, she could have at least picked up a little. Her easel set up in the corner had another failure of a painting on it, and there were more awful drawings spread out on the floor. Every flat surface was covered in papers or books or art supplies, and her paint-streaked clothes threatened to spill out of her hamper. Worse, the ones that stank of fryer grease from the diner were piled on top of them.

And she was even more of a mess. She had pigment on her sleeves and probably splashed across her face. Her hair was all windblown. This man had been the one to make her really believe that she could be beautiful, but letting him see her like this, while he looked like that...

Her breath caught, a choked sound sneaking past her throat.

Fuck him for ambushing her. Fuck him for stealing the higher ground and for making her *want* him again.

"Kate?" He'd turned around to stare right at her, and she couldn't stand it. Not for another second.

The tightness in her throat threatened to choke her. "Can you go to the bathroom or something for a minute?"

"Excuse me?"

How could she explain? "I just need..." She needed him to be somewhere else and she needed to fix this all. Take control of it. She needed to *think*.

Frowning, he narrowed his eyes at her, and he must've seen some fragment of how unhinged she felt. "All right." He set her sketchbook down, and that right there—that he still had it, whether he'd stolen it or found it or what—that was a whole other can of worms, and her frayed nerves came one step closer to snapping.

She pointed at the right door; there were only two of them, a tiny closet and a tinier bathroom—it wasn't as if he could miss it. He slipped inside, lingering briefly, watching her as if he knew precisely the kind of time bomb he was dealing with.

She waited until the door clicked closed and the sound of the fan came on to bury her head in her hands and turn around. With her back to the counter, she let herself slide down until her butt hit the ground.

Until there was no farther down to fall.

Okay. This was not how Rylan had seen this going.

While instant forgiveness followed by enthusiastic reunion sex had been his secret, dark-horse favorite for how this might turn out, he'd never discounted screaming, door slamming, and an invitation to go fuck himself. He'd even imagined a couple of potential middle grounds.

Sitting on the edge of her bathtub, idly scanning the ingredients on her toiletries, had not been among them.

How long, precisely, was he supposed to wait in here?

The drone of the exhaust fan muted any noises that might be coming from outside, but he hadn't heard much of anything. He strained, listening harder, clenching his hand into a fist. She wouldn't have left, right? If she didn't want to deal with him, it would've made more sense to kick him out, not ask him to go sit in her bathroom while she escaped.

His heart squeezed. He was trying to keep his expectations low, but he'd been waiting so long to see her. If he could just get her to talk to him. To give him a chance.

Finally, he couldn't take it anymore. He checked his watch and it'd been a solid ten minutes. With his phone long past run out of batteries and his patience about as empty, he sat up. Checked himself in the mirror. Then took a deep breath and cracked the door open.

"Kate?" What exactly was he supposed to say? *Do I have your permission to come out of the bathroom now?* He rolled his eyes at himself. "You still out there?"

"In the kitchen," she called, and it shouldn't have been such a relief, just hearing her voice.

And oh hell. He nudged the door a little wider and tried to peer through the gap. "Not that I'm not enjoying the décor in here, but..."

The sound of metal clinking on metal carried through the space, followed by a sigh. She grumbled something he couldn't make out, then, louder, "Come on out, I guess."

He poked his head out first, surveying the room. From his angle, he couldn't see into the kitchen, which was a wonder. He'd lived in houses with closets larger than this entire place.

And yet he liked her apartment better than any of them. It hadn't been some designer putting her home together for her. There was no feng shui or flow. Just art. Just *life*, where there had been so little of it in the mansions he'd been told to call home before.

Stepping out, he furrowed his brow. It was subtle, but the place was different than it had been before she'd banished him. Neater. He drew the one side of his mouth up, ready to tell her she really hadn't needed to scoop her underwear off the floor for him, but then he paused. That wasn't the only bit of tidying she'd done.

All the paintings, all of her artwork, were gone. Not *gone* gone, there wasn't close to room enough in this place for her to disappear them completely, but the one on the easel—it had been of a bridge, maybe? She'd tucked it behind her dresser, leaving only the edge of it peeking out. The rows of pictures that had been lined up against the wall had all been turned. Staring at the blank backsides of canvases, he frowned.

The second day he'd met her, he'd gotten her to show him her sketchbook. Only the last few pictures, sure, but she'd barely hesitated before baring her soul to him that way. He'd treated it with the respect it deserved, really looking at her work before passing judgment or commenting, and the next time, she'd granted him even greater access. She'd let him flip through months' or maybe years' worth of drawings.

She'd let him see himself through her eyes, his hollow places filled in by the tender touch of her hand as she'd studied him and captured him on a page.

Now, he wasn't allowed to look.

He worked his jaw against the ache it gave him. He'd lost so much when she'd walked out that door. More than he'd even realized at the time.

God, he hoped she gave him the chance to earn it back.

Squaring his shoulders, he turned to face the kitchen. If she'd been watching him, she buried her gaze back in the pot bubbling away on the stove. Didn't spare a single glance at him.

"Dinner's almost ready."

He swallowed a couple of times, because that was the last of his concerns. "Sounds good."

She snorted. "I promise you, it's not."

"All right..."

Shaking her head at him, she flipped the burner off and stepped to the side. She grabbed one mug from a dish drainer beside the sink, then dug around in a cabinet until she came up with another, larger one in a different color. She sprinkled something from a couple of little foil packets into the pot and stirred, then unceremoniously dumped whatever concoction she'd made into the mugs. Tugging open a drawer, she came up with two mismatched spoons and dropped one in each. "Here you go." She gestured at the soup as if to say *go ahead*.

He had to admit. He was intrigued.

Expecting her to step back, he darted forward, and his skin prickled with heat when she refused to yield an inch. It was the closest they'd been since she'd let him inside, nearly as close as when he'd grabbed her wrist. Only this time she wasn't staring him down or yelling at him. He saw his opening. Ever so slowly, he put his hand to her waist, molding to the soft curve of her frame. Her breath stuttered, and his heart pounded, and maybe this wasn't a lost cause after all. He breathed her in for a moment, the faint scent of still-wet paint weaving together with the roses and vanilla of her hair, drawing him closer.

And he almost leaned in. Very nearly reached forward to take the kiss he'd been aching for these past three months. But for all that her body spoke of invitation, her eyes were terrified, the line of her mouth hard.

He schooled his reaction and reminded himself: This girl was worth playing the long game for.

Holding her gaze, he reached beyond her to take the closest cup by its handle. With it firmly in his grasp, he let go of her side.

She stared at him, dazed, as he stepped back. Every inch of space he put between them hurt, but he could be patient. He could wait.

There wasn't a table or any place to sit in her kitchen, so he turned toward the main room. He didn't find much better options there. The lone chair she appeared to own was a rolling one, pulled up beside a little painted white desk tucked into a corner beside her easel. If he sat there, she'd be worlds away from him.

It was a calculated risk. But after a moment's thought, he crossed the space to her bed. A double, barely big enough for two—not that he'd mind. If she ever let him take her to it, he'd never want to let her go. Having to sleep pressed tight against her... He couldn't think of anything better.

He cast one look over his shoulder at her before dropping down to sit on the edge of her mattress. It barely gave at all, but it would do. Soft, worn-looking purple sheets slipped beneath his hand as he stroked the material. Maybe she'd join him here. Sit beside him.

But instead, she hovered in the doorway, mug clutched tightly enough her knuckles went white.

For the first time, he directed his attention to his own cup, and he had to stop himself from frowning. Its contents were... well, brown. A curly mass of noodles in a murky broth. He poked at it with his spoon and raised a brow. Across the room from him, Kate brought a spoonful to her mouth and blew on it, rosy lips puckering, and he lost the thread for a second, just watching the shape of her mouth.

Then she gestured for him to go ahead. His haze receded, and he regarded his mug again. Her gaze sat like a weight on him as he gathered up some noodles, anticipation like a shiver through his skin.

Shrugging, he took a bite.

This was not a test. If pressed, Kate would swear up, down, and sideways that it wasn't. She honestly didn't have anything else in the house to offer him.

And yet, as he closed his mouth around his spoon, she held her breath.

He'd said so many things, their final day in Paris together. She'd been blind with fury and betrayal, shoving her things into her suitcase and barely able to see through the threat of tears. And he'd talked. Told her his regrets, told her how he'd only lied to her because he wanted her so much.

He'd wanted to be normal. To have this little slice of normalcy, there, in that room, with her. And she had so very, very nearly turned around.

The problem was, he didn't even know what normal *was*. It didn't matter how torn up she was over seeing him, bouncing between elation and rage and every possible emotion in between—if he couldn't handle cheap, terrible noodles—if he couldn't manage to get them down without lying to her...then they were doomed.

He pulled the spoon from between those soft, too-kissable lips, and his shoulders stiffened, his expression going impassive. It took him a hell of a long time to swallow.

"So?" she asked.

His throat bobbed as he managed to get his mouthful down. "Well..."

"Don't lie." And it was supposed to come out light, even teasing. But there was too much history between them. It was too loaded of a statement. Her throat felt raw.

His gaze snapped up to hers, something dark and sharp passing behind his eyes.

Of course he knew this was a test.

Moving ever so slowly, he reached to the side and set his mug down on her bedside table. She stared at the bright red handle of the thing, a stupid freebie she'd picked up in the student union for signing up for something, and she was serving fucking ramen to some society heir in it. Her eyes prickled.

And then he was in her space, warm hands closing around hers, and she'd nearly forgotten how good it felt to be touched. To have this man, the one who could have any woman he wanted—and who probably had—to have him touching her...

Don't. Her mind screamed at her. Don't trust him, don't let him in, don't let him touch you again. But her body went rigid. Frozen.

He coaxed her fingers to unclench, gently prying her mug from her. Twisted to set it on the counter behind her, and that put them even closer. She felt unbearably brittle, like any little thing could cause her to shatter, but the heat of him, the proximity of his body hovering over hers, it melted the edges of her. Fused them together with this vague, impossible promise that he could make her whole.

Taking her face between his palms, he tilted her head up until she had no choice but to look at him. The dazzling blue of his eyes stared back at her, and she'd loved this man so much. For one perfect week, she had.

But she couldn't trust him.

"I'm sorry," he said. "I'm so sorry. For every single thing I did that caused you pain."

She shook her head within his grasp, vision going blurry. Wasn't that exactly what she wanted him to say? What she'd always wanted all the men in her life who had hurt her to say?

His gaze went deeper. "If you don't want me to lie to you about how oversalted and unappealing that soup is, then I won't. I can promise you, I will never, ever lie to you again. Not about anything that matters, and not about your cooking, either, if that's what you want."

A snort of laughter broke through her closed-up throat. "I'd hardly call it cooking."

He didn't let her change the subject or digress. "Whatever you want to call it, then. I won't lie about it."

She gazed back up into his eyes. "Would you have told me the truth about it, though?" Because that had been the problem. When she'd called him out on all his not-quite truths in Paris, he'd sworn he'd never lied to her, not outright, and maybe he hadn't been wrong about that. But he'd kept his silences, muttered vague agreements that dodged all around the questions she'd really been asking him. "Or would you have just said nothing? Just let me believe what I wanted to?"

He stroked his thumbs across her cheeks. "We're not arguing about your soup here."

"No. I guess we aren't."

Sighing, an aching sadness to him, he took one of his hands and braced it on the wall behind her. "So talk to me about something besides soup."

Like all of her strings had been cut, she sagged, leaning back into the wall. It would be so easy to let her head fall forward onto his shoulder, to rest there for a moment. He was clearly ready to give her whatever comfort she wanted, but it wouldn't fix anything. Him showing up here, making promises he'd given her no reason to believe up until this point—it didn't solve *anything*.

"Rylan." She placed her hand over his and pulled it gently from her cheek. "What are you doing here? Really."

"I already told you. I came here for you."

"But why?" And this wasn't the same insecurity from their first night together, eating crepes in the open air on a Paris night. She had some kind of hold over him, there was no denying that at this point. But "Why here? Why now?"

He turned his hand over in hers, tangling their fingers together, and it felt too easy to let him do it. She squeezed his palm, stilling him. Because this was important.

When he spoke again, his voice pitched lower, and his Adam's apple bobbed. "It's funny, you know. I was in Paris for a year before I met you, and the whole time, I was never lonely. I was too angry, too—" He cut himself off with a harsh breath of a laugh. "I felt too betrayed. I'd gone there running from this shitstorm my father had left for us, and I couldn't see anything beyond that. Not even how unhappy I was. I knew my life was empty, but... it was like it almost seemed better that way."

And she had seen that, hadn't she? It'd been lurking in the corners of her vision, all that time they'd spent together shadowed by it. There'd been a restlessness to him, a dissatisfaction he never would've admitted to but which she could all but taste. How else did a man like him get so caught up in something the way he had? How else did he change all of his plans for an entire week, and for what? A girl?

She didn't want to sell herself short, but it didn't make any kind of sense.

"That still doesn't explain—" she started.

"And then you walked into my life, and you were anything but empty. You cared so much about life and art, and you let me touch you…" He trailed off, gaze darting down the center of her body, leaving a low trail of warmth everywhere it went. "And I didn't feel hollow for the first time in so long."

"And so you lied."

"And so I glossed over the details of my life. Because for that moment, that handful of days, I wanted to live in yours. By the time I realized how much I needed you—that I had to come clean with you…it was too late." His mouth twisted up into a painful shadow of a smile. "I thought I was doing the right thing. I'd already fucked it up, so there was no way I could keep you, but I couldn't—I couldn't do it. Couldn't be another guy who'd hurt you."

Her eyes blurred. But she wasn't going to let him see her shake. "You understand the irony of that statement, don't you?"

"There is nothing I regret more than hurting you."

"But you did." There was no invective left to throw behind the words. They were simply there, true and awful and bare. "You broke my heart. Because I let myself think you were different. You only let me see these little glimmers of yourself—"

"I showed you more than I've ever shown anybody else."

Dizziness swept over her, because he believed that. The way he was looking at her, a fierceness to his gaze, he had to.

"I know I showed you more, because it was more than I'd shown myself." He took her hand in both of his. "After you left, I had to face it. There wasn't any pretending anymore. I tried. God, I tried. But none of it was the same."

"So what? You've just been wasting away without me these past few months?"

He shrugged, but he missed casual by a mile. "Essentially, yes."

And that was it. The intensity of his gaze was too much. She suddenly couldn't breathe, and she twisted, tugging her hand away and squirming out from under his arm.

"I'm just a girl," she insisted, retreating. It was a couple of feet worth of distance, but it felt like the world.

"No." His voice broke. "Don't you get it? You're *the* girl. The one who opened my eyes. Before you, Kate, I—" He turned, taking her place with his back to the wall. It seemed like it was the only thing keeping him up. "I was running. I wouldn't let anyone get close to me. And you barreled right through that." He lifted his head. "Two days ago, I took off my father's ring."

A shiver ran down her spine. Right. He'd pressed her hand to the center of his ribs until she'd felt that absence. The place where that band of gold used to be.

"I came here. To New York, to a board of directors meeting to save my father's company, because I'm tired of acting like I don't have any choices anymore. *You* made me want to take my life back again. To find some good in it." His eyes went bright. "I'm tired of living in my father's shadow. I want to be here. I want to fix things with my family. I want to fix things with you."

Her lip quivered. "But what if you can't?"

"Then I'll die trying?"

She laughed, but it came out with a sniffle. "Melodramatic much?"

"Hardly." He licked his lips. "Kate..." He trailed off, hands twitching at his sides like he wanted to reach out again. She took an unconscious step backward. And then another.

Her apartment was such a shoebox, it only took her a half dozen more for her knees to hit the edge of her bed, and she sat back against it heavily.

"This is crazy." The thought finally made it past her lips. "You barely know me, you barely let me know you. We had • just—what? A week together?"

"We were supposed to have seven nights."

"And we didn't even get that far." How could they hope to get any farther? "And now you want to uproot your whole life because of me? It's too much."

"It's barely the half of what you make me want." Rough, he said, "What we had, it might not have lasted long, but it changed me. I think it changed you, too."

It had. In so many ways.

"When you let me touch you, when you let me inside you, it meant something." His words sent molten heat to the center of her. But the sex wasn't the problem. Before she could open her mouth to protest, he swallowed, throat bobbing, eyes darkening. "I still think about it. All the time. How sweet you tasted, how it felt to put my hands on you..."

"Don't." She raised a hand as if that could stop him. Her insides trembled. God, it had been a long three months, with nothing to sate her. He'd started this fire within her from the barest kindling, and she'd had no way to put it out. Only the time to let it burn. Three words from him, and the smoldering embers of it threatened to consume her whole.

"I still have the toys we bought. I'd love to put them inside you again. Make you come over and over—"

It felt like a blow, the wave of need that threatened to knock her over. She shook her head even as she clenched her thighs.

"We *had* something. Something I've never had before, and I was a fool to let it go without a fight last time. Hell if I'm going to do it again. Isn't it at least worth something? All I'm asking is for you to let us try. Let me try, to win you back, to earn your trust."

And just like that, it all bubbled over. The anger and the hurt and the betrayal, and it was so mixed up with how much she had loved him, how much she still wanted him. How much she didn't know if she could ever trust him again. "I don't know you!"

She'd thought she had, but he'd hidden himself at every turn, and so everything he claimed they'd had was ash, scattering at the faintest wind. He'd been just like her father, just like Aaron, pretending to be one thing while deep down he was someone else. Just waiting to turn on her.

He was the reason she'd hardened her heart. She'd learned her lesson, thanks to him, that opening yourself up only led to pain.

She dug her nails into her palms, blinking back tears.

If she let him in again and he hurt her, she'd never forgive herself.

But if she threw him out. If she didn't give him this chance. Would she regret that just as much someday?

She closed her eyes for a long moment, fighting to catch

her breath. She should throw him out. Even if it was only for the night. Having this all tossed back in her face just as the wound had been starting to heal had her reeling. She had to catch her balance—needed time to think.

When she opened her eyes again, though, he was closer. The sight of him on his knees a scant few feet from her...It sucked the air from her lungs all over again.

He worked his jaw, the sharp, perfect point of it flexing as if with a contained strength, a coiled need. "You know me," he gritted out. "Better than anyone in the world. I showed you my fucking soul. I let you draw me. And if that isn't enough..."

She finally heard the undercurrent. *If I'm not enough...*

He shook his head. "Let me prove to you that I'm the man I said I was, deep down. I'll show you the rest of it, too, if you want. The money, my family. Everything. But it won't change anything. The man who made love to you in Paris. That's me. That's all the important parts of me."

A hardness, a tight muscle that had been aching inside her all these months, gave beneath the pressure. Softening. "How?" she asked.

He paused, blinking for a moment. Then as if hit by sudden inspiration, his gaze brightened. Still on his knees, he shuffled closer, reaching out to take her hands, and by God, she let him.

"Seven nights. That's what we were supposed to have in Paris."

"Yes..."

"So give me seven nights more, here, in New York. If by the end of that, I haven't shown you, if I haven't proven to you that I am who I say I am...if you still don't think you can trust me..." He worked his jaw back and forth. "Well, I can't promise I'll go quietly, but I'll go."

She couldn't decide if it was the most ridiculous idea she'd ever heard or the best. "Rylan..."

"Kate. I'm—" The words seemed to choke him, but he got them out all the same. "I'm begging you. Please. Give me a chance. I promise, I will be so good to you." That heat crept back into his tone, making it richer. Deeper. "Remember how good we were?"

The problem was, she did. The summer had been a disaster because of him, but it had had these shining moments she'd remember forever. Standing next to him in a museum, telling him what she saw in a Cézanne, and listening to him break down and start to tell her about his family.

Moments when she lay under him, when his mouth had been on her, when he'd filled her and made her body spark with pleasure in a way she hadn't even known it could.

She was an idiot for even considering it, and even more of one for the way a part of her, a part that had gone unsatisfied for so long, wanted to give in to it right now.

If she was going to think about it, she should *think* about it. Take a day and mull it over. Definitely not let him keep rubbing warmth into her hands, pressing broad fingertips to the skin of her wrists.

She shouldn't be turning her palm over in his to grasp him back. It shouldn't feel this *good*.

As if to clinch it, he dipped his head to kiss her knuckles. "Please."

Really, what were seven nights? She could guard her heart for that long, and take from him all the pleasure he himself had taught her she could ask for from a man. And when it inevitably fell apart, she could let him go without any lingering doubts in her mind. She'd never have to look back on this moment and wonder *what if?*

Shakily, she said, "Seven nights."

"It's not so much to ask."

"Does that include tonight?" It was another not-quite test, because she was exhausted from all of this. Hungry, and not just for the dinner she'd barely managed to eat half of.

Hungry for connection and touch and to just give in for a while. To surrender.

"I suppose that depends."

"On what?"

She held her breath as he drifted his hand up her arm, to her shoulder and her throat before letting it fall down the center of her body. He stopped it with his palm between her breasts, every inch of contact throwing sparks. All the supplication from before disappeared, replaced by the quiet, commanding confidence he'd always shown when they were like this. When he was about to prove to her that he could teach her body to do so much more.

"On whether or not you'll let me lay you out on this bed. On whether you'll let me remind you just how good we can be."

"Seven nights," she said one last time, already dizzy with it.

"Starting with this one." His other hand slipped to her thigh, edging upward with every exhalation.

A beat passed and then another. And maybe she was a fool. But she'd be more of one not to take this.

It was what he'd been trying to show her all along, after all. She deserved pleasure. She had the right to accept it from him.

Swallowing down her nerves, steeling her heart, she placed her hands over his. She gave in to the heat surging through her from this simple touch. To the tiny piece of her that was willing to give this a shot.

Leaning forward, she let her mouth hover just above his. "Then you had better make it count."